Frank Egerton studied English at ╌╌ble College, Oxford.
Between 1995 and 2008 he reviewed books for publications
including the Times, Times Literary Supplement, Spectator
and Financial Times. He teaches creative writing at Oxford
University and was Chair of Writers in Oxford from 2008 to
2010. He is librarian at the Bodleian Latin American Centre
Library and lives in the west of the county. For more
information, visit http://www.frankegerton.com.

Frank's first novel *The Lock* was published in 2003. The
digital edition reached the finals of the Independent e-Book
Awards in Santa Barbara.

"Original, illuminating and absorbing." John Bayley, author of
Iris: A Memoir of Iris Murdoch

"*The Lock* blends a love story with philosophical drama to
produce an intriguing debut... Egerton writes well about
infidelity, ignorance and rivalries that can threaten family
life... He is equally good when it comes to describing place... a
vivid impression of contemporary Oxford. Some fine and
sensuous writing, meanwhile, makes it all nicely diverting."
Sophie Ratcliffe, The Times

"*The Lock* is a classic Oxford novel getting its feet wet in the
mainstream of campus fiction, tiptoeing through dirty realism
wearing some very traditional wellies. This is campus drama
reinvented as soap opera, with a soap's eye for detail and a
realist's relish in the naming of everyday things... Egerton
builds betrayal carefully, the characters, like real people,
contemplate fallback positions even as they present each other
with emotional absolutes." Michael Carlson, The Spectator

Also by Frank Egerton

THE LOCK

INVISIBLE

Frank Egerton

StreetBooks

StreetBooks

First published in 2008 by YouWriteOn
StreetBooks edition 2010

Copyright © Frank Egerton 2008

http://www.frankegerton.com

The right of Frank Egerton to be identified
as the author of this work has been asserted by him
in accordance with the Copyright, Designs and Patents Act 1988.

ISBN 978-0-9564242-0-4

StreetBooks,
3 Windsor Cottages,
Broad Street,
Bampton.
OX18 2LU

http://www.streetbooks.co.uk

Cover designed by Andrew Chapman
mail@awrc.co.uk

FT
Pbk

For Harriet

Part One

**Writing therapy exercises written by Tom Dickens
under the supervision of Dr Martin Calder,
July 2004**

A Time When I was Happy

I remember one weekend about three years ago not long before I decided to sell the business. Jill had been going on at me for ages to take a break. I'd tried to put her off by saying it was our busiest time but she wasn't having it. She knew it was the busiest time as well as anybody. How long had we been together? Seven years and the pubs had been part of my life ever since she'd known me. It was the fact that she was putting her foot down at the busiest time that made me realise she was serious. There was something *seriously* wrong with our relationship.

Anyway, she had these friends from when she was at university. Duncan and Ros. Duncan, or Dunc as he liked to be known, stayed on after they graduated and did a PhD. Then he became a philosophy don and settled down with Ros who was at college with him and Jill and who moved back to Oxford after training as a solicitor.

They had this big house at the top of Jericho near where the iron works used to be. It had originally been owned by the factory and its garden ran down to the canal. They lived a kind of alternative lifestyle. Ros was an earth-mother with a penchant for all things Indian: clanging bangles and voluminous faded tops and skirts. She had this long hair that she either wore down and straggly or up in a coil like a Cumberland sausage. She was nice although I didn't take to either of them to begin with.

Dunc was sort of hearty. His baggy shorts and near worn-out work shirts gave the impression he was still having to make do after the war. He was ex-public school, had thinning hair and thick dark-rimmed glasses which would've looked great on Michael Caine.

So, there we were for three nights, ostensibly free agents,

9

using their house as a base. The idea was Jill would show me the places where she'd been happy. Of course it didn't work out like that. We did go to some of the places but the rest of the time got roped into helping Dunc and Ros. Feeding the chickens and keeping the kids amused mostly.

In retrospect I think Jill and I were relieved to be able to break ourselves into being together gently. If we'd been at a hotel we'd have driven each other up the wall.

I liked the kids. Especially the eldest, Charlie. He had something about him. Despite being the eldest, he wasn't cocky. Neither was he a chip off the old block. He had attitude and could take the piss out of Dunc mercilessly. He had us in stitches – Dunc included – and it was done so dead pan. He was tall but had a tongue on him that suggested someone much shorter who'd learnt to live by his wits.

It was the last night that sticks in my mind, when it was just the four of us and the kids had been packed off to a neighbour.

Dunc had this idea that we should pedal out to a country pub then come back for a late-night barbie after it was dark. Before we set off, Ros decked out the garden with nightlights in coloured bowls and scented candles on spiky sticks.

Bikes weren't a problem because Dunc and Ros had a shed full for friends and visiting academics. Not that they were mountain bikes but you wouldn't expect them to be with Dunc. Like him, they were more 1950s than New Millennium.

Away we went, Jill and I following behind. First Jill in front of me, then when I'd got the hang of things, me ahead. To start with, when we were cycling through the streets, it wasn't so much the novelty of being on a bike that mesmerised me but the sight of Ros's billowing dress. I kept expecting it to get caught in the chain. Great lengths of it flapped up, dipped down, almost got snagged but never quite. It was like my grandad baiting his terrier with a handkerchief.

Then we were on Port Meadow, bouncing along a white track before veering onto the tow-path. Ahead of us was a steeply curved bridge which Dunc turned onto and powered over. He was stood up, legs braced but having to give as he negotiated a series of bumps which appeared to run the whole of its length. You could hear the rattle of his bike, sounding like it was going to fall to bits. Every couple of bumps he cried, 'Yo!' in triumph.

'Mad boy!' shouted Ros as she side-stepped off her machine.

I pedalled hard to get to the bridge before she did. I thought, Wow this looks great. I had this rush of adrenaline and felt I hadn't had such fun in ages.

Around the corner I went onto the narrow bridge just as Ros was going, 'Ride him cowboy!'

There was a line of what looked like wooden ribs going all the way up. I got over the first which made the seat ram into my arse and, fortunately, sent me leaping into the air. The front wheel skewed against the second and I leaped forward over the handle-bars legs apart, landing on my feet as the bike thwanged into the side. It was like I'd been winded but my first thought was, How the fuck did I do that? I had to check my crotch and the insides of my thighs to make sure I hadn't sustained some horrific and so far numbed injury.

I let out a yell of 'Whaaaa Heya!' in relief.

'Maaad Fucker!' went Dunc. Ros collapsed into a heap of agonised hissing laughter. Jill, looking worried, was dropping her bike and coming towards me saying, 'Tom! What happened? Are you OK?'

Once I'd straightened the forks we were off again. A short straight then a section where we had to haul the bikes over a couple of stiles – the tow-path in between ran through the garden of a pub I'd looked at once with a view to adding it to the chain. It would have been the first outside London. But it wasn't the one we were going to that night.

After that there were more meadows. The girls stuck to the path. I followed Dunc cross-country, which included a stretch of ridge and furrow. It was hard on the legs and I was still wobbly from the accident but I was just so exhilarated, bobbing up and down after Dunc. He was extraordinary from behind: standing up all the time, driving the pedals down then shooting back up again. His legs were milky white which was odd for someone who lived in shorts. There was an erectness about him and every so often you'd catch sight of his beaky nose and black glasses. He looked like a scout master.

Soon we were on the road, bowling along towards the pub. Dunc and I parked up and had to wait for the girls.

'It was bloody brilliant,' I said to him. 'Shit,' I panted. 'Absolutely amazing.'

'Simple pleasures,' he said.

'I know, that's what's so good about it. It's like being a boy again. I swear I haven't felt like this since I was ten. It makes me realise how out of proportion everything's got.'

'Well, you'll have to come again.'

'Did Jill tell you why we wanted—'

And then the girls were there.

I kissed Jill as we went inside.

And I remember that pint. Hedgecutter. Dunc handed it to me. It was in a handle. It was medium brown and it had this really hoppy nose. It was clear as the evening light. I took the first sip. No hop until the after taste. Good length. Fruity. A taste like an infusion of hazelnuts. Cellar temperature which on a hot night like that felt like it had been in the chiller. Only I knew it was natural. You could tell this guy knew how to keep his beer. I downed half a pint in seconds. It slipped down wonderful.

I felt so happy.

I also knew then what I had to do. I had to sell the business. Get rid of all of the pubs. Get back on the other side of the bar.

I knew too, at that moment, could feel it like the beating of my heart, the singing in my veins, that everything was going to be all right. That Jill and me, we were going to be alright.

The Source of my Pain

It was Christmas Eve last year. I was at my pub in Clayfield. I'd bought the place along with a ruined mill which I'd done up as a home after I'd sold my share of the London pub chain. I was living at the pub, the Castle, because my manager, Andy, was in jail. A lot of things had gone badly wrong even before the worst things happened.

Sarah had gone back to the Folly that morning. The previous few days had been hell. She wasn't eating properly, only nibbling bits and pieces. She was very thin. We both knew we couldn't go on like we were. She and Griff were going to have to sort things out between them before anything further could happen with us. She didn't want to do that, saying she'd had it with Griff, couldn't go back. I told her she was deluding herself if she thought she could simply walk away.

There were other times when she said that we had no future. 'That's it,' she'd say. 'That's us. I'm off.' And she'd go on standing or sitting where she was.

I said what about the property, her possessions, let alone the fact that she and Griff went back half a dozen years. She couldn't walk away. She owed him.

Besides, I liked him. I didn't believe these drinking binges of his were anything other than unhappiness at the thought of losing her.

I didn't tell her about when he'd come to see me.

The night before she left, he phoned the pub and they talked for over an hour. When I asked her what he'd said, she replied that he was being 'unusually cooperative' as if she was talking about a naughty school kid.

She was docile that night. She seemed to pull herself together.

She said she knew I was right about her returning to the Folly. She was calm and ate a meal of grilled goat's cheese with me. She was happy in a funny sort of way, or so I thought. She read a book upstairs when I was behind the bar. She was in bed when I went up. We didn't make love.

In my heart I was glad it was over for the time being. I told myself that as far as the future was concerned, I would take it as it came. But inside I was experiencing relief: the last couple of weeks with her had been a strain. It wasn't the situation with Griff, it was her. Mood swings, playing games, trying to impose some sort of structure on my life I couldn't fathom.

Anyway, that night I was up at about five-thirty having had a long nap after the lunchtime session.

I switched the gas fire on in the Lounge and stoked up the real ones in the Public Bar and the Tap. There wasn't much else to do because the lunchtime had been quiet. People were still not sure how to take Sarah being there, by daylight at least, and some of them were boycotting the Castle because of Andy's carry-on.

I pulled myself a pint of Wicca Winter Solstice and went through to the Tap. I drew my favourite Windsor armchair across the flags to the fire. I sipped. It was dark, roasted and spicy. There was a chocolateyness about it like a mild. Only Solstice was headbangingly strong. You couldn't manage more than two before the world became a bit unpredictable. I intended to ration myself to two: one then and one at the end of the night before I crashed.

I'd turned out the lights after I'd done the fire a few minutes earlier. There was just the light from the logs and the faint glow from a streetlamp further up the road. As I looked through the window I suddenly realised it was snowing.

I leapt to my feet and went over to check I wasn't seeing things. It must have been snowing for an hour or more. The flakes were like goose feathers. The ground was white.

Then I heard my mobile going in the Public Bar.

I went through. It was Sarah. She was calm to start with – disturbingly so, like a digital announcement.

'Tom. Come out. You've got to come out.'

'But it's snowing.'

'I'm not joking, Tom.'

'What's the matter?'

'It's Griff. You've got to come.'

I knew that something was wrong. And yet, I didn't believe it could be *that* wrong.

'What do you mean?'

'He's drunk.'

'Is that all?'

'Isn't it enough?'

'Is he trying to hurt you?'

'Yes but I think he's beyond that.'

'Well what do you want me to do?'

'I want you to collect me.'

'What, and you come back here?'

'Jesus, Tom. Anywhere. With you or with Fiona. I don't care.'

'Why can't you drive yourself?'

'I don't know where he's hidden the keys. Besides, he's padlocked the lodge gates.'

'Oh for fuck's sake!'

'Look Tom, I mean it about Fiona.' Her voice was sounding desperate all of a sudden. 'Just come and collect me. I've had enough, Tom. I've had all I can take. Don't you understand?'

I knew she was trying to manipulate me. But I gave in.

'I've got half an hour before opening time. I'll have to clear the snow off the car. Be down at the gate in fifteen minutes, all right?'

'OK.'

'Make sure you're there on time.'

I returned to the Tap and finished the Solstice.

*

In the yard I reached into the outhouse and grabbed the coat I used when the dreymen came then nipped round the side of the pub to open the front gates.

As well as the snow there was a frost and I had to use some

15

force to open the boot. When it gave the rubber seals crackled apart. I collected the de-icer and scraper.

As I worked, I thought about the time I should've been having in the Tap in front of the fire. I'd been looking forward to those moments all day. All the last fortnight in a way.

The main road out of the village was gritted but the side road across the Marsh to the Folly was untreated. The BMW's wide tyres have good grip, though, and I was outside the lodge in about five minutes. I got out and tried the gate. As Sarah had said it was locked. There was a huge chain around it and the post, secured by a gigantic padlock.

Griff never did anything by halves.

I went back to the car, intending to call Sarah but realised I'd left the mobile at the pub.

I decided I wasn't going to faff about so I climbed over the gate and started up the drive which rose diagonally along the side of the escarpment.

The snow felt comfortable under my boots and I listened to and felt the scrunching sound they made as I walked. The shapes of the first line of trees and shrubs along either side of the drive were different to the unruly ones behind. These were cedars and rhodies and yews – specimen trees the Victorians must have planted. Griff and Sarah never bothered to do much with them – Griff liked them looking romantically out of hand – and yet they retained a kind of natural dignity which was even more apparent in the snow.

Near the top, immediately before I passed under the arch, I stopped for a moment and looked up at the tower. I couldn't see the battlements because of the trees and the effect of the blistering security light which forced everything beyond its range into blackness. I could just make out the tracery of the enormous second-floor window through the trees. The lights were on but they weren't bright. The trees and the security light somehow made the window look like it was shrouded in mist. The snow came at me in slow lines out of the black. They were soft and wet and inexorable.

It was only as I was about to move on that I saw the shape on the ground. It was near the outer edge of the security light's beams. It was big but not human from that distance. It was made bigger because the snow around it had melted or been disturbed. At first I thought it was a dead deer.

I walked over to it. It was in a small clearing beneath the trees and the snow was beginning to cover it. It was Griff.

I knelt down and shook his shoulder.

'Wake up you stupid fucker!' I shouted.

How long had he been there? How long did it take for a drunken man to freeze to death on a night like that? All I knew was that the Solstice was making me feel like a brass monkey.

I pulled him over. He came easy, despite his weight. He'd been half-over my way in any case. It was as if his body wanted to end up facing me. His head lolled towards me. His eyes were wide and smiling. His nose was smashed in and loose so it smudged across his cheek. His mouth opened, the lips twisting as if they were made of rubber. A red bubble began to form rapidly over his mouth, expanding, distending, then popping. Seconds later a great burp irrupted from him, its smell of puke and whisky mushrooming into my face.

I jerked myself away and, without getting up, threw up on the grass.

I heard footsteps on the snow and looked up.

'My God,' said Sarah. 'Oh, Jesus, no!'

She was staring beyond me in disbelief.

'What happened?' I asked, dragging myself to my feet. I wiped my mouth on the sleeve of my jacket.

She suddenly seemed to realise that I was there. I couldn't catch her expression properly because she had her back to the light, but I thought I could see fear in the way she held herself.

'I don't know,' she said. Her voice was faint.

She said something else. I didn't catch it. I tried to retrieve it. It came back to me as, 'You've got to believe me. I didn't know.'

Shit, I thought. 'What did you do?'

I began to walk towards her.

'What?' she said.

'Calm down,'

'What?'

'Let's go inside. You'll freeze—'

'No.'

'Come on.'

I was close enough to grab her.

'You bastard!'

Her tiny shoulders wriggled out of my grasp. I lunged at her. She went for me like a cat. Her fingernails slashed across my face. One of her fingers cut into my upper eyelid and I let out a howl.

When I was able to see, she was running off down the drive.

'You fucking stupid bitch!'

I began to chase her.

At the bottom she hauled herself over the gate. Balancing her stomach on the top bar and flipping herself forward.

I thought she had fallen but then I caught sight of her running off down the road.

Her footprints soon left the road and headed into the wood.

I thought I was damned if I was going in after her.

I returned to the car. I put my foot on the accelerator and drove fast back to the pub where I called the police.

I remember thinking as I drove that if she froze to death, it'd be no bad thing.

Sarah's Diary

Tuesday 9th August 1994 – Debbie's House, Norfolk

I've decided to keep a diary.

For the second time in my life.

I wanted to keep one again before now but Daddy's words when he found out about the first served as a warning. I suppose I could have begun one at any time and kept it hidden, especially since I started at boarding school but I couldn't quite believe he wouldn't find out. How stupid can you get although I'm having these sort of half visions of him suddenly bursting into my bedroom here as I'm writing.

I know that's not going to happen with him a couple of hundred miles away but I'm still worried about where I'll hide the book when I get home. I know it's irrational but I can't help feeling that I'll look guilty and he'll know I'm up to something.

I decided to keep this diary yesterday.

In the afternoon Debbie's mum gave us a lift to Yarmouth where we did some shopping and then holed up in a pub on the seafront.

We went into Smith's to check out some CDs and I thought I'd buy a notebook and write a diary because Debbie has piano practice for two hours every morning.

It feels like the right time. Something logical but nevertheless strange has happened to me since starting at boarding school. I've grown away from home. Not a long way but enough to notice. It's like the girl who used to go to day school is still doing that and I'm someone else who's thinking what it must feel like to be her. Then when I'm at home in the holidays – which are just the same as always, in a way – I can't quite believe that life's so different for me. I'm Sarah on my school holidays but there's also a new me who's living this amazing new life for huge chunks of the year!

Before boarding school too my friends lived locally. It's good having a friend who lives a long way away. I didn't imagine that would happen when I went. I felt homesick for a start and couldn't believe the other girls would take any notice of me. I thought they'd all be very sophisticated. Some are but most aren't – not when you get to know them.

Debbie is one of the more sophisticated, oddly. But underneath she's vulnerable – and kind. She's an actress. Last winter she played Ophelia. I couldn't imagine anyone having the confidence to do that in their first term. Like me, she arrived for the Sixth Form. She got the part even though there were girls auditioning who had been at the school for ages and who'd been in loads of plays before.

I helped out with the set and did some make-up.

That's how I got to know Debbie. Then her brother Peter was killed in a car crash and she wanted to confide in me. I'm good at listening. We'd also got drunk a few times during rehearsals and knew we were on the same wavelength. Plus I don't get as pissed as Debbie and can put things back together when she's out of it.

The day before yesterday, we went for a family walk along the coast after Sunday lunch. We were strung out along the lane in pairs chatting. For most of the time I was with Debbie's dad. At one point he put his hand on my shoulder and said, 'We're very grateful to you for what you did for Debbie. She's told us how you were there for her.' I put my hand on his arm for a moment. It seemed right – though it always seems odd when that sort of thing happens with a man my father's age. It's because it never happens with him.

Do I miss my dad? Yes, but I'm not sure now if it's the idea of him I miss or Daddy himself.

Strange how hard it is to write the word 'Daddy'.

Anyhow, I've managed to write several pages without him breaking the door down. I quite like the feeling of being disobedient. Writing to myself seems such an innocent pleasure. I wonder why he hated it? I also wonder whether he did. Sometimes after an 'episode' he'll tell me I shouldn't take any notice of what's been said: he says he blows up but then it's all gone the next day. How odd it would be if he'd forgotten what he said. Because it lodged in me and has been there ever since.

I can hear the sound of Debbie practising because all the windows are open. Outside it is hot and beautiful. There is a breeze coming off the North Sea which makes the curtains billow. I think I'll change into my bikini and swim in the pool for a bit. I need to cool off after the excitement of being so wicked.

Thursday 11th August 1994

Two days since I first wrote in this book. I feel I've betrayed it already. Trouble was I got into this novel Debbie showed me. On Tuesday afternoon her mum gave us a lift into Norwich because Debbie had a hair appointment – getting ready for tomorrow – and a check up at the dentist (she asked me if Dad ever did freebies for friends – I said that was a laugh). Before we left I decided I needed something to read. I told her I'd go book shopping in Norwich. She said that was a waste of money. What was the use of having friends with loads of books if you couldn't borrow one? True. It was amazing looking along the shelves. Such different authors to Dad's. Will, Debbie's dad, likes eighties stuff by writers like Martin Amis, Julian Barnes and Tom Wolfe. Debbie suggested *The Comfort of Strangers* by Ian McEwan. I hadn't heard of him and the date in the front said 1981 – when I was three! He was still writing, Debbie said.

What's good about it?

You won't be able to put it down. It's a bit – you know—

She was right – both ways.

I finished it when we were slobbing around in her bedroom yesterday afternoon. She was lying on her bed reading *A Pair of Blue Eyes* by Thomas Hardy (one of our A level set texts) and writing a song. She was wearing her favourite denim shirt and combats. She looks cool when she wears things like that. She looks like she's tough and doesn't care. When she dresses like that she's got that, Fuck you, take me as I am look that Tracy Chapman has (who Debbie thinks is God – I'm waiting for the right moment to tell her that Tracy must be as old as Ian McEwan).

I was curled up in a really comfy armchair.

What do you think then? she asked when I closed the cover.

I'm still in shock. I'm not sure I ever won't be.

Oh come on, it's not that bad. It's not as if you care about the characters. It's the story – it's like a thriller.

With sado-masochistic sex.

Yeah – it certainly broadens the mind. I didn't know what I thought about that when I read it.

It's kind of gross.

It's weird.

So why did you want me to read it if the characters are like Mister Men and it's full of bizarre sex?

I don't know. Devilment?

I pulled the cushion from behind me and threw it at her. I didn't throw hard but I was angry – angry-confused. I still am.

She was fine about me throwing the cushion. Her calmness made me feel so much younger than her. We talked about the book for a bit. She said she wasn't being a mischief maker by suggesting it, she just wanted me to try something different. She said it wasn't about characters, nor the sex, but the fact that it was a totally compelling story. What she found fascinating was the idea that you could be made to read something you didn't want to. We agreed that was *really* disturbing. I said it was an example of evil genius (well, maybe not evil, more dangerous) and tried to compare Ian McEwan with Mr Knight in *A Pair of Blue Eyes*. Not a success.

-- -- -- -- --

Back from a coffee break. I went to the kitchen where Debbie's older brother, David, had the same idea. David was second oldest before Pete died. He's twenty-three and doing a doctorate in music at Manchester (such a talented family). He's home for a couple of weeks but still works religiously from nine to five. Debbie says he plays the sax and will probably provide some moody late-night music if it's warm enough to barbecue on the beach when Karl gets here. David looks so mature. He's got a more rounded face than Debbie, or any of her other brothers and

23

sisters for that matter. He has these soulful eyes which remind me of Wynton Marsalis.

Now I'm back in my room, I realise I'm still confused by the twisted genius of Ian McEwan. Although I agreed with Debbie that the book made you want to read something you didn't like, I knew when I was saying the words they were only half true. It's not that I could identify with a woman who risks breaking her back to get sexual satisfaction. It's that I found the man, Robert, compelling psychologically. His silence, his black clothes, his kind of gay posturing in the bar – all these things repelled and attracted me.

I felt like you do when an older person is talking about how childish wanting to do something is and you think, Well actually I'd still get off on that (but you have enough sense to keep quiet).

It was also scary. I'm not sure I like the me the book appealed to. It feels like a naughty secret. But I don't know whether I should be ashamed or what I should feel.

God! It's so unsettling writing down your deepest thoughts. Daddy must never find this book! Not that he read the one he tore up. I can hear him saying, You've got such bloody peculiar writing. It's a wonder you get anywhere at school. Maybe that's it – you're really as thick as two short planks but they give you the benefit of the doubt.

I sometimes wonder if I should talk to Debbie about Dad and home. I tell myself I will, when I'm drunk enough. But I can't let myself get that drunk – not so far.

Talking of which, we went to this amazing pub last night. David drove us. It was an old mill. It was huge and its outside walls were planks of wood. It's supposed to be ancient and it's on a river in the middle of nowhere. Just cornfields stretching as far as the eye can see like the Canadian Prairies.

David left us to talk on our own for a lot of the time. He got together with some friends from when he was a boy. Debbie filled me in on who was coming to stay for the weekend. There's Karl, obviously, and some others who left last year I know slightly from the play but who Debbie knows really well. Then there's a couple of boys from other schools Karl knows.

Where are they all going to stay? I asked.

Well, if all goes fine and dandy, we'll crash on the beach – and if it's wet we'll pass out in the barn. It's going to be a mega brilliant party either way. And who knows, babes, this might be the weekend you pop your cherry.

Monday 15th August 1994

Never a truer word spoken by Debbie. A lot has happened.

Karl and his friends arrived on Friday night. Most of them came down from London by car, although a couple, Danny, a farmer's son who's starting at agricultural college in September, and his girlfriend Priscilla, had to get a train from Lincoln to Norwich. I'd never set eyes on Danny before (he was at prep-school with Karl). He's a wild boy. He couldn't drive here because he's lost his licence for being three times over the alcohol limit. His family are rich and he told everyone that he is paying for *La*(!) to have extra driving lessons. (I wonder if he's rich *enough*: slap on the wrist, Sarah.) I didn't speak to Danny much and when I did I couldn't understand him. He's always smiley. But he was pissed out of his head.

Debbie was over the moon at seeing Karl. I think she was trying to play it cool but when you're rushing to the mirror every other minute before he arrives, guzzling wine and looking at the clock when you're not looking in the mirror, you give the game away. She hadn't seen him for three weeks because he'd been staying with his dad in Los Angeles. I hadn't seen him since the end of term. I was amazed. During the play and when he was trying to catch up on his work for A levels he got thin and was as pale as a ghost – with funny wispy bits of beard on his chin in between the times when he was told to shave them off. Now he's tanned and hunky – on the way to looking like Brad Pitt.

As well as Karl, there was David and his and Debbie's five siblings (although Tamara was only allowed to be with us until her bedtime – she was furious on Saturday night when Will came to collect her from the beach – I expected her to sneak back, though she didn't, poor little thing). Then there was Andre,

Karl's brother, and his girlfriend Sam. There were Teddy, Andi, Art, Groover, Ricky, Ronan, Irma and... Bob.

On Friday night everyone had drinks by the pool so people could swim and cool off until all the guests arrived. Then we had this scrummy curry that Diane, Debbie's mum, made (spoilt or what!). It was so good. It wasn't strong but mild and creamy. But still curryish.

Afterwards we drove to the pub David took us to and stayed there sitting on the terrace till closing time.

I chatted to pretty well everyone except Bob. I had no idea what was going to happen. All I knew was I felt good. It was amazing being talked to by these older people. It was like being lifted out of one life and into another. So unfamiliar. I can't imagine someone my age talking to me and feeling the same in a year's time. Unbelievable.

-- -- -- -- --

I hardly spoke to Bob all day Saturday either. It wasn't that I didn't know him (I did – about as much as I knew any of them), only that he'd always seemed far older than the rest. Kind of untouchable. I never thought he had any interest in me. He's tall and has long brown hair, parted on the left side. He's handsome when he looks at you with his green eyes but when he doesn't he's merely striking. He's striking because his features are defined (though his nose is a bit big) and because you can tell his body is pretty fit beneath his loose clothes. I don't mean sexy-fit, or not just that, but fit-fit. He was the school's top tennis player. People said he could get to Wimbledon only he's too much of an academic. If his As are good enough – which they will be – he's going to Oxford next year, same as Karl, only doing Classics. After that – he's got his life all mapped out – he wants to go to Harvard Business School. In his year off, which starts in a week's time, he's going to work on a sheep station in Australia (great timing, Sarah). Last year he was going out with an American girl called Lorna who was as tall as Jerry Hall. They were a couple with presence. Like the school Charles and Di. But that's over now.

How do I know these things?

Hum, he told them to me on Saturday night and when we walked along the beach on Sunday afternoon.

The barbecue was wonderful. Debbie's family have a beach hut half-a-mile from the house. Their lifestyle is set up for barbecues. They'd got crates of beer and wine which had been chilling in a special fridge in one of the old stables. They've also got a huge ice-maker that Will bought when a local hotel closed during the recession. Then there's a chest freezer full of meat. And boxes of fruit and vegetables were collected from Yarmouth that morning by Diane.

We loaded all the stuff into an antique Land Rover and headed off to the beach about seven.

By nine I realised that Bob and I had been chatting for an hour. I can't remember how we began. He was suddenly sitting there beside me, a little way off from where David was beginning to hot up the charcoal in the empty oil drums. Bob had been the first in to the sea and then at some point Andi, Ricky and I were gossiping only we weren't alone because Bob was there in a wettish Lacoste shirt and swimming trunks. After a while Andi and Ricky were laughing together and Bob and I were in our own private world.

We got food and came back to the others but didn't join their conversation. The time whizzed by – no it sort of glided past, without any effort from us at all. When it got darker and cooler people started scavenging the beach for driftwood and David lit a fire. Before the moon faded Bob and I went swimming with the others because Debbie shouted it was glitter time. It was extraordinary. The sea was full of plankton. When you jumped up the water sparkled as it ran off. I watched it spilling over my breasts. With Bob it ran off his chest and then whooshed over the bulge in his trunks. Everyone was screaming with delight. Bob put his arms around me and kissed me.

When David began playing his saxophone we were lying together looking up at the sky. Bob had given me his white jumper which was like a rug. Even though the sky was dark you could tell the clouds were thickening. By the time the rain started I had fallen asleep.

We helped put things away in the beach hut and Land Rover then raced back to the house. Debbie told us to keep the noise down and opened the doors of the old barn in the disused farmyard. Someone got a CD player and put on Björk *Debut*. The Land Rover arrived with the supplies of alcohol. A couple of joints were lit and some night lights. Bob got his sleeping bag from his car and we snuggled up in a corner by a stack of logs and watched the others.

When people began to pair off he whispered, You're so small.

I didn't know what to say. I tried not to panic. I willed my being thin not to ruin everything.

I meant slim, he said.

Not too thin?

'Course not. I've wanted to be with you since I came over to see Karl at the theatre last November. It was the night of the dress rehearsal. You were putting make up on Debbie and I thought, Wow!

Wow! The word echoed through my brain. The idea of him thinking, Wow!, about me.

I knew he was going to ask if I wanted to make love. I instinctively did what I'd done on the only other occasion that someone had asked me this. I asked him if he had a condom. The other boy had been so drunk he hadn't understood the question. In a couple of minutes he passed out. When I asked Bob I half expected he'd say no and that would be that. But instead he kissed my forehead and I was aware of him reaching across me for his jeans. Then we took the rest of our clothes off.

And it was— It was difficult and awkward but still amazing somehow. We made love again the next morning and that was far more amazing but the first time was indescribable. Although I think the best bit was waking up together and realising we'd made love.

Before it happened again I put on my T-shirt and went across the yard to the bathroom.

It was the first time since my life had changed that I'd been on my own. I looked in the mirror and then I had a pee and a shit and I felt like an animal. I was just tingly body and hardly any mind. I hugged myself and afterwards went back to Bob and made love. And it was like the whole of him inside me. It was like I was devouring him and him me.

Saturday 20th August 1994

Bob got his A level results on Thursday. Straight As! He'll be going up to Oxford in October 1995. He said he hoped I'd come and see him. He was being typically modest. You have to guess what he means a lot of the time. He seems to be saying he hopes we'll have a future. I told him that he'll probably fall for some *Home and Away* type beach babe. He thought I was joking as if he couldn't possibly go for *that* sort of girl. I didn't like to remind him about Lorna.

It's been a week of not writing this diary because of Bob. I'm now on the train going back home, via London. I've spent the times I should have been writing either talking to Debbie about Bob (she skipped some practice sessions, she was so fascinated) or wandering along the shore thinking about him.

Almost Debbie's first words on the subject were, You're a dark horse. Though I could tell she was treating me with new found respect. She's working on the assumption that I pulled Bob. I've tried protesting but the idea is completely fixed in her head. It's as if she can't imagine any other variation on *girls pull boys*. From my point of view the fact Bob chose me is far more exciting – and puzzling.

Whenever Debbie asks me how I feel I say things like, amazing or brilliant (which are true), but the main feeling is utter bafflement. I suppose it's maybe the result of having been to an all girls school for such a long time. I can't get my head round the idea that the most desirable boy ever chose me. I wonder if I've missed something about myself.

Before, I thought of myself as a dutiful daughter, averagely naughty when away from home and a hard working student – I have some academic gifts but my good results in exams have been hard won. I've always thought of myself as holding my own in social situations but being on the sidelines of things, even so.

So what am I like now? It feels dangerously big-headed asking this question. It implies that I can suddenly be someone different. Where is this train of thought leading? The conclusion that up to now I've been needlessly timid? That from now on I should be more assertive? But these things wouldn't be me. It would be better for me to think I'm in the process of changing, of growing into being me.

And how strange this new aspect of me is.

Bob and I spoke on the phone three times this week. We talked not about love but what we'd been doing, the weather, packing for Australia, David and Debbie, what a lunatic Danny was – getting to know each other. He also sent me a love letter – well a card. It was the picture of Ophelia by Arthur Hughes – she has an oval face, very pale, and the river is slicked with pollen, there is a rather unrealistic bat flying towards you on the left. It was used by Karl for his Hamlet poster to emphasise the fact that Debbie was the opposite of the traditional image of Ophelia. We studied it when we did the Pre-Raphaelites last term too. Before Bob sent it, I thought it was a disturbing image. It's still that but beautiful as well. I can see the resemblance. Inside he wrote, *When I saw you in the make-up room, I thought, My God, it's the girl in the poster. How special she is.*

I shall use it as a bookmark for this diary. What a lot there is for Dad to read. Though I wonder if he'll need to snoop. Won't it be obvious I'm different? Debbie said I was. I guess you can't avoid that. I'll never look at a painting or read a book in the same way that's for sure. Whether it's *A Pair of Blue Eyes* or *The Comfort of Strangers*, I'll now know something of the experiences the adult world assumes you know about. At least Bob has put paid to my brief Ian McEwan/Robert fixation.

Will Dad want to snoop? I don't know. I'm not sure he's that calculating or intrusive. This year has changed the way I think about him. This week seems to have distilled my feelings. It's not just been Bob but my decision to talk about home with Debbie.

More about that in a while – I'm going to get a sandwich and maybe a beer.

-- -- -- -- --

We haven't even reached the outskirts of London and I'm nervous.

I thought the beer might help but I've got into training in Norfolk and it's had no effect.

I broached the subject of home on Thursday.

That morning Debbie skipped the second hour of her practice. We got together a picnic and raided Will's wine cellar. Then we loaded up a couple of bicycles and pedalled inland for a bit so Debbie could show me one of the round towered churches before heading towards the coast again. We'd decided on a spot she showed me last week. We reached the little hamlet and leant our bikes against the railings between the deserted pub car park and one of five cottages. The place was as dead as the pub which only opens in the evenings. We still chained the bikes.

We were both behaving differently from the last time. Then it was a new experience. Now it was familiar and I had the sense that we should have been more adventurous – somewhere new might have helped us to get over the end of party feeling.

Beyond the last house was a T-junction and on the other side of the road we had to climb a style and follow a footpath through some scrubby wood – called a 'car' according to Debbie – Beckham Car. The ground under the trees was wet in places although it hadn't rained since Saturday night. When we got to the dunes we covered the baskets with a rug and opened a bottle of wine.

We didn't eat for ages. We just lay on our tummies, looked out to sea and guzzled.

I won't know what to do when you've gone, Debbie said after we'd started on bottle number two.

You've got all this – and your brilliant family – and what about Karl? He's coming next week, isn't he?

I know but there's been something really special about having you here. You're so easy. You fit in. And then, of course, there was Saturday night. Debbie grinned at me, knowingly.

I flicked sand at her – only a little – with my index finger.

What's that for? I'm not taking the piss. I'm happy for you girl.

Oh I know you are. I've loved being here too. You've made it mega.

I realised that there were tears in my eyes.

Debbie put her arm around my shoulder. Hey babes what's the matter?

Nothing. It's nothing at all. I'm happy.

You don't look it.

I am, honest. I'm happy here. I didn't say anything else for what seemed like ages. Debbie didn't speak either. If she had maybe I wouldn't have said anything about home. But I did.

I don't really know how to explain but it's not just leaving here that's upsetting me but the thought of going home. How things are there.

Debbie didn't seem as surprised as I expected. Do you want to talk about it?

A little.

I'm all yours.

What could I say? I told her that whatever I said would probably sound stupid when put into words, but maybe the best I could do was give an example of the sort of thing I meant. I said I was keeping a diary and that Dad had torn up the one I'd started when I was ten and humiliated me. Whenever I tried to find words I found myself drinking.

I felt like a traitor. I felt like someone was yanking open a door in my head and catching me betraying them.

It probably doesn't seem much, I said when I finished.

Nonsense – it sounds pretty grotesque. It's a bit like an assault. Is that the only kind of thing he's done? Debbie was looking at me suspiciously.

It's not like that, I said. He's never touched me. There's never been anything physical or you know—

Sure but it's still brutal. Barbaric. What's his problem?

34

I don't know. He has these— 'Episodes' Mum calls them. He gets these moods and everyone suffers. Even Alex can't stand up to him – at least not directly. Alex goes off and does stupid things. It's his way of coping. But Dad doesn't mean to hurt people – he's not malicious, he's got this terrible energy. He's a powerful man. Sometimes he can't control himself.

Which was about all I said.

I asked Debbie if it was OK if I didn't say anymore. She said, Sure. But when you want to talk again, remember I'm here. Give me a ring. Write me a letter. It's a real bummer you haven't got email.

She didn't hassle me, although I found myself working hard to try and get back to even the awkward kind of day we'd been having before I confided in her. At some point we both fell asleep.

Things got much better after that. Bob and Karl rang to tell us their results. They're both going to Oxford. We had a celebration on the beach that night – just us two roasting vegetables on the barbecue and drinking wine and smoking a joint. We fantasised about being with the boys in Oxford in a year's time – even though we agreed we were both realists.

-- -- -- -- --

Which is where I'm going to stop. I want to finish on a happy note. I'm two hours away from home and I'm jittery and don't want to be there. If only I could phone someone in London and stay here for a few days. But who could I phone? Karl will be in Norfolk by now and Bob will be flying over the Far East. Even if there was someone, I couldn't change plans. It would cause too many problems at home. It would draw attention to me. Draw Dad's fire. I've just realised I didn't phone Alex to see how he's done in his As. Sorry Alex. (But then he didn't phone me – hope that's not a bad sign.) Hope you're OK. Will my failure to phone be commented on? If Dad knew I'd forgotten because I was too busy thinking about Bob, he'd probably say that if having a boyfriend was going to send me into a spin it would be better if I didn't have one. No, he wouldn't say that, of course I know I'm being melodramatic. But he'd pass some sideways comment and make me feel he'd said it. Perhaps I'm being unfair. Home can tear you apart. In a way, it's a good thing Bob's going to be over in Australia. I don't think I could handle him coming to stay just yet. When he rings it'll be difficult enough.

The train's coming into Liverpool Street. When I was in Norfolk I imagined I'd write this diary every day at home as a secret act of defiance. Now I'm almost there I'm not sure I have that much courage. I don't know when I'll write again. But I'll end on that happy note: Debbie and me visiting the boys in Oxford.

Tom's writing therapy – begun July 2004

31/07/01 – A Tuesday

I'll remember that day for as long as I live. It was a day of euphoria, being brought back down to earth, of rapidly deciding to be philosophical and of the bottom falling out of my world.

I turned up outside the offices of Busby Busby and Linklater with barely a couple of minutes to spare. Jill hadn't been feeling well and I made her breakfast in bed. I also nipped round the corner to get her some Codeine and Paracetamol tablets. She said she had an evil stomach bug, although she looked pretty good to me. I'd been struggling to catch up ever since. Now it was almost midday.

Busby-Linklater were accountants and FAs specialising in licenced and entertainments premises. I'd been put onto them by Len Banks my mentor and stuck with them through all the years of helter-skelter growth – from one-pub outfit, through the arrival of the venture cap boys to its present incarnation. A twenty-seven pub chain serviced by its own brewery, Dickens's. The business was centred on London but in recent years had spread out nicely along the south coast and across the Home Counties.

People said you couldn't put a cigarette paper between the big three Pub'n'Ents accountants but I always felt Claudette was gold dust.

The offices were in a little no-through alleyway off Dean Street. Once you'd pressed the buzzer and been let in you found yourself in a narrow flagstoned passage that led to a courtyard and a bit of lawn and flower beds. Before you reached that, though, you had to take this higgledy-piggledy flight of stairs to the first floor. There were several pine doors leading off the landing, each with a brass plate. By the time I got up Claudette was coming through the first of these to greet me.

'Tom!'

She threw her arms around me. As usual she smelt of top-of-the-range perfume and cigarettes. I heard the sound of her lips smacking the air next to each ear.

'Don't you look *well*,' she said, giving *well* an instinctive stretch as if it were an expensive silk shirt she was interested in buying.

'I had a weekend away in Oxford, with Jill.'

'Oxford? How delightful. How *is* Jill?'

'In herself, fine, although today she's got one of these nasty stomach bugs.'

We were inside her office and she was indicating the chintz sofa by her desk.

The room, like all the offices I'd seen there, was almost completely bare. The floorboards, panelling, sash windows overlooking the alley – all had been stripped back to the wood. The only furniture was Claudette's massive Victorian desk, the sofa and an oak chest against the panelling in between the windows.

The paint above the panelling was a yellowy cream done so it looked faded. There were spot lamps in the ceiling. I'd never known them to be switched off because what with the alleyway and the tall buildings opposite the office was naturally fairly dark.

Even Claudette's desk was bare, except for her laptop, the docking module for a handheld, a slimline matt black phone and a gargantuan gun-metal ashtray. All the gunk of office life was kept out of sight in the rooms behind the partners' offices. Although on the odd occasion I had a peek at these back rooms, I'd have said they were pretty minimal too. I sometimes teased Claudette that staff must be chosen on the merits of their tidiness and aesthetic sense as well as their abilities as PAs.

I loved the place. Its sheer eccentricity. I felt I was keeping in touch with a time when there were real characters in the business. People of Len Banks's vintage. None of these modern offices down by the docks. This was theatre, certainly, but theatre that tapped into the traditions of London life – just like my pubs did, especially in the early days.

'Want a coffee?' Claudette asked once I sat down. She was grabbing a cigarette from the top drawer of her desk and lighting it. She drew a hunk of smoke deep inside. You'd have thought she hadn't had one for a week.

'Not for me, I'm awash with the stuff.'

'Me too. So how can I be of service?'

She heaved the ashtray off the desk and clunked it on the floor boards beside her end of the sofa. She sat down and swivelled towards me. I always found it surprising how agile she was. I somehow thought that being a smoker her muscles would have started playing up by now. She was sixty if she was a day. But then she looked very trim. She was a couple of inches taller than me and in clothes like her figure-hugging black velvet dungarees and cream silk shirt she could be taken for someone half her age. Her hair – short, boyish and subtly blond – added to the effect. It was only her skin that gave the game away, especially when she was under a spotlight. You'd have expected her to have organised the lighting better but she never seemed bothered about disguising her skin – apart from make-up, obviously. Her indifference about her face was another thing I liked about her.

Yes, her skin. Smoker's skin. Not exactly orange peel but puffy with clearly-defined pores beneath the make-up.

'You're not going to believe this but I want to sell up.'

'Uh-huh.' This had a nasal quality as if she was biting on a solid tube of smoke. She wasn't going to be surprised. 'The whole thing? Could be tricky. You've got options that mature a few years down the line.'

'As much as I can get rid of.'

'What's brought this on?'

'To be truthful, I want to spend more time with Jill. Besides which, the nature of the business has changed. It's not what it used to be.'

'It's the venture capital people, isn't it? I did warn you what would happen.'

'I know but they seemed decent and on my wavelength.'

'Not the right attitude, Tom.' She blew a stream of smoke past my left ear, her lips skewed, her eyes looking straight at me. I got the impression she was wondering why she ever bothered with me.

'They've done well for me, though, I'll give them that.'

'They've eased you out of your business—'

'Not true.' I was angry at that.

'Oh no? And they won't have done as well for you as you think. Bet ya!'

I gazed at her, holding her triumphant stare.

'That hurts, Claudette.'

'Only playing straight. As always.' She stubbed out her cigarette and reached for another pivoting athletically on her buttock.

'OK. But if they haven't done as well as they should have, doesn't that reflect badly on you?'

'Not at all. You signed the contract.'

'Which you drafted.'

'Huh-uh. Your hot-shot lawyer did the juciest bits. Much of it against our advice.'

I remembered there being something of a barney between Claudette and Mo. It'd been the one time I'd gone against Claudette. But I was damned if I was going to admit it.

Looking back now I suppose I'd have to concede I *was* blinded by what the venture capital company was offering: the opportunity to double-up my empire.

'We submitted a report. Which was ignored – like you ignored me when I said the venture people would change the nature of Dickens's. Once you signed we just had to make the best of it.'

'Look Claudette, let's stop sparring. To be quite honest I'm not that fussed about the cash. As long as I clear a couple of million, I'll be as happy as Larry.'

'Two million,' she mused. Her latest mouthful of smoke began to trickle out between her lips in ragged wisps before being decisively pulled back in.

'We'd better get some figs.'

By which she didn't mean fruit.

'I'll get Marcus to do a CD. How are you fixed for lunch?'

'I kind of assumed we'd do the usual – only this time it would be a very special sort of celebration.'

'Terrific. Usual it is. I'll have Marcus order us a cab too. We can run through the disc at Fagin's. Don't look so worried. I'm sure we'll sort out something.'

31/07/01 – A Tuesday, Part 2 (after breakfast)

We were turning into Shaftesbury Avenue from Dean Street. As usual Claudette was desperate to keep her hands occupied. She had her handheld and mobile out and was tapping away at both.

Before the taxi arrived, she told me that next week she was flying to New York to see her sister. I often wondered how she coped on planes without cigarettes. A sleeping pill probably – that or got blind drunk.

Her busy fingers were bone white, not a trace of nicotine. I once asked her what her secret was. Pumice stone? Some special preparation? She said, 'Whisky. At the end of the evening I pour myself an extra-large measure to help me sleep. I dip my fingers in for four minutes then suck them clean.' I couldn't tell whether she was having me on.

While she was talking to someone called Donna about an outfit in Margate I stared at the people in Charing Cross Road. There weren't as many as you'd have expected. The traffic was light also. Maybe the tourist numbers were down. Bad for business, although the home-grown crowd was keeping us busy – or so I'd been led to believe by my partners. Having spoken to Claudette that morning, I couldn't help wondering whether they were hiding something.

The cab pulled off Whitehall into Victoria Street then turned left and a couple of streets later we were outside Fagin's.

Although you couldn't actually see New Scotland Yard, people got the joke as soon as Fagin's opened seven years before. I was proud of it. It was the first pub I decided to theme explicitly. What I liked was that I didn't go mad like my partners nowadays – I struck the right balance between tradition and gimmicks. Up till then the only obvious link between pubs and brewery were names like Pickwick's and Copperfield's. Inside, the decor merely implied the characters. In Pickwick's there was tasteful Inn and Road House paraphernalia, coaching prints and a John Bull statue.

This formula worked but by the time I acquired Fagin's, or the Red Lion as it was called then, I felt we needed to move with the times. My original ideas were conceived during the recession of 1991 when people reacted against the crass 1980s. By the mid 1990s things were a bit different. We, that was me and Rajiv, my Master Brewer and right-hand man of the time, liked the look of what Wychwood were doing in Oxfordshire with goblins and New Age imagery: fun beer names and artwork on the pump plates that was pure Glastonbury. We renamed our session and premium ales, Some More, Artful and Dodger, got the same artist that worked for Wychwood to do some grotesque paintings for the plates and then took things just that little bit further. Rajiv got a latex puppet technician to make one-and-a-half times life-size figures of Fagin, Bill Sikes and his dog. The dog looked particularly devilish. And that was it. For the rest we stuck to what we knew: Victorian truncheons, handcuffs, prison doors and prints of trials and executions. It was a sensation. It even became at one time the haunt of the Yard's senior officers.

Claudette and I were shown to her favourite table in the smoking part. I naturally ordered beer while she asked for her customary bottle of champagne.

We agreed we should talk business before the meal so we could enjoy ourselves properly. I got the waitress to disconnect the Wandsworth Gaol Patent Cell Lamp above our table so that Claudette could plug in her laptop.

I remember that as Claudette got her machine going my mind began to wander and I thought that people looking at her in the glow of the computer might be forgiven for thinking she was a high-tech felon made by the puppet guy. I considered making a joke about it – I'm sure she'd have appreciated it – but couldn't quite summon the energy. I was suddenly feeling nervous. What would happen to Jill and me if the figures didn't add up?

I could see Claudette was examining some graphs. After a

while of me sipping my beer and casting my eye over the place to make sure everything was being done properly, she swivelled the laptop towards me.

'OK,' she said, 'that's the little bugger. That one in the middle.' She slipped her cigarette round without burning her fingers and tapped the screen with the filter tip.

I hated figures. OK you had to live with them in business. I'd written dozens of reports based on figures. I'd extrapolated, I'd concluded, I'd recommended. But by nature I was hands on. I understood the bottom line, how to pull in my belt, how to tighten the day-to-day management, how to sell beer to retail outlets to buoy up the pubs side, how to motivate staff – all those sort of things. Figures left me cold.

'You'd better talk me through it.'

'Basically this shows how the pubs your partners control are doing. You'll notice the curve's not nearly as steep as the one next to it. I think your partners have expanded too quickly.'

'I don't doubt that. They're greedy sods.'

'Whereas this steep curve shows the pubs you're still managing directly are going from strength to strength.'

'I know what I'm doing.'

'I know, darling, you're mustard, but the trouble is, they know that too.'

'I don't follow.'

'They know full well they're expanding too rapidly. What they're relying on is you keeping the whole enterprise afloat while their new ventures prove their sea worthiness. If you say you want to sell, they'll do two things. One, they'll make you sign a document saying you won't set up in competition with them in any of the towns they're operating in over the next five years.'

'That's not much of a problem.'

'What? Not even a little pet project somewhere nice? Lake District, maybe?'

'I don't know, we'll see. What I hate about these people is their mean attitude. Men and women who've worked for me have gone over to competitors or set up on their own and I've said good luck to them. It's what happens in business. My view is you take it on the chin. You might have to work harder, be a bit more imaginative, but that's the nature of capitalism. It's what drives things forward. What my partners are doing is the pits. It's like these Americans that sue everybody—'

'I know everyone's not like you, Tom, we've established that. The second thing that's going to happen is they'll say that because of the poor performance of the new pubs the group's overall profit is down and, consequently, so is the value of your shares. The shares you can dispose of immediately, that is.'

'How much?'

'I think you'll get your two million. But for me, that's not the point. In three years time I reckon you'd get five for your pubs and a further two or three for your options. If you sell now, you'll no longer have any say in how things are run. Once they lose you, they'll reduce all management decisions to the lowest common denominator – profit.'

'They've had a good go at cheapening the concept as it is.'

'There'll be a lot more of that.'

'I'll have to grin and bear it. The options'll go up, at least.'

'I wouldn't bank on it. These sort of people have the habit of finding interesting ways of keeping the profits of inconvenient sleeping partners down and, hey-presto, magicking their own sky high. You'll get something. But far less than you deserve. You built the company up. Without you, they wouldn't make a penny.

'How certain are you about the two million clear?'

She turned the laptop back towards her and lit her fourth cigarette.

After about five minutes of her machine clicking and rasping away, plus one call to Marcus, she said, 'Pretty sure. Say ninety-five percent.'

I was happy with that. Very happy. In the past, even when her certainty level had been as low as seventy, she'd never let me down.

I raised my glass and she raised hers.

'Let's turn off that thing,' I said, 'then celebrate.'

Claudette's taxi dropped me at Charing Cross where I got the tube to Highgate.

I'd realised at the pub I was running behind. I'd told Jill no later than four. By the time I was coming up the steps onto Archway Road it was nearing five. I'd considered phoning but decided it was probably better to assume she was sleeping and let her be.

Two minutes later I was inside the entrance to the flats, crossing the hall and heading for the lift. We lived in a modernist masterpiece. A Grade I listed block of some sixty-five flats. It'd been built in 1935 by a Russian émigré architect for an industrialist who wanted to provide quality affordable homes for his employees. The philanthropic ideal went by the board almost immediately. Middle-class people wanted to live here and demand soon priced ordinary workers out of the market. Who could blame them? One of the highest points in London. Smashing views. A three acre garden, swimming pool, tennis and squash courts. Then this beautiful, experimental building. White slab facades without detail save for the windows and scrolled concrete fronts of the balconies. Minimal but somehow unmistakably sensational. And inside, the original specification was all mod cons. Snappy enamel and steel kitchens and bathrooms, cork tile flooring, long picture windows that concertina'd open, fitted cupboards and storage space with roller shutters. Even integral fridges cooled by a central condenser in the basement. On the ground floor communal areas like the tea room and winter garden.

Flats have continually been snapped up within minutes of being offered for sale – if they even get onto the market. We were getting letters from people asking if we would give them first refusal all the time. We'd been lucky ourselves. We were looking for somewhere when there was one of those rare windows of opportunity when confidence in London property dips for a month or two at the beginning of a lacklustre year. London held its breath but we had the dosh and we were laughing.

I didn't realise there was anything wrong until I got to the kitchen. I'd had the manager at Fagin's look out a special bottle of champagne and I wanted to put it in the fridge (a modern replacement, sadly) straight away. I thought that if Jill was feeling a little better, the bubbly would do her good. My news would lift her in any case.

As soon as I was inside the front door I put down my carrier and had a pee in the loo. We used this one off the hallway as the guest lavatory so there was nothing in there to alert me. Walking along the passage, I noticed the living-room curtains were open, so I realised Jill must have been up. I remember thinking this an encouraging sign.

It was only once I'd stowed the champagne in the freezer drawer that I saw the envelope on the butcher's block: pale blue, milled paper, oblong, the kind Jill liked which I bought her every Easter.

I didn't open it but ran out of the room to our bedroom. There was no Jill and the bed was made. I stared at her dressing-table. It didn't look right but I wasn't sure. I rattled up the shutter of her wardrobe. Like her dressing-table what I saw was inconclusive. She'd obviously not taken much with her. Had she taken anything, other than what she'd have worn if she'd gone out to the shops? I didn't think so. It was only when I went into the bathroom and checked the cabinet above the sink that I was forced to admit that she'd gone away somewhere for the night. But then she hadn't done a bunk. You'll clutch at anything when you know you're in trouble. I could taste her absence. It was acid like beer that has sat in the barrel for too long.

I returned to the kitchen. She hadn't sealed the envelope. I read the letter then threw up in the sink.

Dear Tom,

Thanks for getting the tablets. I did feel awful but it wasn't a bug. Only nerves.

The trouble was I couldn't make up my mind.

I knew I wanted to leave but couldn't quite bring myself to do it.

You've said I'm a coward and I never get to the point. You're right about both.

I really thought that last weekend would be a new beginning. Instead it made me realise I couldn't go on anymore. It's not your fault. It's me. It's as if someone's flicked a switch.

I'll be at Jemima's cottage. She's away in Thailand for a couple of months. I've taken a fortnight off work. Don't try and ring – the answer machine'll be on.

I'll be in touch soon and we can discuss it all then.

Please don't blame yourself. It's one of those things.

Love, Jill

When I'd rinsed my mouth I read the letter again. I supposed she was trying to be kind by saying, *It's one of those things.* She could be like that: awkward in her attempt to sugar the pill. I also felt she was trying to avoid taking responsibility for her decision.

Looking back there's a gap of two hours or so in my memories of what happened next. I think I probably just sat at the breakfast bar and stared into space. I remember having a bath later that evening. It wasn't bedtime, only about eight o'clock. I decided to have a bath because I wanted the comfort of hot water. It was a method I used for years to help me cope with stress. All that happened this time was I noticed how many things she'd taken from the bathroom.

Afterwards I went through to the living-room and got myself a beer. I kept a stash of bottles in what I called the cellar, a zinc-lined Arts and Crafts cool cabinet which ensured they were exactly the right temperature. It was one of the many pieces we collected for the flat. We were never slavish about only buying things that were of the right period. We went for whatever took our fancy from Arts and Crafts to Utility, reasoning we were being true to the democratising architectural spirit that had produced the flat, without limiting ourselves unduly.

I was staring at a dozen Wobbly Toms, a bottled version of Dodger, for which Rajiv used a slightly sweeter malt to compensate for that sulphuriness you get when you bottle. It was our biggest-selling bottled beer. There was national front-page broadsheet advertising and export markets all over the globe, including China and Russia. Rajiv originally christened the beer Mr Dickens. It was supposed to be a one-off to celebrate our fifth anniversary. But someone in marketing took it up and it was rebranded under my Christian name with labels depicting cartoon images of me with a glowing nose, dressed up as one of the fictional characters. The character changed every three months. The bottles in the cabinet were Mr Bumble.

I took the top off one, poured the beer into my favourite mug, placed the bottle back in the cabinet and slammed the door shut.

I paced up and down a lot that night. At sunset I couldn't help but stop and gaze at the breathtaking scene. We were on the seventh floor. Our picture window opened onto the whole of London, that night bathed in fire.

On the three middle panes I'd had an engraver do little pictures of my London pubs with their names underneath and lines pointing to where they were. If you stood in the centre of the centre pane they all lined up more or less right. I was going to have them done at my height but Jill said that would be selfish – as well as big-headed. So I had to look up at them. I think the engravings probably contravened the planning laws. My urge to smash the windows certainly would have done. I resisted the temptation.

At eleven I phoned Claudette. I couldn't think of any one else. It was a mistake. She sounded comatose. I wasn't even sure she'd registered what I'd been saying until she commented, 'Sounds like you're a million down already.'

I imagined her sitting at home, her fingers dipped into her last glass of the evening.

Sarah's Diary

Friday 9th September 1994 – Home

This is my first opportunity to write since I returned from Debbie's. Which is not literally true. No one has stopped me from spending hours alone in my room studying. I could have written it then. How many times did Mum and Dad come up? Mum once, Dad never. But I can't write under such circumstances. I need to feel free. Here I am sitting on a lounger by the swimming-pool, Major by my side. Mum and Dad in Oxford for Daddy's college weekend. Alex in the village smoking dope with Jerome. Min at Helen's riding ponies. This feels like open space.

OK so when Dad's in Bath at work and Mum's off doing hospital flowers, don't I have space? No, because I can sense their presence. Somehow the possibility of them coming back unexpectedly seems too risky. I couldn't write under a dictatorship. I couldn't be brave. How did Anne Frank manage? That's courage. Though I suppose she must have had the support of *her* family.

It's a beautiful day. The sunlight is full out but it doesn't burn you. Its light is rich like egg yolk and there is no haze or glare. The sun is lighting the world as it is. It's September light. It's everything strong and defined. I remember one afternoon at school when I was about nine lying on my back on the far sports field looking up at the sky. It was after lunch, although I'd still eaten blackberries from the hedge. Everyone else was playing nearer the school. I could hear their cries. Above me the sky was bright blue, perhaps just a bit of whitish haze really far up. There was a jet flying over. Watching it making its leisurely trail I completely lost the sound of the others. Maybe they'd all stopped for some reason. Anyway they weren't there. Only me, the plane, the sunlight and the taste of blackberries. Perfect. I associate this light with the autumn term, my favourite. A new beginning.

Next week I'll see Debbie again. I miss her so much. We speak a couple of times a week and that's great although I don't feel comfortable. I can't speak in the same way I could in Norfolk. That was even easier than school. I know she can tell I'm different but understands. When she was away in St Lucia we didn't speak, although Bob's phoned four times from Australia. He's having a brilliant time. I think I might be falling in love but I won't tell him yet. Besides our – whatever it is – has hardly stood the test of time. Wish I had email even though Bob phoning hasn't been as bad as expected. Dad's been too preoccupied with what Alex is going to do to notice who phones me and how often.

How blissful life is! I feel so warm and snuggly out here. It seems incredible that there was unhappiness today. When Mum and Dad left almost the last words he said were, Well, burn yourselves to death then, I don't care! Which could've sounded like mildly bad taste. He'd been giving us his fire prevention lecture. In the end he confronted us with the consequences of our inadequacy, hurled poisoned-tipped words at us. I think we could all see and feel the flames. He had broken off from his lecture when Min started humming and Alex got the giggles, real wide-open-mouthed goose-hissing laughter like he was still stoned from a couple of nights ago. Mum persuaded Dad not to get in the car. Peter you can't say things like that. You don't mean them.

I wanted to ask the others, why give him the opportunity to get at us?

Sorry Dad, said both Alex and Min.

Shush! said Mum. Peter, please just say your piece and we can all not worry.

He came back, staring straight at me. At least you've got some sense, Sarah. All I want is for someone to check the cooker, sockets and lights when everyone goes to bed. As he spoke his head shook from the reasonableness of what he was saying. That's not too much to ask, is it?

No, Dad.

Good. He smiled at me.

Come on, Darling. Mum took his arm. And be good you lot.

Mum, we all groaned.

This isn't 1930, Mum, said Alex. He and Mum grinned at each other.

Push-me-pull-you.

It's like Major's coat.

Dear Major, he's such a roly-poly old Labrador even though he's only three and a half. He hates the heat. I call him Scruffy when no one's about. I wonder if the others have pet names for him. If so he must be very confused – or very intelligent. I cringe at the name Major. Better than Thatcher, I grant you. A lucky escape. Quite apart from the chilling connotations of the name, she was female (although the puppet of her on TV pissed in the Gents). The dreadful thing is, he has this gormless look. With the right glasses, even Norma would be fooled.

Poor Major. When you stroke his coat the way it wants to go, you can make it look glossy, smooth, untroubled. But ruffle it the other way and it becomes choppy, inelegant, unkind. You see the blotches underneath, the loose flakes of skin, a wart, once even creatures hopping about (not fleas – worse) which resulted in him having to be anointed with some really evil-smelling stuff.

Our family life is like Major's coat.

Smooth Coat – Smoothish

The day I came back from Debbie's, Mum picked me up from Bath station. She was waiting on the platform. Dad never does that. He's either late or sits in the car outside the main entrance with the engine running, looking grumpy. He once got a parking ticket when collecting Alex. Alex had stopped at the kiosk to buy a Coke. It was this act that was to blame for the ticket, according to Dad. Alex said that when he came out Dad was still remonstrating with the traffic warden. Why didn't Dad move to a parking space, was what I said?

Mum's good about doing things like waiting on the platform. It's partly because she's basically a kind person, partly because she really does have this old-fashioned sense of doing the right thing. Alex wasn't joking when he said it's not 1930. He says it rather a lot in fact but it's still true.

Mum was brought up in the house where we live. Her father, Grandad, was a gentleman farmer. I can't remember him but from what Gran says he had the same outlook as her and she's sort of like Barbara Cartland only on a pretty modest budget. (Gran doesn't like talking about money, which is fine with Dad: he gives her the monthly allowance that was agreed when she made over the farm but none of the promised extras. Unless Mum kicks up a fuss which is not that often. When she does, she fights harder for Gran than she does for anyone else in the family; i.e. *us*, the kids.)

Our house is big but not huge. Debbie's place is much bigger even though it's an Edwardian bungalow. It goes on for ever and it's called a Manor. So it's a bit odd that Mum was brought up to behave like minor royalty.

I was pleased to be back in Bath. I wasn't looking forward to home but it's great having a home town. It's changed so much since I started boarding school. Changed in my head.

That Saturday Mum said she wanted to do some shopping for the weekend. Did I want to go with her? Not much, so she said she'd park in the multi-storey then meet me outside the Abbey in an hour. I said, Fine.

I walked through the gardens alongside the river towards Pulteney Bridge. The borders are pretty boring – it looks like the gardeners buy a job lot of the same flower in just one colour, red – but the bridge is brilliant. You think of bridges with shops on them with classical facades happening only in France or Italy but Bath has one.

It's funny how little I noticed the buildings as a kid when we came here to shop, and when I was at school it was just the place you escaped to when you felt brave enough to skip an afternoon. Which for me wasn't very often. Then it was the shops and cinemas I noticed. I liked the old-fashioned cake place off Milsom Street and later the off-licence along Sydney Road which seemed miles away from anywhere. I must have spent my childhood not looking up. Now I think what a beautiful town it is. All the history. That Saturday I wandered the streets, losing myself in the surprises round every corner, especially the out of the way ones like a Georgian bridge between two buildings over a cobbled alleyway. Something else you wouldn't expect in the West Country. I got to the Abbey a quarter of an hour early and Mum was late. I spent the time gazing at the angels and dragon's teeth around the west door.

I felt much calmer as we drove home.

How's Debbie? Mum asked as we were heading up Landsdown Hill.

We were passing a small development of mini-Georgian houses that must have been put up in the sixties. When I was a little girl I used to think I'd live in a house like that They look a bit tacky now but when I was small I loved their smoothness, their tininess. A complete contrast to the medieval crookedness of home (nothing's straight) – though I didn't think of it like that then. It just seemed bulging and jumbly.

She's wonderful, Mum.

You look so much better. You needed a break. You've been working like a mad-thing. It's not good for you to put in so much effort early on. You'll peak too soon.

I've got into everything, Mum. Work's brilliant. It's different from when I did Os. Then I was like a parrot. Now I'm finding out things for myself.

You're so different from me when I was at school. I always seemed to be hopeless. Rather like Alex.

We didn't say anything for a bit. Mum often drops her bombshells at the end of paragraphs. I think she believes they'll stand out less there. Instead they blow the atmosphere to pieces.

What happened? I said eventually.

Not much, according to Dad. But Alex says there are plenty of courses he can do with the grades.

Well come on Mum what are they?

D, E, F.

Wow!

Exactly, I was amazed he got any of them from what he'd been saying when he came home.

He hadn't said anything like that to me. But then he did have a special relationship with Mum.

Which courses is he thinking of?

I don't know, you'll have to ask him. But he doesn't seem worried.

What about Dad?

He was annoyed to start with.

Furious? Incandescent?

Annoyed. But everything's fine now.

Rough Coat

The first person I saw after I took my bag upstairs *was* Alex.

I'd just come into the hall and was about to go and help Mum in the kitchen when he staggered through the side door from the

56

garden.

I could hear Dad in his study. When I'd gone up he'd been shouting at someone down the phone. Now his voice was still loud but more reasonable. Evidently he was doing all the talking.

Oh shit, I said when I saw Alex.

Well that's a nice way to say hello tuh— He was going to continue but his voice broke up into bad speech difficulties. He bendy-toy'd onto the bottom step and sat with his body arched forward, his legs wide apart, his elbows resting on his knees and his head in his hands. The manoeuvre was executed without any thumping or bumping. It had a sort of improbability about it – that and a comic elegance, enhanced by his long thin limbs.

I stood over him. Come on Alex, up! I said. I had to get him upstairs.

No reaction.

Oh Alex, please.

He turned his head with his hands and his face swivelled towards me. He was grimacing as if the whole rubber body'd incoherence thing had been a joke. Only I knew it wasn't.

You didn't ring, he said with alarming clarity.

I'm sorry. I just forgot. I feel awful about it.

Suppose Mum huh—

Yeah. Sorry.

Ho hah—

His head was back in its navel-gazing position.

I knelt down and took his face in my hands. I kissed his forehead and nose. I put my forehead against his and rubbed gently.

What are you doing, boy?

We looked into each other's eyes. His whites were crazy paving with red cement.

What is it? What've you taken?

Hope.

Not just dope. Come on.

Temazepah—

Jesus! Idiot.

Suddenly his arms were around my neck and he was

sandpapering my cheek.

Come on. Stop it. I tried to wriggle away.

He was mumbling. I felt like Esmerelda to his Quasimodo.

Come on you idiot.

I managed to extricate myself.

Will you stop calling me a fucking idiot!

It was extraordinary. He sounded perfectly normal. But the effort had been too much and his eyes began to cross.

Behind me I could hear Dad's voice shouting again. I sensed he was about to slam the phone down. I panicked. I got behind Alex and tried to haul him upright by climbing the stairs backwards.

I must have pulled him against the hard edge of one of the steps because he started howling. The pain energised him and he got to his feet. I grabbed his arm and he lolloped upstairs after me.

I got him into his bedroom and then into the bathroom. I pulled his shirt over his head and sat him on the loo. I ran a little warm water into the sink and got him to stand over it. I eased his head into the water and massaged his scalp. I wasn't sure if I was doing the right thing but I wanted to get him clean. His hair stank of dope. He looked as if he hadn't washed it for a week. I shampooed his hair. I listened to his breathing. I wanted to know if he was going to be sick. Instead the washing seemed to calm him.

Smooth Coat

Dad was on the phone to someone else when I got back to the hall. He was telling a story to someone. I heard, Yeah, I know, absolutely unbelievable. Couldn't believe it. You wouldn't get away with it in a novel. I presumed he was recounting what had happened in the last conversation.

In the kitchen Mum was preparing Saturday supper. She was peeling carrots. I could smell roasting beef.

What's for Sunday lunch, then?

Figs and Parma ham, corn on the cob with pesto sauce, spaghetti carbonara and green olive ice-cream.

Jees, what's that in aid of?

I might have guessed: Rick, Dad's partner in the practice, was coming over with his new girlfriend who was Italian.

Your Dad didn't want to miss out on his Sunday roast so we're having it tonight. He thought it would be a welcome home meal for you too.

I felt *so* flattered.

Dining-room? I asked.

Of course.

Is the table set?

No, Min's gone riding.

I wondered how many of the tasks I usually did Min had actually done while I'd been away. I imagined Mum did most of them. Min hates being told to do things. Like Alex she's a rebel only unlike him she's able to get away with it. Criticism is like water off a duck's back. Most importantly she doesn't drink or smoke dope and so can argue herself out of anything with absolute single-mindedness. Even if she did drink or smoke dope, I couldn't imagine she'd be any different. She doesn't like arguing, mind you: she prefers to just get on with what she wants and sod everyone else. Do I wish I was like her? A bit I suppose. Most of all I wish Alex was like her. He's so vulnerable.

The dining-room was still, like a chapel. It's only used a couple of times a week and is kept spotless by Una. Whenever you go in on your own it makes you feel calm. It smells of polish from the table and the bare floor-boards around the edge of the carpet and of stone from the big fireplace. I love setting the table. I select the mats and put them out first. The mats have hunting scenes on them. That day I was in two minds whether I should give 'The Kill' to Dad or Min. Dad's never been hunting in his life but likes to show solidarity with that kind of thing. Min, I'm sure, will be starting before long. I'm amazed she hasn't already.

Then I select the cutlery, pinching the sides of the handles between my thumb and forefinger and laying them in a tea-towel before transferring the bundle to the table and positioning them. The glasses come from the corner cabinet which smells of polish and old wood. It's not a soft, fusty smell but clean and nutty and hard as if the last four centuries have cured the wood. Each glass is given a polish before being put in place.

In the winter I also light the fire.

I'm glad it's only me that likes these tasks. They give me such pleasure.

Back in the kitchen I de-stringed, topped and sliced the runner beans Una brought up from her husband's garden.

When Dad came in I was lost in a trance brought on by the smell of their juice and by Mum's easy chatter.

You'll never guess what that lunatic woman's— he began and I thought he's full of some scheme to do with the practice or the City Council and he's going to rant. But then he saw me.

Sarah. I didn't know you were back.

I looked at Mum, as did Dad.

I thought you were coming back late this evening. Pen you never told me—

Honestly, Peter, you're so wrapped up in that planning business.

She rolled her gaze towards the ceiling and tutted theatrically.

Well, Dad said, it's tremendously important for the future of the practice— and I thought he was going to go on.

Instead he gave me an enormous hug and kissed my forehead and both cheeks.

Sarah, how are you? We've missed you, haven't we Pen? How was Norfolk? And how's Will?

He'd met Debbie's parents at speech day and immediately took to Will. He admires anybody who's good at business. Not that Dad is that good at business, I don't think. Although he says he is. But it's Mum's money. He admires Will because he's made a killing with his software company.

I looked at Dad and was kind of overwhelmed by him.

And I felt guilty because I'd told Debbie he has 'Episodes' and written about him in my diary.

Rough Coat

Min was cutting it fine, as usual. Although how she gets out of her riding stuff, showers and makes herself look as cool as a cucumber in fifteen minutes is a complete mystery. We heard Helen's Mum's BMW draw up on the gravel at seven twenty-seven, Min and Helen calling out the arrangements for tomorrow as Min crunched to the front door and then there she was – just as I was draining the veg – looking tall, willowy in a flowing fuchsia dress and most definitely *not* fourteen.

Hi Sare, she said when she realised it was me. I didn't think you were coming back tonight. Is there anything I can do? Where's Mum?

She gave me a tight little peck on the cheek.

Mmm, beef!

Mum's upstairs – freshening up, babes.

Babes! She gave me an Oh *please* look.

Out-of-the-way, out-of-the-way.

I plonked the joint down on the kitchen table.

Anything I can do? Table laid?

Min! We're serving up!

I know how much you just *lurv* it. She sashayed out of the room. I'll get Dad.

I poured off the juices for the gravy, feeling like Cinderella, although I enjoy getting the food ready. It helps me steady my nerves.

OK all under control? said Dad coming through from the hall. Smells good. Shouldn't it still be in the oven, though?

As you say, Daddy, all under control.

I gave the gravy a stir and put the meat back in the oven.

Um, Yorkshires, said Dad.

Shoo!

I'll go and open the wine.

All done.

Check it then.

As he left Mum arrived. Have you seen Alex?

He's in his room.

Is he? I poked my head round his door and he wasn't there. Must've been in the bathroom.

I finished draining the veg and putting them into serving dishes. I suddenly wanted to crack myself open and let myself out like I was one of those Russian dolls. I told myself to keep calm. I opened the oven and turned the roasties even though they were coming out in about half a minute. I wanted to burst. I wanted to leave me to it – this dutiful me, the one that just *lurved* all this getting the meal ready. I wanted to skip off down the lane and magically meet Debbie and have a pint or get stoned. I wanted to be anywhere but here. Although if I had to be anywhere in the house I'd rather be here.

I wondered whether I should go and check on Alex but couldn't move. He'd be alright, I told myself. He always was. But then what about D, E, F and all the drugs? Had I done the right thing leaving him? He seemed to improve before I came down. But I couldn't help thinking I'd been selfish – after all I did know how vulnerable he was. Every time I smoothed things over, I was just being selfish, wasn't I? I wanted everything to run smoothly. But it never did. It always span out of control.

Right, Mum said, shall I take these through?

Push-me-pull-you.

Dad carved, as usual.

I let him serve everyone else – everyone else except Alex – while I busied myself fetching things from the kitchen and putting the saucepans in to soak.

By the time I got the roasting dish in the sink I'd summoned up enough courage to go and see if Alex was alright, but I knew I was too late. It occurred to me I'd been deliberately deceiving myself, pretending to be looking for an opportunity but finding it only when there was no hope. But then why would I do that? The summoning and the indecision, not to mention the realisation I'd missed my chance, were all agony.

I knew I had to get back in time for Dad to serve me.

He was putting a gigantic hunk on Min's plate when I arrived.

Mum had put on a CD – Leonard Cohen.

Just a little for me, Dad.

Nonsense, you've had a long day.

No really, I'm not hungry. *Tiny piece*, I said putting on a little girl voice.

Pen – your daughter's turning into a vegetarian!

I felt angry and embarrassed.

Yuck! went Min.

Don't bully her, Peter.

Doesn't matter, I said to Dad, and the moment I did I thought, But it does, it *really* does.

How's that?

I looked at my plate. The meat was thick and bloody. I knew it would taste nice and I'd loved cooking it. I just didn't much feel like eating it. I felt defeated. I wanted to sulk.

But there was a fiercer self inside too. Another Russian doll struggling to get out. It wanted to smash the plate on the floor or stuff the blood-soaked strips of leather into his stupid mouth. I hated the thought I could think that.

Mum poured me some water when I sat down.

Don't eat it all, she whispered.

I smiled thanks.

What she didn't say but I knew she meant was, He doesn't mean it.

Push-me-pull-you.

Min, can I have some wine?

'Course, babes. She was speaking with her mouth full. She seemed annoyed I'd brought her out of her chomping stupor. She crashed the bottle onto the table, as hard as she dared, gave it a shove and it began to tip. When I stopped it, I swear she looked disappointed.

Then, just as *Suzanne* started playing, Alex wandered in.

Better late than never, said Dad.

Sorry I'm late. Alex was subdued but OK. He even looked cool, I thought, with his newly-washed hair, and had had the sense to put on a clean shirt.

He wasn't simply cool-cool but like a cool breeze streaming into the room.

I felt Dad could sense this too. He sounded as if he meant 'Better late than never'. I stared at the two men and it occurred to me how much they loved each other, deep down.

I cut a piece of meat, not a big piece – I didn't feel that confident – but big enough to be a celebration.

While Dad cut Alex's meat everyone else was silent. I listened to the music. Mum told me once that she and Dad loved this CD because they'd bought it on vinyl when they got together. I imagined what it would be like if Bob and I got married – or lived together anyway. Would we be like Mum and Dad in twenty years time, having supper with our kids and playing Björk *Debut*?

Have you been taking drugs?

Min was staring slyly at Alex who'd sat down opposite her.

Fuck off, he said.

I couldn't believe it was happening.

Don't swear please, said Dad.

Yes, don't Alex, said Mum.

Anyway, said Dad, have you?

Have I what?

Been taking drugs?

Why don't you fuck off too, Dad. Alex sounded chilling. I thought, My God, they hate each other. How could I have got it *so* wrong?

D'you hear that, Pen? Your son just told me to fuck off.

Mum didn't know where to put herself.

Dad wasn't looking at her anyway. Look sunshine, he said, jabbing his fork towards Alex, if there's going to be any fucking off here, it's going to be you. Now, apologise to Min or get out.

It was only then that I noticed Min. She was still in her meat trance. She seemed completely oblivious to what was happening.

I got up from the table.

Dad and Alex's voices were getting louder and more angry.

I apologised to Mum as if I was going to the loo. I was but I sort of knew I didn't want to pee.

I felt like my head was about to burst. Not only my head, but my chest, tummy and abdomen. It was like the doll inside me wanted to burst out. I locked the door, lifted the lid and put my fingers down my throat. The softness gagged on them. The skin of my palette felt dry and like it was sticking to them, like it might come off. I coughed and felt saliva and the skin suddenly slippery. I rammed my fingers harder then pulled them out. The puke streamed out of my mouth and splashed into the water. I was amazed how digested it was. And then I felt a wave of pleasure. A warmth. An anaesthetic. I flushed the lavatory. I went to the sink and rinsed my mouth. As I straightened up I was overwhelmed by a feeling of cleanness. I was empty, pure inside. I was slight. I was like an egg. I was smooth as a shell. I was calm, infinite and strong. I went back to the dining-room a different person.

Tom's writing therapy

04/08/01 – A Saturday

The Saturday after Jill left I drove out of London on the A12. At Chelmsford I took the A414 for Maldon. Just beyond Danbury I turned down the B1010 and followed it through Hazeleigh and Rudley Green to the B1018. I crossed over and set off along the lane that takes you to Cooper's Creek and the River Blackwater. But instead of going all the way I took the left turn half way along and headed north back towards Maldon.

Almost immediately the lane passed over the Mundon Wash. I knew this route like my own face, could recite the names of the farms – lovely names like Copkitchen and Bramble Hill – could hear my grandfather's voice telling me them. Over to my right the land began its gentle fall to the river and I caught sight of Northey Island. I came to the ash and oak standing either side of the road. I could hear – can still hear – Grandad's rhyme: 'If the oak shows before the ash, there'll be a splash; if the ash's before the oak, you'll see a soak.' This was said by a man who'd spent fifty-five years in Essex but still retained his Norfolk accent. I can hear Mum chipping in her version whenever she heard him tell his. 'Oak before ash, summer splash – ash before oak, summer soak.' 'It's neater that,' she'd say, hamming up her usually light Yorkshire accent. 'None of this iffing and showing business. To the point Grandad.' 'Ah, but you can't beat Norfolk for poetry, can you girl?'

We used to take Grandad down to Cooper's Creek when he lost the use of his legs so he could watch the coming and going of the tide.

Near the town I passed the sign to the site of the Battle of Maldon – one of the subjects I was able to write well on before I decided to chuck in my history degree. I was always good on battles, especially primitive ones. With battles you can see the way things stand. You can make clear sense of strategy and tactics. Although there's no absolute rights and wrongs – just like with people-history – with battles I found I could speculate about what might have happened if so-and-so had done such-and-such much more easily. Battles are practical common-sense things. It was when it came to teasing out the different levels in social history or trying to work out how two people interacted in the political arena that I came a cropper. I sometimes wonder whether I'd fare any better now if I went back to finish my degree – as I occasionally consider doing.

Anyway, after the sign to the battlefield, I went straight over the ring-road roundabout and hung a left into a newish estate. The farmhouse was around the next bend. The road dipped down to a stream and on the opposite side was the farmhouse to the left of the road and the engineering shop on the right. Both buildings looked mightily incongruous in the middle of all that self-conscious eighties residential vernacular. The fact that Grandad's farm was the real McCoy only made the fake detail – the chalk lump, timbering and pargework – seem all the more bolted on. The engineering shop stuck out for different reasons, although Dad went to a lot of trouble to disguise it with shrubs and trees.

I pulled over to the side of the road and switched off the ignition. I'd had no fixed idea of where I was driving when I left Highgate. I'd not exactly intended to end up here, although I wasn't surprised by the route I followed either. I suppose, looking back, the act of driving was as important as anything – I often feel calm behind the wheel – although I also needed to touch base. It was like I needed to confirm I was me.

The farmhouse was clay lump painted white and this together with the depth of the walls and the bold roundness of its shape – not a single corner was pointed, no door or window opening had a straight edge – made it look like it was made of icing sugar.

Great Grandad moved there in the Depression. Up till then he'd been a tenant farmer up by Beccles. But around 1930 Great Grandmother inherited a chemist's shop in Chelmsford, the town where she'd grown up. She said he could buy a farm with the cash from the sale of the business so long as they moved to Essex. They were only there five years before he committed suicide. Grandad never talked about his father but according to Dad, Great Grandad never settled. Added to which he couldn't make the land pay. I suppose it was a different kind to what he was used to.

When he took his life he wasn't in debt but soon would have been. Oddly enough, his death was probably the best thing that could've happened for Grandad and his brother, Uncle Ted. They weren't much interested in farming and so they sold the land and one of the cottages and set up as welders and mechanics. Grandfather, his young family and Great Grandmother lived in the farmhouse while Ted moved into the remaining cottage which was no longer needed for a farm worker. The original shop was converted out of a corrugated iron barn.

Grandad and Ted were craftsmen – and artists in their own way – and were soon coining it. They did farm machinery, obviously, but their big success was a contract to service Council vehicles. Then when the war came they took it in turns to go over to Lakenheath and work on the planes in one-week-on, one-week-off shifts. It was knackering but the money was exceptional.

Dad didn't join the business until the early nineteen-fifties. By then he'd done his National Service and had enrolled on a Guilds' Diploma in Light Industry and Book-Keeping which would take him three years at night school. During the day he worked as the firm's apprentice. I don't know whether he ever considered doing anything else but I suspect not. I think he knew a good opportunity when he saw one and decided he'd learn as much as he could from the older generation while developing his own ideas through his studies. He was very respectful of Grandad and Uncle Ted, introducing new ways only gradually and leaving a respectable interval between Grandad's retirement (Ted died a couple of years before) and putting up the new shop.

I can just remember being taken to see the old one coming down. I had to stand with Mum at a safe distance as if it was being blown up. Whereas in reality Dad and the two lads, Wal and Richie, were dismantling it piece by piece with such tenderness that hardly a rusty washer got lost.

The funny thing was it wasn't so much Mum as Dad who wanted us to stand back. In fact Mum would've probably been easier about me being closer. She had a sort of you-can't-alter-the-future outlook on life. Dad, on the other hand, has always been a stickler for safety. He'd never have forgiven himself if the wind caught a loose sheet and it sliced me in two. At the time, I guess I didn't understand Mum and Dad's different temperaments and assumed it was Mum spoiling the fun.

I think it was that day I kicked her in the shins. I caught her wrong so my toes rather than the sole of my rubber wellingtons connected with her leg. I howled the place down and had to be carted off home, missing out on one of Granny's longed-for high teas.

As I sat in the car looking at the old farmhouse and the shop, I began to feel sad. Remembering my childhood and the stories Grandad and my parents told me reminded me of little fantasies I had about Jill and me having kids. We never really discussed children apart from testing the idea on each other now and again. Once when we were going for a walk near home this tiny boy whizzed past us out of nowhere on a skateboard and flicked a V. He deliberately skewed in close to my ankles making me jump against Jill and nearly sending us both over. 'Little fucker!' I said to her. 'Kids, eh? Who'd have them?' 'I bet you were like that once,' she said. 'And you never know, one day I might make a dad out of you.' Not that she'd ever put up any explicit signs pointing in that direction before and wouldn't do after but I felt so close to her at that moment. There was something real there and we both knew it.

Coming back to Maldon suddenly made me realise what I'd lost in ways I never imagined it would.

It was then, on the spur of the moment, I decided to see Dad. I needed to tell him about Jill.

*

Dad lives about a mile from the shop in a brick detached Edwardian house with about half an acre of garden. He and Mum bought it in the late sixties not long before I was born. It isn't as big as the farmhouse – three double bedrooms, one single – but Grandad used to take the piss out of Dad about it without quarter. It's in a fairly up-market area and our neighbours when I was young were a doctor and bank manager. Grandad used to say Dad was getting 'High-blown ideas, boy' and would sell the shop next and move to the Costa Brava.

I love the house. Mum made it a real home.

When Dad opened the door I was as surprised as him. It was only when I saw him that the fact I was there and intending to tell him about Jill hit me.

'Tom, what are you doing here? Nothing's wrong I hope.'

'No Dad. I was just passing – on my way back from a meeting. Jill's gone to stay with Jemimah for the weekend and I thought I'd come and see you.'

'That's good of you. Well, don't stand there, come in. I've got the kettle on.'

There was a lovely display of chrysanthemums on the hall table. Dad is amazing about keeping things like that up – things Mum used to do. For a second I expected her to come through from the kitchen.

As I followed him down the passage I realised my surprise visit had settled one thing I suspected about him. He was wearing his old tweed jacket Mum bought when I was a little boy. He'd always loved that jacket but even so I couldn't help thinking his wearing it was a bit morbid. It seemed to me it was indicative of the depressed state he went into when he lost her and which he's never entirely got out of. I'd bought him a new jacket the previous Christmas. A real cracker – just his colour, light-weight like he preferred but a really top quality, hard-wearing cloth. I even got the tailor to put leather patches on the elbows and strips round the cuffs. Whenever Jill and I came over he was always wearing it but I felt it wasn't ever looking worn in – despite the material. Now I knew the truth.

As he attended to the kettle, I put my hand on his shoulder.

'Good to see you Dad.'

*

'Dad, I've got something to tell you.'

It was now evening. Dad had suggested we went out for a meal and offered to do the driving.

The Marney Tower stands on its own about half-way between Messing and Easthorpe and has been a favourite of his for as long as I can remember. It's changed precious little since I first went there when I was fourteen. Before then he and Mum and occasionally friends went there without me. The place took on a kind of mythical status and I remember being unbelievably proud when I was finally allowed to accompany them.

Outside, it's a beautiful warm brick with old grey timbering. It's a low building with an unusually tall barley-twist chimney. Inside there are flagstoned floors and a massive fireplace. There are hops above the bar and copper-topped tables. Only once, for a period of about five years, has it fallen into the hands of an unsympathetic landlord. It wasn't that he changed the way it looked but he was clearly in the wrong business. His fondness for his product made him surly and occasionally violent. He was evicted by the brewery in Mum's last year. It always seemed to me a blessing that she and Dad could go there a couple of times and enjoy a nice atmosphere before she passed away.

That night we were eating our mains – chicken for Dad and beef Wellington for me – accompanied by pints of Abbot. As usual the beer was proving a difficult one to define. I grew up on it, after all, and I could never recapture the purity of my first pint when I was bunking off school. I could still taste the distinctive fruitiness but couldn't put a name to it. It was simply a familiar combination of flavours. Although its pleasing effects also had something in common with Dad's old jacket (now replaced by the one I bought him) and how it affected him because the beer reminded me of being there with Mum.

The way Dad looked at me when I said I had something to tell him immediately knocked my confidence. He was surprised for a millisecond then his green eyes sparkled. He hid his emotion quickly but I was in no doubt I'd glimpsed it. I could guess what was behind it: marriage or children. Of course he would have liked me and Jill to marry first because he wanted us to have what made him so happy. But if we stayed as we were and had a kid he'd have still been over the moon. Having kids was the Big One. Given what I'd been feeling earlier I assumed his twinkling eyes were about children.

I panicked. I couldn't tell him about Jill, could I? It would have hurt him too much. It wasn't the right time. I couldn't do that to him when we were all cheerful with our food and pints.

'I've decided to sell up,' I said.

He was taken aback, I could tell, but I knew I'd succeeded in deflecting him from the emotional stuff and he was engaging with the business issues.

'The business?'

'Yeah, the whole shooting-match. Well as much as I own.'

'I don't know what to say.'

'Well I hope you'll be pleased for me.'

'I dare say. But are you sure about it? What will you do? What does Jill think?'

'I haven't told her yet. But I know she'll be pleased. She's been on at me to spend more time with her for ages.'

'There's time and time. Don't think I'm interfering but you can't just click your heels, you know. I've seen people from the Chamber of Commerce sell up a good business and sit on their backsides for a bit thinking they've got all the time in the world to find something else. Well some do but some take a fall. They find they've spent too much of their capital rewarding themselves for selling so well, or else inflation catches them out. You know, they suddenly realise markets have moved on faster than they bargained for and their capital isn't going to buy them a business that'll give them half as much income as they're used to. It's a dangerous time, when you've sold up. Unless you're careful the days turn into years before you know it. Anyway, you'll be bored to death and drive Jill up the wall. She'll be begging you to get out from under her feet.'

72

'Quite a speech,' I said, though I wasn't knocking him and he understood that.

'I'm bound to be worried. It's that you've done so well. I'm proud of you and don't want you to come unstuck.'

'I'm grateful for that Dad. I really am. It is a bit of an unreal time. It's good to have someone bringing you down to earth.'

He smiled at me. 'Even so, I haven't said well done, have I? I haven't even asked how much you're getting, if you don't mind me asking. I'd quite—'

'No, Dad, I don't mind at all.'

As we talked business our different sides of the conversation meshed together tightly. He could see where I was coming from. He'd voiced doubts about getting the venture capital at the time and had considerable sympathy for my disenchantment about the way the company was going. He was impressed by the sum I was getting. Though I didn't explain about the options. I reckon I'd mentioned them to him before, thinking back, so he didn't raise them either because he'd forgotten or didn't want to burst my bubble. I suspect the latter. He'd made his speech and now wanted to bask with me in my glory.

I love my Dad. He's my rock. It's corny to say so – a million princesses must have used that expression up and down the land – but it's true. It is for me just as it was for Mum. When she campaigned for branch libraries she showed a flair and commitment Dad could never have matched but without his solidity she could never have done it.

I take after her as far as chancing my arm is concerned. Or rather she was who I got the confidence to try different things from. Not that it was always obvious she was adventurous when I was young. To me then she was often simply a librarian. The campaigning didn't start until I was in my teens.

Looking back I think Dad was probably embarrassed when she began, although he didn't let that stop him supporting her. He would have given her a little lecture – same as he gave me that night – but as soon as he realised she was serious and had thought things through, he was behind her.

As we chatted I forgot Jill – quite got into the part I'd decided to play. Instead I slipped back into those other rites-of-passage moments that I'd shared with him and which he carried me through. There was my decision to give up university, my choosing the pub trade, my first pub on my own, buying the flat with Jill – loads of other times too.

The funny thing was I'd never consulted Mum about things like that first: not often anyway; though maybe when I began going out with Jill. Mostly the protocol was to talk to Dad then he'd discuss things with Mum who'd have a word with me afterwards. It wasn't that Dad was patriarchal, far from it, but we both wanted him to take that role.

He has quiet authority. It's not simply his engineer's precise manner but his capacity for love.

I wonder now whether I wasn't in a state of shock that evening. I should have trusted that love and made a clean breast of Jill leaving. Dad's love was big enough when I did eventually tell him four months later but I couldn't help feeling guilty. He wasn't stupid and must have been hurt I'd kept quiet that evening at the pub. I'd led him into a conversation and emotional responses under false pretences.

*

The guilt began that night when I was lying in the bed I'd had since I was fifteen. I lay awake reflecting on the evening and Jill – she was coming back into the picture as the effects of the Abbot wore off. In the foreground, though, were bits of what Dad said. His voice was both balm and a reminder I'd not been straight with him. It also provoked the thought I'd let not only myself down by not spending enough time with Jill but my family as well. My ancestors.

Of course Dad wouldn't have wanted me to feel like that but there's gravitas in that voice. It's the accent. He's of that generation that was caught between two vernaculars – in our family's case, old Norfolk and my Estuarine vowels. Both Mum and Dad flattened out their native speech considerably – in order to get on, I suppose. In the fifties, I guess, it was what you did.

The fact it somehow made me feel a bit of a lout wasn't intended. Nor would Dad have deliberately courted the deep respectfulness Grandad had towards him for all his taking the piss out of Dad.

As I fell asleep, I felt like an idiot quite honestly.

Part Two

Sarah's Diary

13*th* Feb. '98

I found my old diary this morning when I was clearing out my room. I didn't put it in a box with the other stuff because I'm going to read it tonight. Instead I put it with this one inside my overnight bag. Old habits die hard! Not that there's any need for concealment now. In fact Dad's been pretty amazing over the wedding. He's mellowed – towards me, at least – and I'm learning to trust him more. I suppose we have an adult relationship at last. I know I've certainly grown up a lot in the past four years.

I'll read through my diaries in bed. These days I read for hours anyway before falling asleep. There's so much inside my head, the only way I can get it to shut up is reading. I don't suppose the diaries will have quite the same effect but finding the other one put the idea into my head of going through them and that's that.

I flicked through the first few pages when I discovered it (after asking myself why I'd abandoned it in my room when I left home – I didn't come up with an answer but I'm thinking about it). Some of the things blew me away. I wasn't shocked: I just freaked at how vulnerable she was. I wished I could go back and tell her not to worry. That everything would come good in the end. But maybe things wouldn't have come good if something like that had happened. What I've gone through has been like a series of trials which have made things come good.

But before I read there's an evening with uncle Vern to endure – not exactly a trial by fire, that one, more a damp squib. He's a cat vet. I'm being unfair, of course, but you can't help thinking of Harry Enfield's 'Nice But Dim' whenever you see him. There was one time, a couple of years ago, when I saw another side. But mostly he's our family joke. Dad's always been a riot about him, making loaded comments whenever he's come to stay, right in front of him, playing to the gallery of us lot, making us nearly wet ourselves trying to keep from laughing. It's cruel. But even when we've all been at each other's throats beforehand, Uncle Vern is one of those people who's guaranteed to unite the family (poor Mum excepted – her 'dear' brother).

Ah well, maybe it'll be different tonight – now I'm so much more mature...

August 1995 – Tuesday 29th

It's almost a year since I last wrote this diary.

I didn't plan not to write. I just lost the will, somehow. Partly it was because of going back to school. Partly, I was shocked at having written so candidly about myself and my family.

Writing was a release but once I started my final year doing As I felt I had to take things more seriously. What I'd written seemed to be a bit like the licenced anarchy in *Twelfth Night*. It was letting off steam, a necessary bit of mischief at the darkest time of the year (summer holidays in my case) before I had to confront the harsh realities of life.

All of which might also be said about the other thing that happened then. At the risk of seeming coy... No, I'll say it, the chucking up. Which didn't stop when I was back at school and performed the same function as this diary only on a day-to-day basis. It seemed to help me get through. Although I'm better now, calmer, I believe it somehow saved me from myself. It was as if I was able to concentrate all my shit feelings into a couple of moments when I simply threw them up.

I expected to get thin but didn't. No more than some of the other swats. I certainly wasn't like Henrietta in Year Eight who became like a skeleton and had to be hospitalised. For me, it all seemed perfectly rational. There were just a few times I lost control, and they were terrifying, but I don't want to talk about those.

Finishing As and enjoying a long hot summer in a household that appears to be on an even keel for once – my last summer holiday as a child I suppose – seem to have cured me. I know I'm living in a Fool's Paradise because I have things I now need to broach with Mum and Dad. I think it's the thought of what's going to happen next that is making me write. I don't want to start throwing up again. That's history. So I write.

Mum and Dad are still aglow with pride at my two As and a B. Little do they suspect their dear little daughter is about to ambush them. But it's now or never. With Alex living in Bath – out of sight out of mind (out of his mind and seducing all the girls who come to admire his body and his flowers) – with Min suddenly looking up to me, and with me the golden girl in Mum and Dad's eyes for the first time in my life, it's got to be the right time.

So why am I feeling like someone standing on a precipice about to jump?

I want to jump. I *need* to jump. I know I can fly. There is nothing to fear.

...A little later, after a quick saunter round and round the garden.

One thing I've noticed is how like stories last year's entries were. I was puzzled at first. At the time I just wrote. I didn't think further than the need to express myself. It's only with hindsight that you can see *how* you wrote.

In the garden, I wondered where that came from. I suddenly remembered Miss Allison. I was twelve and she told us how she wrote out her life as a story with dialogue and everything and how this helped her to stay sane. At the time, I thought she was exaggerating but now I'm pretty sure she wasn't.

So last year, under the covers of my mind, it was like she reached out in the darkness across the years and touched my hand, gave me something to heal myself with.

Thursday 31st

I told Mum and Dad what I'd decided when they were in the study drinking sherry. They have taken to doing this in between Dad getting home and Mum preparing supper. If it's nice they sit out on the little terrace.

They must have started this ritual before I came back from school, although on my first night they didn't do it because there was champagne by the pool and a special meal to celebrate me leaving. When it happened the next evening, I assumed it was a one-off but it soon became clear that they were deliberately making time for each other.

I tried talking to Min about it but all I got was that it was *cool* knowing exactly where they were. She's taken up smoking. Not a lot but she seems to like lounging by the pool and enjoying a couple at about that time. She's so brazen. I've never found the courage to smoke at home even now. There would be too much hassle and I don't want to have to deal with that. I'm sure they know I smoke when I'm out with friends but as long as I don't flaunt it, they're OK. It's a kind of tacit understanding.

Their sherry trysts are the sort of things that make you wonder if they've been to Relate. You are baffled as to what's brought them on. Was Alex really so disruptive he drove them apart? I suppose one reason Dad used to be tense was the recession and that's well and truly over. I know Dad was very worried in the early nineties about some shares grandfather made over to him. Alex reckoned he might have to leave Radley. Then there's the never-ending battle over the site next to the new surgery. There was quite a kerfuffle about it this time last year but things have gone quiet again.

It's good Mum and Dad are more together. Yet I still find it spooky. It's like Dad's had a head transplant. Mum would have always liked to have sherry moments but he was always firm about the period before supper being *his* time. When he was attending to *important* things.

For me yesterday, just like for Min, it was good to know where they would be. I also knew they would be calm and relaxed. You should see the grins (somewhat smug) as you tiptoe past the terrace.

Not that it was terrace weather. It had been gloomy and wet all day. It was cold too. I couldn't believe it was summer – ish. I found myself tricked into thinking it would be dark by four and there would be a cosy log fire in the sitting-room.

The weather almost cost me my resolve. Or at least that's what I told myself. And yet, the well of resolve could not be capped. There was something in me that continued to live. So much so I felt it had me by the scruff of the neck and was hauling me towards the study. The feeling fed itself. Knowing it was in me gave me confidence. It wasn't like I was carrying out a plan but instead I was describing what was so obviously true. I had that belief in myself that Debbie has when she goes on stage. No, I wasn't carrying out a plan, I was making things happen and responding to circumstances like an animal, my whiskers sensing the fine changes in the air, helping me to judge the situation.

Mum and Dad were sitting on the two-seater sofa by the French windows. On the coffee table was an expensive bottle of sherry which had been chilled in the fridge and was standing on a silver dish.

Dad said, It's our star child.

Mum flung her arms out for me to come and kiss her. As I followed her lead, I heard her saying, I bet you've been thinking about what to buy for Danny's. Danny was Dad's partner when he started the practice. Now he was in Australia and from the look of the photos lived the *Dallas* dream. Gigantic Andrew and Fergie mansion, swimming pool, fleet of Volvos on the drive and a heli-pad. I'm due to start my gap year there in October. Before equally exotic stop offs with friends of parents and long-lost relations in New Zealand, KL, Caracas and New York. Kindly meant and appealing for about two minutes but basically a spoilt brat's global zig-zag towards total prathood.

Not exactly, I said, pulling myself up from Mum. Actually I wanted to have a chat.

Mum looked at Dad.

Dad said, I'll get a glass, and Mum patted the sofa beside her. You sit here, darling. Beastly weather.

Dreadful. I felt really cooped up.

Mum told me how the bulb went in the sort of cupboard she uses as one of her hospital flowers HQs. Technical services had more important things to do (keeping people alive) and so Mum's morning was purgatory.

There's a horrible side to me that's surfaced since I've been home that makes me want to poke fun at Mum. Before, she's always been picking up the pieces after Dad's explosions but now he's been lobotomised there's no drama to deflect attention from what she does – and what bugs her. I find myself asking, Is that all? I hate myself for being such a snob. She brings cheer to sick people's lives.

Dad poured me a sherry and sat on the stool opposite. He was still wearing his work clothes: pin-stripe suit, maroon striped shirt and Oxford college tie. He looks more like a merchant banker than a dentist. He even looks too grand for Bath City Council. Alex says he gets really freaked when Dad comes to see how he's getting along.

After we'd all clinked our glasses and said cheers, Dad asked, So, what did you want to talk about?

I'm sure I gulped, but then I said, I want to go to art school.

Bit of a show stopper, said Dad.

What do you mean, art school? Mum asked.

I don't want to go to Edinburgh. I want to go to art school. I've thought it through.

Jesus, Pen. We've got one Community Gardener and now we've got an art student. What's Min going to end up doing? Mucking out horses all day?

Peter! What kind of art school? To study—

Mum shrugged and stuck out her bottom lip.

You see I don't know anything about art schools.

Well, to start with I'll have to do a foundation year, locally. Then I'll have more idea about what I want to concentrate on and where the best place to do it is. I'll apply in the spring and go next autumn.

You mean this foundation thing would start next month. But you're flying to Australia.

I know. I'm sorry. I don't want to go.

How selfish. After all the trouble we've gone to. What do you mean, you don't want—

I'm sorry.

Have you thought about Danny and Eileen? What are they going to think? Art school? Jimmy's training to be a corporate lawyer and Janice is something big in Qantas.

She's an air-hostess, said Dad.

I looked at him and though he didn't smile with his face I thought I could see one in his eyes. I was amazed. I thought, He's really not against me. He's interested. What's he thinking? I could feel his interest. I didn't trust him. He picks you up then drops you. But I knew I had to encourage him.

I know, I'm sorry, Mum.

I could have laughed or dug my heels in. I decided a modicum of looking pathetic would do the trick.

Dad leant forward. So you'd be doing your foundation course in Bath, would you?

Yes, at the Tech.

Has that got much of a reputation? I mean do people in London take it seriously?

Yes, I think so.

Why are *you* taking it seriously, Peter? A few Nissen huts on the outskirts of Bath instead of Danny's spread in Oz. I can't believe it. If I were your age Sarah, I'd jump at the chance. You'll love it when you get there. Won't she, Peter?

I don't know, he blustered.

He looked at her and I imagined him wondering how the person he'd been enjoying a warm intimate moment with up to a few minutes ago could behave like such a lulu.

I've talked it through with Mr Sissons. I went to see him last week and he's explained how I apply and what to think about.

So, *that's* where you went.

Nice of you to talk about it with a complete stranger before telling us.

That's not fair. You met him at the Open Day and again—

Oh *that* Mr Sissons. I thought there was something wrong with him—

You liar!

I beg your pardon.

I confess, I lost it for a minute or two. Mum winds me up nowadays. She never used to.

Dad then stepped in. I think he was concerned I shouldn't throw away my advantage.

Look, he said loudly, I think this has come as a bit of a shock. Obviously. But it's also obvious that Sarah's serious. I don't necessarily think art school's a good idea but we're going to have to talk it through properly. I don't think this evening's the right time. What I suggest is a truce. OK? Then we can talk about it again tomorrow night or over the weekend.

Mum shook her head. I think it's ridiculous. But she wasn't going to argue with him.

She finished her sherry. I'm late. I've got to magic something up for supper, haven't I? She looked at Dad defiantly.

And I've got to make some phonecalls.

Which left me doing the dining table. Before I went into the study, I wondered how I would be feeling when I did this. In the end I was buzzing with excitement that tingled through my whole body.

Supper was tense, even so, with Mum, Dad and I making an effort not to start bickering. Min sensed the atmosphere right away. Her response was to pile huge amounts of mustard onto her food. She reckons Mum and Dad can smell her breath, I thought.

September 1995 – Friday 1st

Today I had a lie in. I could tell from the light coming round the sides of the curtains that it was just as bad outside as yesterday. I dozed for a bit then put a CD on. I lay in bed thinking. Not too hard – I let the thoughts form and float around for a bit then listened to some of the music. It was the Waterboys *Fisherman's Blues*. I'd set random play and the last track came on early. The WBs have paled a little recently. I was big on them in my O-level year on Alex's recommendation. But *The Stolen Child* is still really tingly. It's sung by this old Irish guy and it's got a sort of ballad feel. It's a poem by WB Yeats about faery folk tempting a human child to their enchanted island. The husky lilt of the man's voice blows you away.

It makes me think of Bob. He's staying on the west coast of Ireland with a friend from school. It's the last leg of his round-the-world trip. He tried to persuade me to go out there but I couldn't do it. I had to get art school sorted out as soon as I knew my results. I thought it would look as if I wasn't serious if I gallivanted off to Ireland. He was OK about it. I'm going to meet up with him and Debbie and Karl in a couple of weeks. I wonder if we'll still be interested in each other. Has there been anyone else? Not on my side. There was a boy who was interested in me at school but I couldn't start something in the middle of my exams – even if I wanted to.

Thinking about Bob and his year off, I did wonder if I wasn't being stupid not taking one. People say it changes you. Would I feel differently about art school after all those experiences and broadened horizons? But that's just it. The way I feel about art school is like knowing it's the right thing really deeply. Not that I didn't find myself stretching and feeling all cosy and warm and thinking for a second or two that Australian sunshine was very tempting indeed.

I stayed in bed until I could be sure Mum had gone to Bath General. I didn't want to bump into her particularly. She was so out of order in the study. I couldn't believe it when she said I was selfish. Think of the money they'll save! She's been in a funny mood, off and on, just recently. A time of life thing, I suppose.

I spent the rest of today lazing about and reading, apart from jogging and swimming. I read *The Commitments*. I thought it would bring me closer to Bob. It didn't work. It wasn't romantic at all. It was too much of a riot for that.

At about five, I retreated to my room to think about my strategy. It could only have been about ten minutes before I heard someone coming upstairs. Then there was a knock at my door. I knew it was Dad. The fact he was there turned out to be the least surprising thing.

* * * * *

I looked at my diary which was lying, closed, on my desk.

My first thought was to hide it but then this seemed a clumsy idea that would only draw attention to itself and make Dad think I was up to something.

Come in, I said, as nonchalantly as I could.

He was wearing his work clothes. I caught a whiff of cold tar soap.

Hi Sarah. Mind if we a chat for a few minutes?

Of course not. Sit down.

I indicated the bed.

I stayed seated by the desk. When he knocked I'd been facing the window, staring at the tops of the trees. Now I swivelled to face him.

He looked slightly flushed. He's not as fit as he used to be. His breathing was fairly heavy and he seemed agitated. I sometimes wonder whether he drinks at lunchtime. You can never smell any drink on his breath, though.

I didn't look at my diary but I was aware of it the whole time. Every now and then I noticed him looking at it but I'm not sure it would have occurred to him that what he was seeing was a diary. It's an exercise book after all.

The diary he tore up was quite obviously a diary.

Did he remember tearing it up?

I really don't think so.

For him, I imagine, it was just one of so many episodes in which he played a fatherly role. I'm sure he believed he was doing it for my own good. Can that be right? Perhaps he simply lost it and blotted out the memory. People aren't very good at remembering things they're not proud of.

I remember when I was staying with Debbie last summer, I wrote that it would be ironic if he'd never given the incident another thought because it made such a deep impression on me. So deep that the earlier time overlaid this afternoon. It's odd how events stay with you. This afternoon was completely different to when I was ten. My father would never have knocked then. He did as he liked. Now he treats me with a certain respect. Yet I'm in a way forever the little Sarah who was hurt by him. The diary episode was something destined to overshadow us, always, I suspect.

I got hold of this.

He held up a copy of the Tech prospectus.

And?

I think it sounds quite good.

Really?

I had a look at the place.

It's a lot better than Mum made it sound.

I know, I've given talks there but never saw the art department.

It's pretty modern.

I could see that. I phoned up some of the London colleges to check out its reputation. They all seemed to praise it.

You've been even more thorough than me.

Look, how much do you want to do this, Sarah?

Very much indeed. I'm absolutely certain.

One can never be absolutely certain about anything.

I know that, *Dad*. But you know what I mean too.

Sorry.

I've really got into art over the last year. I didn't expect to. English was always my favourite subject but somehow art has taken over. It's to do with creating things, expressing myself. It's something in me answering what we learnt at school. Art A-level taught me so much about myself.

I wanted to say much more. My words seemed inadequate.

Dad smiled at me.

There was a time when you were passionate about being a dentist.

I know, Dad, but that's not the same.

I know, I know. And being an artist isn't about garrets anymore.

No, it can lead to a proper career. You can design for businesses. You can specialise in the science side. Graduates get jobs as technicians in industries like ceramics and textiles. You learn skills that business people need.

Not all arty farty.

No Dad.

I didn't tell him that I quite fancied being what he called 'arty farty' for a bit.

Even so it's a big thing for me to accept.

Of course.

Though I'm actually not as much against the idea as you'd think. Not like Mum. She's got pretty worked up.

I couldn't believe her the other night.

I think she's just terribly disappointed about your year off, that's all. She's not really very interested in academic stuff. The idea of you going somewhere like Edinburgh is important, of course, but that's because it's, I don't know, *Edinburgh*. She's been looking forward to the social aspects of you doing well. I suppose she can't understand why you don't want to do all the fun things she would have loved to do herself.

Yeah, I know. But 'selfish' was a bit much.

I'm sure she didn't mean that. I'll have a word with her later.

I'll tell her what I've found out. I've also done a bit of research into the position with Edinburgh. It looks like you can defer your place for another year and so long as you play straight with them, letting them know what you've decided by such-and-such a date, they'll be fine about it.

I know what my decision will be.

OK but if you want my support—

Yes, I understand, Dad.

Good. One thing – I take it you'd live here.

Yes.

I had visions of persuading Mum and Dad to pay for a room in Bath but these also involved Mum being on my side. I envisaged us doing the painting and decorating together as compensation for her disappointment about me not going to Oz. Now was the time to hold my tongue.

You could in and out with me.

Yeah. Then there's the bus.

From the village?

Yes, the one that comes past here only runs twice a week. But I could cycle to the village and leave my bike at Jerome's.

Well, we'll have to see about that. We'd work out something anyway.

He stood up.

I've got some phonecalls to make before we have sherry. I'll try and talk your mother round. OK?

I don't know what to say.

Nor do I, to be quite honest. It's just, I've always believed that you, at least, know what you're doing.

I was so shocked when he said that.

Dad!

He smiled at me. I kissed him and gave him a huge hug.

When he'd gone, I thought, I don't believe it. I think I'm really going to art school!

And yet there was a voice in my head saying, What's he up to? What's in it for him?

While Mum and Dad were in the study, I went down to the sitting-room and tried phoning Debbie. Diane said she was out with Karl. I'll call tomorrow. I can't wait to tell her. And Bob, of course.

Tom's writing therapy

16/08/01 – A Thursday

The Surtees was a beautiful 1920s pub which had remained in the same family for three generations. It was situated on the A21 just to the south of Bromley. Although nowadays it was surrounded by housing, when it was built it would have stood on its own – a real genuine road house catering for the burgeoning motorist market. Ideally placed for those going on a jaunt to the Kent countryside or those more adventurous souls whose next stop was Dover.

Jill and I made it our stopping off point whenever we drove to Sevenoaks to see Jemima or Jill's mum, Cath.

To look at it from the outside, you'd think it was nothing special. It was a squarish building with nice but restrained stone-mullioned windows. The only hint that there was something more than met the eye was in the detail. If you looked closely at those windows you noticed they were still the old metal-frame originals with decent-sized brass handles on the inside. What was more, the brass was polished and the frames shone. It was the same story when it came to the pair of wrought-iron boot-scrapers either side of the front porch.

The front door was panelled oak with gleaming brass furniture. The mechanism of the handle had to be felt to be believed – smooth and positive. And although the door glided back on its oiled hinges you could tell it had weight.

These details set the tone of the pub's interior. There was nothing fancy. A flagstoned vestibule and two quarry-tiled main rooms with worn but spotless art deco rugs. There was oak panelling and stout bars, stone and tiled arched fireplaces – always on the go in winter (they gave the place a lovely smell) – and the original stools, tables and high-back Rennie Mackintoshlooking chairs.

There were prints of hunting scenes which picked up on the Surtees name and the fact the local hunt used to meet there regularly in the old days. In the smaller room was an amusing feature known as the 'Horse Power Alcove' which had engraved scenes of motorists and motor cyclists in the top lights above the main windows. There were contemporary prints of racing cars and aeroplanes.

What struck you about the Surtees was not just the decor but the love that went into keeping it clean. Even the urinals were a pleasure. Big china step-ins with copper and brass pipework and fittings.

The beer, it has to be said, was good but indifferent Harrow Pale and Brewer's Choice but in surroundings like that you would have settled for gnat's piss.

The Surtees was the natural choice for our first meeting. When we made the arrangements Jill and I were in complete mutual agreement. I took this as a good omen.

It wasn't until I opened the front door that I realised there was something wrong.

I was keyed up and hadn't noticed the new layout of the car park nor the banners across the building. In any case these weren't exactly tell-tale. The pub was a road house and had always boasted a big car park. And Harrow, though a bit sleepy in my opinion, was a long-established commercial brewer and if it suddenly decided to enter the twenty-first century and put a couple of ads up that was hardly earth-shattering news. If I did clock there was something, I probably thought, good for them.

It was only when the door mechanism grated and I looked at the handle that I realised things were different. It was more like bronze than brass. It was dirty.

The sound hit me next. If there'd been a vestibule it would have been muffled. There were never that many in as a rule anyway. That the Surtees stocked below density – well below – was one of its charms.

Before I realised the full extent of the transformation I saw Jill sitting in the far corner of the vast room. She was talking into her mobile. She looked as black as thunder.

Jesus, what the fuck's happened here, I thought?

'Jesus, what the fuck's going on?' I said to her when I reached her table.

'Hold on, *Tom's* here,' she said into the phone. 'It's outrageous!'

I suddenly realised she was directing her anger at me. When she got annoyed her delicate face pointed itself into a sort of bird's head: a bit beaky and her eyes – usually so fine and light – became beady, hard.

'Yeah, of course it is. I just can't believe it. They've vandalised the place.'

'What do you mean, you can't believe it? It's your bloody flaming company.'

I whipped round, then round a bit more trying to find where the bar was. And there above it were pennants for Pickwick's and Tupman's Strong.

'What the fuck? What've they done to my Surtees?'

'It's not the Surtees anymore. It's the Nathaniel Winkle.'

*

'Denney told me they'd got somewhere down this way. He even said it was the Nathaniel Winkle. But I was burying myself in the brewing and existing pubs. In a way, it's my own fault. I just left them to it.'

It was half and hour later and we were sitting in the Raven about a mile along the road towards the city centre. I can't really tell you what it was like. The table we were at was sticky and the beer was wet. I think Jill was on South African Chardonnay which she didn't usually go for. She obviously needed an alcohol hit.

She pushed her hand towards mine but stopped when she realised what she was doing.

'It's not your fault. I'm sorry I jumped to the wrong conclusion.'

'That's all right. But it is my fault, in a way. I've been really

96

stupid. What did Declan say?'

'I don't think I made much sense. I sounded like a hysterical—I *was* a hysterical woman. I was beside myself.'

'Understandable.'

'I gave him the right address – I hope – and he might be able to find something out on the Web but I said I'd give him another call tomorrow morning.'

'I should think it's above board. Denney's sharp but careful.'

'But if he did get planning, there's got to be some back-hander involved. Or a sweetener, maybe?'

'Well, you've got to prove it, haven't you? In any case there might be some perfectly legal government incentive scheme in play. You know, less favoured area.'

'Hardly.'

'Yeah, you're right. Anyway, don't hold back because of me. If any of your heritage contacts can nail us, go for it.'

'Don't worry.'

Despite her harsh words, her face was much softer. There was just the normal level of determination that gave her features purpose. Some strands of hair to the left of her parting were squint a little so you could see into the honey layers beneath the highlights.

I wanted to touch her. If this was the morning before she left, I'd touch her and she'd let me. Since then there'd been the letter – but that didn't say anything angry – there'd been her absence. There'd been a couple of phone calls. We hadn't had words, except when we were at the Surtees which didn't count. I knew she was a no-go area. Why? What had changed? It's taken a couple of years to understand. If I do, even now.

'Anyway, it wasn't why we agreed to meet, was it?' she said.

'No.'

'You look tired.'

'There's been a lot to sort out.'

'How's that going?'

'OK. Claudette's on the case. Money should be through in about six months. They're trying to drive a hard bargain but Claudette's up to them. Although there'll probably come a point when I'll walk away. I won't fight to the bitter end.'

'You'll still be rich.'

'*We'll* be rich.'

'Don't say that.'

'I don't mean *us*. I mean I'll see you right. If that's what you want.'

'We'll see. It's a bit early to be talking like that – about the money side, I mean.'

'You obviously haven't talked to a lawyer.'

I think she had though. She looked a touch guilty. I wanted to hug her.

'Do you feel better for having sold?'

'Yes. Yes, I do. It's not my business anymore. You only have to look at the Surtees to see that. It's not fun anymore. Denney and his lads haven't got any ideals. Or rather, their ideals aren't about brewing and pubs. They're not *pub* people. They're vulture capitalists.'

'I'm pleased you're OK about it.'

Again she nudged her hand towards mine.

'I'm fine.'

'I'd be very sad to think I made you do something against your will and then left you.'

'Don't worry. As far as the pubs are concerned, you did me a favour.'

'I'm *so* relieved. Thanks for not making it hard.'

Her saying that was very nice I thought. Although there was a part of me that took it like a kick in the balls. She was trying to sugar the pill as usual. A part of me felt I should've been more aggressive. We were both being so fucking civilised. But then what was the point of rowing? She'd made her position very clear. I'd known what was on the cards six months, maybe a year before. I thought I could have my cake and eat it, I suppose. She gave me enough rope—

I still felt torn, though. I was still up for getting her back.

'I've decided that the flat's yours. It's a down payment. There'll be cash when the business goes.'

'I don't want the flat. Nor your money.'

'Well, it's what you're going to have. You'll need somewhere to live.'

She looked away from me. Into her near empty glass.

'I think I've got somewhere.'

'Oh.'

'Yes, I've talked to my boss. The trust's recently taken over a big estate near Mum and Jemima. I can manage the project, if I want. There'd be a lodge thrown in. I'd have time and space. There's a lot of restoration to do. The whole thing could take five years.'

She'd never wasted any time.

'Looks like I'm going to be your tenant then.'

She looked at me and our smiles turned into laughter.

I didn't take her hand but stared into her beautiful eyes.

'You could always come back with me tonight.'

She held my gaze. 'We'll see.'

As she said the words, I knew I'd made a mistake. It wouldn't be difficult to fall into bed together. We didn't hate each other. But if we did go to bed it would be the end. It wouldn't be right and we'd only realise how far apart we still were. Bodies still lustful but minds badly aligned.

The possibility of her coming with me stayed throughout our next drink making our conversation warm and sentimental and lovely.

But I was relieved when she had the strength to say she was going back to Jemima's.

And as I drove away, I thought, 'There's hope.'

Sarah's Diary

Tuesday 19th

I intended to write yesterday but was wrecked from the weekend plus there was so much to sort out in my head.

I got the train to London on Saturday morning. Then I took the tube to Leicester Square. I found the pub, Copperfield's, straight away.

It was on the other side of the square from where I came in. It was a tall Victorian-looking building with arched windows in rows that got smaller the higher up they were. The arches were supported by stone columns. It was like looking at five different sized viaducts stacked on top of each other. The brickwork was ochre but there were bands and zig-zags of red and blue. The bricks in the arches over the windows were angled so they looked like teeth. The name Copperfield's was done in gold letters but wasn't as large as on some pubs. The reason the place stood out was it looked like it had just been built. The bricks were so bright. It seemed incongruous amongst the shabby older buildings and the slightly tacky modern ones. It was a real fantasy.

I loved it – loved the shapes and colours. It was extraordinary to find the original architect's drawings in the lobby as you went in. They were protected by security glass but were lit up and there were notices explaining what had been done to restore the building. There were also racks with leaflets about the project. I thought it was so cool to find a pub with an architectural conscience. It was brilliant. At one point I dragged Bob out to have a good look at the drawings. The delicate colour-washes and fine detail fascinated me – on paper you could see each column had a different top to it, something you didn't notice from the ground.

Inside, Copperfield's was sort of themed but not clumsily. Not that you could tell straight away because it was packed. There was a curious bronze sculpture of a cottage built into an upturned boat in the centre of the enormous space which Karl said was inspired by an old black and white film of the book. I'm not sure I've ever seen it but the image did seem familiar. Then there were big recesses around the side, each decorated with pictures and bric-à-brac representing themes from the story. We ended up squeezed together at a long table in one of these which had prints of trials showing earnest lawyers and frightened defendants. There were odd, almost creepy wooden mannequins leaning from the walls, one with a judge's wig on and others with black caps and gowns.

Seeing the others was pretty amazing. It seemed so strange to be getting together as adults who had left school. Meeting Bob was the most amazing thing of all.

He was waiting for me by the door from the lobby. He looked so tanned and fit, I almost didn't recognise him. He always was fit but in a boyish kind of way. Now he looked like a man. He was wearing black jeans and a brown suede jacket, open so you could see how muscley his chest was beneath his black T-shirt. The only disconcerting thing was, I thought I could detect his hair was thinning at the front. I forgot this almost immediately because the overall effect of him was just, Wow!, but it's true, he's lost a lot of hair.

It's weird but I can't really remember what I felt about Bob when I was on the train up. I was nervous, but then I always am when I'm going somewhere to meet people – it doesn't matter how well I know them. It's partly excitement, partly that I can never imagine being inside a situation before I'm in it. I always think I'm going to be awkward and won't know what to say.

My feelings about Bob, though, were different to my usual social insecurities. I reckon I intended to keep a bit of distance between us, to start off with, anyway. Until I worked out how I was responding to him. I thought he, Debbie and Karl would be together when I arrived and my reunion with him would be lost in the general greetings.

Thinking about things now, I realise quite clearly that the image of the person I'd been fantasising over for the last year hadn't changed with the passing months. We were the same two people making love for the first time or, in my imagination, making love in my bedroom or an unknown bed in an unknown darkness.

It was the dawning realisation that I would meet a stranger that I remember now from my train journey. It was the placing of a blank face on a roughly sketched body – clothed anonymously – and wondering what he would be like. Eventually it was simply unfocussed excitement and heightened perceptions. Then, suddenly, there he was.

Was I nervous about how he would respond to me – the way I look? Surprisingly, no. I've been quite easy about my shape since leaving school. Mum and Dad being relaxed has helped. In any case, they're so into each other, they hardly notice what Min and I get up to. And then, I've got better at disguising how much I eat – something made easier by a new informality at meal times. We help ourselves more rather than Dad serving us. I exercise choice. I can exercise too.

I'm thinner than I was when Bob went away. Too thin Bob said once over the weekend. That didn't put him off, though.

But before I saw him, I suspect I wasn't too bothered if he found me a little unattractive. The brake would be welcome.

When we saw each other whatever our plans or preconceptions were didn't matter. He looked great and I threw my arms round him. We kissed and hugged and couldn't believe that we were together again.

I just remember us pressing so tight against each other. I don't know how long it was before we became self-conscious and moved away. We were both gasping for air. My heart wasn't pounding exactly. The blood was sort of whooshing round my body. No, it wasn't blood, it was pure energy. It was almost overwhelming. I couldn't have predicted that.

Sounds came back to me first. The hubbub all around us. I looked into the room then back at him.

I kissed him and said, Where are the others?

He looked puzzled for a moment. I don't know, he said, Karl said he was going up to the bar and Debbie was trying to grab us some seats. Let's go and find them. Do you want me to take your bag?

I'm OK.

*   *   *   *   *

The house is so quiet. Everyone's away: Dad at work, Mum at the hospital, Min in school, Alex – wherever.

I went to Bath with Dad this morning so I could go to the college library and register at the department. I couldn't believe I was actually doing those things, although my excitement has been tempered somewhat by mixed feelings about Bob – not to mention all the other different kinds of echoes from the weekend.

Why does life have to be complicated? At least I haven't thrown up again. I'm just not eating. I couldn't. If I keep myself from being sick I'll easily get back to normal once things have quietened down.

Since I got home – I caught the bus to the village then had a brilliant walk in the September sunlight – I've been writing. I used to feel uncomfortable doing that when my parents were just at work but today the place is so deserted I didn't give opening up my diary a second thought. It's only partly the absence of my family. I'm much stronger now too. I'm beginning my life.

I think today has set the pattern for this week – my in-between time. I'll write then read some of the books on my reading list before my parents get home and we have sherry together. I think Mum's beginning to accept my going to art school.

I want to write about the weekend, though, despite feeling strong and happy. I want to go through the tensions and my feelings as if by writing them out I can make better sense of them.

I'm not sure about Bob and I'm worried for Debbie.

Wednesday 20th

We sat squeezed together in a row for about half an hour (apart from when I took Bob to see the drawings in the lobby) – it was quite fun, what with being pressed against Bob. Then Karl suddenly leapt onto the table, jumped over a couple of people, skipped towards the opposite corner and hovered by a group of four who were getting up to leave.

What the fuck is he doing? Debbie asked before she had time to realise what was going on. He's mad!

OK let's go, said Bob. He's got us a better table.

Brilliant! shouted Debbie. She looked at the startled and mildly angry middle-aged couple opposite. She raised her shoulders and made a sweet face. Sorry.

Sorry, sorry, said Bob and I to the other people at the table.

We made our way round gingerly, deciding not to follow Karl's example.

Cowards, said Karl.

It's alright for you, said Debbie, you're not wearing a skirt.

Would they see any more?

Fuck you. But well done for getting this.

Space at last, said Bob.

Yeah, I get a bit edgy when I'm hemmed in like that.

I have to say that Karl did look paranoid. He didn't improve over the rest of our time at the pub, let alone the weekend. He's really thin again. He's tanned from having spent the summer in Los Angeles but is different from a year ago. He was quite a hunk then but now looks weedy. By Sunday he looked ill. He's got a drug problem, was Bob's conclusion. He's going to look out for him when they get to Oxford. It's so hard to believe that one of our friends is in trouble like that. It makes summer '94 seem *so* innocent.

OK, I know Alex has his moments but I don't think of him as being an addict, somehow. He's so unpredictable you can't rely on him being anything for longer than a few weeks. The last time I saw him, he was as sober as a judge. He needs to be to keep up with his harem.

But with Karl there's something serious about his habit. Something committed.

Anyway, once Bob and Karl finished rhapsodising about their new surroundings, we decided to stay for another couple of drinks so we could enjoy our new-found freedom before heading off to McDonald's and pigging out on burgers and chips – and strawberry milkshakes for Debbie. At five we were going to see a French double-bill at the NFT. Both Debbie and Karl are film devotees at the moment. Debbie needs to be for her course at Warwick and as for Karl, movies, as he calls them, are in the blood.

Bob did the next round and I went up to the bar with him to help carry the drinks. While we were there he tried to persuade me to have a bitter.

I looked along the bar towards the pumps, straining to read the labels, without success. They were too far away.

I did have a half when I was staying with Debbie last year, I told him. The day before I met you.

We kissed.

Did you like the bitter?

It was OK but I prefer lager.

It doesn't taste of anything.

It *does*.

He still got me to have a pint, though. Dickens's Sesh, he called it.

You should have bought her Premium, said Debbie.

Oh come on, I want an appetite for my Big Mac, I said.

Those bottles you live on are pretty poky, babes. There's nothing to this stuff.

Babes? said Karl. What's *that* about?

I always call her babes, as you well know.

I've *never* heard you call her that. Karl shook his head.

You're out of your box.

I thought I could detect real irritation in her voice. It was the first time I'd noticed it. I know they have their moments but in public they seem so in love. Mainly because Karl is always deferential towards her. He worships her.

Here goes. I clinked Bob's glass.

Down in one, OY, OY, OY!, he went.

Is that Aborigine? asked Karl, his face creasing up as he hissed out the words.

No, that's the Hakka, you wally. And that's Maori.

You need some air, said Debbie.

Pardon me.

So, what d'you think? Bob asked me.

It's alright.

He looked disappointed. I could get you something else.

No, no – it's good. Just different, that's all. It's smoother than the one I had in Norfolk.

Not as good as Some More.

I looked at Karl blankly.

Can I have Some More? Geddit?

Don't take any notice, babes, he's not making any sense. These two boys were out on the piss last night and they went to this place where they served beer called Some More and when you go up to the bar, you say, Can I have – ta, da, di-da, di-da?

You've missed out the crucial bit, said Bob. The pub's called Fagin's.

Oh, I *see*. Oh, Fagin's – *well*. What's with all this Dickens *stuff*?

It's a chain.

Fagin's was *really* wild. Karl looked about him and reached across the table towards the main part of the pub. His fingers curled as if he was clutching a tennis ball.

It was light years away from this shit. There were these really bizarre puppets – one was a dog. You wouldn't believe the dog, would she, Bob?

As he asked this, he gave us a mad-looking sneer – spookily

canine.

Actually, I prefer here, said Bob.

I thought he was beginning to lose patience with Karl.

Fagin's is pretty naff.

OK boys. Debbie tapped the table. That's it, we're off to Mac-D's. Finish your drinks everybody. We need more blood sugar.

*   *   *   *   *

After McDonald's we went to see the French films which were brilliant.

I'd never been to the National Film Theatre before. The buildings themselves were really odd, though. I liked the glimpses of the Thames we got as we went up and down the walkways. But the concrete, or whatever it is, is so cold and grubby. It's like I imagine the Soviet Union was before the fall of communism. It seems ironic that the buildings are places where the human spirit is celebrated.

And although the Film Theatre is nice inside the way you reach it makes it look tucked away. A bit like it's some sort of basement storeroom that's been cleared out so that a new-fangled medium can be experimented with. The computer rooms at school were like that.

I'd never been to a film with Bob before – obviously. I wondered what he'd do. Would we hold hands or would he put his arm round me? It was a totally new situation – in more ways than one. Thinking back over my teenage years I suddenly realise I've never been going out with anyone when the opportunity of going to the cinema has arisen before. Or else they weren't around at the right moment. I've never had the proverbial back-row experience. I'm deprived.

Bob drew me close, kissed my forehead and nuzzled my hair to start with. Which is about all I remember. From the moment the films started I was transfixed.

The first was Jean Renoir's *Une Partie de Campagne*. The story was good – and poignant – but it was the images that excited me. There's one moment when the camera is mounted on a boat and you get this incredible view of the wind sweeping across the surface of the water. You also get the sense of the boat gliding away from the beautiful willows on the bank. It was quite magical and it didn't matter that it was black and white. I also remember light spilling through trees, dappling the ground, its brightness intensified as the wind touches the branches.

These visions made my heart ache. They almost made me give up going to art school too. When such exquisite effects have been captured, what is there left to do? How can one ever hope to convey that light through art?

The other film *Jules et Jim* was as much of a revelation, although I got more involved in the story with this one. I loved the amazingly fluid camera work but the images weren't as natural as the ones in the Renoir film. I can feel *Une Partie de Campagne* when I think about it. It's entered my soul.

Of the two men in *Jules et Jim*, I have to say I preferred Jules. Neither were my type exactly but he simply seemed so gentle and kind. It wasn't his fault that the Jeanne Moreau character was wild. Is Bob like Jules? I think he could be but this weekend he was louder than I remember. He's excited about Oxford and he's buoyed up by his gap year but even so, I hope he won't get too brash when he starts university. It's probably just Karl's bad influence.

I thought Jeanne Moreau was stunning. Her role was a real *actress's* one. Such range, such vivacity and elegance, such mischievousness, so self-destructively awesome. She's beautiful. She carries a little weight but can get away with it.

I've just looked at myself in the mirror. My shape is very different from hers. She has a strong frame, an athlete's – or maybe a dancer's – physique. If I put on weight it shows as fat. It sags. Whereas with her it's somehow banded taughtly into strong sinuous curves.

I've always been the same. Fat doesn't sit well on me. When my face is slim you can see the fine structure of my bones but a tiny bit of weight makes me jowly or hamster-cheeked.

I don't begrudge Jeanne Moreau her body. We're all individuals. I need to stay slim to look good. It's simple.

But maybe watching her did unsettle me a little on Saturday night.

Thursday 21st

When we left the Film Theatre we crossed Waterloo Bridge and caught the tube to High Street Kensington.

Karl's dad, Rick, has a flat a few minutes away. It's on the top floor of a large Victorian house which Karl's parents bought when they got married and started a family. They converted it into flats and sold off the ones on the other floors in order to finance Rick's second film. The gamble paid off in that the film was a huge success, although as Karl told us on the tube, it was also the beginning of the end of his parents' marriage.

Karl could remember all the building work going on and then the next moment, or so it seemed – Karl was only four – the family was off to LA. They had been there barely a year before Karl's mother, Enid, decided to come back to London.

Karl said that to start with he was really excited about having two homes and didn't realise his father and mother had split up for almost a year.

Karl told us that Andre, his older brother, had memories of their parents rowing and their dad's drink and drugs binges but that he himself remained blissfully ignorant. It was this that made it very difficult for him to accept his parents were no longer together. He said it's almost as if he still can't believe it. He has these nightmares about his parents fighting and his mother walking out and taking him and Andre with her. Then he wakes up and tells himself it's only a dream before realising that Rick and Enid divorced nearly fifteen years ago.

Debbie said he cries in the night like a little boy sometimes.

Karl didn't really see his father again until he went to public school. His mum remarried and he and Andre were brought up in a big house by the Thames in Richmond. But when he went to our school his dad started jetting over about once every term and taking the boys out for weekends. Then they went on holiday to LA and began dividing their time between parents.

I remember Karl's dad giving the school a talk about film-making in my first term. He was one of its most famous old boys. What he said was really interesting although the way he looked was pretty naff. He wore a baseball cap, oversize sweatshirt and these amazingly baggy jeans. He also went about with a fold away scooter just like a kid.

Anyway, when Andre started at the London School of Economics he moved into their dad's old flat and now Karl's started using it as a base too.

This weekend Andre and Sam were away on the Isle of Wight sailing so we had the place to ourselves. It's a beautiful flat, although I can't imagine Rick in it. It's old-fashioned. A bit like home. There are loads of antiques and paintings. Karl said the stuff belonged to his grandparents – Rick's folks – and that Enid was responsible for the country house decor. When Rick started returning to England he planned to have the flat completely re-designed but the boys wouldn't let him. It was their childhood, Karl said.

That night, we decided to order a take-away. Karl got some beers and wine from the fridge and we chose from the menu of what he claimed was the best Indian in west London. Once Debbie phoned the order through Karl said he was going to the off-licence to get some special wine – the *only* wine that would go with the meal – and to score some drugs, before the take-away was delivered.

If you don't mind me saying, he's a bit out of it, Bob said to Debbie after Karl left.

She stared into her glass for a moment. No, I don't mind you saying. I think basically he's OK but this last time in LA unsettled him. And going up to Oxford too.

I'm going up to Oxford.

And you're Superman – we know.

He looked miffed but then he deserved the put down. He'd sounded so smug.

He's not as confident as you, Bob. He's bright but he's scared of failing.

News to me. Anyway, what happened in LA?

Oh I'm not sure I should tell you. But maybe I should, if it helps you understand. But promise you won't let on you know.

Alright, I promise. Bob took a long drink from his bottle of beer as if he was somehow sealing the bargain.

You know his father's always gone in for adolescent floozies?

Bob grinned. Yeah, Karl always reckons they're secretly after him.

Whatever. But it seems this time Rick's fallen for someone nearer his age. She's called Veronica and she has these two teenage kids. Karl felt Rick was paying them too much attention. It's as simple as that. Now do you understand?

Debbie had taken the wind out of Bob's sails. She can be very good at doing that to people. It's the clear way she puts things. Totally straightforward. They've got no comeback.

Yes, I suppose. I don't imagine I'd much like it. Even so, you ought to watch the drugs.

And you won't be smoking this evening?

It's not the same – you know what I mean.

She poured herself some more wine. Lets change the subject. Tell us all about the art school plans, Sarah.

I was startled when she said that. While they were talking about Karl, I was curled up on the sofa against Bob, content to smoke and sip beer and listen to them. I was also replaying images from the Renoir film and studying the landscape painting above the mantelpiece. It had some people on horses in the foreground but its true subject, as far as I was concerned, was the English countryside. As your eye moved to the left the ground fell away, opening up a view of a valley with fields and woods and streams, cottages dotted here and there, and in the far distance a little village made up of brick houses and a stone church.

I was feeling comfortable, safe, happy.

I yawned. Sorry.

Were you falling asleep there? Bob gave me a squeeze and kissed the top of my head.

Not really. I'm still a bit overwhelmed by the films, that's all. Weren't they wonderful!

I knew you'd like them, said Debbie.

Perhaps you should think about film school – or media studies like Debbie, said Bob.

I instinctively ignored him. I don't know why. I suppose I feel proprietorial about what I've decided to do.

I've got a place at the Tech, I said to Debbie.

Wow, that's brilliant! Why didn't you say so earlier? You're always such a dark horse.

She got up from the floor and gave me a hug and kisses.

As she settled again, Bob said, I *think* I approve.

Don't listen to him. He's just in a funny mood. So, what happens next?

I start a week on Monday.

Wow!

Term's already begun but they're cool about me joining late.

So what will you be studying? asked Bob.

Anything and everything – I've told you.

Not, something and nothing?

Shut up *you*, I said.

Yes, shut the F up! You're so negative. What's the matter with you?

Bob looked at me and smiled. It was a nice smile, not hostile. He looked at Debbie and shrugged then looked back at me. It's just that you're launching yourself into uncharted waters.

Pomposity or what?

Edinburgh would've meant security – a proper academic structure.

I know what you mean.

No you *don't*. Don't listen to him, do your own thing, babes.

No Debs, I didn't mean it like that. I know what I'm doing, Bob. I know it inside here – I pointed at my chest.

It's a heart school thing.

I could have flattened him when he said that. Piss *off*! I'm being serious. Maybe I'm not getting the words right. But it's what I want to do and nothing's going to stop me.

Go girl! Telling your parents – that sounded scary. That's how serious she is, Bob. You haven't met her dad, have you?

It was awful to begin with. But, it was only awful because it's such a big decision and I had to think it through properly. Mum and Dad were actually quite good about it.

I'm just worried for you.

Don't be. I *know* what I'm doing.

Of course you do, most of the time. It's this foundation course, though, that sounds vague.

Anything and everything?

Yeah.

It's only a jokey way of describing it.

I felt a bit woozy then. I was surprised how parentish he sounded and forcing myself to respond convincingly had taken me away from the comforting place I wanted to be in. My nausea was due to the dizzying effects of having to stand up for myself when I was hungry and had drunk tons of alcohol and smoked too many cigs.

Anyway, I said, let's skip it for the minute. We'll talk about it tomorrow, if you want.

Spoil sport, said Debbie.

Me? said Bob.

Yes, you. I want to hear all about her course and you wade in and wreck things. You've tired the poor girl out.

I've got it, I said, let's talk about Oxford.

I'm sure you've got lots of things to say about *that*.

I winked at Debbie.

Just press the button and put your feet up, babes.

I made as if to press his stomach. OK he was tongue-tied for a moment but only for a moment. He hardly drew breath until Karl came back.

Sunday 24th

I couldn't write about the rest of last Saturday yesterday. It wasn't that I didn't have the opportunity. What was supposed to be the start of a family weekend to mark my going to the Tech disintegrated when Dad went to a last minute meeting about the site next to the new surgery. Whereupon Min decided to go riding and Mum set off for the hospital. Alex was nowhere to be seen.

I went for a long walk then slept in the afternoon – having bought a bottle of red at the village shop and consuming it under a tree. Sad.

I reached the conclusion that some things were better off not being written but tonight couldn't stop myself from getting out my diary. I tell myself that if I put everything down in black and white I'll confront what I am and maybe that will bring me to my senses.

I want to start college clean.

*   *   *   *   *

Karl bought some evil skunk. It smelt repulsive in the flat next morning. But at the time we must have been too drunk to notice. Debbie put the take-away in the oven for a bit while he skinned up and Bob and I opened more wine and beer.

Karl was already even weirder than when he left. He admitted later he'd shared a spliff with the guy he bought the stuff from.

I didn't want to get too stoned although I decided I could handle a few puffs before the meal to give me the munchies. I was hungry anyway but there's nothing quite like the effect of dope on the palette and stomach. You become ravenous and food, especially spicy food, tastes divine. Then I thought I'd probably smoke a little more after the meal to spice up our love-making. Not that I really needed it for that, either.

The stuff was strong. The hit it gave you was awesome. Although you couldn't smell it much, you could taste and feel it. It was hot and raspy on your throat and had this amazingly herby zing.

Then Karl produced some tabs and wanted us to try them. It was a bad move.

I knew Debbie'd taken E before because she'd told me but she wasn't keen. She said it would spoil the evening.

Bob gave a decisive thumbs down and I tried to decline gracefully but ended up in a fit of the giggles because Bob sounded so outraged and Karl started taking the piss out of him.

Bob and Karl began arguing. Debbie brokered a truce and we got the take-away out of the oven.

It was brilliant. For my main I had lamb Korma and the almonds and coconut and cream just exploded in my mouth.

It was when Bob caught Karl trying to slip a tab onto my plate that the row got going again. Bob told Karl to fucking pull himself together. Which was like a red rag to a bull.

I hated that bit of the evening. Karl was trying to drive a wedge between me and Bob. He was saying things like he didn't know what the fuck I saw in Bob or he knew I wanted the tab really.

I was drunk but not enough not to feel the tension that had been building since we got to the flat. Maybe the dope made it sharper. I looked at my friends. My lover for God's sake! Even Debbie. They were all so full of rage. It was like some Bosch caricature of them. The only things missing were snaky tongues and lizard tails. I wanted to shout at them to stop but I also didn't want them to turn on me.

After a while Debbie suddenly got up and told me we were going to the kitchen to finish our meal in peace. Bob said he was coming too. She told him to stay where he was and make it up with Karl.

I stood up. I took my food, my glass and a bottle of Karl's

special wine – the full effect of which was rather lost – and followed her into the kitchen. Then I said I'd be back in a minute.

Inside the bathroom the noise stopped. I sat on the bath and tried taking deep breaths. But I couldn't stop the feelings. I knew the only way I could get calm was throwing up.

* * * * *

Making love with Bob was great. We did it four times. I couldn't believe it when I counted on Sunday morning.

We made love again after he came back to bed, having made us a cup of tea.

On Saturday night he apologised for the argument once Karl fell asleep on the floor and Debbie and I returned.

We both told him we were fine. Debbie because she's cool and me because I chucked up. We said it wasn't Bob's fault.

I don't think I remembered throwing up until after we made love for the fifth time and were dozing. The memory made me feel guilty, although I was pretty sure Bob hadn't noticed anything on my breath. I'd rinsed my mouth out thoroughly and rubbed toothpaste into my gums with my finger. Not, I suppose, that I really needed to because of the curry and dope.

I felt I'd let myself down. It was like I'd broken my run of virtue. It was like losing your virginity – not like it was when that happened to me but the way people of my parents' generation said it ought to be. And perhaps being sick like I am is just another sort of rite of passage for some people that one day will be accepted as quite normal.

No, thinking like that scratches my brain as if my thoughts were pulling the wrong way.

I would go as far as saying that chucking up was necessary that evening to ease my feelings of tension. It enabled me to cope. That's what I told myself on Sunday morning and what I half believe now.

As I lay beside Bob I thought about Karl. Again it seemed unbelievable that he should be addicted to drugs – if he really is.

117

I wondered whether I should think of myself as being somehow similar to him in that I needed to be sick to cope. I told myself I was being melodramatic. It was a one off. I'm not going back down that road again.

Tomorrow I'm off to the Tech. I have so much to look forward to.

Tom's writing therapy

15/03/02 – A Friday to 18/03/02 – A Monday

The next six months were a bit of a blur to be quite honest.

I think I suffered a kind of progressive delayed shock. The enormity of what happened only gradually began to hit me and got worse and worse until about Christmas 01 when alcohol pretty much obliterated the whole of the next three months.

The money from the sale of the pubs took longer to come through than I hoped. In truth this wasn't that much of a surprise but it had the effect of putting off the full realisation that I'd actually disposed of the business. If there'd been a sudden, clean break I might have got things into perspective earlier.

Then, of course, there was Jill. There wasn't a clean break there either. We spoke over the phone twice a week and I reckon we probably met a dozen times at least before the New Year. Nearly always in pubs, but not the Surtees, obviously. (I still can't bring myself to use the new name, even though I'd once considered it for another venue.)

As far as that disaster was concerned there was precious little that could be done. I was right about Denney – he'd been sharp but careful, as usual. Careful enough to ditch the blade well before anyone noticed the planning laws were carved up the way he wanted them. Careful enough to do his slicing with the precision of a surgeon so you couldn't work out where the bits had been taken out. Back-handers had to be involved but as I said to Jill, you prove it.

And Jill accepted she couldn't. She became as easy about the Surtees as she was about chatting and meeting up. Living in her lodge and getting stuck into her new restoration project seemed to make her as happy as a pig in clover.

Her outlook forced me to see things her way. We were a

couple who were making a success of what people often say they want to become after breaking up – friends. Personally I believe with hindsight my friendship was somewhat false. It had an ulterior motive. By playing her game I was biding my time until she was ready to make another go of our relationship. By deluding myself in this way I again put off facing the truth.

Throughout the autumn there were times when I realised what had happened. My reaction if these occurred at weekends was to hole up in the flat with a full cellar. When they struck during the week I threw myself into the exploration of a series of unlikely schemes. I found out alot about computer games design and eco-friendly cemeteries, to name but two. The former with a view to backing an old friend who had bags of ideas but no dosh. The latter I considered after reading an article about some guy down near Bristol who converted an old barn into a chapel and was burying people in a field and planting trees on top of them. He was making a fortune. He'd converted another barn – some way off from the chapel one – into a house that looked like a palace. When I read about him was the first time I toyed with the idea of moving out of London and making a new life in the country.

It also got me thinking back to when Jill and me's relationship was at its best. We were about two years in. It was before the venture cap boys and she was still at the V&A and both of us seemed to have lots of weekends free. For about a year we used to take off on Friday nights armed with walking boots, waterproofs, the appropriate OS maps and a couple of pub guides. We knew the area we were heading to but not where we'd stay. As we drove along she read me details of different establishments then she tried the ones we liked the sound of on the mobile until she got us a bed for the night. It was such a simple time. We were both fascinated by the architecture of old pubs and although I didn't know much about nature or ancient churches, I could tell a good landscape when I saw one, and loved learning about wildlife from her. Flowers, birds and trees. We tried identifying fungi but neither of us were much cop at it. We'd be in the organic cemetery if we'd eaten any.

We both loved being in the open air. Mornings and afternoons on the footpaths, whatever the weather, with pub lunches and suppers. It was a real eye opener to try the new beers being produced by the micros tucked away in the shires. It was a time of innocent pleasure and dreams.

It was during one God awful weekend in early November 01 that I decided to retrace my steps to some of the places we'd stayed at. When I came out of my stupor the following Monday, my first thought was I must be mad. But the idea wouldn't shift. It occurred to me that returning wasn't morbid. It would be a way of finding the me in those breaks. When we did them Jill's input was colossal and I think it's fair to say I felt she shaped them the most. And yet, the idea of weekend escapes was mine originally. I'd grown up in the countryside, pretty much, and it was the semi-rural background we shared that intrigued us about each other in the first place. I saw revisiting as a way of putting my stamp back on the experiences so, in a sense, I could start the last four years again.

*

I can't say the trips were an unqualified success, although the last was eventful and led in, as it were, to a life-changing moment. The first three – Bugsworth in Derbyshire, Loweswater in the Lakes and Clovelly down in Devon – were largely scuppered because it was the wrong time of year. We'd visited all three in the summer or early autumn. And thinking back Jill and I probably stopped our jaunts after November anyway, what with the run up to Christmas, the miserableness of the English countryside in winter, as far as good walking's concerned, and the prospect of skiing in January.

Why I didn't give up after Bugsworth, I don't know. I think alcohol made me fixed in my ideas. I decided what I was going to do and that was that. The flaw in my logic began to dawn at Clovelly but – thankfully, in a sense – I wasn't completely put off. There can be few bleaker experiences than a seaside resort in storm force gales in December. Particularly when you have a treasure chest of happy summer memories from your last visit.

The pattern of my stays was set at Bugsworth. A long lie-in, sleeping off the hangover from the night before, followed by a walk or drive to wherever was recommended for breakfast – the pub having stopped serving hours ago. Then a liquid lunch and a bag of dry-roast followed by a knackering couple of hours trying to work out which footpaths Jill and I took (I couldn't believe how out of condition I was). I'd crash out when I staggered back to the pub. Later I showered, hit the bar, nibbled a bit of supper then retired to my room with a bottle of red, a pint and a double whisky.

I suppose I derived something from these experiences. Leaving London behind was a tonic. It was good to be doing something recreational I'd dreamt up myself. I was giving my single life shape, even though it was seriously blurred round the edges.

One thing that really surprised me was how isolated I felt. Pubs were my manor and before this series of trips I considered myself to be more easily sociable in one than anywhere else. But these weekends were different. I ended up sitting in a corner downing my beers and working my way through a stack of newspapers, computer game coding manuals, eco-friendly cemetery literature and what-have-you. Whenever I was at the bar I felt self-conscious. I got the impression people couldn't work me out. Not surprising, looking back. Here was this reasonably good-looking guy, brand-new Porsche Boxter, expensive clobber, holing up for a binge weekend with a cart-load of technical stuff.

But it wasn't only the fact that I stood out that left me tongue-tied. It was to do with being without a defined role. Let's face it for most of the previous twenty years when I'd been in pubs I was either behind the bar, the owner of the place or out for the night with my girlfriend. I hadn't had to make polite conversation since I was in my early teens.

My social inadequacy shook me. I couldn't place the cause exactly, like I can now. I was living the experience without perspective. But I reckon it had the effect of undermining my confidence even further and I guess it probably didn't help the boozing either.

It was Clovelly, though, that was the killer. Afterwards I was still determined to carry on with my plan but the notion of having a few months off before starting again in the spring did make it through the anaesthetised outer layers of my brain. Stopping was in any case made easier by Christmas and New Year which I spent with Dad and Rajiv and his family respectively.

The less said about the time with Dad the better. I had to break it to him that I'd split up with Jill. He was kind but when I went off to try and sleep in my childhood bed, I couldn't have felt more like a child if I tried.

The couple of days with Rajiv were a riot. He'd set up a micro in the outbuildings of his croft in Galloway and cracked the problem of putting decent flavour into a heavy whilst still allowing it to be chilled and remain a bit gassy. He wasn't giving much away but it was down to oats, apparently. I was envious of him, I freely admit it. He and Gina had made the place beautiful and the little nippers had gone from sounding East End to more Scottish than the Scots.

From the New Year on I did my drinking at home until I went down with a nasty flu bug. During the next few weeks I sobered up. Afterwards I had the blues – very bad blues indeed. Then in early March with the days getting longer I suddenly got it into my head to go back to Llanthony. What clicked about Llanthony was the time of year was right. It was one of the first pubs we went to on our weekend escapes. To find it by accident, as it were, seemed like a blessing on the whole enterprise. By returning I was getting back into the idea that something of my past's magic would rub off on the present – and in a way it did. Though not in any way I could have predicted.

*

The time since I had the flu had seen the stirrings of a fresh beginning for me in any case. The blues were partly the result of me sobering up. A kind of beer and wine drinker's cold turkey.

But underneath the leaf mould of my previous life new shoots were starting to poke up. I had a go at taking myself in hand. I did a few sessions at a local gym and bought a mountain bike to whiz up and down Highgate Hill on.

So, when I set off in the Boxter for the Welsh borders I was determined to get something positive out of the experience.

Before driving over Hay Bluff to Capel-y-ffin and Llanthony I stopped in Hay itself. When Jill and I were last there I sussed out the dealers who kept brewing-related stock. This time I came away with a leather-bound early edition of Thomas Melsom's *The Gentle Brewer*, a seminal work written as a reaction to the growth of industrial practices at the beginning of the nineteenth century. Basically he was urging people to preserve the cottage character of ale production. So what's new? Nothing under the sun. His was the Bible of micro-brewers in the know.

I also bought a paperback *Spy Who Came in from the Cold* which I'd not read since I was a teenager. I loved it then, inspired by the old black and white film with Richard Burton which was masterful. It was the only le Carré I was able to get to grips with. I always felt with the later ones that he was trying too hard. Whereas in *Spy* he kept things pared down. As I say, the book really hit the spot at school and it didn't disappoint that weekend. It and *The Gentle Brewer*, I felt, would make for better reading than computer games and planting trees on top of dead bodies.

The weather was outstanding as I drove towards the Gospel Pass. It had been hot and sunny all week and would continue being so for a good few days yet. There's nothing like a spring heatwave. Everything's so moist from winter. The landscape stays lush and as green as new peas rather than getting tired or parched, as in the summer. The sun's different too. It gives the land that sort of egg yolk glow which is never richer than in late afternoon.

Up on the bluff there were masses of cars and people. There weren't the usual kite fliers because there wasn't a breath of wind. That afternoon people were simply strolling about or sunbathing. From the top the land fell away and you could see for miles right into Wales.

As I cruised the plateau I gradually caught up with a couple of cyclists. The nearest was a young woman with beautiful, glossy long chestnut hair. She was dressed in only a green cropped T-shirt, khaki shorts, white socks and trainers. In front was a man who was a good deal shorter than her – even smaller than me, I reckoned – all done out in maroon Lycra with white and black flashing, knuckle and knee defenders, goggles and a go-faster helmet. He looked like an over-protected child. Both people were cycling hard. As I was about to overtake I couldn't help noticing the woman's black thong peeping over her waistband then dipping out of sight. She had a beautiful bum. I remember that for a few moments my heart fluttered and it was like I was having breathing difficulties. As I sped towards Capel-y-ffin I wondered why women hadn't worn thongs when I was that age.

You can't see much of the priory as you approach from the north, just the odd glimpse. It's only after you turn up to the car park that you realise what an extraordinary place you've come to.

It's this ruined priory – dark grey stone, arches, towers and stepped-down remains of high walls – sitting on a valley floor in between steep hills with the sky like a roof overhead. You can't help thinking, this place hasn't changed since it was built – the way the valley looks, that is. You're seeing it as the monks did. When Jill and I first found it we looked at each other and I don't think we spoke another word for ten minutes.

The pub itself is like a big lean-to up against the walls of some of the priory's ancillary buildings. The guest rooms are in one of the old west towers of the church. The pub was originally a shooting lodge fitted out in the early 1800s and if memory serves, was once used by some eccentric Victorian as the HQ of his utopian community – doomed to failure of course, as these things always are.

On my way to the car park I stopped the Boxter for a bit and stared at the ruins in wonder. I wanted that moment inside me forever. For a moment I wished I could go back in time.

When I was walking across the courtyard with my bags the two cyclists arrived and shot past on their way towards the Chapter House where they screeched to a halt and dismounted. Seen from the front, the woman was a real stunner. Lovely strong body and white teeth. She was laughing. They were having a race I think. Seeing how happy the two of them were made me sad.

*

The following day I made breakfast with a good fifteen minutes to spare.

The previous evening I had a couple of pints before supper, a bottle of wine with and took just a last pint to bed. I had enough to help me sleep – I slept like a baby – but not so much that I was laid low when I woke up. I was definitely turning over a new leaf.

My room was the one Jill and I had back in 01. With the other pubs I booked different rooms quite deliberately. I thought there was retracing your steps *and*... But when I phoned Llanthony the room at the base of the tower was the only one left. Curiously I wasn't disconcerted by it at all. Maybe its familiarity put me at my ease. It was a lovely room. It was dead simple – just white painted walls, heavy Welsh furniture, some exposed stonework and this amazing arched window with stone mullions and leaded lights. The view was this dinky little veg garden at the back of the farmhouse that adjoined the priory which would have done Peter Rabbit proud.

After breakfast I set off across the fields northwards then climbed the incredibly steep slope to Offa's Dyke. I was astonished how much fitter I was. True I had to stop for a rest at one point – no hardship, the sight of the priory church was magnificent – but it was only a minute or two before I was off again.

Not before, though, noticing two bikes tearing along the lane towards Crucorney, one rider almost camouflaged, the other looking like a flying streak of mulberry juice.

I didn't think much as I walked. I lost myself in the chess board fields stretching away towards Gloucestershire and was content to be healing. I shuddered when I remembered what a wreck I was only a few months before.

I had lunch at the pub then walked on the other side of the valley. I got back about four. I changed out of my walking boots by the car. The cyclists were loading their suitcases into their battered four-wheel drive. I smiled at the woman. She seemed a bit pissed off, I thought.

After that I crashed until seven.

*

The pub was packed. It was a fairly small space and quickly felt full at the best of times. But that night there were more punters than usual because of the warm weather. Up to nine o'clock they were able to sit out among the ruins but after that it must have got nippy and they all crammed inside. I was OK. I had a table in the corner by the stairs which was reserved for me. I could have eaten in the dining-room but always preferred the bar. When the hoards arrived a couple of people asked if they could take the other half. Of course I said be my guest. By then I was well away. I'd had an excellent dinner, some superb Border Ballad and was well stuck into a bottle of not unpalatable Côtes du Rhône and *The Spy Who Came in from the Cold*.

It must have been ten when I was aware of someone saying, 'Mind if I join you?'

I looked up. I was prepared to be a bit off-hand because I reckoned I'd done my Good Samaritan act. It was the girl with the long chestnut hair.

'Yeah, of course.'

I reached for my jacket and *The Gentle Brewer* which were on the chair beside me.

I looked around for another seat.

'There's only one, though,' I said. 'I can't see another.'

'That's OK. It's just me.'

'Right.'

She settled herself down. She was wearing a short black denim skirt and a turquoise Thai silk shirt. She put her bag under her seat, raised her pint and said, 'Cheers, then.'

'I thought you left this afternoon.'

127

'Richard did. I've got to man the fort.'

'Oh, right. What d'you mean, man the fort. What fort?'

'Rich's phrase, I hasten to add. Public school, Dick is. Dead posh.'

She laughed.

I warmed to that laugh when I heard it the day before. It was both girly and womanly. There was a huskiness mixed in with the more infectious trilling notes. I found the fact the woman whose laugh it was was sitting there next to me all of a sudden, rather amazing. Difficult to take in. Part of the magic of the priory and valley. The effect of three pints of Border Ballad and the best part of a bottle of red. Call it what you will.

'I'm a book buyer.'

'You don't say.'

'I do.'

'Yeah, well I'm confused. The book buying bit's not exactly unusual round here but I'd got you down as a couple of cyclists on holiday.'

'That too.'

She giggled then gulped down some cider. As she drank she kept her eyes on me over the top of the glass. They were bright and smiling. Mischievous. She was playing with me.

'It's better than down the road,' she said, looking round. 'There was supposed to be music in the other pub but the band didn't turn up. Good thing, really, as everyone seems to be here.'

'Probably the band as well.'

'Yeah.'

'So you buy books and Richard's—'

'Richard's my boss. I'm his trainee. He had to go home to see his mum who's sick.'

'Right.'

I was about to say, Not a couple then, but on reflection didn't think it would be appropriate. That they weren't an item made sense, of course, because when you thought about it what would a lovely young woman want with someone who dressed like that – even if it was only for cycling? Still she worked with him, so they must get on.

OK, I admit it. I'd been a bit jealous of old Richard and was relieved to hear they weren't going out together. Not that I fancied *my* chances.

'Sorry to hear that.'

She smiled. I guessed she was wondering if I was sincere.

'The book buying, though— What, you're on a buying trip?'

'Yeah, we come down for five days or so and make a bit of a holiday of it. Richard's mad on cycling.'

'I'd never have guessed.'

She ignored me. She was definitely devoted to this Richard guy.

'We cycle over to Hay and then visit some of the more esoteric dealers who live out in the sticks. Then at the end we drive round and pick up the books.'

'You mean the countryside's crawling with book people as well?'

'A place like Hay's always going to attract dealers who like working from home.'

'I suppose so.'

You could tell from the way she spoke that books were a serious business for her. I liked that. I suppose that if I was pushed to it, I admired her loyalty to Richard too.

'Where's home then?'

'Near Norwich. Richard owns a big manor – he's one of the ones who likes to work from home. But my home's Rochdale – originally.'

'Right.'

I wasn't surprised she said Rochdale. There was a definite accent but way off in the background. It reminded me of my Mum's, although it was a sort of cross between Yorkshire and Mancunian. It turned out she'd been a student at Oxford. She'd worked in London training to be an accountant before chucking the whole lot in to deal in old books.

It was funny, I thought, how each generation tackles this business of accents differently. Her approach, like that of a lot of young people was akin to Mum and Dad's. Only she wasn't going for RP so as to get on. Her voice was well-spoken, anonymous, bright, clear – perfect for the sort of customer who'd buy books from a manor – with just a hint of regionality to give her a touch of street cred.

'I'm from Essex but my grandad was from Norfolk. Not far from Norwich, as it goes. It's a good side of England. Although I'm warming to the west.'

'You on holiday?'

And that was it. We were away. I said I'd get us another pint before I told her about me and when I came back the conversation just flowed. I don't know why, exactly. I was attracted to her but that wasn't it. You can fancy someone and the chat can be as flat as a pancake. It was simply one of those magical gifts from the gods that comes your way only a handful of times throughout your life. Everything that should have gone against us getting on slipped away. Age, principally, background – she couldn't abide beer, my knowledge of the kind of literature she liked was zilch – these things weren't important. We talked about everything and anything. The subject hardly mattered. The evening reminded me of my first date with Jill.

When the last of the other punters left at about two she asked me if I wanted to go cycling with her the following day. She added that Richard's bike would be the perfect size.

Although I said yes, I couldn't help thinking I should have made an excuse. It wasn't the pain of having lost Jill that was beginning to kick in that made me think that. It was the fact the evening had been so wonderful, I couldn't imagine tomorrow being anything other than an anti-climax.

*

We met for breakfast at nine. I don't know what the other guests thought about us sitting together, if anything, but it gave me the kind of thrill I hadn't had in ages.

Kim appeared in black shorts and yellow top. She looked as fresh as a spring flower. You'd never believe she'd been up half the night boozing. I wish I could say the same about me – although I must have looked better than I would've done a couple of months before.

We both went for coffee and the full English.

After we started tucking in, I said to her, 'There's one thing bothering me, what's Richard going to think about me borrowing his bike?'

'He'll be fine. It's not his best one. That stays in Norfolk. As long as you don't crash, he won't care.'

'Well that's a relief. It was just that what with all the kit, he seemed a bit of a fanatic.'

'He may look like that but underneath he's dead sound.'

I liked the more pronounced Rochdale accent that was beginning to emerge. I felt I was getting closer to the real Kim.

After breakfast we set off along the valley towards Capel-y-ffin. Kim decided we'd go there first and return along a track that followed the sides of the hills higher up. Then we'd head for Crucorney before doubling back for some serious off road. She said we'd be about ready for lunch once we did that.

I said I'd need an ambulance.

It was an extraordinary day. By ten-thirty it was hot. Not sweltering but a lovely dry heat with just a hint of fresh breeze to take the edge off. There was the scent of the countryside – not always welcome – but mostly this wonderful verdant earthy smell that invigorated you in a kind of subliminal way. There was the visual beauty of the green and the sunlight coming through the trees. There was Kim's bum but I tried not to look too hard now I knew her.

At Capel-y-ffin we stopped and looked round the church. It was tiny but had incredibly thick walls which kept it as cool as an ice-box.

'Didn't you come here with Jill, then?'

'No. We decided that would be too much of a good thing. We left it for another day.'

Kim smiled at me in sympathy. She was such a warm person.

We sleuthed the pair of Eric Gill gravestones in the churchyard – at least I think we did. They were very restrained and you'd hardly guess they were by the great man at all. If they were the ones, Jill would have loved them.

The cycle into the hills was OK and I was surprised at how well I coped. The mountain biking around Highgate had done more good than I thought. I even coped with the off road later on which took us back from Crucorney towards the priory via a series of drove routes and rabbit runs that went so high it nearly had us nipping along Offa's Dyke. I hadn't had such fun on a bike since the evening Jill and I and our friends cycled across Port Meadow in Oxford – another fateful occasion.

We were hardly a mile from the priory when we reached a large oak wood. There was a gate across the path and I expected Kim to get off and open it. Instead she veered to the right and headed for a section of wall which had fallen over. I was a fair way behind her and before I turned off she'd already rethought the situation and shot up the hill, twisted round and was burning towards the gap. I say 'gap' but the stones were still piled pretty high. I thought, what the hell does she think she's doing?

I was so preoccupied I almost came a cropper on a giant molehill. I'd just about recovered myself when she started bumping over the outer edge of the fallen stones. She stood up as the bike juddered under her. Then, nearly at the top, I thought she'd been stopped dead, only it was immediately obvious this was intentional. She bounced the bike onto the top of the heap, bounced again and was off down the other side.

When I got to the gap and dismounted, she was standing opposite me saying, 'Not tempted, then?'

'Show off. Though I've got to admit it was impressive. You oughtn't to do it in shorts, though, should you? If you fell, you'd be cut to ribbons.'

'I've always had an impetuous streak.'

'Yeah, well just be careful.'

At which point I stumbled on my gingerly way up.

'You're the one at risk.'

'OK, OK. Here, can you take the bike. This is the sort of moment I'll do something that gives Richard heart failure.'

When I was safely over she started wheeling her bike through the undergrowth towards the path.

'Lost your sense of adventure?' I said.

'Not really. I didn't think there was much point in getting back on. I want to show you something.'

After a few hundred yards there was an even narrower path going uphill through the trees. We dropped the bikes and started off on it. About a minute later we were suddenly in a sort of clearing around a derelict cottage.

'Isn't it sweet?' said Kim.

'It's as enchanted as everything else in this valley. Yes it's lovely.'

We were going through what had been the front door. We both froze. We saw the owl at the same time. It was perched on a beam end jutting out over the fireplace.

'Shit,' I said as it began to lift off.

It swooped at us.

We ducked down.

'Fuck,' said Kim but I could tell even in that split second that she wasn't as afraid as me. She was almost laughing.

I was still looking up through my crossed arms. The wings filled the tiny cottage. I saw the scowling angry face, the claws, felt the wind from its wingbeats. Then it was gone.

'Jesus, that was close,' I said.

'It was magnificent.'

I looked around for its mate before venturing further. With the benefit of hindsight, I don't think we'd been in much danger. It felt like the bird somehow squeezed through the door directly above our heads but in reality it must have got out through an old bedroom window.

Even so I was mightily relieved to see the back of it. My heart was thumping. It certainly felt like a close call.

'God that was fantastic.'

Kim turned to me. Her eyes were bright with excitement.

That we should be in one another's arms and kissing within seconds was inevitable, I suppose. Whether it was or wasn't, it *was* indescribably amazing.

Somehow we were soon on the ground over by the hearth which was covered in deep moss like a bed. It was like a fairy story.

133

Then she was on top of me, her top pushed up over her breasts, and she was opening the leather pouch on her belt. She produced a condom and held it towards me like she was tempting me with a sweet.

I took the condom.

*

When we got back to the pub we feasted on a couple of Shropshire Blue ploughmans that could only be described as gargantuan. How Kim put away so much food and still stayed slim was a marvel. I remember wondering if I was ever like that. I suppose I must have been but it was as hard to imagine then as it is now.

After we ate I fetched us another couple of pints and we dozed on the grass for a while. Occasionally I opened my eyes and squinted at the row of arches along the north side of where the nave had been or the ragged outline of the tower above the crossing. The sight of these together with the feel of the March sun were as unreal as the fact I was lying on the grass hand in hand with that beautiful woman.

Every now and then I took a sip of my pint. Kim got me drinking cider which I hate as a rule. But the stuff they served at the priory was like nectar. It was pure apple yet with a sharpness that made it as clean as the Bavarian-style wheat beer Rajiv cooked up to celebrate the Millennium. It was poky too. After two pints it was a wonder I could ride a bike let alone do anything else.

We cycled a little five mile off road circuit Kim knew on the opposite side of the valley, then came back, adjourned to my room and made love.

In fact over the next eighteen hours we made love I don't know how many times. It was like being a teenager again. I couldn't believe it. And it wasn't simply making love, it was the chat as well. It was like we'd known each other all our lives or come out of the same mould. It was also like time stopped. In that timeless place we were outside time. We suspended our disbelief.

Of course what we were doing couldn't last. We both accepted that but in those hours it didn't matter. Everything was possible. Even though we probably wouldn't set eyes on each other again we'd always be together in a funny sort of way. We'd found each other. We couldn't *be* without each other. We were eternal. She is a part of me just as I am a part of her.

It was only next morning that the veil lifted a fraction and she provoked feelings in me she's never provoked before or since. The feelings made me realise that what was eternal about us was on another plane. It wasn't in the hum-drum world.

It was about six, beginning to get light. Kim was lying on her back, the bedding pretty much thrown off her. She was fast asleep. I gazed at her body, her lovely smooth, creaseless skin. Her form was that of a mature woman but her texture was that of an angel. I tingled inside until I shed tears. I felt old. For a moment I felt like I was a dirty old man.

*

Later that morning we said goodbye.

*

I drove back to London by a different route, via Crucorney and Crickhowell, Ross-on-Wye and the Cotswolds. A mile or so beyond Burford I turned off the A40 and headed for the village of Clayfield which I'd read about in one of the trade papers. It was, apparently, an historic village of pubs – one of them being ripe for a makeover.

Although I didn't know it I was about to start the second remarkable series of events that happened that extraordinary weekend.

Sarah's Diary

*November 1995 – Monday 7*th

On Saturday I met Debbie at Reading station. She's in London at the moment working for a screenwriting agency in Soho – not far from the pub we went to back in September. That weekend seems such a long time ago now. So much has happened. Both good and bad. No, all of it good but one thing was vv hard.

Debbie's reading film scripts. When they come in she goes through the first thirty pages – no more, no less – and writes a précis. It's on the strength of this that the scripts get read by someone else, or not. Can you imagine? Such power!

She does this until Christmas and in the New Year flies to LA to see Karl and his dad. When Karl comes back to Oxford she'll stay on, working in a studio for three months. She'll just be a dog's body but it'll be amazing fun. She'll love it and it'll be the start of her glittering career.

Karl's really freaked about the whole thing. He has drug-fuelled visions of Rick ditching Veronica and shacking up with Debs. Shacking is her word not mine. It's perfect for Rick.

Debbie tries to reassure Karl there's as much chance of her sleeping with Rick as there is of Tom Cruise winning an Oscar but that doesn't work. So she tries to make a joke of it and that's even worse. He accuses her of being insensitive. Which is itself a joke. Is suggesting she'd seduce his father sensitive?

I can sense another break up. Though she'll have to wait till she's finished at the studio. But she'll have to do it before the summer when Karl's supposed to be joining her on the travelling part of her gap year. I guess she'll be hoping he'll be in the States for Easter. If not she'll have to end it by phone which won't be much fun for either of them.

What tangled lives we lead. As I've written before, it's weird how everything's changing so fast. But it is. I've already taken the lead with Bob. That was the reason Debbie and I were meeting up. Going to the pottery was an excuse to sort Mum and Dad who wanted me home for Gran's birthday. I never imagined the pottery would turn my life upside down.

Debbie looked fantastic. Her hair was cut short – not that it's been long for quite a while. She had most of it off, chopping it from almost waist to collar length, on the last day of the summer term '94. Will was furious. Now it's kind of elfin but also sophisticated. It's taken above the ears and high up the neck but because her hair's so strong and wilful it has real movement. All natural. She's stunning. She had this long black overcoat which she wore open and a black, ribbed top with slinky, velvety dark green leggings.

I felt positively under-dressed in my dungarees and Oxfam overcoat.

You look like a film director, I said to her.

And you look *so* art school.

Which was, I suppose, as it should be, only she ought to have said, *so* like a potter, if she'd only known how things would turn out. Then again, perhaps she was right after all and I'm counting my chickens.

Before catching the bus to Aldermaston we had a beer in the pub opposite the station. We were going by bus because the local trains were cancelled due to track maintenance.

We were both drinking bitter. Since the weekend in London I've become a convert. It's cheaper for a start and I'm beginning to get into the taste too. Not that there's one taste. The range of different flavours is one of the most fascinating things about it.

You're smoking roll-ups, said Debbie when I produced my tin.

'Fraid so.

Don't apologise, girl. I think it's cool. I just never thought you'd smoke them – a nice well-brought up girl like you.

I've changed quite a bit.

That's for sure.

I couldn't look her in the eye for maybe a quarter of a minute after she said that. When I did I knew she was going to be OK about Bob – she wouldn't be judgmental at least. You can never tell how friends are going to react about things you've done when you meet them face-to-face. People change from when you speak to them on the phone and when you actually see them.

I should have known Debbie wouldn't judge, though.

Yeah, I said, finally looking up.

Do you want to talk about it? She sounded a touch over-eager but I couldn't blame her.

It was pretty awful but not as bad as I expected.

You'd made up your mind, you mean.

Yep.

Was he surprised?

Of course he was.

I mean, that you carried it through.

Coping with his surprise was the hardest thing. He had no idea I was going to finish it.

People who don't know you – and let's face it, how many times have you actually *seen* Bob? – always underestimate how determined you are.

I think I downed nearly everything remaining in my glass when she said that. It made me feel confused. I was proud in a way. Proud to be thought strong. But also worried. I sometimes think I'm too stubborn for my own good. I make myself do things that are bad for me. Sometimes I wonder whether the things I think are really in my best interests – like going to art school – aren't misguided. Am I a self-destructive person? I don't know. I mean, who would give up a man like Bob? Was I mad? I only know I had to end it.

Thanks.

Debbie smiled at me. She said, It must have taken some courage.

I lit a roll up, which I'd only just managed to put together because my hands were so shaky, then I lit Debbie's Silk Cut.

I didn't feel brave. I felt cruel. But I decided it was the best time to go ahead. I could have let it run for a while. But that wouldn't have been fair. Now at least he can start a new life at Oxford. He'll meet someone really academic who's interested in the same things.

Why did you end it, really?

He'd changed. From when we first slept together at your place to when he came back from Australia, he'd become someone else.

He was a bit full of himself, maybe. But probably it's both of you who've altered.

You're so right, as always.

There are a lot of things I'm not right about. I've got my own problems to sort out, haven't I?

How is Karl?

He's OK. I'm going to see him tomorrow.

Will Bob be there?

I don't think so. But he's been as good as his word about keeping an eye on Karl.

Don't.

What? A little twinge, babes?

Piss off. I tried to look outraged.

We both laughed.

Couldn't resist. But it's true, he's looking out for him. Otherwise, I think he'd have been sent down by now.

You're joking!

Nuh-huh. There've been times his mind's been completely AWOL.

Sad. I can't believe what's happening to him.

Don't I know it.

At which point I got us another couple of halves – I only got halves because the bus was due in about ten minutes. We talked about Karl and Bob and how oddly things were turning out. Then I said, Shit, we've got to go!

Debbie played devil's advocate by saying we could always hole up in the pub. But I told her we couldn't do that.

Looking back I'm so pleased I did. I could so easily have given in. I was sorely tempted.

* * * * *

So, what's this place gonna be like? asked Debbie as we headed out of the city.

I've noticed recently how every now and then her speech becomes Americanised (especially when she's had something to drink), like the way she said 'gonna'. It isn't surprising, though, given she works for an American company. Somehow I can just see her ending up there and developing a transatlantic purr.

Search me.

But you're the art student. You know these things.

I'm not that keen on pottery, to be honest. It was just an excuse to meet up. Pottery's dull – all those lumpy shapes and drab colours. It's not really art at all. It's a craft.

Well that's pottery in the bin. You are getting firm opinions in your old age. So why *are* we going to—?

Aldermaston.

How could I forget. Nuclear bombs and all.

And pots.

And pots. Anyway, answer my question. It better be good. We could've spent a very pleasant afternoon in that pub.

It wasn't that good.

A better pub, then.

In Reading?

Anything's gotta be an improvement on this bus. It's freezing and it stinks of— She lowered her voice. Puke.

What are you whispering for? I whispered back at her. There's no one else on the bus. And the driver's as deaf as a post.

We began giggling like schoolgirls.

We're too well brought up, aren't we? said Debbie when we calmed down.

Speak for yourself.

OK, so where were we? Going to a pottery for no good reason whatsoever.

Not true. I've got to report back to Glen.

Who's Glen?

He's the lecturer that told us about the pottery being part of Berkshire art-thingy.

What? Isn't he going to it himself? Sounds ominous.

He went yesterday and took three or four students with him.

But that's not the point. I've got to be able to talk sensibly about the place because he's in overall charge of our course. I told him I was really keen to go but I'd make my own way.

And hence we have to traipse out to the sticks.

You're becoming too urban. You're forgetting your roots.

My roots, babes, are Jamaican.

You know what I mean. Besides there's a thumpingly good pub in the village. Glen said so. And Glen likes his ale.

Now you're talking!

*   *   *   *   *

I hope this bus drops us by that pub, said Debbie a few minutes later. Otherwise I'm gonna have to break someone's door down.

Ssssh! Don't think about it.

I thought you said it was only five miles away.

It is, as the crow flies.

Flying isn't what I associate with this bus.

I didn't expect it to go the scenic route.

You live and learn, girl.

We sat in silence for a while, both trying hard not to think about needing a piss. I tried to concentrate on the countryside but somehow ended up thinking about Bob and for the first time since last weekend wondered whether I did the right thing. The thought of him looking out for Karl had lodged in my mind. Since the weekend in London, I'd portrayed him to myself as this insensitive, self-centred bigot. Of course, I knew I was being unfair but I allowed my thinking to be dominated by the odd disdainful look I glimpsed or the memory of a sarky comment. It's strange how these infinitesimal moments obsess you and get so big they blot out all the good.

But Bob looking after Karl didn't square with this distorted view. Maybe too, needing a pee made me suddenly less confident. Or maybe talking to Debbie about breaking with Bob was forcing me to think about the bigger picture. When you talk to a friend, you can't help wondering how they see you. Debbie didn't need to say anything against me. The things she might think – or how I imagined them – were just there, brought to life by me speaking.

I suppose you could say my conscience was catching up with me. When I'm at college – absorbed in my work, not yet good enough friends with anybody to confide about Bob – I'm able to sustain my selfish certainties about how things are. You can't stay like that with a real friend. Someone who really knows you.

As we were coming into Aldermaston and Debbie said Yes! and punched the air, I was wondering whether I'd not only decided to split with Bob but had held myself to it because it was the simplest option. Wasn't I just opting out of all the grunt I'd get from Dad if Bob came to stay or if I went over to Oxford too often? OK, you could be positive and say that that meant I wasn't ready for a full-on relationship and had therefore taken the right decision. Or you could say that I was so wrapped up in my college work there wasn't any room left for Bob (partly true). But it could also be described as cowardice.

When we were gingerly stepping off the bus then whizzing across the green to the pub, it occurred to me that in my own estimation I'd gone from hero to wimp in half an hour.

Thinking about these descriptions of myself now, neither seems true. They were like masks – masks that remind me of the experiments I've been making with different media on my foundation course. I sometimes wish I could suddenly grow up without all the hassle of trying things out with paint and photographic paper – and emotions.

Friday 11ᵗʰ

I've had to take a break from writing.

I wrote the first bit on Monday night before going to bed – nowadays I can write when Mum and Dad are in the house. I sat up till four the previous night reading the book Sinéad gave me. It was as good as I expected – well, ten times better really – but I needed to let it settle before I started making notes. I finished those last night then read an article she recommended which I managed to copy at the department library. The other books she suggested won't be here until next week. The library's having to get them under the inter-library loan scheme.

When I've read them I'll know what I've got to do about my future.

I'm still enjoying my course, though. I'm working on a painting of Pulteney Bridge and doing a project on the Renaissance, plus some photography. The work takes my mind off food. I know I'm thin but I'm not chucking up, nor exercising and I feel strong.

And tonight I'm writing again – and will be over the weekend too. This time, I'm writing not because I need to sort things out but because I want to assert myself. By writing down what happened I want to make it even more real. I want there to be no going back. I want to encourage myself. I want to be me, to let out the person I know is inside.

*   *   *   *   *

When we came out of the loos, Debbie suggested we have a pint to set us on the right track.

I can't take you anywhere, I said. Look, we'll have a quick

scoot round. I'll take a couple of notes and we'll be back here in no time.

Do you even know where the pottery is?

Good point. I'll ask the landlord.

While I went up to the bar Debbie went and stood in front of the blazing log fire.

When I'd got directions I signalled to her across the packed room, pointing at the entrance.

It was so nice in there, she said as we went outside. That bus was cold, girl. I can't believe we're not staying. They've got Dickens's Old Curiosity.

It's really catching on. It's everywhere in Bath. It's a good pint.

Well, what are you waiting for?

We'll be back. We've got ages. The landlord said he closes when the last customer's left but no earlier than three. And did that crowd look like they were planning to go anywhere?

When's the bus?

There's one at four.

OK – just a quick scoot remember. You said. Now, where is this place?

From the little green and the duck pond we walked along the main street which sloped gently up to what looked like the lodge of a stately home. Like the pub the low houses and cottages on either side were built of brick and had clay tiles. Even on a dull cold day like Saturday, the walls and roofs had a warm earthy quality.

Picture post-card village, I'll give you that, said Debbie. It reminds me of home. Where are the bombs, by the way?

I don't expect they're in the village.

Dad said he knew people who came on the marches.

I can't imagine my dad knowing anyone like that. He'd have thought it was all a communist plot.

Dad knows a lot of people from around Reading who marched. Computer people. You may find it hard to believe but it's been England's Silicone Valley since the sixties.

Wow! I didn't know that. Wasn't he tempted to come over?

Marching's not his thing. I reckon he was more interested in fitting in. You know, keep hold of the job in Cambridge. There was a lot of prejudice against him to begin with.

I remember you telling me that once. It's unbelievable – it's sick.

It's just sad.

That's the polite way of putting it.

Whatever.

Anyway, here we are, I said, looking at a sandwich board on the pavement saying Berkshire Countywide Arts Festival, then up at the pottery sign which was hanging from a bracket above the entrance like the place was a pub.

Cool sign, at least, said Debbie.

It showed a man's face encircled by leaves. It was as if he were looking through a gap in the foliage. His face was gentle and sad. His eyes were his saddest feature – filled with compassion as if he was witnessing a tragic event he could do nothing to stop. The leaves seemed to swirl, though there was no blur of movement. The effect came from just the way they were arranged and the way the light caught the angled surfaces, as if the wind was bending them, carrying them round in an anti-clockwise direction. The leaves were from all seasons. There were fresh new ones, rich mature ones and yellow and orange autumn ones. There were leaves spilling out of the man's mouth. The leaves were from different trees and there were also some grapes and white flowers and red holly berries.

The sign took my breath away. It reminded me of one of the moments in *Une Partie de Campagne* when the man you wish the woman would elope with pretends to be a faun and springs at her from behind a tree.

When we went inside, the first thing I saw was a wall-plaque showing the same image. Underneath was a quotation from Dante which read, 'The eternal gardener's leaves, enleafing everything...'

Heavy, said Debbie. But it's an excellent design. You lost your tongue or something?

It's just amazing, that's all. I hadn't expected anything so beautiful.

I have a bad feeling about this.

I thought it would be mugs and stuff.

Well, there are a few of those. Debbie pointed to the other side of the room.

I couldn't see what she meant at first because the tiny pottery was full of people. But when I squeezed my way through, there, set on a work bench, were examples of mugs, bowls and goblets showing the different stages of throwing, glazing and decoration.

I stared at one of the bowls. Its pattern was abstract, a dance of shapes in blues and reds which shimmered like polished metal. Although when you changed the angle at which you were looking they suddenly became three-dimensional as if you were looking into a pool or through glass. Inside were slivers of gold and silver and dense spots of colour which were spreading out like ink in water. There were star bursts and blemishes which could have been fossils or pieces of semi-precious stone.

For a while I was totally absorbed in the bowl. Then I had another surprise. There was a man's voice behind me saying, Sarah. I turned round although I imagined he meant someone else and there was Uncle Vern.

* * * * *

Uncle Vern, I said, what are *you* doing here?

My innocent question made him look almost panic-stricken, although such a response was not unusual for him. Oh, I was up this way. My friends have gone out to lunch. It's a long story. I'll tell you in— But first— He bent forward, somewhat awkwardly because of the box he was carrying, and kissed me on both cheeks. How nice to see you, Sarah.

Nice to see you too Uncle Vern. This is my friend Debbie.

Uncle Vern reached round the side of me and shook Debbie's hand.

Pleased to meet you. Do you live near here?

No, London.

My turn to ask you what you're doing here then. Oh, I suppose it's something to do with your art course, Sarah. Are you a fellow student, Debbie?

No, I said, Debbie and I were at school together. Now she's in the film business. Though you're right about the pottery and my course. As I was coming over here it seemed like a good opportunity to meet half way.

Pen told me you weren't going to the lunch. But what a co, you being here of all places.

Yeah, spooky.

Shall we go and stand by the entrance? I think we're in the way.

That's better, Uncle Vern said, once we decided there was no space inside after all and went out onto the pavement.

I didn't know you collected modern pottery, Uncle Vern. I nodded at the box.

For a moment he looked as if he'd been caught doing something naughty. I half expected him to say, Don't tell your mother.

I don't. It's just it's such beautiful work. I've never seen anything like it. The lustre they use is quite outstanding.

We've only seen a couple of things, but they were mind-blowing. Don't you reckon, Debbie?

Actually it's a lot better than I expected.

It's mega! Completely different from what I imagined too. The stuff they make at college is dead boring. This is art.

You've changed your tune, said Debbie, and she had a go at tickling me through my overcoat.

Debbie!

I pulled away.

She composed herself and turned to Uncle Vern. Sarah said she thought pottery was just a craft on the way here.

True, I'm afraid, Uncle Vern. OK, I admit it, I was wrong. *So* wrong.

There's no need to go over the top. It's still only pottery.

Now, who's the philistine? It's cosmic!

I think I ought to let you two look round, said Uncle Vern. He seemed perplexed by us.

I hoped we didn't seem drunk. I didn't want him to pass that on to Mum and Dad, let alone Gran.

Is there much to see? asked Debbie.

There are other rooms further along, then the woodshed—

Woodshed? she said.

For the kiln. You've got to see the kiln. That's a work of art in itself.

We'd better get going then, I said. We've only got an hour before our bus.

Uncle Vern looked at his watch. I could give you a lift, if you hurry.

No, we're going to a gallery in Reading – part of the Countywide scheme.

Pen said you were missing the tea too.

I know, it's *such* a shame.

I could feel Debbie willing me to shut up.

You still haven't told us what's in the box.

It's a bowl with one of their abstract designs on it.

He glanced at the box then looked at me, his face changing, opening up and it was as if he were losing his inhibitions and speaking to me directly for the first time.

But it had something. I'd never seen anything like it before. It was like staring into a rock pool when I was a child. I lost myself in it. I fell in love with it.

He looked at Debbie then at me again and smiled. He suddenly looked embarrassed.

Anyway, I ought to be getting on. I'm parked at the bottom of the hill.

I kissed him goodbye, still surprised by how kindred he seemed in those few seconds when he spoke about the bowl. I'd never felt like that about him before.

Nice to meet you, he said to Debbie, and shook her hand.

He's quite a strange man, she said as he was heading off. He's your mum's brother, right?

Yes.

Do you get on with him, as a family, I mean? You both seemed a bit awkward together, like there was a history there.

Sharp eyes. He's a sort of family joke. Dad and Alex really send him up. But Mum adores him, after a fashion. Gran does too but she can't stand him being around for long. That's why he's only going to the tea. It's because he's gay – though no one knows he is for sure.

It did cross my mind.

Did you notice how funny he was about who he's staying with?

Sure did.

I glanced at my watch. Shit Debs, we'd better move.

You're OK. Enjoy looking round. I could tell you liked it. I'm interested too. Just as long as we get a pint in here. Then maybe we can have a session in Reading.

*   *   *   *   *

And the pottery was magical, wonderful – words cannot describe how fresh and exciting it was.

First of all, I picked up a leaflet which told me its history.

The building was a blacksmith's shop right up until Sinéad, the potter, bought it in 1965. Although she mostly left it as it was, some stable doors and places where rooms were open-fronted were bricked in. I found it so odd to think that horses used to be kept in what now looked like a cottage. I guess it always did look like that. So you'd be walking along the High Street peering through people's windows (as you do) and suddenly there would be a horse standing on straw and beyond, out in the yard under a makeshift roof, the red glow of the forge. There was a photo of one of the Victorian blacksmiths standing by this dangerous-looking contraption in the leaflet. Not that the forge was actually much different from Sinéad's kiln.

One of the extraordinary things about the building was its floor which was made up of small wooden squares, worn smooth and yet with hardly any dips because the wood was so hard. Apparently these squares were really the tops of stakes, or piles, made of hornbeam which were driven into the ground a hundred and fifty years ago. They'd withstood all that time with horses trampling over them, not to mention peeing on them! Wild.

The three rooms along the street were very simple. In the first two there were old workbenches, which looked Victorian but weren't, deep china sinks with brass taps and foot-operated potter's wheels which looked far more elegant than the dumpy electric ones at college. In the far corner of the second room was a large cast-iron woodburner with a stack of logs beside it. The stove wasn't lit on Saturday – the crowds generated more than enough warmth.

From the first room, an open staircase went through a hole in the ceiling to a loft where the finished work was stored.

To begin with I was surprised by how few tools there were, but then I noticed along the backs of the benches there were jam jars containing brushes and wooden implements and in between them were rags and funny little clay stands and bungs. The place had an extraordinarily appealing simplicity and I could really feel the creative atmosphere, although if I'm honest, I was barely able to imagine the incredible skills needed to make such beautiful objects. I still can't and hope like mad this won't be my undoing.

Then there was the smell of the clay – so earthy and yet so clean and purifying. It cut right through the haze of perfume and sweat and stale cigarette smoke produced by the people.

I liked the fact that although the rooms had clearly been tidied up for the open days, the spatterings of clay and pigments on the walls and windows had been left alone. They made the pottery feel lived-in and alive.

For a while I completely lost myself in the smell of clay, the look of the rooms and the loveliness of the pottery. Then I met Sinéad herself.

Saturday 12th

The third room was full of shelving set at a variety of heights to accommodate different sized pots. It's here the pieces await their first firing. I learnt from Sinéad that beforehand they are left to get 'leather hard', at which point they are trimmed or have spouts and handles added.

I found the phrase 'leather hard' fascinating. It's so appropriately descriptive but also disturbing somehow. The tongue almost feels like leather hard clay when you say it.

Beyond the third room a short passage leads into the yard. Some of the bigger pots are stored in sheds open to the elements. Sinéad said a few years ago she got a commission to make these gigantic vases – as tall as a person – which formed part of an exhibition that accompanied a trade delegation to Russia and the vases were not only stored in these barns but thrown in them as well. Making them must have required so much knowledge. Then there is the woodshed which looks massive, like it could be part of a timber yard. And, of course, there is the kiln.

I met Sinéad in her office which is on the other side of the yard passage. From what I could tell, the office is the beginning of her cottage.

I'd had a look at the pots in the drying room and was just about to head into the yard when I noticed that a door saying Private was ajar. I saw a woman standing by a large dresser which was strewn with papers and photographs. There were more photos and designs pinned to its shelves and others hanging from the shelves in bulldog clips. The woman was prodding at the papers as if she was searching for something. Her movements, though, weren't hurried but deliberate –- calculated, I should say. Her head was bowed slightly and this emphasised her long platted ponytail which almost reached her waist. Her hair was a vivid mixture of grey, chestnut and red.

From her plat my gaze returned to her hands. Her fingers were long but not fine. They were thick and looked very strong and sinuous, as did the hands themselves and her wrists. Yet they weren't man's hands. They had feminine grace.

The woman was speaking to someone behind her. She had a gentle voice and I heard her say, I don't know, I must be getting old. But there was nothing resigned about the way she said the words. Instead they sounded playful and perhaps both mocking and self-mocking.

Suddenly a man came up to her and put his hand on her shoulder. Nonsense, Sinéad. But don't worry, it'll turn up. Anyway, I've really got to go now. I've outstayed my welcome as it is.

He kissed her on both cheeks and as he opened the door further I knocked on it.

Looking back, I wasn't at all aware of what I was doing. I was just totally taken up with the pottery and the need to talk to Sinéad.

You've got another visitor, said the man.

Sinéad looked from him to me. She smiled at me and said, Hello.

Hi, I'm one of Glen Williams' students. The one that couldn't come yesterday?

Oh yes, he mentioned that someone—

Bye Sinéad, said the man, from behind me now.

Sinéad gave him a little wave. Bye Tony.

Come on in then. What do you want to know?

I felt a little flustered by her friendliness. I felt guiltily self-conscious about having imposed on her.

I'm sorry I knocked.

She looked surprised. Knocked?

I glanced over my shoulder. It says Private.

She laughed. Oh you don't want to take any notice of that. People do, thank God, but I'm always here for friends and students and anyone else really. The problem I find— Sit down.

152

She swept her hand towards an ancient swivel chair by her desk.

—is knowing what to do with myself on days like this.

I can imagine – so many people.

It is a bit awe-inspiring. The funny thing is, though, that if I go out there, no one recognises me, so I smile at people and most of them probably think I'm a lunatic, although one of them might ask if I'm the potter and we'll have a chat. But really I end up feeling that I'm in the way most of the time and retreat in here. Anyway, that's enough of that. What can I do for you?

I hardly know where to start.

What do you like making?

For a moment I considered lying. But I couldn't. What I'd seen in the pottery and my responses to it were too important for that.

I have to confess I've not much enjoyed pottery classes.

But now?

I know it sounds silly—

Why don't we have a coffee?

That would be nice.

She crossed the room and filled a kettle at another of the deep china sinks then plugged it in.

Pottery can be pretty boring at college. People play safe.

She rinsed a couple of mugs as she spoke.

Glen would shoot me for saying so, but that person he's got at your place is frightfully dull.

I smiled when she said that. I *know*. I thought it was just me.

Of course not. Glen's good, though, but he spends all his time being an administrator. Trips like the one yesterday are supposed to fill the gaps but it's terribly hard to keep that momentum going when students go back to college. All those lumpy bits of green tableware that would smash a banqueting table if you dropped them!

Is it a technical thing? I mean do colleges make that sort of stuff because they don't have the right equipment?

No. I think it's more that it's the way it's always been done. The approach is supposed to ensure that students can at least produce something symmetrical. Well, I know things can go horribly wrong if you try and make things that are too fine and glazes can end up disastrously up the creek, but even so. If students aren't taught to push themselves and try different things it's hardly surprising if they don't take to the craft.

Craft? Is it an art or a craft? My friend and I were talking about this on the bus here.

She spooned coffee into the mugs and poured the hot water.

Milk?

Please.

Would your friend like a coffee?

I don't know. I think she'll be OK for a bit. I tried not to look at my watch and promised myself I'd pay for all the rounds in Reading.

We can go and find her in a minute — I could show you round. Point out things you might not have noticed so you can impress Glen.

Brilliant!

Sinéad handed me my mug and sat on a stool opposite me.

For me— What's your name?

Sarah.

For me, Sarah, pottery is definitely a craft.

But the things are so beautiful.

Can't crafts produce beautiful things? Have you ever looked at a hand made basket?

I'm not sure.

There can be beauty in a simple thing.

But surely pottery's different? The way *you* do it, anyway.

Not really. Potters and basket weavers both use natural materials. Both use hand skills which they've learnt over a long apprenticeship. Both have to have artistic judgement when it comes to shape and texture. And both, crucially, have to repeat quantities of what they produce to make a living.

But the designs out there are unique. I looked at two mugs and although they were the same shape and colour, each was completely different.

That's true. But they're still repeats. The processes we use do allow variation and I like to think there's some art there but we rarely produce work that's figurative or conceptual. Our work doesn't say anything in the way that paintings and sculptures do.

When I looked into one of those bowls out there I thought it said *everything*. And what about the man and the leaves? He's magical.

As I said, we do *some* art. Sinéad looked at me and laughed. I love the man and the leaves. It works – although sometimes I think he's taking being a god too seriously and I call him Alan, after Alan Bates the actor. Probably before your time. But to me that makes him more human.

I didn't know how to react when she said that.

Sacrilege?

It's just that the image reminded me of a film I saw recently – *Une Partie de Campagne*.

Wonderful film.

When I came out of the cinema I was totally overwhelmed. It was the light. The shimmering trees. The sunlight. I love painting but the film somehow defeated me. I thought how could you ever hope to compete with that. But when I looked into that bowl out there I realised you could capture such light.

Thank you. It's exciting when someone gets so much from our work. It makes everything worthwhile.

How many people work here?

She seemed surprised by my question and the shift in direction – as I was myself. I could suddenly see myself working here. I suddenly so wanted to.

About five of us. But it varies. We can't go over seven, though, or we become a factory and the European Parliament imposes lots of expensive conditions.

Do most people come here and train up?

Most – though occasionally we get people who've worked elsewhere.

Could I work for you?

She looked at me intently for a few moments then smiled.

It depends, she said. You'd have to go away and think very hard before that could happen. And there'd have to be a vacancy, of course. If there was, you'd have to ask yourself lots of searching questions. Do you want to become an apprentice? In which case you'd have to forgo college. Would that be a good idea? What would your parents think? Do you really understand what working here would involve? You'd have to do lots of reading and imagining before you could even begin to appreciate what it would be like. You'd have to understand that the craft bit is terribly important. People that make a go of it here find the routine therapeutic and fulfilling in its own right. But there have been some who didn't last because they were disappointed when they realised that there's a gulf between the beautiful pieces we make and the way we make them. You'd have to think about all those sorts of things – and *more*.

What she said was a lot to take in but I was high on the atmosphere of the pottery and felt I could focus on the things she said needed to be done and that I could do them. I then wanted to ask her my next question.

And you do take people on straight from school?

I have done. But there have to be good reasons for doing so.

Right.

I suggest you think about what I've said and read up on pottery then, if you're still interested, get back in touch.

What should I read?

She reached towards her desk.

This for a start.

She handed me a book about her work. I looked at the back cover and saw its price was twenty pounds. I leant forward for my bag.

You can borrow it. If you lose interest, just give it to Glen and he'll drop it back.

Thank you.

I'll write down some other good books you might try. You also ought to have a go at making pottery with Brian, even though he's not imaginative. If you can persuade Glen to teach you, so much the better.

OK.

But don't be in a rush. If you were to apply to me, you'd be making a big decision. You can always put it off until after art school. In the meantime you could see if we had holiday jobs in the summer. Your decision's got to be informed and above all right for you.

I understand that. Thank you.

Although she was saying things that were intended to make me cautious, I felt as if the day was like a revelation. It felt far too real to be anything other than my destiny.

Now, said Sinéad, let's go and find your friend and I'll show you round.

We found Debbie in the yard standing by the kiln. She was talking to a very short man with blond hair and blue eyes. As we approached, she said to him, Here's my friend.

The man looked at us and smiled. He stretched out his hand first to me, then Sinéad. Tom Dickens, he said. Pleased to meet you.

He spoke with a sort of Cockney accent and was immediately warm and smiley. His name sounded familiar.

Debbie and me, he said, were just consoling each other about playing gooseberry. My partner's trying to track down the potter.

Oh, said Sinéad, that's me.

God, I've found you first. Isn't that always the way?

Is your partner Jill? From the V&A?

That's the one.

She did phone and say she might be here. Why don't you go and find her and I'll meet you in fifteen minutes in my office.

Fine by me.

I'm just going to show Sarah and Debbie the kiln and things.

She broke off and shook Debbie's hand. Hello Debbie.

OK, said the man. Well, good to meet you Debs, and we'll see you – he nodded at Sinéad – in a quarter of an hour.

The office is to the left of the passage. Marked Private.

After the man was out of earshot, Debbie said, Do you realise who that was?

I shook my head.

Only Tom Dickens of Dickens's Brewery.

No! I don't believe it! I said. (Even so, meeting Mr Dickens seemed no less magical than the rest of that afternoon.)

Sinéad looked puzzled. I don't know who Tom Dickens is, she said, but his girlfriend is a curator at the V&A and she's interested in buying some of our work for the Modern Masterpieces section.

Wow! I said. Don't you want to see her right away? We could wait.

I could see Debbie was shocked by this.

Not at all. Showing students round is just as important. So, this is the kiln. The 'Beast'.

*   *   *   *   *

When we got to the bus stop we discovered there was a five-thirty back to Reading. It was by then four o'clock.

Fortunately, the pub was still open so I bought us a couple of pints of Old Curiosity and a bottle each of Wobbly Tom to take home.

Cheers, said Debbie. Unbelievable meeting the man himself.

We stared at the labels showing Tom Dickens dressed as Miss Havisham.

It's the day, I said. I shouldn't think I'll have another one like this, *ever*.

That's a bit over the top. But the pottery was good, I'll grant you that. Sinéad was nice too.

She's fantastic.

I looked at Debbie and raised my glass.

Let's say cheers, Debbie, to Sinéad's pottery. I know what I want to do.

*   *   *   *   *

It was only later, on the train back to Bath, that I thought about what I'd say to Dad.

I rolled another cigarette and felt my stomach tighten into nothing. I was glad I'd only had some dry roast.

Tom's writing therapy

18/03/02 – A Monday

I found Clayfield easily and as I entered the village was immediately struck by how many big houses there were. It was evidently a prosperous place. But there was also something reassuringly jumbly about the little cottages in between the larger properties.

The stone was pure Cotswold, although I got the impression the Cotswolds had petered out a couple of miles earlier. The land round Clayfield was flat. River valley. I'd seen on the map that the Thames ran nearby.

I promised myself a nose round and a walk down to the river after lunch.

Looking back, having lived here for a couple of years, I know how different the kinds of stone used for each house are. There was a talk in the village hall on the subject not long after I moved in. Apparently there isn't much good stone locally so it was bought in from wherever it could be obtained. And as the village is on the cusp of four counties (Oxon, Glos, Berks and Wilts), what was bought varied considerably.

But on that March day the even golden glow of the houses was a reflection of my inner state after Kim.

The pub I was looking for, the Parker Arms, wasn't hard to miss, although there were, as the trade paper article stated, a number of licensed premises to choose from – seven to be precise. At one time, it said, there'd been twelve, an extraordinary number for a village like Clayfield. It was all down to the good old Beer Act of 1848 and the fact that in Victorian days Clayfield boasted a thriving cattle market.

The Parker was just over the cross-roads in the centre of the village. It was a large edifice in between a smaller pub and a row of cottages and shops. Its style was Carolean, I would say, with two round, Dutch-looking gables with stone spikes on top. At ground-floor level were a couple of deep bay windows, and above each was a balcony reached from the bedrooms by a door set in the middle of stone mullions. The doors should have been iron-framed with leaded lights but weren't. They were cheap wood-and-ply painted black gloss. They were like the fire escape doors you get on those terraced flats along Western Avenue.

Even so, at first glance, the Parker could have been one of the village's big houses and you could see its potential as an upper-mid to upmarket hotel, restaurant and county-set hostelry.

I parked the Boxter on the street, although there was a car park sign pointing down the coaching alley. I wanted to enter from the front and work through to the back.

The food blackboard by the entrance – a lovely heavy door with brass furniture – advertised several decent mains at ludicrously cheap prices, with the promise of plenty more inside. Another board said B&B £20 per person per night.

And inside – it was chaos. I don't mean that disrespectfully but there was no system. You could tell from the dust on top of the cigarette machine, next to which stood a gleaming antique brass umbrella stand, that there was no fixed cleaning itinerary. I imagined the cleaners just did what they felt like.

The tables in the big front room were all over the place and the furniture was nothing special. Then there was the bar. In 1965 it would have been state-of-the-art. And although the beer pulls were nice – probably about the only things left from a Victorian layout – the optics were set out like someone was trying to take the micky out of a landlord who had a skinful the night before.

The staff were lovely, young girls mostly. They were friendly and eager to serve. But they obviously weren't under any direction. They had bags of potential but hadn't been taught anything. There were loads of oopses and giggles and squints at glasses or the way they'd laid out a table because they simply didn't know the proper way to do things.

It was like the landlord (nowhere in evidence) had got his daughter's school friends round to help out to give them

something to do. Which of course was more or less how it was –
on a permanent basis.

Nevertheless there were a lot of punters in and they *seemed* to
be enjoying themselves.

I peeped into the snug at the back which had a good intimate
feel to it. I bagged a table by the way through so I could see both
areas then got myself a pint of Growler (a lovely dark bitter with
more than a hint of roast chestnuts that weighed in at a
respectable 4.8%) and a newspaper from the end of the bar.

As I settled I gave the two men sitting next to me the once
over. One had his back to me – he was obviously tall, middle-
aged and balding on top. The one facing was again clearly a tall
man, but younger (early twenties, maybe), somewhat overweight,
with long unruly blond hair and cherryish face.

They were chatting about land and crops and foot and mouth
but every now and then leant into each other and their voices
went quiet.

As they spoke, I noticed one had a rural accent whereas the
other, the one with his back to me, spoke in a rather cultivated
way. The latter's voice reminded me of someone but for a while I
couldn't think who.

Instinctively I turned to page three, took one glance at the
half-naked lovely then flicked over to four and five. Looking at
the girl felt like betraying Kim. I immersed myself in a
supposedly in-depth interview with the estranged boyfriend of a
minor Royal but gave up after a couple of minutes. The guy was
trying to say the princessette was a loony but in my opinion he
was the one with the problem. He was a plonker.

I shut the paper and looked into the main room. I tried to
envisage it divided up into more intimate spaces. Panels of
what's known in the trade as stable partitioning would do the
trick, I thought, although given the target clientele, you'd have to
do something bespoke. The stable dividers idea but the look of
dark panelling. I'd want to make the area around the big old
fireplace particularly special.

The trouble was when it came to something really top of the
range I didn't have enough confidence in my concepts without

Jill. I was good at my sort of pub, of course – larky but upmarket – and I was also good at broad brush and once the exchange of ideas got going could come up with some hum-dingers but I needed Jill's assuredness in order to get off on the right foot. She was also great at bringing me down to earth. She added a lot of subtlety to my plans. I'd learnt so many new things from her but couldn't yet manage on my own.

It was odd realising, as I tried to picture a new Parker, how dependent I felt on Jill. Especially given my buoyancy after Kim. After all, it wasn't as if we'd ever done any pubs together, Jill and me. What I learnt from her came from one project – our flat – and our little dreams when we were off on our pub weekends. In those days we fantasised about me selling up and taking on a country pub which we'd design together. We used to sit in bars and rejig them in our minds over the course of the evening.

Why was I there anyway? Well, what I'd read about the village of pubs and the Parker had somehow stuck. And when I was thinking about my route home during breakfast the idea of calling in on Clayfield simply knitted itself into the picture. I thought it'd be a treat. If I'm honest it was a sort of game. A way of giving myself something fun to do and also a means of getting back into thinking about what I was going to do with the rest of my life. A nice project to exercise my brain. That was all. Nothing serious.

Just as well, really, because the design side of things wasn't working. Staring into that room made me feel like a savage. A theme-pub numbskull who'd been briefly elevated to rarefied heights. Who then blew it and couldn't hack it on his own. I suddenly felt I had more in common with the guy who'd bonked the princess than I cared to admit.

For diversion I turned to look at the blokes sitting next to me. The red-faced boy was reaching into the pocket of his suit jacket which was hung over the back of his chair. He was saying he ought to be getting along.

He produced a floppy disc which he slipped onto the table. He patted it like it was a beer mat and he was about to try the flipping game then slid it over to his friend under his hand.

162

He lowered his voice somewhat. 'Let me know what you think.' He nodded meaningfully.

Does this guy think he's a gangster? I asked myself. I wondered what was on the disc. There'd been something stagily self-conscious about the way the man half-concealed it. It was porn, I decided.

'Sure. You won't stay for another? A bit to eat?'

'Got a full afternoon of calls and Mum did me sandwiches.'

The red-faced man got up followed by the one with his back to me. They shook hands. As the younger man headed for the door a bloke came into the pub. I heard them go through what I took to be the Oxfordshire version of the universal greeting.

'Hi ya, Andy,' said the guy coming in. 'Alright?'

'Alright, Sam. You?'

'Alright.'

The exchange sounded rich and fruity and Andy's accent was more pronounced all of a sudden, almost West Country.

The man who had his back to me was reaching into the pocket of his tweed jacket, also hung over the back of his chair, for his wallet. He was stood up and twisting round. Our eyes met and he smiled at me. He wasn't smiling because he recognised me but out of natural friendliness but when he smiled and I smiled back we recognised each other.

'Good God,' he said. 'Tom Dickens.'

*

We were now sitting at Colin's table with fresh pints of Growler in front of us and a couple of ploughmans on the way.

'Cheers,' he said and raised his glass. 'Well I never.'

Colin Jannaway and I were at London University together. We both studied history and spent our first year in the same hall of residence. Of course, I dropped out after that but we got on and I saw him a couple of times after leaving. Once when I went back to see him and some other college misfits and another time when he came to the pub in Tring where I was working for Len Banks. After that we lost touch. I think we suddenly realised we were in different worlds. He decided to study hard and I was working like stink and had a yen to make a fortune.

I say we were misfits – and we were. Colin was a bit of a country squire, even then, and pretty aloof. But you could tell inside he had a heart of gold. Besides he liked his ale and we shared a passion for Shane MacGowan and the Pogues.

The reason for the squire stuff wasn't immediately obvious. His home was on the outskirts of Grantham and his dad had a very successful Mazda dealership in the town. But then, when you dug deeper – or rather when he poured out his life history to you in the uni bar – you discovered his dad had been set to inherit a chunk of prime Lincolnshire farmland. Only his dad's passion was for motors. He signed his share of the family business over to his younger brother in exchange for enough cash to set up his first franchise – Sunbeam, if I remember rightly.

Colin had never forgiven his old man. I can see the contempt in his face as he told me that when quizzed his dad just said, 'Well, how was I to know you'd be interested in farming?' (When do dad's ever get it right? Colin's father was doubtless cut up by his son not wanting to go into the car business.) 'But he shouldn't have sold his share,' Colin used to say. 'He could have rented it to the family. You don't sell farmland. It's your heritage. Farming's in the blood.'

'Cheers,' I said in the Parker Arms over fifteen years later. 'It is a bit, well I never.'

We looked at each other for a few seconds in silence. Stunned for a moment, I guess.

Then Col said, 'I drink your beer.'

'Not mine anymore.'

'What, you've sold up?'

'Yeah. Though until my erstwhile partners judge it's the right time to let the cat out of bag it's still hush-hush. It's a question of consumer confidence.'

'Does that mean an end to Wobbly Tom? I do hope not. I collect the labels – soak them off.'

I was touched by that.

'We're still negotiating the fate of Wobbly. With luck, it'll survive. It's a market leader and besides if it continues, I'll still get an annual income from the business – copyright for my mug.'

'Whew!'

I felt his relief and again was touched.

'Anyway,' I said, 'that's enough about me for a minute. My life's been in the public domain. How about you? What have you been doing for the last fifteen years?'

'It's seventeen actually – I think.'

I did a quick calculation in my head.

'Christ, it is and all.'

'Time really does fly.'

'Well let's skip the depressing stuff. Tell me about you. Do you live here for a start?'

'Yes, yes I do. My wife and I moved here four years ago. I got my farm.'

He grinned at me, although what with his smallish mouth with its down-turned corners, his deep round chin and basset-hound eyes, the expression looked somewhat mournful. Still, I knew what it meant from years ago.

'I don't believe it! You stuck at it! Did you get the old man to sell the motor business?'

'You've got a good memory.'

'It's part of what I do, remembering things about people.'

'No, dad's still clinging on up in Grantham. He's tried to take a back seat but can't do it. He's always interfering with his managers. He can't sit still that's his trouble.'

'Know the feeling.'

'Bet you do. No, we rent – from the council. We've got a smallholding. Twenty acres.'

'That sounds alternative, Col.'

'It is a bit. But we only do it part time. Fiona, that's my wife, does some accountancy and I'm a land agent, three days a week.'

'A land agent. Is that what you went into after college?'

'No. City. Stocks and shares. It was thrilling for a couple of years. All that loot. Big bonuses etcetera. But then I got bored, decided to do land agency by correspondence course. I got a job with a big London firm and studied in the evenings.'

'But how did you end up here with a smallholding?'

'Well, working for the big firm was all very well but it was pretty unreal. We used to look after wealthy investment clients – like pension funds, plus one or two rich Arabs – who owned landed estates. But it wasn't proper hands-on land agency. We were based in Mayfair, for God's sake! We'd go on estate visits, of course – in company Range Rovers – but mostly concentrated on legal work and accounts – tax planning, that sort of thing. My boss used to say we should never get bogged down in the shitty stuff. Instead we just phoned up expensive contractors and got them to do it for us.'

'Sounds ideal.'

'Not for me – nor Fiona. She's a country girl. Her father used to farm down in Somerset in quite a big way. He's dead now. Farm passed to her brother. She's the youngest of four – brother and three sisters. Although she decided on a career in the Smoke, she's always secretly resented the fact that the farm went to John.'

'Families, eh?'

'Anyway, to cut a long story short, we'd had Ben and Nat—'

'You got kids?'

'Nine and eleven.'

'Congratulations. Lucky you.'

'You don't have any?'

'No, not yet.'

'Still plenty of time.'

'Yeah.'

'Well we both decided that London wasn't the place to bring up children and started looking at our options. We thought about buying somewhere but neither of us were happy with that idea.'

'Why not?'

'We didn't want to burn our boats. What would we do if we found we'd made a mistake? We decided to sell our house and invest in shares. After all, we both had experience of money markets.'

'You'll have had a bumpy ride recently, though.'

'Sore point. Although things'll pick up eventually. The silver lining is we love what we're doing and where we are. The kids adore the fresh air. The farm's surpassed our expectations – even if the government hasn't.'

He glanced at me and rolled his hang-dog eyes towards the ceiling.

'The government? What have they got to do with it?'

Col shook his head.

'Oh it's just we had such hopes. Another long story. Basically Fiona and I became fairly active in the Islington Labour party in the run up to the 1997 election. We were disillusioned with the sleazy Conservatives. It was also to do with guilt and a feeling that all the money we were earning was somehow a bad thing – morally.'

'It's funny you should say that. Now this might not sound very convincing coming from a man who's just sold out for a couple of mil.'

Colin whistled and then said, 'Well done you.'

'Thanks. But the thing is, what I've gained in money, I've lost in emotional terms. I've lost far more, emotionally, than two mil could ever buy, in fact. I lived with an angel, only I was too wrapped up in my business to let her know how special she was.'

'I'm sorry.'

'It was my fault. No one else to blame.'

'They're taking a long time with our ploughmans. Sorry about this.'

'No problem. I'm enjoying talking.'

'I'll get us another couple of pints in a minute and chivvy them up.'

'Anyway, Jill and me's a long story too. The upshot is that after six months of drinking myself into oblivion, I'm beginning to think I'd be better off getting out of London. Starting a new life. Maybe even—'

I broke off. Saying I hoped I'd get Jill back would have been going too far. Tempting fate. It also wouldn't have felt quite as right as a day or two earlier, what with Kim.

'It's about living a simpler life, isn't it?' I said instead.

'That's what we thought. And it's working well. We feel we've taken a stand and are upholding the values we fought for in Islington. We're very angry with Tony. Still, as a historian, I should have known better. It's like Cromwell and his lot after the Civil War.'

'That's a bit over the top, isn't it? I mean Tone's a big fish today but he's not that important in the grand scheme of things, surely?'

'No, you're right. But it's the same principle of betrayal. I found a passage in Winstanley when I was re-reading *The Law of Freedom* which summed it up—'

He looked towards the ceiling like he was studying the overhead fan and started spouting at me. I was amazed – though no one else seemed to think it unusual.

'—"Well, let it appear now that thou hast fought and acted for thy country's freedom. But if, when thou hast power to settle freedom in thy country, thou takest the possession of the earth into thy own particular hands, and makest thy brother work for thee as the kings did, thou has fought and acted for thyself, not for thy country; and here thy inside hypocrisy is discovered."'

Yeah, I was amazed alright. It was like sitting with a street preacher. Was that a tear I saw glinting in his eye?

'I'm impressed.'

He fixed me with his stare. He was serious. 'Substitute "kings" with "Conservatives" and Tony's sham is plain for all to see.'

'No, no I've got you, Col. Having said that, politics isn't exactly my bag. Though I think Gordon's doing wonders for micro-brewers. But that's another issue. Basically I think you and I have reached similar conclusions, only by different roads. Besides I was never very good at the philosophical background to the Civil War. I was better at battles. I can see Cromwell was a decent general.'

'He'd have been nothing without Fairfax.'

I shrugged. 'Ah well,' I said, 'it was a long time ago – when we did the history course, I mean.'

My second reference to time passing seemed to bring him back to the here and now. He frowned his dark bushy Willie Whitelaw eyebrows and nodded at my empty glass.

'I'll get you another,' he said. 'And find out where our ploughmans have got to.'

*

I watched Colin as he went up to the bar. He'd put on a little weight since I'd last seen him, though not nearly as much as one might have expected. He certainly didn't look like a City boy would've done at his age. And apart from the bald patch on the top of his head, his hair was still thick and dark, hardly a whisper of grey.

At the bar he grumbled good naturedly about our lunches to a couple of blokes he knew while the girl serving finished pulling someone else's pint. She'd obviously picked up on the fact he was going on about the ploughmans and became increasingly flustered. When she eventually turned to him she was evidently relieved to hear the mock angriness in his voice when he said, 'Wake up Katie!'

She began to explain something about Tara and a crisis in the kitchen. (Over two bread and cheeses? But then again, the place *was* heaving.)

As they bantered the toss, my mind began reviewing what we'd been talking about. Winstanley, for a start. I could barely dredge up a single fact about him. There was one word that did suggest itself, though, and that was 'communist' – which would explain my general ignorance of the man. Whilst I've never had much interest in politics, I've always been sure about two things, even in my teens. Firstly that socialism's a good thing, in so far as it means you give everybody a fair crack of the whip. And secondly that the only runner in the economics stakes is capitalism.

Which was, I suppose, why I was a bit freaked when Col started spieling Winstanley at me. A sort of knee-jerk reaction – although it took my brain a while to catch up.

I began wondering what this Fiona was like. I wondered too about the Islington Labour party and Tony's cronies. In any event, it was clear there was something bizarrely mixed-up about Col – just like in the old days. I was perplexed by the glint of fanaticism in his eye as he declaimed Winstanley but also pleased he hadn't changed. I mean how could you square taking a council smallholding – in all probability depriving a deserving family who'd grown up in the village – and your wedge of what, half a mil, in the bank? I ask you. How was that scenario helping freedom in they bleedin' country?

The more I go through life, I thought to myself that afternoon in the Parker, the more I'm convinced we change very little fundamentally as we get older. I mean, take me and my mistakes over Jill. The truth is I was a prat with women when I was at uni, just as I was a prat with them now. I hope to God I'll learn – you've got to, haven't you, otherwise you'd top yourself – but I have this sneaking suspicion that I won't.

Sitting there in the Parker I recalled Col and how incongruous he was when he came out on the piss with me and the other misfits. There *we'd* be in our leather jackets and stupid hairstyles – ranging from shaved to punk revival to New Romantic to dreadlocks – and there he'd be with his army-officer crop, tweed jacket and baggy cords. The amazing thing was he got on. He was fun to be with. Full of paradoxes though he was.

My thoughts were interrupted by his return with our beers.

'There you go,' he said. 'And the ploughmans'll be out pronto. Cheers.'

*

'This place is on the market.'

We were about finished with our ploughmans which had been well worth the wait. Tara, the chef, was that good, she made the likes of Gordon and Jamie look like amateurs. She works for me nowadays. Her salad was a delicate mix of rocket leaves, radicchio, fresh finely chopped chives and basil, baby sorrel and Swiss chard leaves, finished off with just a hint of grated fennel. Her home-made beetroot pickle had to be tasted to be believed. The cheese, Witney Blue, wasn't one I'd heard of before but turned out to be a very passable Dolcelatte substitute. The tannins in the Growler complemented the food, especially the pickle, wonderful.

'Yeah, well funnily enough I read about it in one of the trade papers. That's why I'm here.'

'Thinking of buying?' Colin suddenly had a big grin on his face. 'That's fantastic.'

'Wo! Wo! Col, slow down. Sorry to disappoint but I was just toying with the idea. You know, fantasising. What if?'

'But is running a little pub in the country something you're considering? Generally?'

'It's one option. I've tried quite a number on for size over the last six months, believe me. Virtual zoos, biodynamic vegetable production, organic micro-brewing—' I paused. '—Eco-friendly garden gnome manufacturing.'

'I don't believe you.'

'I jest, Col – about the last one.'

'There's another pub for sale in the village, though, that might interest you. Got some good barns too – for the micro-brewery.'

'It's just a day-dream really, Col—'

'No harm in taking a look.'

'It'd be a bit of a busman's holiday to be quite honest. Most of the time I think I'd be better off trying something completely—'

'Come on, sup up. What've you got to lose?'

'You got shares in the place?'

'No. But it used to be my local and it's been shut for the last year. It's been a fair saga, I can tell you. I do have another property on my books – derelict, all but. You could do that up as your house.'

'*Steady*!' I said.

But he wasn't to be deterred. He looked at his watch.

'You're in luck. I can spare you another hour.'

*

The Castle was on the outskirts of the village, a quarter of a mile or so on from the post office and newsagent. It was a low

171

building that looked to me as if it was two or possibly three stone cottages knocked together. There was nothing to suggest it was a pub apart from the Osney Brewery tile with its colourful narrowboat logo beside the front door. There was no sign or nameplate – even the statement about the landlord being licensed to sell alcohol had been painted over (badly, as it goes, because you could still see it beneath the white).

And, of course, the Osney tile gave nothing away. The brewery closed down years ago but people who own a house that used to be one of its pubs seem to like keeping the tile.

'So what's going on?' I asked Col as I tried to peak through one of the grimy bay windows.

'No need for that. We can get in.'

He produced a key and tried to unlock the door, only the mechanism was stiff.

'Go on, you bugger!' he said through gritted teeth before it finally gave.

I began to repeat my question but he interrupted me.

'Let's get inside first.'

He shut the door and switched on a light. We were in a narrow flagstoned passage with doors off leading to the bars and a serving hatch at the far end for off sales. The place obviously hadn't been touched for decades because passages like this with their hatches were lost when pubs went open plan from the sixties onwards.

'I like,' I said. 'Though seeing this only makes me want to ask more questions. Why the clandestine stuff for a start? And how come you've got a key? Are you the agent?'

'No but when the specialist pub lot had it they roped me in to show people round – they were based in Bedford and needed a local man. They forgot to ask for their key when it was transferred to an ordinary agency.'

'What, so it's being sold as domestic?'

'Yep, it's under offer as such. And there's planning permission for three houses in the garden.'

'So it's on the market at what, two, two-and-a-half times pub value?'

'Thereabouts. The place used to be run by a lovely old chap who died five years ago. He'd been here since the fifties. Anyway his nephew inherited, said he was going to make a go of it but in reality ran the business down. He then put the pub up for sale saying it was bankrupting him, dissuaded anyone who was interested with his tales of ruinous returns, before applying for planning permission. Not surprisingly he got it.'

'It's an old dodge but works every time.'

'Well, shall we have a look at the first bar?'

'Lead on.'

We went through the left door which had a brass plate on it saying Public Bar. The one opposite, I noticed, had signs saying Tap and Through to Lounge.

Col switched on the lights which were a pair of funny-looking wooden wall brackets that had what once must have been red shades with hunting scene panels. The material on the shades had wasted away to virtually nothing and the panels were faded, looking like pieces of ancient vellum covered with indecipherable symbols. The brackets appeared odd I soon realised because they were half-eaten by woodworms. These creatures had also feasted well on the ancient beam over the inglenook fireplace.

I noticed there was about a foot of soot in the grate mixed in with twigs and straw which the crows must have poked down.

There were the remnants of spiders' webs hanging from the ceiling in great black ropes by which anyone with Tarzan-like inclinations could have swung themselves across the room. The spiders no doubt made their excuses and left ages ago. Who could blame them? There was little light coming through the filthy windows and the room stank of something rotten.

The bar was on my right at the top end. It was stone built with a slab of oak above. Behind it was a beautiful Victorian pub sideboard. It again was oak and although let go – it couldn't have been polished for yonks and was badly dried out – seemed free of worms and could be brought back. It had racks supported by twisted columns, panelled cupboards and a mirror that was of sufficient quality to still be in good nick. It was patterned round the edge with flowers in lovely delicate colours and had paintings of different kinds of nesting birds in the corners: blue tits, wrens, goldfinches and robins.

'I'm surprised the nephew didn't get shot of this sharpish.'

'I know. I dread seeing it gone every time I come in. There used to be some superb prints on the walls. A few of them were supposed to be pretty valuable. A Victorian horse painter used to be a regular here in the 1880s and sometimes paid his bills with a watercolour. They went months ago.'

'Criminal.'

I tapped one of the flagstones with my foot to reassure myself it was real.

'I can see the place's appeal. It would be Jill and me's local if we lived here, without a shadow of a doubt.'

'People in the village are devastated. Everyone loved this pub and would like to see it saved. There's a campaign and some quite large pledges have been made – but as time passes it becomes ever harder to keep cheerful.'

'Which is where someone like me comes in.'

'Tempted?'

'It's a nice place, I'll give you that. But even I've got to be careful with my money. My dad gave me a lecture about that, you know, only the other day, bless his heart.'

'But if you could add value—'

'You'd have your work cut out to—'

'Well not necessarily. You could build one house – the garden's pretty big and one house wouldn't intrude – build some hotel accommodation instead of homes nearer the pub and convert the barn into a micro-brewery. There's the campaign money too. How about that?'

'If I bought I'd like to own it outright and leave it as is.'

'Just as you like.'

'But I'd have to see some figures.'

He beamed at me. I thought he was getting carried away. I tried to calm him down.

'I mean, just for interests sake. Maybe I could advise your campaigners.'

Still, truth be told, I was beginning to get a tiny-weenie bit tempted. I could imagine it being the very thing to tempt Jill with too.

'Let's go and see the Tap and the Lounge and this barn then.'

I smiled at him then raised my finger.

'No false hopes, mind.'

He nodded as if he got the message.

'Absolutely not.'

He looked at his watch.

'Right, we'll have a quick deco at everything else here, then there'll be just enough time for me to show you the mill.'

*

It was the mill, I suspect, that decided me. Even though it was a good two weeks before I actually *took* the decision to buy.

Col parked his Land Rover at the top of the mill lane. We were about half a mile outside the village.

'I was going to drive us down,' he said. He was unfastening his seatbelt then reaching into the pocket of his tweed jacket. 'But on a day like this, it would be madness not to walk it. By the way, you haven't got to be anywhere this afternoon?'

It seemed late to be asking but I let it go.

'As long as I'm back in London before dawn tomorrow.'

'Good.'

He produced a mobile.

'Change of plan,' he said as he tapped in a number. He proceeded to cancel his next appointment and phone his wife to say we'd be round at four-thirty for some home-made cake.

It took us twenty minutes to walk the lane. There was Tarmac for only a hundred yards then the surface was gravel with decent-sized pot holes, getting deeper, the further we went.

Col talked me through the wild flowers as we walked. Most of them I knew, although I let him do the guide bit. He obviously thought I was irredeemably urban. The banks were thick, and I mean *thick*, with violets. It was unbelievable. There were primroses too, in *abundance*, and wood anemones in a copse, plus dog's mercury, celandines, lords and ladies, to mention but a few.

At one point we surprised a fox sunbathing on the tin roof of an ancient hut. He moved like a jaguar.

There were a pair of buzzards, a heron fishing the stream and loads of yellowhammers – more than I'd ever seen in my life.

Eventually we rounded a bend and there was the mill. Bang slap in the middle of nowhere.

The building itself was a treat. It was a shell basically. 'Do what you like with it,' Col said, 'as long as you keep the outside the same.' It was a beautiful box waiting to be filled with goodies. It was a project fit for me – and for Jill, of course. She'd love it, I was convinced of that.

It was Victorian, just our period, but done in a timeless vernacular. The stone was Cotswold, oddly. I say oddly because it was further away from the Cotswolds than the village. But then, Col explained, you wouldn't have expected anything else, given the estate-owner who built it.

'This place was on the route of the Victorian Squire's daily walk, so he would have wanted it to look fitting. Having said that, it always makes me think of Hardy's Dorset and *Tess of the D'Urbervilles*. You know, where Angel and Tess spend their honeymoon – if I remember rightly.'

'I've read him, but not that one.'

Before showing me inside he took me to have a look at the pond and wheel. You could see the bottom of the former quite clearly. It was about six inches below the surface of the water. It was like staring into a barrel of slip clay – something I'd seen at a pottery Jill and I visited ages ago. It was silted up but as Col said, it would dredge.

The wheel was magnificent. Its paddles only just beginning to break up after nearly half a century's neglect. A good local carpenter and it would be as good as new.

Inside was pretty much only one room, the kitchen. There were more but they looked derelict. The old boy who died in the mill a couple of months before had retreated to the kitchen in his seventies – twenty years ago. There was a bedroom he used upstairs but people used to reckon there were many days when he didn't bother to go up to it. The other rooms were simply let go – totally unheated – and the furniture had been gradually sold off to pay his living expenses.

'I used to visit him regularly,' said Col. 'Lovely old chap. Full of stories about how things once were. He used to have a straw rope factory here before the war. That's what that big pole barn was.'

I wanted to quiz Col about the factory but he was in full flight.

'It was amazing seeing him: tie, tweed jacket, grey flannels – all filthy. The room stank of tea, though, mostly, which was rather nice. Reminded me of my grandfather's. It smelt like that because the tin kettle was always brewing on the range. A sweet, herbal, stand-your-spoon-up-in-it kind of smell.'

Of course, I knew exactly what he meant. It was the same smell as in Grandad's house. I liked the idea of that smell. It seemed like an almost universal memory when Col told me it. Part of the strange process too that was sealing the bargain.

And afterwards?

We walked back up the lane. Had cake at Col's. Met Fiona and the boys. Saw the smallholding. Then Col gave me a lift to the Parker where I collected the Boxter.

What can one say?

It was a red-letter day. A day that changed my life.

Part Three

Beside the Beast

It is a warm August evening and Sarah sits beside the kiln in the pottery yard. She has been working for Sinéad for four months.

She started shortly before Easter and, although not religious in a churchy sort of way, couldn't help thinking the symbolism was appropriate. It was, she felt sure, a rebirth.

Not that the move to Aldermaston was easy – which birth is? As she expected, her parents were dead against her going. But because their response was inevitable she did the groundwork well. She contacted Edinburgh and asked if the university would keep her place open if she became a potter for a while rather than doing her foundation year. The admissions officer said that was fine so long as she met the deadline for her final decision. So, when her father made the point that by working for Sinéad she would be throwing away her academic career she was able to set him straight.

At college, she first persuaded Glen to give her the chance of working with him rather than the hapless Brian, then – much to her relief, it has to be said – showed an aptitude for the craft (or art – call it what you will) that genuinely impressed Glen and confirmed her calling.

When her father phoned Glen he was sympathetic but also an enthusiastic and implacable supporter of her.

It was her mother's reaction that Sarah found most difficult to bear. Her father was angry but at least he didn't give up on her. He was always ready to argue. Always trying to persuade her to change her mind, whether by coaxing, bullying or being shamelessly manipulative. She threw up less often after confrontations with her father.

Not that encounters with her mother always felt like

confrontations. Mostly it was her mother's cold hostility that upset her. It was as if Sarah had done something scandalous that brought shame upon the family.

Pen was at a loss to understand her daughter's point of view. Doing the foundation year had been bad enough but at least Sarah was at home and Pen had been sure she could talk her daughter round in time.

Pen had also felt that Sarah being at home made everything less public. She found herself telling friends that Sarah was studying art because she wanted to do something more constructive during her gap year than mere travelling. Pen could make a virtue of her daughter's perverseness. She put a shine on reality that blinded everyone, including herself, to the facts and what they revealed about Sarah.

Sarah wanting to be a potter was bad enough, but the thought of her moving away from home really unsettled Pen. It made it seem that she herself had failed and that everyone would know this. She was suddenly powerless. She had lost control of her daughter. Her simple hopes of shopping expeditions together in Edinburgh evaporated. To say one's daughter is at Edinburgh is romantic. To say that she is a potter in a village near Reading that was famous for ban-the-bomb marches is not.

Pen expressed her feelings indirectly. She did not go so far as to leave the room when Sarah entered – only once or twice – but might as well have done. She spoke to her daughter but it was clear that there was one kind of speech before she came in and another the instant she appeared. Sarah could see the concern at her mother's altered behaviour on the faces of her father and Min. The effect was even more marked when friends were visiting.

It was strange that someone who wanted to keep Sarah's intentions well under the carpet was doing much to raise people's suspicions. But then Pen felt that what was happening was obvious and so she needed to express her disapproval publicly. People would then know that it was none of her doing.

Yet it takes a while for friends to realise for certain that there is something the matter. They are quick to rationalise what they see into something less serious than it appears. It is not comfortable knowing that other families are in trouble, particularly if the family in question is a by-word for stability and sortedness. Even Peter and Min were able to think their way round admitting the severity of Pen's reactions.

The only person for whom Pen's attitude was as poignant as a dagger was Sarah.

She took the blame upon herself. She knew she was a disappointment. Not that she was going to change the way she was. She couldn't do that even if she wanted to. And this self-knowledge only made everything worse. What she could do was try and carry her mother through these situations by being attentive and helpful. She tried to make amends with all the energy she could find. And sometimes she succeeded for a time. Her mother would smile. Once or twice she gave her daughter a supportive hug.

But the cost to Sarah's well-being was high. Whenever she detected her mother's hostility her breathing became broken, irregular. Her oesophagus tightened when she started to eat and she sicked up the food as soon as she could. Throwing up was by now second nature but it still seemed to repay her with a healing rush of endorphins and adrenalin. It was when she returned from being sick that she was able to find the most energy for placating her mother.

This vicious cycle of cause and effect was Sarah's curse. Yet it was her way. Her reactions were not confined to her mother, as we have seen. While at one time Sarah could never have imagined that Pen would ever cause her to throw up – indeed she had been her unwitting healer – she had long responded by being sick when faced with other stressful situations. At school it became the means by which she advanced herself. She would always take the blame for any lack of knowledge or flaw in her thinking or expression. It was up to her to do better and she was determined to do so. Chucking up fuelled her, and in a curious way it gave her the strength to better herself.

It also stained her teeth, made her throat burn, kept her awake at night, obsessed her, made her thin. But in turn the pain of these things and Sarah's embarrassment at them were helped by throwing up, and, when she could, by smoking cigarettes and drinking beer or wine.

But for now the rewards outweighed the penalties – though there were occasions, increasing in frequency in an insidious but inexorable manner, when this was not so.

Sarah sits beside the kiln in a beam of hazy light from a hurricane lamp hanging from a rafter. When she said she was happy to keep an eye on the kiln, Sinéad lit the lamp for her, saying that she might want to read something.

Sarah got some magazines from the office for appearances' sake but is not looking at them. Instead she looks up at the stars that are just beginning to appear in the darkening sky. Or else she studies the cover of the hardbacked exercise book – black with a red spine – which she bought earlier in the week.

She wonders whether she should write about her father's visit. She has got out of the habit of writing and is in conflict with herself about whether she should start again.

She stopped writing after she decided to become a potter. Working with Glen and reading the books Sinéad recommended took up nearly all of her time. These things and the sheer excitement of what she was doing. She worked long into the night at the college. Travel and finding the wherewithal to pay for it also ate up her time. Occasionally her father gave her a lift home if he had a council meeting. But mostly she had to get a taxi. She paid for this out of her savings and the money she earnt by doing two hours serving in the college canteen each lunchtime. She enjoyed the work. She had no need of a lunch break herself – all she required was a slice of cucumber or a lettuce leaf from the salad bowl – and felt that by working with food she might be doing something to conquer her fear of it.

Her father seemed quietly impressed by her initiative in the face of his refusal to act as a regular taxi service. Her mother was embarrassed. But by the time Pen decided that she would pay for the taxis herself it was too late. Sarah bluntly refused the offer.

Sarah reaches tentatively towards the sealed up opening of the main firebox. She can feel little radiated heat and touches a firebrick, prepared to pull her hand away quickly. It is warm only. She is astonished that hardly any heat escapes from the kiln. The temperature inside is over 1000°C. She remembers the sweat pouring off her and the other potters as they fed the fires throughout the day. In the end they could hardly get close enough to put in the logs.

She again looks at the diary. She left the previous one in her room when she moved to Aldermaston. She didn't hide it in a cupboard but left it on her desk under a couple of Ian McEwan novels but still perfectly visible. At the time she arranged the books she imagined one of her parents being unable to resist the temptation of having a read. In a way she was willing one of them to do so.

But, so far, nothing has happened about the diary. At least, her parents haven't said anything about it and she thinks that she would have known if her father had read it and was keeping quiet when they met the other day. He would have given away something.

She imagines opening the diary and beginning to write. She tries to detect signs of wanting to sick up the cereal bar she ate about a quarter of an hour ago. She'd not intended to eat but was exhausted after the gruelling day and weakened.

She remembers how anxious she was when she first started writing a diary – for the second time, that is. Her apprehension now, though, has nothing to do with the fear of describing her parents' behaviour. She feels justified in doing that, no longer feels a traitor. She believes she got to know her parents through the writing and to know herself and how she should deal with them. She thinks that self-preservation is important. How could she exist fully as a person without standing up for herself? And she tells herself in moments of objective candour that she is not at war with her mother and father, that the period of misalignment will one day pass and they will be able to coexist. Then her diary writing will be seen for what it is, an act of love. You do not expend energy and precious life trying to understand those you do not love.

No, her suspicion of writing a diary now comes from a fear of regression. Despite her preoccupation with food and her relationship with it, she has generally become a far less introspective person over the past year. She is practical, pragmatic, looking outwards, getting on with things, a doer.

At the back of her mind lies a fear of going back to the uncertain Sarah, the person who was at a loss. That person does not accord with her new-found confidence. And yet she also knows that she is at the same time still lacking in confidence. She is both strong and weak. Assertive and self-effacing. She is a paradox.

She decides she has a long way to go before she will be able to say she has achieved even a measure of self-knowledge.

She tells herself that she is both strong enough to progress through writing and weak enough to benefit from it.

She opens the book, takes a pencil from one of the many pockets of her dungarees and starts to write.

Sarah's New Diary

22/viii/96

Dad took me out to lunch a week ago.

He phoned a couple of nights before, full of the joys of spring. He and Mum went to a Greek Island for three weeks. Makes a change from Normandy and Daddy's annual grouse slaughter with Mum's cousins near Braemar.

Why didn't he take us to a Greek Island?

Anyhow, he and Mum obviously did a lot of heart-to-heart, wallet-to-wallet while they were out there.

The former activity concerned us lot, of course. When Mum told me they were going to Greece, she said that Dad was taking her there to cheer her up after a terrible year. I felt like saying, well don't look at me, but didn't. Thinking about it, I should have said, don't look at *us*. OK, none of us are doing what she expected but then whose kids are?

At least we keep her entertained.

And Alex is cool. I can understand his horticultural experiments in the council greenhouses were an embarrassment, as was his dismissal, but he's picked himself up. To those of us who've had faith in him his appointment as a gardener at the so-called *Eden* Project is no surprise. I think he'll go far. So what if he smokes dope. Everybody does and he loves Cornwall. I'm going to stay with him next month.

Can't Mum see he's not stupid? He knows he was dumb growing the plants but he's learnt his lesson. A few weeks of What's life all about and gigantic spliffs but then he picked himself up and got a new job. He wants to be a gardener not a neurosurgeon – so?

It'll do him a power of good not to be working for Daddy.

Meanwhile, Min has followed in my footsteps to public school and caught the acting bug. *Who's Afraid of Virginia Woolf* next term, playing Martha. Mum said couldn't she play Honey when Min told her the plot. Mum thought Honey sounded *much* nicer. Poor Mum, she didn't know which was worse, a dope-smoking gardener, an anorexic potter or a daughter who likes pretending she's a foul-mouthed bitch in front of six hundred people. *Pretending?* She's type-cast.

Before Greece, Mum asked me to talk to Min. I was supposed to say she should get her exams first then be an actress. Mum showed not the slightest awareness of irony until I said I *was* the obvious role-model for Min. Then she was just miffy.

I don't understand Mum. Things turning out unexpectedly was always a feature of our family life. There's nothing new – except that the unexpected is happening far away. Which, I suppose, if I'm honest, is the key to how she feels: none of us are there for things like family meals anymore. These were the times when Mum could restore order. Of course, it never was like that for us – we were only behaving in a superficially civilised manner and I was throwing up – but I think mealtimes made her feel as if it was. Now all she's got are hospital flowers, Dad in his study, and she's lonely. I imagine she broods and feels frustrated that she can't do anything. But then showing her displeasure in such an infuriating way doesn't help. Why can't she accept us for who we are? At least we know what we want to do.

I mustn't go on about her.

I wanted to write about Dad's visit. I'll do so after a cigarette. I've got hours to go before I can leave the kiln.

Dad didn't fancy the village pub. Instead he took me to an upmarket foodie place near Hungerford. He said Uncle Vern recommended it when he stayed last week. You could have knocked me down with a feather. I can't remember when Vern actually *stayed* at home. My first thought was, Gran must be ill but Dad said she's fine – 'fighting fit' was the phrase he used. Dad wouldn't elaborate on why Uncle Vern stayed, although later it turned out that it was connected with the wallet-to-wallet part of Mum and Dad's holiday (yawn).

Before Dad arrived I decided I'd try and persuade him to give the local a go. I wanted him to see the village. I thought maybe I'd be able to get him to look round the pottery after a couple of drinks, then go over to Helen's and see my room. But Dad's mind was made up. Vern didn't think much of the pub, apparently, said it was too noisy.

Uncle Vern's preferred choice was a beautiful Georgian coaching inn, built out of what looked like Bath stone, which inside was a weird mixture of old flagstones, big fireplaces, dark wooden bars, and minimalist chic.

We moved from the Pickwickian main bar, where we chose our expensive food, to a bleak conservatory which was all stainless steel furniture, huge thick white tablecloths, and overhead spots strung from a cat's cradle of tramlines. On each table was a tall stainless steel flute with a priceless-looking orchid in it. The type of thing I imagine Alex grows.

The food, though, included options that looked big but amounted to virtually nothing. And, best of all, there was Dickens's on handpump. Dad didn't approve of me asking for a pint but didn't say anything – to start with that is.

When I began at Sinéad's I kept hoping Tom Dickens would turn up but he never did. When I asked her about him, she said his partner had left the V&A for the National Trust. Sad.

So what's this in aid of, Dad?

He was tucking into grouse and veg – if it's after the Glorious Twelfth it must be grouse – and I was psyching myself up for Caesar Salad without oil but with the anchovies, eggs and cheese (just for show). Dad had already put away an exotic variation on the prawn cocktail while I chased an olive round a dish.

My leading question was a diversionary tactic, I suppose, looking back, and I thought I knew the answer already.

You ought to eat more than that. Have some bread.

I shook my head.

He was staring at my hands.

You can wear dungarees (suitably smart ones) and a baggy sweatshirt in a fancy restaurant on a warm day, but not gloves.

I attracted his attention with a lip and eye smile. A necessary and dangerous attempt to make him look away. Once you've established eye contact you can't keep your mouth shut for long without looking mad. And he's a dentist. He's also my father and no matter what I've done I'm still the apple of his eye, but even so. He must suspect, I thought, but now I'm not so sure. He gave nothing away, although that's no guarantee of anything.

Do I think he knows really? Do I wish he suspected?

Don't know. Don't know.

He must suspect, I thought, and then became invisible – to myself and therefore to him. I didn't shrink to nothing. I didn't hide. It's difficult to explain. It's eyes mostly and gluttonous, conspiratorial glances at his plate – and mine which I attack with the gusto of someone half-starved. I attack with knife and fork but rarely does the food get near my mouth.

No bread, thanks. I don't eat much during the day. Especially today – Helen's having a dinner party. Roast beef.

I don't know why I bother.

I'm not being ungrateful – honest, Dad. It's such a lovely place and this is superb. Besides—

I paused and patted his hand. I don't ever remember doing this before. My hand was under the table when he realised what had happened.

He seemed pleased.

I really appreciate you coming to see me. Perhaps you could have a look round the pottery when you take me back.

No, I'll probably have to shoot off.

Dad.

We'll see.

I knew he wouldn't come in.

I still don't fully understand why you're here, though.

I was all ready to justify my decision to work for Sinéad. I didn't want a row but was prepared for a controlled firm exchange of views. With a touch of indignation – I couldn't be expected to finish my meal after being upset, could I? What he actually said surprised me.

He put down his knife and fork and looked into my eyes. His stare was gentle, although there was apprehension there too.

You think we're against you, don't you?

I don't know what I think, to be honest. Apart from being sure that I'm doing what I want to do. But it wouldn't be surprising if I did feel you were against me.

Yes, I accept that. Mum took it very badly. But *I've* tried to fight your corner, both when you've been there and when you haven't.

Most of the time.

I smiled at him and he smiled back.

I appreciate that, Dad.

It's not easy, you know, being a parent.

It's no picnic being a child, particularly when you're grown up.

I do understand. But, you know, Mum and I had certain expectations. Then suddenly we're in the thick of it and everything's being turned upside down.

Especially shopping in Edinburgh. She could try Truro.

That's unfair, Dad snapped. But then he chuckled faintly. His eyes were smiling.

Is she any better after the holiday?

Yes, and no.

I was a little disappointed. He'd got my hopes up. I imagined she had rethought things.

She's still very angry. I've never known her like this – although it's under the surface. She keeps it well hidden much of the time.

When we were on Skiathos I thought she'd come round. We talked through what had happened – we talked about lots of things – and there were flashes of frustration but on the whole I believed she was beginning to reach some sort of acceptance. It was only when we got home that I realised she still has a long way to go.

I wish she understood. It's so painful knowing she disapproves.

Dad looked somewhat flustered. He poured himself some more red wine from the half bottle he'd ordered.

The thing is, I know from what I saw in Greece that she will come round. What I want to say is that I'll make sure that her depression – or whatever it is – won't destroy either her love of you lot nor what you're doing. That's why I'm here, to reassure you of that.

I felt like crying but couldn't let myself. I am grateful to you for that, I said, but I don't understand why you won't look round the pottery.

I'm sorry. I suppose it's partly that *I* need to go one step at a time, partly that I do genuinely have to get back. I've got a patient to see at the end of the day.

He looked at his glass.

Perhaps you'd better have that – unless you'd like another beer.

The wine's fine.

You know, it's a funny thing but it still seems odd women drinking pints of beer. I remember when I picked you up from a party ages ago, and there you were, a great mug in your hand.

It was cider then, now it's bitter.

I never liked bitter. What do you like about it?

We talked about beer and pubs for a while and it was great to be just chatting. I felt that he was taking a genuine interest in me and how I lived my life. He wasn't judgemental and I think I persuaded him that people of my generation aren't all out of control (apart from poor Karl). He seemed to appreciate that pottery involved hard work – mega hard work – and complete single-mindedness.

I felt happier talking to him than I had for ages. I forgot about the hurt caused by Mum. It was just me and my Dad doing something I always used to imagine we'd do when I was young and thinking about being grown up but which I lost hope of ever doing. It was like a coming of age.

I enjoyed myself so much I forgot not to eat. When I realised what had happened I excused myself and went to the loo.

When I came back Dad had ordered coffees and a glass of pudding wine for me. Even though I hadn't eaten in a restaurant with my parents for a couple of years, he remembered I liked espresso and Vin Santo.

Cheers, he said, taking back the glass with the last few drops of the red in it and raising it.

There is one other thing that came up when we were in Greece which I wanted to talk to you about.

I was puzzled by his tone. He was smiling still but he sounded suddenly more detached, businesslike.

It's nothing to worry about. Just a formality really but there might be something for you to sign.

Sign? I don't—

Don't look so worried. You remember we told you ages ago about some money Grandad left you all.

I nodded. A trust fund for each of us.

That's right. You inherit the capital when you're twenty-five. In the meantime I'm entitled to the annual income and can borrow up to half the capital for certain specified uses – so long as you're in agreement.

He looked at me expectantly, as if he hoped I'd put him out of his misery.

I didn't recall the bit about him borrowing the money but I had no objections.

Of course I agree. I couldn't not – I don't know anything about business.

Your Uncle Vern's a trustee and he's all for it.

Are you going to ask Alex too?

Yes, but I'm not quite sure how to go about it.

I could ask for you, if you're not getting on.

Dad was even more serious all of a sudden.

I'd be grateful if you didn't mention the trust to him for the time being – until I judge it's safe to do so, in fact.

He's not stupid, Dad.

No, although he does have a drug problem. What Vern and I are trying to do is think of a way of getting his approval for the scheme without alerting him to his right to sell his interest.

I'm not sure I understand Dad. Can I sell my interest?

Yes, but please for God's sake don't think of doing it. You see, if you wanted to raise money now you could sell your interest to some loan shark for a third of its value. Suppose your part of the trust's worth a hundred thousand—

That much?

Well, that for argument's sake, but the funds are quite substantial. I can't remember the exact figures. But anyway, *if* the sum involved was a hundred grand you could sell today for thirty. The trouble is, you'd then have to sign over your right to the full hundred thousand in order to get that thirty. Then, when you turned twenty-five the loan shark would collect the hundred.

That's appalling. Is that legal?

Perfectly, so long as you sign an agreement to that effect.

Jesus!

Now do you see why I don't want Alex to know the full details?

He's not completely out of control, Dad. But OK, there's a slight chance that he could lose it and do something stupid.

He's far from stupid. But like you say, it's better to be safe than sorry. And, by the sound of it, he is getting himself sorted out. But I couldn't forgive myself if he blew all this money. If he can make a go of this Eden thing, the trust money'll be the making of him. It's his future.

It's OK Dad, you've persuaded me. Anyway, what are you going to use the money for?

Oh it's this business with the second surgery. I had to go to appeal to get approval for change of use. I still haven't got it but it's now merely a formality, only the business has cost so much that I don't have enough left to develop the building.

I don't understand planning.

Nor do I – and I'm part of the process.

Dad laughed. He attracted the attention of a waiter.

Before the waiter returned, he put his hand on mine.

Thanks, Sarah – for agreeing to the loan and for keeping things to yourself. You don't know how much this building scheme's cost me. Not only in terms of money but emotionally. Your mother's been very supportive. And it's a very good scheme. I'll pay you a dividend, of course, when it's sold.

You don't have to do that. The trust's a small fortune in any case.

We'll argue about that when the time comes.

I suppose you'd say we agreed to differ. I felt very grown up saying things like, The trust's a small fortune in any case.

Although I didn't understand much, I'd taken on board a fair bit and it just seemed like an adult thing to do to be talking about so much money. It crossed my mind on the way home that one day I was going to be rich, and yet that day seemed a long way off.

I was right about Dad not coming into the pottery when we got back to the village. I could have laid bets on it and won a fortune. But as he drove us home, he and I chatted together in the amazing warm way we did at the restaurant. I loved him so much when he left.

I still love him. But I don't entirely trust him and wish I did. It's not that he hasn't stood up for me over the past year – he has – but not all the time. It's as if he has to struggle with himself and sometimes wins, other times loses. He wants to believe in me. He has all the right instincts. But often he can't let himself stand up for me and he sides with Mum. In many ways he's such an emotional man. He's stern and a pillar of the community a lot of the time but he's a romantic at heart.

Romantics can be cruel sometimes. They promise more than they can ever hope to deliver. I can't decided which hurts most, his see-sawing or Mum's relentless resentment.

Still, I enjoyed seeing Dad. And I'm grateful he came. I'm still basking in the warmth of those easy chats about nothing in particular. Those moments are hope for the future.

Larkin got it about right, though!

Dear Sarah

Dear Sarah,

It's getting to the time when I start writing about us and I'm afraid because I don't understand what happened. I thought it was all going to be so good.

Having read through my first paragraph I realise that it won't make much sense to you. The thing is I got very depressed after Griff died and you ran off.

Of course I was also depressed about the way I'd behaved towards you. That was the worst of it.

Then in the background there was all that stuff about getting ripped off over the pubs and Jill leaving me.

In order to try and make sense of what seemed like a catalogue of disasters and whatever the opposite of the Midas touch is, I went to a doctor and asked for help. He suggested I should try writing about some of my experiences. I'm not sure he bargained for the reams of stuff I've ended up doing – and I'm not finished yet.

I remembered you once said that you'd written a diary like a story when you were at school and how it helped you. That wasn't in my mind when I started writing out the last three years but it may well have been at the back of it.

The writing <u>does</u> help. I've come to realise my limits. As a human being that is. I haven't exactly come to terms with who I am yet, nor tried to think if there are ways of bettering myself in the long run. But facing up to some of my failures has been salutary.

It's like staring at yourself in the shaving mirror after a night on the piss. The light seems so bright and undeniably you're looking at the face of a middle-aged man who inside his head still thinks he's in his twenties. There's nowhere to hide.

You said that when you looked in the mirror you saw someone else – someone big and fat when in reality you're as thin as a rake. Well I had the opposite problem – I'd look in the mirror mostly and think, Sorted! When in fact I was a sodding mess.

Anyway, I'm about to start writing about us, as I say. I'm a little scared, if I'm honest.

When you ran off into the snow I thought I could read you like a book. In a way that feeling still persists. I somehow don't want to give it up. But I fear that writing is going to make me see everything differently.

I wish you were here to help me. To help us understand each other.

I did think of you when you ran into the wood and I drove off, contrary to what you might think. I realised that if you died it wouldn't be instant. There would come a time when the cold anaesthetised you but before that there would be suffering. You were frightened too.

I didn't want you to die…

I know that if you were ever to read this, you wouldn't believe me. And you'd be right not to.

What I'm saying is I'd dearly love to turn back the clock. But I know I can't and that the only way I can make sense of things is by writing them out.

I'm thinking about you, Sarah.

I'm sorry.

With love,

Tom

Tom's writing therapy

24/05/03 – A Saturday

The day I first met Sarah was a beautiful one. It was a day of exquisite early summer weather, of Morris dancing, folk music, Col's pageant... But above all it was *the* day the Castle reopened its doors and Castle Bitter was launched.

I'd given up on gimmicky beer names and theme pubs. This time round, everything was simple. WYSIWYG. What you see is what you get. Only one bitter to start with – the Best. A cunning variation on the traditional recipe of Pale and Crystal malts and Goldings aroma hops. It had that lovely refreshing hint of hazelnut you get in Hedgecutter, with honey overtones and a full caramel finish. It was nectar! Dreamt up by that Einstein of brewing, Rajiv, and hand-made under his supervision by yours truly and Andy. Principally by Andy, who Rajiv said was a genius-in-the-making.

I awoke to glorious sunshine filtering in through the Arts and Crafts embroidered hangings Jill gave me as a moving in present. She was due later for the festivities. She'd intended the hangings for my dressing-room or somewhere else where you wouldn't need proper curtains. But I decided they'd go in my bedroom straight away. Since moving to the country I was a new man. Back to a sensible drinking pattern, up early every morning, and happy to welcome in the daylight, rain or shine.

The room was still to be decorated. Its walls were unpainted plaster, the floorboards were bare and there was no furniture, save for my bed from the flat. The mill was coming along but I'd concentrated the lion's share of my energy and resources on the pub and microbrewery.

I was out of the house about half an hour after I first opened my eyes. A quick cup of tea, a polish round my face with the electric razor and I was away. I'd usually have toast and Frosties but I couldn't have kept anything down that morning and decided I could fuel up at Andy's or Fiona's if I changed my mind.

The sun was well up but a lot of the time I couldn't see it because of the trees in the hedgerows along the lane and the copse which ran along much of one side. When I'd first seen the mill that day with Colin I hadn't realised how tucked away it would seem when the trees were full out. In places the lane was like a tunnel.

The sun wasn't hot exactly – yet. You could tell it would be and it *was* warm but it was comfortable too and there was a bit of a breeze. The feeling that morning reminded me of a print Col and Fiona had in their hall. It was of a painting by John Nash of this big cornfield with dark trees all round it. You can't see the sun but it's slicing through a break in the trees and bisecting the corn diagonally into areas of shadow and bright yellow light. There's also a strange hole in the middle of the corn, the shape of a giant matchbox cut out of the crop, which I've never understood. But the point is the feel of that picture is so like that Saturday morning. There's a stillness and a sense of the night lingering but there's also this amazing expectation. There's an exhilarating, almost terrifying energy rushing into that painting as there was that morning. It was wonderful. I felt like jigging up the lane.

The spring wild flowers had come and gone but there were new ones now. Cow parsley was thick and frothy. I say cow parsley but I suspect Col would tell me it was some other sort of plant from the same family. There was bedstraw which Fiona taught me about and loads of wild clary. There was also, thinking about it, this slender frondy thing in little groups. Just green spikes with tiny yellow flowers dotted along them. I meant to look it up but I forgot all about it until now.

I wonder also if it came up this year. If it did, I didn't notice. The depression was at its worst in the spring.

Anyway, in no time at all I was at the road then bounding into the yard at the Castle. It was a picture. We'd found this bloke, friend of Andy's, who could do anything. It was just him and his brother – and another brother when they needed an extra pair of hands. They re-roofed the place, pointed up the outside walls, did all the internal woodwork and plastering. But their masterpiece was the barn. They'd never so much as thought about a micro before but to Doug and Rod it was no problem. Doug worked out the layout even before I came up with a rough sketch. The rep from the firm up in Leeds where we bought the kit was astounded.

There was one of Doug's cousins to do the electrics, Doug's oldest brother to do the plumbing and their dad, Percy, took on the beer garden.

Percy was a mine of information and had drunk at the Castle all his life. He had photos of the place from the fifties onwards. Basically it hadn't altered since then, although it'd got shabbier. What I wanted for the pub was simply to do it up as if we were still living in 1955 and I was a new young landlord with a bit of dosh but only enough to make the place spruce. I'd had it with theme pubs. I wanted something absolutely natural.

A journalist from one of the trade papers said the Castle was a masterstroke – taking theming in a new direction. The first of a chain of Tom Dickens artisan pubs but he couldn't have misunderstood more if he tried.

That May morning the pub looked outstanding. There was something virginal about it. The sandblasting and repointing had given the stone a new lease of life, taking off the careworn layers to reveal the stunning colours beneath. And what colours: as the guy who gave the talk about stone in the village hall would have put it, there was burnt toffee from the north of the county and ochre from the Cotswolds with the sun locked into it. There was grey from Wiltshire – because without grey the other colours aren't half so bright – and a curious lemon yellow from Berkshire. As I say, the original builders bought in stone from wherever they could, used anything that came to hand.

The pub looked new-built – still does, although it will never again be quite as it was that morning. As Col said that night, it's like the set of a film of a Thomas Hardy novel. I'm prouder of the Castle than anything I've ever done.

After marvelling at the pub's beauty I set off towards the barn, pausing only to look at the garden, which was divided into two areas. The first, by far the larger, was separated from the yard by a low wall and had a border along two sides planted with English cottage flowers. The foxgloves were already well away. We'd chosen oak benches – expensive, very, but last a lifetime. Steps led up to the smaller area which was Andy's vegetable patch. I don't know where he found time to get that sorted but he did. I suspect Percy gave him a hand. If I was in the business of max stocking density, that bit would be benches as well. But that's not my game. I want to give the punters space to relax in, not pack them in like sardines.

The barn was an oddity. Far older than the other buildings at this end of the village, it was, according to the local librarian, all that remained of Clayfield Castle's home farm. The mill that previously stood on the site of my home was part of the same estate.

The front of the barn had thick stone walls and these massive oak doors. The place was still being used by a farmer as a grain store when I was thinking of buying. There were some signs in one of the outhouses which must have been put up at harvest time telling pub patrons to park properly so the tractors and trailers could get through.

I had Mo check out whether the guy had some long-term right to use the barn. He said yes, so I was expecting a spot of trouble. It could have jeopardised the whole deal. In the event the farmer was as good as gold. He said he'd only been using the place because it was there – his father had used it before him. I told him that legally that was the problem. Even so, he agreed to dismantle the bins, adding, as a bit of a joke, that I could have the barn back in exchange for a barrel of beer every Christmas. I said, "Your on" and we shook on it. He's been a regular since we opened.

I bought the bins off him too. They were perfect for converting into the hygienic fermenting rooms.

It was the back bit of the barn that puzzled me, though. It was built of old-looking brick and timber. And according to Doug the brick *was* old. Tudor was the verdict when he took a sample to the county museum. The look of the back was like an Essex barn and it made me feel at home every time I walked from the mill to the pub by what's known as the Castle Footpath. I would have taken this route that morning only there were cows in one of the fields and I wasn't enough of a country person again to feel easy with them.

Doug had cut a little door into one of the massive oak ones for easy access when we didn't need to use the fork-lift. I opened this door then went inside and slid the main ones open. We wouldn't be using the fork-lift but I wanted to let in natural light. Doug had taken the big doors off their hinges and mounted them on runners to gain space.

The smell of the fermenting beer was fantastic. I checked both vessels and the yeast was like a gigantic layer of custard on a rich trifle, just as it should be. We got the particular strain we liked from the National Collection of Yeast Cultures in Norwich. Both batches were on target for racking up next morning. We'd got four batches done for that weekend, two for the coming week and the stuff in the vessels for the following weekend. This was overkill and much would probably go to waste – we had a mild and a premium on as guests too, both local – but what with the opening I was leaving nothing to chance.

I remember patting the fork-lift before I checked that Andy'd sterilised the mash tun and pipes properly (he had). Andy'd nicknamed the fork-lift, Bronco, and he used to whoop like a buck-jumper when he rode the thing. It was like it had a personality.

My big sadnesses about that weekend were that neither Rajiv nor Claudette could be with us. He'd had to get back to his own pub for the bank holiday. It'd been lovely to see him and to have the pleasure of benefiting from his knowledge and boundless inventiveness. She was in New York seeing her sister.

He and Andy had hit it off. There was just one awkward moment. Within minutes of their meeting Andy said, "I thought your lot didn't like alcohol." I wondered if this was evidence of the rural racism the papers were full of. I was surprised because of Andy's right-on green credentials. I don't think he meant any offence, looking back. He just expressed himself clumsily.

Rajiv certainly took no offence. No doubt he'd heard everything in the East End. He simply explained how his ancestors were in fact part of the Muslim minority but that his grandfather had been an anglophile civil servant who converted to Christianity and decided he was better suited to life in the 'Old Country' after Partition. He added, as he always did, that the family joke was that the grandfather turned to Christ only out of an unquenchable thirst for IPA.

After that, Rajiv and Andy got on like a house on fire.

Once I'd inspected the pipes, I took in some last deep breaths of the malty atmosphere, closed the doors and set off for Fiona's. I didn't disturb Andy. He'd probably got someone with him, and besides, he'd need all his excess stamina for the weekend.

*

I saw Fiona and the boys from a long way off. As usual the family was up with the lark.

I'd taken to calling on Fiona and the boys quite a lot recently. I valued chatting to her – she was mostly very easy to talk to. I valued the company and the family atmosphere.

Fiona was outside the hen houses in the old orchard when I first spotted her then she disappeared inside to collect the eggs. Ben and Nat were tipping food from a sack into a tin trough for either Ben's pony or the dozen or so sheep. I didn't know which until the pony's eager arrival and the sheep's utter indifference – they just kept grazing – settled the matter.

There was no sign of Col, which was normal because he tended to go into Burford to do his land agency office work early in the morning. Or, if it was a smallholding day he'd be up in the woods round Griff and Sarah's looking after the pigs. He'd usually have a cup of tea at the Folly afterwards.

At that stage, though, I hadn't met Griff and Sarah. They were simply names.

And on this occasion I knew it wasn't either land agency or

pigs that was behind his absence, but the finishing touches to his pageant and the marquee for the lectures.

As I approached, the boys stopped pouring out the feed and patted the pony. Then they took a corner each of the bag and shook down the contents before carefully folding the top over so it was closed neat and tidy. Lovely kids.

I imagined they'd carry the sack into the barn but instead Nat suddenly pointed at his brother and barked out an order, whereupon Ben put his hands behind his back as if they were tied and started marching across the orchard. Nat picked up a stick, rested it on his shoulder like it was a musket and went left-right-left-right along behind. By this time Ben was obediently lining himself up against the fence. Nat came to a halt about ten yards away with a lot of stomping of feet. He raised the gun to his shoulder, aimed and fired. Ben forgot he was tied up, clutched his chest, shrieked, fell to the ground and lay still. Not content with this result Nat aimed again and fired, over and over. Each time he went 'Bang!' Ben screamed and writhed about.

I was mildly shocked by what I saw. I knew Col wouldn't approve and besides it wasn't the sort of game the boys usually played. True Nat had the instincts of a little tearaway but his energy was generally channelled by Col and Fiona into useful things. Or else he just hared about. You could imagine him as a long-distance runner one day. He'd go round and round the orchard, scaring the sheep maybe, but with no malice in him. Bags of staying power.

When I was still a little way off I called out 'Morning boys' to stop the shooting.

Nat didn't bat an eyelid but continued firing.

It was only Fiona coming out of the hen house, setting down the egg basket, and shouting, 'Boys, for goodness sake, that's enough!' that made them stop. They both looked at her angrily but then saw me and came running. I opened the gate and went into the orchard.

'Hi, Uncle Tom,' said Nat.

'Hi, —cle T—m,' said Ben looking at the ground.

Nat held the stick up with both hands like a Red Indian brave

205

giving thanks to the spirits of his ancestors for a stunning victory.

'It's a musket,' he said.

'I thought it probably was,' I said, trying to give him a *Tell me something I don't know* look.

'I'll take that,' said Fiona and whisked the stick away.

For a second Nat glared at me as if he was blaming me for throwing him off guard.

He made a lunge for his mum who hid the stick behind her back.

'No, Nat. You know your father doesn't like that sort of thing.'

'He and the vicar do it.'

Fiona smiled at me.

'That's different. Now get on with you. Put that bag in the barn, please. Go on.'

'I'd say you got off lightly,' I told her as the boys ran towards the trough.

'Give me strength.'

'He's got a point.'

'Hi Tom.'

She kissed me on both cheeks.

'Isn't it a beautiful morning!' she said.

'It's gorgeous.'

We looked at the orchard, at the sheep, the pony and the boys.

Nat was playing the strong man with the bag of feed.

'Let Ben help, Nat,' said Fiona. 'Little sod,' she muttered and smiled fondly. 'He'll be twice as bad tonight.'

'Are you letting them go to the pageant?'

'Try and stop them. But honestly, mixed messages or what?'

'Col says it's going well, though.'

'Oh, it'll go down a storm.'

I wasn't sure if she was being sarcastic.

'Now, will you come in for some tea?'

'Love a cup.'

She called towards the barn, 'Come on boys, breakfast. Oh, and bring the egg basket, will you!'

*

206

'All set?'

Me and Fiona were sitting on the little terrace by the back door. The boys were inside making toast and listening to the farming programme on the radio. This, another country programme called Open Country (which I've quite got into myself, lately) and the Archers were their favourites. Col didn't allow television, although there were computers in the house. Since being back inside the boys had forgotten the mock execution and things were returning to normal.

I blew on my mug of tea.

'Yeah, thanks. I've got a good feeling about today.'

'So you should, you've worked bloody hard.'

'I try.'

'You know, it's funny, but I wasn't sure about you or the pub project when I first met you.'

'Uppetty incomer?'

'Hm, that's why it's funny, I suppose. We've only just arrived ourselves.'

'Everything's relative.'

'Though I am from a farming background.'

I was about to say I was a country boy myself but didn't. It didn't take much to make Fiona defensive about her country credentials and this wasn't the first time her response had jarred me. I was learning to live with this aspect of her. Also, it struck me that her sensitivity maybe had something to do with her not being entirely comfortable here herself. Despite the farming pedigree, I thought she'd become far more of an urban person than either me or Col.

'I guess I must've seemed a bit of an oddball.'

'Not oddball, exactly. To be quite honest I think the root cause was all the money!'

She laughed, lowered her head and looked up at me with her blue eyes. The skin around them was wrinkled but not with age. Her look had the appeal of a child because her eyes were so clear, her skin so fresh. It was like she was saying, *Am I being naughty?*

'I did wonder what you thought of me. It must've been odd

someone from Col's past suddenly turning up like that – let alone moving in virtually next door.'

'I was apprehensive about that. Though not for Colin's sake – more for mine. It's difficult to explain but the way you affected me had something to do with someone with lots of money coming here, and, yes, a person who we were connected with. I don't know, I thought it would make me feel frustrated with where we are, what we've got.'

I was thrown by what she was saying, although it was consistent with the other signs of dissatisfaction I'd detected.

'I thought you were worried I'd lead Col astray.'

She shook her head and smiled. 'No.'

'But you've got other rich friends – this Griff bloke's loaded by all accounts.'

'Seems to be. But he's different. He's an artist, a bohemian, quite different from the London crowd. Whereas you – well I thought you were going to bring Fagin's to Clayfield.'

'Not a chance.'

'Well I know that now. And, like I say, it's a brilliant place and you deserve every success with it.'

'Thanks – I reckon it's got a chance. Andy's mustard.'

'Yes.'

She drank the rest of her coffee. She was frowning and quite obviously nerving herself up to say something. It was almost impossible for her to conceal her emotions.

'As far as leading Col astray—'

She put her mug down, leant forward and took my hands in hers. Her hands were strong but the backs were so smooth-looking. Like the rest of her skin, soft and golden – the hands of a girl in the full bloom of youth not a middle-aged woman with two kids.

'You know, Tom, I wouldn't mind if you led him astray.'

I laughed and she let go of my hands. I confess I hadn't been expecting her to say that. For a moment, I'd— Well, it's better left unsaid.

'Serious?'

'I am pretty, yes. Don't get me wrong, he's still the centre of my world but he's started to go off at a tangent and I feel I'm being left behind – not a long way, but—'

'Winstanley, I presume.'

'I'll be glad when the pageant's over to be honest. I'm looking forward to getting him back.'

'It's going to be quite a day, what with one thing and another.'

'A good day for you – I know loads of people who can't wait for the Castle to open its doors – Griff and Sarah included. They're coming down from the hills.'

'I'd love to see their folly.'

'Ask them – they'd love to show you round. You'll like them. Sarah can be hard work sometimes, but they're both great.'

'I'll look forward to meeting them. And you never know, if Col's in the mood for celebrating later, I might even get him rat-arsed!'

24/05/03 – A Saturday, continued

I intended to write that Saturday all in one go like when I wrote out Hay-on-Wye and the Priory. I made sandwiches specially, so I wouldn't keep driving myself and getting near-psychotic. But once I'd reached the point where I was about to start on the day proper I balked. I thought that if I got a drink of water I'd be able to get going again but even after a glass of the finest water in Oxfordshire, I still couldn't think straight. There was too much going on in my head. Too many mixed up emotions for me to separate out without a breather.

Talking of the water from the bore-hole, I've begun thinking about the practicalities of a scheme I first thought of eighteen months ago. It was something for the medium to long term in any case but it got completely lost when Andy was banged up and Griff died and Sarah— Well, just, And Sarah.

Anyway I started thinking again about piping the water from the mill to the micro the day before yesterday. I won't do it for a while even so but I can't help feeling my renewed interest's a good sign. I emailed Mart about it and he said he was impressed.

The other thing I thought about was writing to Jill. It was something I'd considered doing the day after the opening of the Castle – before, well before I'd even heard of writing therapy (I mentioned this to Mart too and he was fascinated). That Sunday night after the opening I let myself go and had a bit to drink. I sat out in the beer garden under the stars with my punters listening to the folk singers and the diddley-dee. I thought about what I'd write to Jill the following day. I could see the letter so clearly. Only the next day I had a hangover and writing didn't seem such a good idea. I was too self-conscious, I suppose.

But the day before yesterday, the memory of the letter came

back to me and I decided to write it out. It was more an exorcism than anything else.

Though I've re-read it again and again since, and I sometimes think I'll send it to her now, the idea seems preposterous somehow and I doubt I ever shall.

Letters attached to Tom's account of Saturday 24th May, 2003.

Dear Jill,

It was lovely to see you when you came to the opening of the Castle. You looked fantastically well. Life in the Lodge and new job – well, not so new now – is obviously suiting you. Everyone loved meeting you. They're a good crowd, aren't they? It was funny about the girl from the pottery.

Anyhow, I'm writing this at home after sitting out in the garden at the Castle under the stars and thinking about things. I had a few pints of Best, needless. I've lit a fire in the big old grate in the "living-room" because it's cold now. I take your point about flagstones but if I go for underfloor heating the problem's solved, isn't it? Let me know if I'm being too glib.

I probably am. I've got bags of ideas but I need people who know what they're talking about to keep me on the ground.

You know, last winter – the winter before last, actually – time's a blur. Well, that winter I went off the rails. I didn't tell you, though you might have guessed, because I didn't want to worry you. I missed you. I blamed myself for mucking everything up. Sorry.

I got out of my depression, or whatever, by going back to some of the pubs we stayed in years ago. Retracing our steps was a mixed blessing. Kill or cure. A high-risk strategy. Memories came flooding back.
I remembered things like how we used to fantasise about

doing up a pub together. We'd combine our two sets of talents. I wasn't much of a designer, really, but you could shape my concepts into something workable, and I know the business through and through. We'd have made a good team, I can't help thinking.

I suppose what I've done to the Castle is a tribute to those times as well as the pubs I went to with Mum and Dad. As you say I've gone for an understated look (me, understated, you've got admit that's a first!) and yes, you're right, I really have tried for one that's properly sympathetic to the village. It's brilliant that people seem to like it. But best of all was what you said about it. You paid me the biggest compliment anyone's ever paid me.

My only regret is that what I've done's come two years too late.

I should have sold the chain and downshifted ages before now. I'm dead sure that if I had we'd still be together. After all there was no malice when we parted. It was just that because I'd spent so much time on the business, I'd let the relationship dwindle – not to nothing, but to something that was basically only a friendship, not a partnership. And that was my fault.

Now I have what we wanted but I don't have you.

I also don't really know how to say this, but it's not simply that I don't have you that makes me so sad, it's the fact that we're not a family. I'd love you to have had my kids. I never communicated that properly, did I? But I felt it, I really did.

That we didn't quarrel when we split up is a two-edged sword. On the one hand it's nice that we can still be friends. On the other, it makes us not being a family seem so unnecessary, somehow. It cuts me to the heart.

The life I've got now is simple and, I think I can go so far as to say, wholesome. I'd love you to share it.

With <u>all</u> my love, my dearest Jill,

<u>Tom</u> XX

Dear Tom,

Thank you for your letter.

I was very touched by the things you said about our happy memories and how you wanted us to be a family.

I would have liked to have had our children too. Clayfield is the perfect place for them.

But, you see, you shouldn't beat yourself up about us.

It wasn't only you who was burying yourself in your work. No, burying's the wrong word.

It's that when you're young you've got so much energy and so many ideas and you need to get on and do something with them.

It wasn't as if we didn't create something lovely together either. We did and that was so valuable. I really do think you ought to sell the flat, by the way. You having found the mill and pub makes now a good time.

I think perhaps I'm not expressing myself sensitively. I was prone to that failing.

The bottom line, I suppose, is that we had a fantastic time

but it wasn't the right time for us as far as settling down together.

But, given that these facts have had such power to hurt, it's rather wonderful we can still be friends.

Accept that gift, Tom. It's not an inconsiderable one. I value it enormously.

Above all, don't blame yourself.

With all love,

Jill X

Dear Tom,

Thank you for your letter.

I was very touched by the things you said about our happy memories and how you wanted us to be a family.

I hate the thought of you going back to places we stayed at. I can imagine you were blaming yourself all the time. You mustn't do that. We split up because we'd both reached that stage. I think the fact that we're still such good friends only goes to prove it.

I do value your friendship, you know. In many ways it's the most valuable thing I possess. If it's all I ever have from you again it will be enough.

However, I do know what you mean about not talking about children. We did in a way but never quite, if that makes sense.

I can also understand how difficult it must have been for you to write what you did about having a family. You're very brave, Tom.

Do I think we could get back together and become a family? I don't know. My heart says yes, but my head puts obstacles in the way of going back – back not backwards, don't think that. My funny head. I'm sorry.

That's not a no. It's a maybe.

Please don't get your hopes up too much.

I'm going to see Jemima in the Cayman Islands tomorrow. Only for two weeks. I wish I wasn't going. But at least I'll have time to think things through.

I'll be in touch when I get back. I promise.

All love, Tom,

Jill X

24/05/03 – A Saturday, continued

It's been three days since I wrote the letter and two since I composed the replies. I'd intended to write about the opening of the pub and so forth but I got this idea into my head that I might put Jill out of my mind by pretending she'd turned me down.

It didn't entirely work. When I'd finished I read the letter and it didn't sound quite like her. It had that willingness to take the blame she has but there was something amiss. I tried writing it again but this time the feeling in me was similar to the first time I wrote something for Mart, like I was being taken over. I wrote a hopeful letter.

And, although neither sounded right when I read them through the first time, when I came back to them they did somehow seem real. Of course they can't both be real but I can't decide which aspect of Jill my original letter would connect with. What does she feel about me? I can never tell, even after three years. Perhaps she doesn't know herself. There doesn't appear to be anyone serious on the scene. I'm mystified. It's strange how writing opens up these possibilities. I think the therapy is supposed to guide you to the truth. That is, if a patient writes two different kinds of letter like I've done, they're supposed to know, deep down, what the right one is.

At least I wrote the cheerful one last and that could be a sign I suppose. But I don't want to get into mumbo-jumbo land.

Yesterday, I couldn't write anything. I went for one of my usual long walks along the Thames to Kelmscott. It's September now. The time when Sarah's and my love was still fresh and young. It was odd regretting Jill but always being reminded of Sarah by the particular type of light that comes this end of summer.

I'm writing this as a warm-up exercise. Just tipping out my thoughts. It's designed to get my writing mind going. A little like the free-indirect exercises. I'm going to get a glass of water and then see whether the gambit has worked.

*

It was gone midday when Jill arrived at the Castle so I had ample opportunity to go through everything with Andy and Tara and the two casuals, Jimbo and Emily.

I was pretty sure we'd need the extra staff but no matter how many times you do launches, a couple of hours before the off you always end up being convinced that no one'll turn up. That morning was especially bad. The confidence drained away. The trouble was the venture was such an unknown quantity. My uncertainty grew like compound interest paid every minute on the minute. For two pins I'd have cut and run.

I didn't let my feelings show, of course. Just convinced myself that Jimbo and Emily were going to think me a complete prat when they were clicking their heels all weekend.

My panic was made even worse by the enthusiasm of the kids – the four of them were utterly sold on the project and gave the impression they'd work till they dropped. They bloody nearly had to.

I was particularly impressed by Tara's attitude. She'd walked out on the Parker a fortnight previously over a dispute involving walnut oil. I told her we wouldn't be offering food for six months (the conversion of the outhouse into a state-of-the-art kitchen was the one thing yet to be done) but she still said she wanted to be in on the ground floor. I had my doubts, expecting a prima donna, but she got stuck into straight bar work like a Trojan.

I couldn't work out whether she and Andy were having a fling, though. If they were they weren't letting their emotions touch the surface. True professionals, both.

When Jill arrived we'd been open over an hour and it was three yards deep at the bar.

*

Jill looked radiant. She no longer wore highlights in her hair which you'd have thought would have made it duller. Not a bit of it. She was working outdoors for part of the week nowadays and exposure to the sun was bringing out the full range of natural colours. There were bits of blond, of course, especially near the front, but there was also quite a lot of coppery red which was a surprise. And the blond strands were totally different to the dyed ones. You could tell they weren't synthetic. The sun had given her a healthier-looking complexion too which somehow set off her eyes. The blue looked bluer and that lovely clarity her pupils and whites have, even after a night on the wine, was clearer still.

Then there was the change to her physique that the outdoor life was bringing about. She was still slight but there was substance now and she didn't look like she'd blow over in the wind.

I was dumbfounded. The very occasional, moderate attraction to Fiona I experienced which was stirred up a little that morning vanished.

Jill had told me on the phone that she was doing a couple of days a week assisting the estate manager of the National Trust property with a view to changing her career path. She also mentioned a hedge-laying course. But I'd expected nothing like this transformation.

I showed her as much of the pub as I could what with the crowds then gave her a tour of the micro before we set off for the mill *en route* for Col's pageant. We took the Castle Footpath at Jill's insistence. We'd done it when she first came to see me and she wasn't going to let a herd of cows put her off.

'So, what do you think?' I asked as I climbed over the style at the top of Andy's veg patch. She was ahead of me.

She stepped forward, threw her arms out like she was doing an Al Jolson impersonation and said, 'Its breath-taking. Sublime. As I told you last time, you've landed on your feet, Mr Dickens.'

'Yeah,' I said, literally landing on my feet. 'It's wonderful but I was wondering what you—' But then I could see she was winding me up.

We were standing pretty close now.

She looked at me as if she was asking herself whether I really didn't know what she felt about the pub, as if I was fishing for compliments. I remembered this kind of thing from before. I sometimes didn't understand why she couldn't just say what she thought – good or bad. I sort of knew this time that she would say something positive but it was like she thought my ego was big enough without her having to pump it up. But I needed reassurance. On the one hand, yes, I had a lot of faith in the project, wouldn't have undertaken it otherwise, but I was also shit scared. It may have been irrational but that was the way I felt.

As I stared back at her, I remember, I felt a little disappointed. She was so gorgeous and new – and was embarking on new things too – and yet there was still a lot of the old Jill underneath. It wasn't that her unwillingness to pay a compliment was a terminal fault but it was something that grated and that afternoon it brought me back down to earth.

We could only have been standing there like that for a couple of seconds but I remember distinctly the thoughts that shot through my mind. It was like the way she looked at me switched on a bank of emotions which went with a forgotten but familiar situation.

What came next, therefore, really floored me.

She smiled at me. She said, 'I think it's perfect. I think it's *brilliant*! It's the best thing you've ever done! It's light years away from the theme pubs. It draws on the aesthetic and ethos of the pubs you told me about which your parents took you to.'

'I don't know what to say.'

'Your pub chain was good but—'

'I needed to break into that market if I was going to make any serious dosh. I was thinking about the future, trying to free myself for something better – you know. I'm proud of my theme pubs but they weren't what was in my heart. A means to an end.'

'Ssssh! I know and that's what's so fantastic about here. And it's more than just being about pubs you used to know.'

She came even closer to me.

'You could have tried to impose Essex décor and it would've been disastrous. You've shown such sensitivity to the village *and* its heritage.'

She reached out to me like she was going to pat me on the head. Instead she smoothed my hair away from my forehead. Then she bent down and kissed my forehead and then my cheek. She pulled away a little and smiled at me intently.

'Well done. I'm so proud.'

I knew she didn't want me to kiss her back and I didn't. But a whole new bank of emotions were switched on and it was painful not to be able to take her in my arms. I could have cried.

Instead I took her hand briefly, just to start her along the footpath, and said, 'Come on, let's go and see the mill.

As we walked towards the field with the cows I was expecting something like the stampede scene from Ken Russell's *Women in Love* (a favourite film) but in the event they were up the far end.

I didn't say anything and neither did Jill.

It was only when we got to the mill that she said, 'Where did the cows get to?'

I glanced up at her. She was about to giggle.

'*You!*' I said.

*

Jill loved the mill. It was nine months since she was last there – the time it takes to carry a baby. On second thoughts, Mart, I'd better not go down that one. She was as impressed and complimentary about it as she'd been about the pub and micro. It was funny seeing the place through her eyes. To me, not much had happened since well before Christmas but Jill coming made me realise just how much had been accomplished.

It was when we were leaving the mill that Dad phoned. I pulled the mobile from my back pocket and flipped it open.

'Dad,' I said and I was immediately aware of Jill turning away from me and wandering round to the mill-pond. It was the sort of discretion she always used to show whenever he phoned when we were a couple.

'How are you, boy?'

'Alright. Jill's here.'

'How is she?'

'Fine form. She loves the pub.'

'Oh, good.'

I knew he couldn't make out what was going on between us.

'I would have liked to be there with you, you know.'

'Yeah, of course I do.'

'And I'll be up to see it all soon.'

'Of course, whenever you want. I know you don't like openings.'

I could hear him chuckling away to himself. He'd been able to get away with not coming to my launches the first couple of times but then I twigged. He'd never attended one of them. But he always rang and he always came to have a good look round a few weeks later.

'Gaynor was saying she fancied seeing where you lived only the other day.'

The name Gaynor had first been mentioned about a year ago. I didn't take much notice to begin with, maybe thought it was nice Dad had a new friend, if I thought anything. It was only last autumn that the penny dropped. They'd sort of teamed up together. You could have knocked me down with a feather. But when I got over the shock I was pleased for him.

I couldn't remember having met Gaynor, although Dad insisted I had. She was the widow of a crony of Dad's from the Chamber of Commerce, Leo Corfield. He had a jewellery business in Hatton Gardens but he made his big killing selling off his arboretum. He was passionate about trees and bought about twenty acres on the edge of Maldon to grow them on. Only he wasn't so sentimental about his saplings to refuse two mil for the privilege of seeing them flattened and a chic low-rise development loom up in their place.

When I met Gaynor I had a dim recollection of her and Leo sitting at our table at the Marney on one of the few occasions when people joined us.

'I'll tip you the wink when it's a bit calmer – might be a long wait, mind.'

'Get on with you – still, I'm pleased it's going well.'

'I was scared this morning, Dad.'

'You, scared? I don't believe it.'

'I was, honestly, but everything's looking good now.'

'I know it'll be a success. And Tom?'

'Yeah, Dad.'

'I'm proud of you, you know.'

I was choked.

'Thanks, Dad. I really appreciate the sentiment. And, seriously, no time's soon enough for you and Gaynor to come and see it.'

When we said our goodbyes, I had tears in my eyes. I wiped them away and went to find Jill.

'Sorry about that,' I said.

'No problem. How is he?'

I looked at my watch.

'Alright. I'll tell you on the way. We'd better hot-foot it to Col's pageant.'

*

The number of people in the Castle Field was astonishing. There must have been at least two hundred. There were familiar faces and I recognised fifteen or twenty who'd been at the pub for opening time. But what was really surprising was the number of visitors. It wasn't just that a mass of faces weren't familiar – that meant nothing, it was a big village – but that the field next door was jammed with cars.

The New Age throwbacks with their canine all-sorts were in evidence, of course – someone obviously hadn't told them that Grunge died a death in the mid-nineties. But these were the minority. The most striking thing about the gathering was how normal everyone looked. The kinds of people there became evident during questions after the talks by Col, the Oxford don and the vicar. Each person announced themselves before speaking. There were teachers – from all points of the compass, as far as I could see – members of various trade unions, some of whom described themselves as 'delegates', a *brother* from the UK Communist Party, a National Health Service manager from East London and a couple of Free Miners from the Forest of Dean. Then there were the visiting teams of Morris men who were prancing about beside the beer tent non-stop. Everyone seemed completely wrapped up in what was going on. Col had evidently tapped into a substratum of society that was alive and well but which I never knew existed.

Jill and I surveyed the scene from the rise at the end of the Castle Footpath before making for said beer tent where I'd caught sight of Fiona. I was a bit hacked off to be quite honest, to start with, by the fact that there *was* a beer tent. I felt Col had dissed me – until I twigged that the outfit running the thing was connected with this strange sect of Leveller fanatics. The micro was the Cornet Thompson Brewery and the ale was Burford Three, which some punters evidently thought well amusing.

Us lot – that is, me, Jill, Fiona, and Fi's friends – were a small band of bemused outsiders. Fascinated but also sceptical, on the edge and occasionally satirical. We were like the old lags at a school sports day.

When we joined Fiona, we found she was part of a gang of about a dozen or so who formed a distinct group half-in, half-out of the tent. From there you could get a decent butchers of the Morris men and the goings on inside the marquee, which had its sides rolled up.

A number of the people I recognised. There was Phil and Jean from the Parker who I'd got to know through having stayed there a few times while the pub and mill were getting going. My judgements about the Parker the first time I saw it were substantially right – it was chaotic. But I'd learnt a lot when I was on the premises. That kind of jumbliness was what went down well in the village. People were suspicious of anything slick. And while I'd taken this knowledge on board, I'd not sacrificed everything I learnt in the Smoke. Attention to detail, but behind the scenes was what I was aiming at at the Castle. I was fortunate that people like Andy and Tara were on the same wavelength.

There was Bill Prendergast, a gay solicitor, who was a howl or an utter pain, depending on his mood. Also present were Sally, a nurse, Graham, the property developer who'd done the tower for Griff and Sarah, and Steve, who had a beard, wore shorts, rain or shine, and loved his ale. The source of Steve's income was a mystery – to me, at least, and if anyone else knew, they weren't saying.

But centre stage was a man that had to be Griff. He wasn't especially tall – though taller than me, obviously – but was built like the side of a house. His head was shaved and his skin milky pale. I noticed how he tended to stand just inside the tent. He looked fit and strong, despite the weight he was carrying, but was evidently an indoor man. He too had a beard but whereas Steve's was neatly trimmed, Griff's was straggly and prematurely grey. When Fi said Griff and Sarah were coming down from the hills she hit the nail on the head. He was a mountain man. A Welsh hill-billy. His eyes were beady and jet black, small for his head like currants jammed in the face of a snowman. He was wearing a blue boiler-suit, open to his navel, exposing his carpet of a chest. He had gigantic work-boots on which looked steel-capped. In his left hand he clutched something blue and woolly which I couldn't make out to begin with but which turned out to be a bobble hat. A lot of the time he kneaded away at the hat, sometimes he wore it, at other times it was half-stuffed into the pocket of his boiler-suit. His right hand was clamped round a pint glass, with a cigarette – hand-rolled and smelling somewhat herbal, shall we say – jutting out from between his fingers like a thermometer in a hairy arse.

It was his voice, though, that was the most curious thing about him. It was high-pitched and scratchy. He could say *'course* as if he was gargling pea grit and make *right* sound, when he was agreeing with you, like a threat, spat out through clenched teeth. There was a fair larding of *boyos* and *bachs* which made him seem like he was doing stand-up.

Yet, for all his oddness, he was, from the word go, an obviously warm and lovely man. Clever too – you could tell that.

Even so, it wasn't Griff that I was introduced to first off, but this beautiful black girl standing by his side. And I knew I'd seen her before, the moment I clapped eyes on her. She was stunning.

*

Almost as soon as we reached the beer tent, Fiona was throwing her arms round me and kissing me with an enthusiasm that quite belied the fact that we'd already seen each other that morning.

'I hear congratulations are in order,' she said looking from me to Jill. 'Bill, Sally and Graham virtually set up camp outside the Castle last night. They've been raving about the place ever since they got here. Bill says Cornet Whatnot's gnat's piss compared with your brew.'

Right on cue Bill, who was several people away, raised his plastic pint glass and gave it the thumbs down then pointed in the direction of the Castle while giving the thumbs up and mouthing what looked like 'Yum, yum!' with a dirty great grin on his face.

Meantime Fiona was saying 'Lovely to see you again' to Jill without letting go of my hand. She only did let go reluctantly it seemed to me in order to give Jill a peck on the cheek.

I was suddenly aware of people near me repositioning themselves as if a sizable dog was threading its way between their legs. I looked down and there was Ben. He stared into my eyes for a millisecond before his gaze fell away and became fixed on his trainers, his hands clasped behind his back like he was still expecting to be shot by Nat. He twisted his body to and fro absent-mindedly, keeping his legs dead stiff.

I leant forward and said, 'Hi, Ben. Do you want Mum?'

He nodded without looking up.

I touched his shoulder and he obediently brought his hand round and placed it in mine.

'Fiona,' I said. 'Messenger!'

She bent down and asked him what he wanted.

Before he spoke, he gradually lifted his head and his whole

demeanour changed. He became an important person. 'Daddy says he needs you. It's very urgent.'

'What do mean, urgent? What's Daddy up to now?'

'Don't know. But he said it was *urgent*!'

Fiona glanced at me and raised her eyebrows. 'Goodness!' She stood up. 'Well, orders are orders. Sorry Tom.'

'Not a problem.'

'Let me introduce you to somebody.'

She turned towards Jill and I did the same but Jill was deep in converation with Graham.

'He's such a fast worker,' said Fiona. 'Second thoughts, what you both really need is a drink.'

'Fine, you get off, I'll fight my way to the bar – I'm used to it. Besides I can check out the competition.'

'You'll do no such thing. Honoured guest and all.'

She pushed forward towards Griff who was so obviously Griff and was on the line where the edge of the tent and the outside world met. He was the centre point of our group, the natural focus. I could tell everyone was aware of him, measuring themselves in relation to him.

Fiona whispered in the ear of a girl standing next to Griff. The girl looked round to get the position of Jill and myself.

'You'll have ale, obviously,' Fiona called back, 'but what about Jill?'

I tried to attract her attention but it was hopeless. 'Oh get her a dry white,' I shouted. 'I'll answer if it's wrong.'

The girl, who had long brown hair and pale skin, smiled at me, I think. Anyways, I didn't take her in somehow. She couldn't have been more than a teenager. She was just a gofer. I seem to remember wondering if she was Griff's daughter from an earlier relationship.

Fiona then made a grab for my hand and hauled me forward.

'Tom, this is—' and mentally I filled in the name, Sarah, 'Debbie.'

This stunning black girl turned towards me. Just as somebody's arms, Bill's it turned out, got Griff's neck in a playful lock and a bit of a struggle got going. But the scrap was simply background noise – a couple of clowns employing themselves in some theatrical business designed to show how aloof this goddess was. She didn't bat an eyelid.

'Tom Dickens,' I said, making as if to shake her hand.

She smiled at the gesture but took my hand anyway.

'I know,' she said. Her voice was slightly breathless – velvety not husky – and there was a hint of an American accent.'

'We've met before, haven't we? But I can't think where.'

'I'll give you a clue, shall I?'

I smiled and narrowed my eyes. I stifled the words, 'Yes, please,' although I didn't get the impression she was toying with me. She was enjoying being one up on me but gently – there was no mockery.

She leant down and whispered the word, 'Pottery.'

'Pottery, pottery,' I thought and must have looked absolutely blank.

She made a smiling scowl, summoning up her next clue. She leant towards me again, her dark eyes full of delight. 'A nuclear village,' she whispered. Then she reconsidered, shook her head and said, 'No, that's far too cryptic. Think, the village where they had the ban the bomb marches.'

I was bewildered but suddenly it came back to me.

'I was with Jill,' I said. 'Stone me – she's here – over there. You were—'

'The girl waiting for her friend.'

'Jesus! Well, I'm blowed. I thought at the time, she'll be a stunner. Sorry, not very pc.'

'I think I can just about cope. Compliment and all. Talking of which, I thought you were like, God! So cool. Not to mention the fact I was tanked to the gills with your beer.'

'It didn't show. I wish I'd known. I could've used you in an advert.'

'I'm not sure I'm Dickensian, exactly.'

'No, but we were trying to broaden the base then, get away from the *purely* Dickensian.'

'I remember – the cinema ads?'

'That's right.'

'Did they go?'

'Not really.'

'They were a bit naff.'

'Watch it. I scripted them myself. Hang on, weren't you hoping to be an actress?'

'Film director.'

'Did you make it?'

'Getting there – commercials up to now but I've started on my first feature.'

'Excellent! Any famous ads?'

She mentioned one that was doing the rounds – two penguins, a tiger and a tub of margarine. It had won an award, if memory serves.

It was then that the girl came back with the drinks.

I took mine and Debbie was about to say something to her but before she did Griff grabbed Debbie's arm, pulled her towards him and growled, 'Come 'ere *cariad!*'

By the time she extricated herself and we resumed our conversation the girl with the wine had gone to find Jill – I suppose. I don't think I gave her another thought.

Maybe I remember her flitting about, getting things for people, seeing they were alright. I'm not sure. It would be the sort of thing she would do.

Debbie and I chatted for a bit and she stunned me with her beauty and sophistication. As the beer added to the effects of the couple of pints I had earlier, I began fantasising about getting off with her. It was a day of beautiful women, that day. But as Debbie talked I decided *she* was out of my league. She was something else. I just basked in her beauty for as long as I was privileged to do so.

Eventually, we were joined by Jill and Graham and I met Griff. I got separated from Debbie and found myself squeezing Jill's shoulder and kissing her forehead, made romantic by the afterglow of Debbie. I recall wondering if Jill and I would make love before the day was out.

Then there was the banging of drums and people went quiet. There were the melancholy brass notes of what looked like an elongated bugle and there were men dressed as Civil War soldiers moving among us saying things like, 'Proceedings will commence in the marquee in five minutes. Come on ladies and gents, let's be having you.'

Col's talk and pageant were about to begin.

*

By the time people had taken their seats, the beer tent was nearly empty and we had a clear view of the proceedings in the marquee. Even so, as things got going we couldn't hang back for too long and we all ended up, if not exactly in the marquee, as good as.

And you could have heard a pin drop from the moment the Cornet, a Civil War cavalry trooper in full dress, stood up to kick the event off with a folksong.

I think the seriousness of the audience was what struck me most. Not even Griff could keep up his merry banter beyond a minute or so.

His last exchange was with Graham and Bill just before we set off across the beer tent. 'This'll be good, Graham,' Griff said, 'mark my words. Col tried it out on me after breakfast the other mornin' – 'first, you know, 'thought 'ee'd fipped but the more I thought about it, the more I reckoned 'ee'd got somethin'. Not that I'm going to spread my wedge, though.'

'Such a shame,' said Bill, camping himself up.

'Dirty fucker!' chortled Griff. Then he took a mighty slurp of beer and never uttered another word until the last round of applause.

The trooper had long straggly hair and was wearing a filthy knee-length suede coat – one that didn't have arms and was like an overgrown waistcoat. His trousers were woollen and if it hadn't been for the fact that they were full of holes, he'd have baked. His riding boots were equally dodgy. The look of him was impressive and I wondered where Col had got the gear. It certainly looked authentic – like the man had stepped out of that film, *Cromwell*, with Richard Harris in it.

The Cornet gave the impression of being both battle-worn and poverty-stricken but with defiance in spades.

He had a lovely voice. The words of his song, as well as Col's quotations from Winstanley, were printed on a sheet that Fiona handed out – it was about the collection of these that Nat was sent to find her. The first verse the Cornet sang was:

You noble Diggers all, stand up now, stand up now,
You noble Diggers all, stand up now,
The waste land to maintain, seeing Cavaliers by name
Your digging does disdain and persons all defame.

I expected people to join in but that obviously wasn't the done thing, let alone anyone actually standing up.

On the back of the sheet was an extract from a book called *The Levellers and the English Revolution* by H.N. Brailsford which filled in some biographical details about Winstanley's life and writings – not that much was known about the former, apart from his occupation of common land in Surrey and the fact he ended his days quite prosperous, ironically. The first sentence seemed to sum the man up:

'On Sunday, 1 April, 1649, a band of a dozen landless men with their families camped on St George's Hill, near Walton-on-Thames, and proceeded to dig and manure the common...a peaceful, albeit revolutionary act.'

The Civil War was a period of revolution and proto-socialism but the Levellers were too extreme even for the Puritans. Besides, by then Cromwell and his cronies were the establishment.

There was spirited clapping when the Cornet finished his song, after which Col began his speech. He started by thanking the Cornet and told us we'd be meeting him again later, then he introduced himself before launching straight into a chunk of Winstanley.

'"No man can be rich, but he must be rich either by his own labours, or by the labours of other men helping him. If a man have no help from his neighbour, he shall never gather an estate of hundreds and thousands a year. If other men help him to work, then are those riches his neighbours' as well as his; for they be the fruits of other men's labours as well as his own."'

Col was dressed in black trousers, cavalry boots and a white shirt. His waistcoat was draped over the back of his chair, which was on the right side of the dais next to where the vicar and the Oxford professor were sitting. Col's sword and cartridge belt were slung from the chair too and his helmet was underneath.

The first thing I noticed about Col was how clean and smart his clothes were. He was supposed to be a senior officer who'd been on the road and would have sustained the scars of battle, just like the Cornet, but Col wasn't prepared to slum it on his big day. Col was interested in looking cool.

'Before I hand over to Professor Lockley and the vicar, or should I say, Corporal Tomkins—'

There was a titter from some of us lot but the audience proper merely smiled benignly. It was like a church meeting.

'—I'd like to say a few things about Gerard Winstanley, whose words you have just heard. I shan't apologise for speaking personally about this great man, about his effect on me *personally*, that is, because I think he would have expected nothing less. He was a man of destiny who knew very well that he was speaking eternal truth not simply for his own time but for all time. His words echo down the centuries without loss of power, touching people anew, in fresh ways according to their circumstances, as surely as ever they did the Levellers and Diggers.'

Col's voice was calm but there were moments when he displayed the same fanaticism I'd seen that first afternoon at the Parker.

'First,' Col continued, 'a little background information about me. I suppose you could say that like a lot of people nowadays

I've been searching for *something*. I daresay I always will be but I hope that now I and my family have moved to the country the pain of emptiness will never be as acute as it was when we lived in London. Not that there's anything wrong with London, it was just the jobs we had, the way we lived our lives that was wrong—'

As Col explained about the soul-destroying effects of stockbroking and Knightsbridge land agency I watched Fiona for a couple of minutes, off and on, letting my gaze settle on her before my eyes flitted to the audience then to Col, and I checked out where, if anywhere, he was looking. I clocked Ben and Nat sitting with some friends beneath the dais on our side of the marquee.

I kind of expected there to be more eye contact between Fiona and Col but neither seemed able to look in the other's direction. While Col spoke of London Fiona was watching her children or smiling at her friends but never facing her husband. I noticed how she was standing a little back from Griff, Graham, Jill and Bill who she'd moved to the front of our group with when Col started speaking.

Fiona was standing with her hands behind her back, side onto me, and I saw that although she had finished her wine, she was still holding her glass – it was hanging down, its bowl facing the ground. Her grip was loose and I constantly expected her to drop it. She was also picking at a triangle of skin along the edge of her thumbnail with her index finger, which made the glass bob up and down irritably.

She wasn't happy. I guessed she would rather be back at the smallholding or just boozing away with us lot, or playing with the kids. Anything but listen to Col's obsession. Not that she didn't love him. I was quite sure she did. Alright, I'd toyed with the idea of a fling with her myself but that was only an aid to flirtation. A fantasy. If she'd made a play for me I'd have run a mile. It was the fact that she was firmly-rooted in her marriage that gave me the go ahead for the day dream.

'—Then I read Winstanley,' Col was saying now. 'A friend on Islington council suggested I try him. And I've never looked back. I was transported home to Eden, to my childhood in

Lincolnshire and visits to my uncle's farm. I knew I and my family had to get out, otherwise we'd drown in a sea of cross-currents, muddled thinking. A world where greed is good, where exploiting your fellow man, is good. I yearned for the simplicity of Winstanley's world where it was possible to be clear-sighted. Yes, to call a spade a spade.

'Of course, nothing is ever perfect, and change has not been instantaneous. For a start, there are deep contradictions in myself – I freely admit that. My wife points out that I'm happy on the one hand to read Winstanley, the father of communism, but on the other to work for the owners of landed estates—'

I glanced at Fiona. She still wasn't looking. The skin she was picking had begun to bleed.

'—My wife, Fiona, says that deep down I love the order on those estates, the way of life of the landowners. She's right too – and many of the landowners have become friends. I have to face up to the fact that there are divisions within myself. Things I may never be able to reconcile. But I think Winstanley would understand that. True, we know precious little about him, apart from his writings, but we do know that he wasn't able to practice all that he preached.

'His vision, I'm sure he knew, was an ideal not something that was achievable in his lifetime or in a dozen lifetimes – if ever. But the vision's inachievability does not devalue it. Life is always a trade off between pragmatism and the ideal. For me and my family, downshifting has not been about literally rediscovering Eden, or a new St George's Hill for that matter, because I have to do my land agency, my wife her accountancy, but we have struck a blow for the ideal and with luck we shall get closer to that ideal over time.

'We have re-established contact with the earth, the land, and have thus tapped into the fount of wisdom and decency. As tenant smallholders, we are trying to eschew the worst excesses of ownership and are striving to learn anew how to accord our fellow men the full respect they deserve.

'I shall leave you with these words from Gerard Winstanley, written some three-hundred and fifty years ago and which put the things I have tried to say so much better.

"'When men take to buying and selling the earth...saying *This is mine*...[they] restrain other fellow-creatures from seeking nourishment from their mother earth...So that he that had no land was to work for those, for small wages, that called the land theirs; and thereby some are lifted up into the chair of tyranny and others trod under the foot-stool of misery, as if the earth were made for a few; not for all men.'"

Col gripped the sides of the lectern and leant forward. He looked as if he was going to bow his head but he didn't and I fancied from the way he stared at his audience, his eyes seeming to twinkle with tears, even from where I was, that he wanted to watch every second of his triumph.

The audience didn't disappoint him. The applause was tumultuous. Though when I tore my gaze away from Col and looked at Fiona, it was obvious that her heart wasn't in her clapping even before she was forced to stop by a thump on the back from Griff and congratulatory kisses from Debbie and the girl who'd brought us drinks.

It wasn't until the very tail end of the ovation that Col did at last make a little bow before walking to his seat. As he crossed the dais I could tell his legs were shaking.

Col had a quick word with the Oxford professor who suddenly looked even more out of place than before, dressed as he was in blazer and grey trousers, and now flanked by two Roundhead soldiers. The professor shook Col's hand vigorously, stood up and then positively bounded up to the lectern.

While all this stage bonhomie was going on our group repositioned itself. Fiona said she needed to go and see the kids and headed out the back of the beer tent – though intriguingly, she didn't reappear beside Ben and Nat until the professor's speech was nearly over. Meanwhile Jill came and stood beside me, and Debbie moved to my other side, between me and Griff.

The professor filled in the background to the story of the Clayfield Levellers by telling us about the mutiny of several of

Cromwell's mounted regiments in Salisbury on May Day 1649. The soldiers weren't prepared to serve in Ireland until they got their back pay and also wanted Cromwell to honour the Agreement of the People of 1647, which asked for the scrapping of press gangs, the redrawing of Parliamentary boundaries in the interests of fairness and shorter Parliaments. The Agreement asserted that the People had sovereignty over King and Parliament and stated that 'All are equal before the law'.

The mutineers put the wind up wealthy Londoners so much that Cromwell marched west to sort them out. Meanwhile they'd set off north to try and rendezvous with Levellers from Buckinghamshire. But when they reached Abingdon they decided it would be wiser to change course for Gloucester. Cromwell made a surprise night attack while they were quartered in the pubs of Burford but in the event, only one person on each side was killed. After which three Levellers were executed by firing squad in the churchyard as a warning to others.

What scholars hadn't realised until the local vicar found some old documents in the church archives was that there was another showdown at Clayfield on the very same day.

Previous to this discovery, it was thought that all the Salisbury rebels got to Burford from Abingdon via a ford in the Thames because a bridge a couple of miles from Clayfield was already in the hands of Cromwell.

Now, it appears, a breakaway group of about one hundred spirited mutineers did in fact charge the bridge and get across. But Cromwell's men let them over only to start after them immediately they were on the other side. The rebels rode to Clayfield and occupied the castle which used to be in the field where we were standing – only a bit of its curtain wall remains, incorporated into an eighteenth-century farmhouse. Even in 1649, the castle wasn't much more than a shell after being raised earlier in the Civil War and not surprisingly the mutineers surrendered within hours. The next day, May 15th, two of the Levellers were shot in front of the castle walls.

It was a great story. I'd picked up a little of it from Col, of course, but he'd played most of the details close to his chest. At the end of the talk I'd already decided that next year's beer tent would be selling Cornet Smirk, handmade by the Castle Brewery.

But this was only one thought that preoccupied me during the professor's speech. I was also wondering why Jill was holding my hand all of a sudden and thinking to myself that Debbie really was stunning. Not to mention cogitating some of what Col had said and what downshifting meant to me, and perhaps to Jill. Oh, and looking out for Fiona.

My confused thoughts and feelings were typical of that day, although I wasn't yet as muddled, or beer-befuddled, as I became later.

Having said that I can only just remember – and I'm not sure if this is a false memory or not – that I was brought another pint when the professor was speaking, by the girl I took to be Griff's daughter.

Dear Mart

Dear Mart,

The day of the Castle's opening and Col's pageant stirred up a whole raft of turbulent emotions, as you'll have gathered. It stirred them up at the time and when I wrote about them.

I read somewhere that suicides often do the deed when they're on the up. That is, they sink very low, then when they've begun to get their affairs sorted, top themselves.

Less dramatically, it's when you've got a breathing space after committing yourself heart and soul to a project, that all the things you've been putting off barge in on you.

I'd like to keep writing because when I write these days I don't seem to think. I experience but don't think. I haven't, though, the strength to continue with the story at present. I don't even know whether I can manage this letter.

I haven't written for a week actually and the thoughts about what happened last year have inundated me. What I want to do in this letter is draw a line under that day, apart from apprising you of a few last facts. If I may, I'd like to stand back from it and attempt to distil for you some insights into the way I felt – as well as to work out what I've learnt from reliving them. Not that you're definitely going to read my story, nor this letter.

It's a strange caper this therapy because here I am

pretending to write to you. Also, we've discussed why I should do this. You say further that you respect my right not to show you another page. It's a highly artificial exercise and yet I do believe I'm writing to you, especially when I get going. I'm pointing in your direction. It's the power of the imagination.

To put things another way, even if I'd decided to write to you spontaneously, off my own bat, there's no guarantee I would send the letter. But when I was writing it I would believe I would and so would express things to you – aspects of myself – that I could only express to *you*. My belief enables me to open up a certain part of me. And if I believe I'll send the letter but don't or whether I imagine my way into writing a letter I know I won't send the two situations work the same magic.

You've taught me something, Mart, and I thank you for it.

Before I go on I ought to round off the story of the pageant. Not that there's much more to say. You'll have gathered that the climax involved the re-enactment of the execution of Cornet Smirk and Corporal Hearne in front of the last remaining section of castle wall.

The little drama was done very well. Col was part of the five-man firing party and the vicar was officer in charge. A nice touch this because before taking holy orders the vicar'd been in the army. Saw active service in the First Gulf War. This fact was alluded to in the vicar's speech about where people should go to see the re-enactment and so his later transformation back to vicar for the procession along the Castle Footpath to the church for the service of remembrance affected people deeply.

The only unscripted part was when Nat suddenly leapt up and went 'Dugadugadugadugadugaduga-dug!' at the soldiers waiting to be executed. Most people took no notice – those that did simply smiled indulgently. The only person stifling hysterical laughter was, I think, Fiona.

Of course, I was surprised it was Nat. Ben I could've understood. But then I suppose when you think about it, Nat was feeling important after bringing Fiona the message about the programmes and he didn't have the nous about what was appropriate to the situation that Ben did. It's the quiet ones you have to watch.

And it wasn't just Ben who I failed to pick up on. Looking back now, Mart, it seems like the day was positively humming with signals I didn't receive. I didn't work out who Sarah was, for a start, though all I had to do was ask Fiona. Why didn't I? I suppose it might have been because I didn't like to appear too eager. Maybe because I didn't like to admit that I didn't know who that golden couple were. Because then I'd have to admit that I was the new boy who was going to have to get to know people and be accepted by them, initiated into their world. I think my vanity sometimes doesn't like having to do things the normal way. I like to jump straight in, be a part of where it's at and fill in the detail as and when. That day I thought I *was* there, trusting to social osmosis and my eagle eye for tell-tale signs. Packed full of confidence, I was, fuelled on ale and Class A adrenalin.

I suppose I also assumed that the golden couple would be interested enough in me to announce themselves, if I'm absolutely honest.

But then fate also played a hand with this one. Twice. At one point Debbie asked me if Sarah had had a chance to speak to me yet. I said no and she told me Sarah was the friend who she'd been with at the pottery in Aldermaston. Of course I said I remembered there'd been two of them – which was true, by process of deduction. If Debbie'd been waiting for a friend, obviously there had to have been a friend there. Though I couldn't for the life of me retrieve what she looked like.

Then Debbie said I'd no doubt meet Sarah later, after she finished at the church. I asked if Sarah was religious but Debbie said no, she'd just volunteered as a steward so as to help Col and the vicar.

I suspect Sarah turned up at the Castle when Jill and I went for a walk to the Thames and an early supper at the Trout at Tadpole Bridge. She'd certainly gone home by the time we returned.

It was then that fate played its other trick. I have a rather swimmy recollection of finally having a decent chat with Griff. I mentioned I'd met his daughter. He seemed well chuffed, particularly when I said I thought she looked a lovely girl. He confided that she had taken after her mother who she lived with in a place on the borders called Llann-y-Blodwell. 'Moralistic, she is, see,' he explained. 'Fucked off to the tower with Virgin bloody Mary, she has' (by whom, I assumed he meant Sarah). Whether he did or didn't I joined in with the throaty guffaws which followed his joke. As he laughed he slapped his gigantic leg with his cap.

It was a day of crossed wires and misinterpreted signals. My eagle eye told me what I wanted to see not what was there – story of my life.

It was like one of those pattern pictures that were popular in the late eighties. The ones which looked like wallpaper samples but which you could turn into amazing 3-D images if you focussed in a particular way. They didn't half make your eyes ache but the book of them I had kept me amused for ages. The one that always sticks in my mind was of a pair of rabbits – mother and baby – grazing, if memory serves. It was beautifully simple and touching. The bunnies weren't naturally coloured but, like most of the revealed images, had an iridescent quality.

I remember yacking about these sort of pictures with Rajiv one drunken evening. He'd started off studying philosophy at Strathclyde before switching to chemistry. He reckoned the images behind the wallpaper were like Platonic forms – idealised versions of the things we see around us on earth which we sometimes get a glimpse of through poetry or art or music.

Well, the point is that on the day the Castle opened – as so often with me – I was pretty good when it came to describing the pattern of the picture (though sometimes I didn't even manage to do that – in connection with Andy for instance) but rubbish at letting my eyes discern the truth behind.

I suppose you could take the idea of pattern pictures further and apply the principle to gallery paintings. People talk about reading pictures and it's rather wonderful when you watch a programme on TV where a critic brings a canvass to life. Some teachers have a similar gift. The one that taught me English A-level had it.

But somehow I never quite got there myself on the day of the pageant.

I didn't notice Sarah but took her for someone else. I could tell Fiona wasn't happy but I never imagined she'd leave Col. I decided she was the long-suffering type. I saw Andy with some mates up by the style from the Castle Footpath during the execution of the soldiers. I saw him thrust his arms into the air after Nat's performance and the real guns went off. I saw him but persuaded myself that he wouldn't have bunked off from the Castle. I never even got a quarter of the way to asking myself why he might be there.

I did see myself making love to Jill that night because she'd been so nice to me and that didn't happen.

Poor Jill. Poor me. When I was running my company, I never saw how she was really, either. As I say, story of my life.

Sometimes when I think about that strange day, albeit with the benefit of hindsight, I find myself concluding that everything was there for a man who had eyes to see with. Griff was marked out as a man who death would soon be calling for. Sarah had a danger sign flashing on her pale forehead. There were alarms ringing with every creak of her tiny girl's body.

And I ask myself now, have I learned anything over the past year? Would I make the same mistakes again?

I recall the Shakespeare tragedy I studied for A-level, *King Lear*. There's a character, an old man called Gloucester, who thinks his bad son is good and his good one is bad. He only learns to see the truth after he is blinded and his passionate nature is utterly humbled.

I wonder, am I blind enough to my own ego to begin seeing clearly?

I don't know. Perhaps – and I hope this is the case – I shall learn humility from finally describing what happened with Sarah.

Valentine's Eve

On the eve of Valentine's Day 1998, Sarah writes her diary at her desk in the bedroom that was hers when she was a girl and a young woman.

It feels appropriate to be writing the diary in this room. Not that she wrote much of her earlier diary here and little or none of it at this desk. And yet when she was younger the room was somehow the spiritual centre of her being. It is her space, her home within the home, and so writing the new diary seems fitting. It is the right place in which to be drawing a line under her single life.

She read her old diary last night, together with the opening pages of the new one. She only flicked through the rest of the new diary because there is little of emotional substance there. She gave up diary writing eighteen months ago when her life changed, getting first worse then better, so much better. Since then the entries have been lists of things to be done and presents to be bought for friends, notes about pottery techniques, and visits to studios and exhibitions.

When Sarah was at her lowest, she had no spare energy for writing. When she suddenly became happy she was so taken out of herself that writing seemed an almost alien activity.

Sarah has put on a stone over the previous year, two stone over the past eighteen months, and miraculously the fact that she now has unconcealable curves rarely bothers her. For the first time in her life she feels truly happy. She is content, easy in her skin.

There is a good chance that no long-term harm has been done by her anorexia. Her fiancé, Jamie, has paid for her teeth to be re-enamelled – in London, a good eighty miles from her father's practise. Her doctor says her bone density is reduced but within the range of normality. She may be more at risk of fractures in later life than most people but being aware of this she can take precautions. Her periods have started again and she should be able to have children.

She has told Jamie that she had an eating disorder but that she is fine now. She thinks this news has made him more protective of her, although she doubts she has conveyed quite how serious her illness was, even when they swapped confessions when deliciously drunk and it seemed as if nothing they could ever say would be enough to put even a tiny dent in their relationship.

Her father must have noticed that she had her teeth done but he has never mentioned it. He is too preoccupied with the redevelopment of the second surgery and some tussle with his fellow councillors which is said to be just an irritating bit of procedure and of no consequence. Her father says this as does her mother.

Sarah feels these machinations have sometimes overshadowed her stay. She has felt anger towards her father but cannot sustain it because she believes he is trying his best to keep the business in the background and is in any case being wonderfully generous about the dress and wedding.

When, for example, she and Jamie announced their engagement she expected her father to refuse to let them have the marriage and reception at Jamie's family church and his family home, the Old Hall. But while her father expressed surprise about the proposals, since discussing them with her mother and Jamie's parents he has been wholly in favour.

The worst part of her stay was yesterday afternoon shortly after she and her mother returned from the final dress fitting.

Her mother went to look at Min's horses, having established that Uncle Vern and Peter were locked in discussions about something in the study.

Sarah got changed upstairs before going for a walk but when she came down she heard her father and Vern arguing. Vern sounded far stronger than usual. 'You've got to be straight with them, Peter,' he was saying. 'You've got to be straight with *me*.' 'Are you calling me a *liar*?' shouted her father. His question was a familiar one under such circumstances. 'Of course you're lying, Peter. Do you take me for a fool?' 'If the cap fits, Vern.' Her father's voice was no longer raised but he couldn't help making the words come out loudly. Sarah decided he had the upper hand and was almost proud of him despite being outraged by the fact that the dispute was erupting that day.

It was then that Vern said something that ended, '...tell them myself.' His voice was calm and indistinct. There were more quiet words from Vern before her father exploded. 'You bloody well won't, you despicable little sod. Who the hell do you think you are? You're nothing but a creeping trouble-maker.' Vern protested. Her father then shouted, 'Get out! Get *out!*' at the top of his voice.

Sarah thought the study door was about to burst open. She left the hall, went to collect her gumboots from the kitchen passage and set off on her walk. The argument went round and round her head for about half an hour but after that she began blotting it out by thinking of her dress and some of the happy times when she did this walk as a girl. But most of all she thought of Jamie and what he would be doing on the farm.

She found she was angry not so much with her father but with Vern. Surely, she thought, he could have had more tact than to pick a fight on one of her last days at home. Why was he here anyway? Ostensibly to celebrate her forthcoming marriage with the family but he evidently had his own agenda. It occurred to her that he might have invested in the second surgery project.

She imagined her uncle would have fled by the time she returned but instead he was not only still at the house but apparently on friendly terms with her father again. Throughout the evening she was struck by how kindly her uncle was towards her and how warmly she responded to him, despite her earlier feelings of rage.

She was also struck by how polite her father was to Uncle Vern. She expected her father's usual wicked asides but these were nowhere in evidence.

When Sarah opens her diary at her desk in her bedroom and leafs through it to a clean page, she is considering writing something about the previous days at home and Uncle Vern's argument with her father. But she decides not to. She doesn't want to dwell on unhappy thoughts and besides the row has nothing to do with her.

Her father never discusses business with her. He never used to discuss business with anyone in the family, ever, although she gets the impression that he talks things over with her mum a lot nowadays.

There was the time when he spoke to Sarah of the trust fund he wanted to borrow money from but he's never mentioned this again since she signed some document or other. She can't remember what it was she signed because she was at her lowest then. In any case, she never got the impression that the trust had anything to do with her – not really. If it had, the trustees would have asked her opinion, surely? She rarely thinks about the trust and hardly does so now though it does enter her thoughts fleetingly for some reason she can't explain.

She pushes the trust from her mind by thinking about Jamie and what she is going to write about him. She wishes she had put something down about him before so she had a proper record of their life together thus far. Why couldn't she write about truly happy things, only sad ones?

She will attempt to redress the balance. She will round off her unmarried diary-writing career with a brief account of the happiest days of her life.

Her thoughts return momentarily to the trust fund, then she tells herself that she doesn't need to concern herself with it because she is remarkably lucky. With Jamie she will have all the money she could wish for. She will work still but it is extraordinary thinking of how cushioned life will be. These are scary thoughts and she hopes she will not be spoilt by wealth, is determined not to be.

She realises how lucky she is having Jamie and will never take him for granted.

She clicks the lead out of her pencil and starts to write.

Sarah's New Diary

13th Feb. '98

I want to write about Jamie.

Jamie is my fiancé who I love so very much and who I can't believe I've found.

I want to write about him but hardly know where to begin. It's so much harder to write about happy things than about suffering.

I'm also out of practice and don't think I can ever recapture that mad energy I used to have when words just flew onto the page. Perhaps contentment isn't conducive to writing. Paper and pencil are unhappiness's soulmates.

Not being able to write is the price I pay for being well – which I can live with. But maybe too I've found new ways of expressing my feelings. Can I see angst in my old pots and joy in my recent ones? I don't know but a psychiatrist might.

I met Jamie at Christmas 1996, not even eighteen months ago, and he asked me to marry him a year later on 15th December 1997.

I'd made one or two friends in the village and we used to spend more time than was good for us in the Caiger Arms. Dave, the landlord, was big on lock-ins at the weekend and high days and holidays. That Christmas you could have virtually lived at the pub. Sometimes, like the night I met Jamie, Sinéad came along, though she'd never stay later than twelve.

She liked the ceili nights when local musicians got together and played folk music. I never thought I'd get into that kind of thing but it was fantastic and was all part of the amazing atmosphere of the Caiger. Never mind real ale, Dave wanted to be a real landlord, keeping the old pub traditions alive.

The pub was packed and it was about eleven-thirty. Dave had an extension so the lock-in hadn't started and people were still coming and going.

I remember Sinéad suddenly looking towards the bar and saying, 'Well I'm blowed!' She leant across me and shouted to Dan the forester, 'I didn't know Jamie was home.'

'Neither did I,' said Dan. He squinted at someone in the scrum round the bar and then shouted, 'Is it him? Looks a bit like him – 'cept for the tan and muscles!'

'It's him alright.' Sinéad pointed the man out to me and told me he was the son of the local landed family. 'He's completely different to what you'd expect,' she said. 'He's got attitude – you can see that straight away. The punk gent. I'll try and catch his eye. He's someone you ought to meet.'

How can I describe Jamie that night?

Well, to begin with all I could see was his back. He wasn't especially tall compared with several of the men up at the bar but he somehow seemed taller because he was so slim and elegant. And his hair was long and extraordinarily sleek. It was glossy, beautifully layered and like the fur of an exquisite animal. His hair was the sort that made you want to run your fingers through it.

He was wearing a pinstripe jacket over drainpipe faded blue jeans and as people moved about him I glimpsed a pair of amazing dark brown cowboy boots.

I could see what Sinéad was driving at when she called him a punk gent but he was too chic to be punk. To Sinéad he looked like that but I thought of him as being more like an actor. He was dressing down with the jeans but letting you know he had cash with the jacket. Not that it was designer – my father's taste in Savile Row suits had taught me enough to spot a tailor-made jacket. When we first started going out I surprised Jamie by unbuttoning the cuffs of his jacket and folding them back to reveal his Omega watch and tiny – miniature but strong – wrists.

Every now and then he spoke to people either side of him. What struck me most was how smiley he was. I saw flashes of his white teeth, the crease in his tanned face from in front of his cheek bone to the side of his chin.

It was the smile that made him really interesting. His clothes and his bearing made me think what a gorgeous man, made me want to stare, but the smile gave me hope that he might actually be nice to talk to. It made him seem human.

And then he turned away from the bar and took a sip of his pint.

Sinéad waved to him and caught his attention. His smile was so broad at seeing her he could almost have been laughing. He started to walk towards us.

Sinéad introduced me to him and he shook my hand. His grip was firm but not combative. It amazes me how often men treat shaking my hand as a wrestling match. OK I wear dungarees and my hair is quite short but I'm only a slip of a thing – I was then, especially (and saying that is *real* progress). I think their attitude results from the fact that I make things. Only pots but somehow I'm still put in the same category as blacksmiths and carpenters and even in these post-feminist times that's enough to mark me out as a woman to be stood up to, perhaps tamed. Of course when they've talked to me for a few minutes they realise their mistake. I'm prickly, certainly, but I'm not going to take them on.

But Jamie didn't behave like that. His handshake showed that he thought I was an equal. I felt that the way he shook my hand indicated his honesty and directness.

He remained standing by our table for some minutes. He talked to Sinéad, although he broke off now and then to pick up on some comment that Dan and the others made. And he never forgot me. He would turn to me and it was as if the conversation had been directed at me all the time.

He had been working on a farm in New Zealand in a beautiful temperate valley which reminded him of the best ever days in

England, only they were the norm. Sinéad asked if he'd learnt as much as he hoped and he said, 'Definitely,' with one of his lovely smiles, and explained about New Zealand's free market and the absence of subsidies, and said that as a result people favoured good old-fashioned mixed farming so that they spread the risk.

Dan remarked that this country had been the same before the Second World War. His girlfriend Belinda said she hadn't realised he was so old but Sinéad and Jamie ignored her and agreed with Dan. Jamie continued by saying that when subsidies ended in Britain people would have to turn to mixed farming again. He obviously couldn't wait for this and extolled the virtues of balance and growing grain for both sale and feeding livestock, and in turn using the manure from the animals to fertilise the land. He spoke with an authority and enthusiasm that took my breath away.

Then the last band came on and Sinéad invited Jamie to sit with us. She stood up so he could squeeze in between her and me.

During the music he whispered comments to me about the singing and at one point cracked a joke but it wasn't against anyone – unlike the jokes made by some of the others at our table – but against himself, which I liked.

Shortly after the band finished, Sinéad said she was off to bed. I expected Jamie to move to another table or at least start talking to someone else. But he stayed where he was and asked me questions about myself and I asked about him. The conversation was easy and spontaneous. We must have spent a couple of hours together before he said he ought to be getting home.

He said how much he'd enjoyed meeting me and wondered if I'd like to have a drink before Christmas. I said I'd love to. Not that I thought he'd actually get in touch. I didn't doubt his sincerity but imagined he'd be inundated with other offers and meeting me would get pushed to the back of the queue. Besides, a person like Jamie remembering a tentative arrangement with me was not the sort of thing that usually happened. But I shouldn't have doubted him.

I was wrong when I said I couldn't write about good things. I *can*, although my progress is much slower than when I wrote out my suffering. I started at twenty to eleven and it's now nearly midnight. Two years ago I'd have filled this exercise book in that time.

Also, writing about Jamie is far more tiring than writing about pain. With the latter you're performing an exorcism and after the turmoil of casting out your thoughts comes serenity. If I'm honest, and I don't want to be, it's like anorexia. You feel stuffed full of life, stomach-churning life, and you purge it by writing.

Conveying what it was like to meet Jamie is exhausting because I so want to do him justice. I want to make such a counterbalance to all the misery in these diaries that it will never rise up at me again. Yet with each word I realise how impossible it is to transfer what's in my heart to the page.

It's my own fault – I should have written about him before. There's so much I want to say but if I wrote a whole book I would only be scratching the surface of the past fourteen months.

Fourteen months, the fourteenth of February 1998. The hands on my watch have just passed through midnight and a naughty thought has crept into my mind. Will I dare to carry out my plan? I don't know for certain but suspect I might. I'll let the idea lie for now. I'll try to write a little more about my beloved and then decide.

Jamie did remember to ask me out. He took me to a pub a few miles from Aldermaston which was near his family estate.

He collected me from Helen's – where I still live, notionally, though only for six more weeks – and before we went to the pub, he called at his cottage to show me his spaniel puppy, Rufus. Jamie told me he'd been hoping for a puppy from Rufus's breeder for eons but there had always been such a long waiting list. Jamie claimed that Rufus was the reason he'd come home from New Zealand. I wasn't sure whether to believe him but now

I know it's true.

I thought maybe the puppy would be used as an excuse to get me back to the cottage later but Jamie didn't show any sign of making a move. He was just warm and charming and we talked about what we'd been doing at work and about home and Mum and Dad. He then told me about how his ancestors had first come to the Old Hall over three hundred years ago. His great, great, great whatever grandfather was a silversmith who worked his way up from humble origins and made a killing in the years after the Civil War. I assumed Jamie meant during the Restoration but he insisted it was the Protectorate.

Of course he was right although he didn't know the details well. It was his father who explained how the years of Cromwell's rule were good ones for businessmen, especially the members of the worshipful companies of the City of London (several of whom were patrons of Jamie's forbear). Cromwell was keen to encourage business and trade in order to put the country back on its feet.

I've become fascinated by the story of Jamie's family. I was a little surprised by this to begin with because I'd been made rather cynical about family connections by Dad's clumsy efforts to talk up the one or two worthies who we're distantly related to. But Jamie's family history is *real*. You can see the ancestors covering the walls of the Old Hall and can read their different tastes and aspirations in the additions made to the house over the centuries.

Sometimes it's awesome to have that weight of history pressing down on you. I know Jamie feels this too. He said once that he almost wrote to his father from New Zealand telling him he wasn't coming back. He desperately wanted to live a normal life – as a free man. But he came home to take on his responsibilities and soon he will have me at his side.

We saw each other again in between Christmas and New Year – a lunchtime drink at the Caiger – but it wasn't until early January that Jamie made his move. No 'made his move' isn't right, it makes what happened seem contrived but by then our sleeping together was a quite natural inevitability.

We each went away at New Year, Jamie to Scotland and me to Cornwall to stay at Alex's cottage. I had a brilliant time there. It was wonderful to see Alex looking so well, full of self-confidence and a new-found sense of responsibility. He's been put in charge of part of the Eden Project – the actual gardening work in one area of this big biome – and is the proud owner of a Jack Russell puppy called Tufty.

At the party, I got on especially well with a friend of Alex's called Will. After midnight we kissed and had a bit of a cuddle. He wanted to take things further but I stopped him. He was OK but I could feel he thought I'd sent out mixed messages.

It wasn't as if there was even a half-understanding between me and Jamie but I just felt sufficiently close to him for kissing Will to seem wrong.

The night we slept together, Jamie took me out for supper at a pub in the middle of nowhere about six miles from Aldermaston. It was a pair of cottages knocked into one which stood in a clearing in some woodland. There was a beautiful old bar with oak beams, bare floorboards and a huge inglenook fireplace with a stonking fire. On the other side of the flagstoned passageway was a small dining-room where the most scrumptious food was served, not to mention Château Léoville-Barton 1982.

Jamie came to collect me from Helen's by taxi because he wanted to enjoy himself – to wash away the Twelfth Night blues, he said.

In the bar we managed a pint of Dickens's Best, a pint of Cornish beer I'd tried with Alex to remind me of him and a half of Dickens's Great Expectations, a 7.5% New Year special. Then the wine on top, which seems an amazing quantity now I look back on it, and yet I didn't feel at all drunk at the time and can remember everything as clear as a bell.

It was just all amazingly exciting. I did throw up but only once and then made up for it by gorging on the cheese board without feeling the slightest twinge. Being with Jamie that night was the beginning of the healing which has meant that I've got better and stronger ever since.

After the meal, Jamie asked if I'd like to go back to his cottage for coffee and Armagnac. I asked how I'd get home. He said he could order another taxi or else I could stay the night in one of the spare rooms.

At the cottage, he put a log on the embers of the fire which were still glowing and while he went through to the kitchen to make coffee and let Rufus out, I got the flames going with the pair of bellows which has Jamie's family crest carved on one of the wooden sides. The motto beneath the crest is *Carpe Diem*, or Seize the Day, which seems appropriate to his lot, somehow. Although Jamie himself is an odd, unpredictable but utterly adorable mixture of confidence and shyness.

Above the puppy basket beside the fire was a mobile made up of cut outs of all the different breeds of spaniel. After we'd finished our first glass of Armagnac, Jamie stood up and asked if I'd like another. Before he went to the drinks cupboard, he began twirling the mobile.

I joined him and turned it, then he turned it again, and he took me in his arms and we kissed.

During the night the sky must have cleared because there was a sharp frost. The inside of the window next to Jamie's bed was coated with ice. I remember reaching out and scraping a little away with my fingernails and thinking how old-fashioned the cottage was and how old-fashioned Jamie could be. I loved that aspect of him.

I turned to him and looked at him sleeping. His lovely soft hair was swept back so it and the fine structure of his face made him look like David Bowie on the Aladdin Sane album cover. Although Jamie never seems bothered about his appearance – you don't know whether he'll turn up to something looking impeccable or like a scruff – he can't not be aware of how exquisite he is. Sometimes, for parties, he gels his hair to look like Bowie and sprays on red dye. Then he really does resemble a punk gent. No, then he's like a god. But full of contradictions.

I snuggled up to him and fell back to sleep in his warmth until we both awoke and made love and I knew for a second time what all the fuss was about.

Sarah lays down her pencil and looks at her watch.

She re-reads her last paragraph and smiles.

She glances over her shoulder at her little bed then turns back to her diary.

The time when she used to sleep in this room seems impossibly long ago. She thinks of the bed she has shared with Jamie for most of the past year and imagines Jamie asleep alone without her. She wonders whether he is in fact still up.

When she spoke to him earlier in the evening he said he probably wouldn't go out but she urged him to go and see his friends down at the Caiger, telling him he would enjoy it and it would be better for him than falling asleep in front of the television.

When she spoke to him he was in the lambing shed and in her mind's eye she sees him driving his Land Rover back to the cottage, then coming downstairs after his bath and making himself some supper – sausage, egg, chips and beans. (Whilst it is true that Jamie likes the finer things of life when at a restaurant, when he is farming he prefers his schoolboy favourites.) She sees him sitting in front of the telly with a beer and getting bored. He will have wondered whether to take the Land Rover down to the village or to bike it. She hopes the latter with a taxi home after the lock-in. She hopes too that he will have let himself go. She feels he doesn't see enough of his old friends now he is with her and doesn't want him to one day blame her for this.

She would like to phone him now but knows she mustn't.

She gets undressed and puts on a T-shirt and dressing-gown. She goes downstairs to the snug where the fire is still alight, reminding her of the first night at Jamie's cottage.

She opens the drinks cupboard and moves the bottles round as if she is playing a village fête game until she finds a bottle of Armagnac. She pours herself a large glass and sits on the rug in front of the fire, leaning against one of the armchairs.

She loses herself in the alcohol, the lazy flames in the grate and her thoughts of Jamie.

Her mind returns to the plan that came to her at midnight.

It is February 14th. She should be with Jamie for as much of the day as possible. Although they are going out for supper later on, he shouldn't wake up without her. After she finishes her drink she will go to bed then at seven she will get up and drive to him.

Once back in her bedroom, she flicks through the pages of her diaries, catching words and phrases of her past. She is tempted to add a few last words more to round off her single life for good but is too tired all of a sudden.

She has already written what are, perhaps, the last words she will ever write in a diary.

Tom's writing therapy

11/07/03 – A Friday to 21/08/03 – A Thursday

It took me some six weeks from when the Castle opened to realise my mistake about Sarah.

During those weeks I was out of circulation. The weekend of the launch and Col's pageant I was like a moth on its brief doomed jaunt in the sun. Much of the following week I slept, utterly poleaxed by the stress of getting the pub and micro on the go.

As far as Jill was concerned, I felt that on balance I'd been right not to try anything on and this was born out by the weekly telephone conversations that followed. We were becoming friends once more, which was, I convinced myself, the way forward if there was ever to be intimacy again.

Anyway, during the first week after the pageant, I also learnt that I'd got myself a cracking team in Andy, Tara and the two kids. I'd always intended to let them have their head after the opening but hadn't bargained on how knackered I was going to be. I struggled to do the light supervision I'd planned and most of the time found I was superfluous. Andy had the next couple of batches through the tun and into the fermenting vessels before you could blink – and the product was super.

Tara meanwhile, kept the place spotless, worked like a demon behind the bar and displayed none of the preciousness I'd been expecting.

Oh, and she and Andy were an item.

By the following week I was back to my old self – although, the sheer amount of sleep I needed made me realise that time was taking its toll. A decade before when Dickens's was unstoppable and I body-slammed anything, or anyone, standing in my way, a pub launch was an excuse for a piss up and a lie-in till seven am.

Nothing more.

But last year, for the first time in my life, I imagined the Grim Reaper running his finger down the blade of his scythe. He wasn't ready for the harvest yet, hadn't even picked up the whetstone. He was like a farmer contemplating the harvest in winter-time. It was a long way off but would come and he knew it and I knew it too.

Still, throughout June I threw myself back into my projects. There was the state-of-the-art kitchen at the Castle to be designed and started, beer to be brewed, pints to be pulled (particularly so the kids could have some time off), not to mention my home to be refurbished.

I initiated Sunday night picnics for the pub crew. We'd close at ten-thirty sharp and then take jugs of beer out into the garden with which to wash down the Indian take-aways we'd pre-ordered. The picnics were open to all employees and their partners and were a howling success. Only the barest essentials were done in the pub after we closed, the rest being done by me after everyone else had gone home. The picnics were my way of saying thank you and instilling team spirit. They were richly deserved.

Of course, I saw people during those weeks but I didn't go out much, just went to the odd barbecue and pool party, and made a lot of small talk across the bar. Plus Col and Fiona were also out of circulation. Fiona went down with summer flu immediately after the bank holiday (I wasn't the only one to think there was more to this than met the eye) and Col had his hands full catching up with his land agency and looking after Fi and the boys.

I suppose what I'm saying is that I didn't meet Sarah in that period. Griff came into the pub a couple of times in early June but, it transpired, Sarah wasn't a great one for going out – and Griff wasn't in a hurry to ask me to see the Folly, despite my hints.

Looking back objectively, I suppose I must have done quite a lot of socialising before I met Sarah properly. It's just that in the light of what happened when we met, those weeks seem a little

259

flat, shall we say.

I met Sarah properly when I was working with Col on his coppicing project.

I offered to help him one night when he came into the Castle for a pint – Fiona had recovered by this time but still wasn't getting out much – and he told me how he'd got behind with sorting out a wood up by the Folly for his next lot of free-range pigs. His first batch was on one of Griff and Sarah's fields for the summer, having been over-wintered in another clearing in their woods he made the previous year.

Col was bitching about how he was going to have to take someone on to help him which would mean raiding his capital for the wages and receiving a rap on the knuckles from Fiona. He then said he didn't know how he was going to find someone because the best of the bunch of summer casuals were already signed up.

I patted him on the shoulder and said, 'Look no further, mate.'

He nearly dropped his pint and I realised how cut up about his problem he was.

'I couldn't,' he said. 'I couldn't accept. The work's so menial and I can't pay very much.'

'Jesus, Col, how long've we known each other? I'll turn my hand to anything. And as far as the dosh's concerned, forget it. You'll be doing me a favour. I've started to put on a few pounds and need the exercise. I was oiling the bike only yesterday. And another thing, I wouldn't like to think of Fiona losing it. *Nasty*.'

I got him smiling with this last comment, which was quite something that evening.

He then explained that Griff and Sarah were renting him another three acre piece of woodland about a mile from their house. The area had been used to grow hazel coppice in between the ancient oaks up until the Second World War but had been let go since. Our tasks were cutting down the hazel suckers and the weaker oak saplings, grubbing up the stumps, cutting back the coppice and tidying up the wispy bits on the trunks of the oaks.

Then we'd fence the area and Bob's your uncle.

I said the project sounded doable and was prepared to give up a couple of afternoons a week for a month or two.

He reckoned that was about right but if he needed to get someone else in afterwards, there would be casuals looking for work by then, and in any case we'd have broken the back of the job.

I said, 'Done.'

He said, 'I still can't believe it.'

I repeated, 'Done,' as firmly as I could and we shook.

I remember thinking as I pulled our celebratory pints that Col was a changed man since the pageant. He was jittery and had this hunted look. It could have been that he wasn't able to settle after his afternoon of fame but this didn't seem likely. Equally I didn't think things with Fiona were *that* bad and there were no money worries. I couldn't put my finger on anything but the impression I had that evening persisted the whole time we were working – or not in his case – in the copse.

That summer was a scorcher but I took to the work.

Even though the sun was baking, being in the copse gave you a lot of protection. You worked up a sweat but there was a constant sense of coolness that came from being under greenery. And when there was a breeze there was the soft skittering of the leaves, which soothed you.

I recall the light too. Once your eyes got accustomed the wood was almost normal but the world beyond was bleached. It looked like something unreal, or a hard, hostile, desert place and I was pleased to be safe in my copse.

Working away, cheerfully, a lot of the time on my own, I lost myself in strange thoughts like that. It was wonderful, a great unwinder of all the tension that had ratcheted up since I don't know when. Not long after the venture cap boys started putting their oar in, I suppose. Then the stress of trying to do their bidding, the decision to sell, breaking with Jill, my descent into boozing, buying the pub and mill, and the mad dash to do the pub and brewery.

I ended up at the wood three or four times a week, I loved the work so much. And why not? The pub was in safe hands, the builders were swarming all over the mill. I'd decided to put a swimming pool in the old straw rope factory. I was also converting the other outbuildings into an office and garaging, and having the mill-pond dredged and the banks shored up. You couldn't find a peaceful corner to call your own.

I used to bicycle across the valley, over the Thames and up to the woods, which ran all the way along the escarpment in both directions. I not only soon shed pounds but actually started to feel fit for the first time in years.

To get to Col's copse you had to turn off right about a quarter of a mile from where the woods began and follow the single track road for another mile or so, passing first the gate to the Folly, then a pair of massive brick and stone piers with their vast iron gates that used to be the main entrance to a sprawling mock-Elizabethan pile which burnt down in the 1970s.

The family that owned the place built a new house a couple of miles away and then sold off the Folly, its lodge and about seventy acres of woodland to Griff and Sarah when one of the sons got into financial difficulties with his software company.

The Folly was what it said on the tin and had been on the back drive to the big house.

You couldn't see the Folly this time of year, although I'd given it the once over through binoculars when I was walking on the other side of the river in the winter.

Our progress with the work was slow to begin with because I was inexperienced and Col didn't have his mind on the job. I reckon I was lucky if he was there for one full afternoon a week all told. Obviously he had his land agency and the smallholding but I still thought he was being a bit of a wuss. I say I thought he was a wuss, but I didn't resent his skiving. Actually I preferred being on my own.

I loved just working away and listening to the sounds – trees, birds, animals, sometimes a plane overhead. I loved the rhythms of those afternoons that I established. At five I'd stop and have some tea from my Thermos then at six-thirty I'd pack up and sit on my favourite patch on the edge of one of the fields and drink a couple of bottles of beer I'd brought in a coolbag and contemplate the world.

The place I sat was a bank between the wood and a cornfield. From there I could see the river, the fields and in the far distance the space-rocket steeple of the village church.

I grew to love the valley during those moments of peace.

The valley is amazingly flat and more than two miles wide. The fields either side of the river flood in the winter and people still call this part of the valley the Marsh. Col once took me down to the watermeadows in late autumn and showed me where the snipe were. He told me that curlew nest in the fields in the spring but I've never seen one yet.

Col, being a proper historian, was a mine of information about the valley. He explained to me that it was inhospitable swampy woodland in the Dark Ages but was steadily drained and cleared after the Norman conquest. You can still see Victorian dykes and sluice gates in places. Reminds me of where grandad came from in Norfolk, which is probably why I like it so much.

On the other side of the river, beyond the watermeadows the farming is nearly all corn, including this field of extraordinarily tall corn that a thatcher grows each year. Last summer there was also a bit of oilseed rape and a field of maize. I remember coming across the thatcher's field not long after I moved. I followed the footpath through a gap in a hedge and there were these ancient-looking tractors with strange bits of kit on the back. They were like some of the machinery that turned up at the engineering shop when I was a boy, but even older. And the cut corn was gathered into bundles leant together like it was another century. I couldn't believe it – such beauty.

The maize, though, was an oddity. I remember one time when I was cycling home I saw that someone had painted CAPTAIN SWING in red letters on a sign strapped to the gate across the track that led to it. I asked people in the pub what this meant but no one knew.

The next time I cycled to the wood the sign was gone.

It was that afternoon I met Sarah.

I was out on the bank drinking a beer – a bottle-conditioned Ridgeway Rambler – when I was aware of someone walking towards me along the headland.

It was a girl but I couldn't work out who she was for a moment because her dark hair was short. Added to which she had on a pair of designer shades that, although narrow, still seemed to cover much of her tiny face. She was wearing a simple blue dress, almost black, long and loose-fitting, with some sort of fine pattern on it (miniature red and pale blue flowers, it turned out).

I put down my beer and got to my feet.

As she came up, she held out her hand and I shook it.

'Sarah Vine,' she said. 'We met at Colin's pageant.'

Everything fell into place – sort of – why I hadn't recognised even the girl I thought she was, and who she actually was. She looked a little older with short hair, although her body, what I could see of it, was still skin and bone, making her look like a teenager.

'You've had your hair cut. I couldn't work out who you were.'

'When I was a girl I always used to have long hair then I had it cut off in my late teens – my father was furious. I let it grow back because Griff likes it like that.'

'Was he angry when you had it cut?'

'Good word, "angry". Griff is an *angry* man. Yes, he was but there's not much he can do about it. Besides I can be an angry woman.'

She smiled and observed me over the top of her glasses.

She looked frail but her voice and her expressions were strong and I liked the playful mischief I saw in her eyes. The directness about Griff was odd, disconcerting. I'd used the word, angry, without thinking.

She peered into the wood.

'I thought I'd come and see how you're getting on.'

'Very well. It's hard going but I love the work. Col's not been here today if you were expecting—'

She shook her head and her soft feathery hair rearranged itself slightly. The cut was expensive and glossy – the sort of hair that makes you want to put your hand on it and play with it.

'I know, I spoke to him earlier. He said you'd be annoyed with him for deserting you. He also told me you were doing an amazing job.'

'Kind of him but I don't doubt the old boys who kept this going years ago'll be turning in their graves. I bodge it – so does Col, in a way, but he's got a season's more experience. It's all about selection and judgement, this work. You need judgement to select the stems you're going to cut out completely and those you're going to leave and cut back. You need judgement to select where exactly you're going to do the cutting.'

'Sounds like you've given this coppicing business a lot of thought.'

'Not really. I read up on it on the Net but I suppose what I'm really doing is applying the same way of looking at things as I do when I'm brewing. Not that I'm a genius at that—'

'You must have done something right with Dickens's.'

'Well I had a wizard Master Brewer to do the real work. But let's just say that if you know one practical skill, at the very least you can work out your limitations when you try another – and that's useful.'

'I know what you mean. I don't know if anyone's told you but I run a gallery. I trained as a potter, though, and having that skill helps me a lot when I'm working with artists. It's not quite the same as what you're saying—'

'No, I can see where you're coming from.'

'At least I can tell when someone I'm dealing with has got something or is wasting my time – handy when you're investing thousands.'

'Tell you what, why don't I show you what we've been doing and then we can have a drink together. I've got another beer in the cool bag.'

'Sounds great.'

So saying, she gave me this lovely big grin that made me see her in a completely different light. It's hard to explain but up to that moment, she'd seemed a little, how shall I say, frigid. She was awkward, unyielding, and when I'd glimpsed her at the pageant, thinking back on it, it seems to me now that the impression I'd had was not simply of a teenage girl but of a very *serious* teenage girl. The sort you'd run a mile from at school. But the grin she gave me outside the wood revealed a different person. She opened herself to me and there was a real, flesh and blood person. Attractive too despite the skinniness.

When we came out of the wood I retrieved my half-drunk bottle from the coolbag and opened the other for her.

We said cheers.

She produced a tobacco tin and lighter from her dress pocket and asked me if I'd like a cigarette.

I said no, I didn't. Then I added something that looking back on it seems like pointless bravado. 'Except for the odd spliff.' I hardly ever do drugs. It was as if I was tailoring my words to what I presumed to be her arty personality.

She smiled to herself and set about making an ultra-slim, perfect tube before nipping off the wisps sticking out at the ends. As she did so, we talked about how extraordinary the summer was and how beautiful the valley looked.

Her smile when I mentioned dope made me wonder and when she lit up I thought I could detect the faintest whiff of cannabis.

The smell was always there when she smoked. I remember asking about this several weeks later. She denied there was any dope in the tobacco, said it was a special mixture from a shop in Oxford and offered to roll me a cigarette to try if I didn't believe her. I declined.

We talked for maybe half an hour before she said she had to get back because some friends were coming round. We talked about the Folly for part of the time and she said she'd give me the guided tour one day. She mentioned that Griff was away in London and that she was often on her own in the summer. Griff had another studio – his main one – in London and would spend weeks on end up there.

Before we set off, I offered to wheel the bike down the lane as far as the Folly lodge but she said she'd go back through the fields.

She asked me if I'd be working the same afternoon the following week.

I said, yes, if it was fine.

She said that if she was about she'd come over with a bottle of wine and maybe some food.

'Try and persuade Colin to be here too.'

'Yeah, that might be enough to stop him skiving,' I replied. 'Hope to see you then.'

And in my heart I almost hoped Col wouldn't be there.

Col kept me guessing that Friday afternoon. He told me he might have to leave early but by five-thirty was still there.

That Friday afternoon, not to mention the whole of the next few months, had a kind of strangeness. On the one hand, there was something inevitable about what was happening but at the same time, while the events were actually happening, I hadn't the faintest how things would go.

I suppose the point is that I asked myself, will Col stay or head off? I thought, yes he'll leave, and I can see how the afternoon'll pan out. Yet equally I could see him staying and a different scenario happening. Well, when he did make his excuses and I got the result I wanted, it was then, in the light of the magic I was suddenly caught up in that the events seemed inevitable. It was irrational rationalisation. A beautiful but dangerous fairytale.

It was when we'd already started packing up that his phone rang. He was irritated when he heard who it was. 'I'd given up on you,' were his opening words.

When he finished he explained that Andy was meeting him at the thatcher's field and they were going to watch the harvest. Before Andy started with me he was a seed rep with one of the big multinationals and the thatcher was a mate of his, so it made sense. Andy'd also booked the early part of the evening off till eight-thirty – Jimbo was covering for him. I was a bit surprised that Col had never been to see the field being cut, even so. But what with my elation at knowing he was leaving I didn't say anything about it.

I only went, 'Lucky you, I wish I'd known.' And if it had been any other day, I wouldn't have been pretending when I said this. It would've been fascinating.

'Are you OK to pack up without me?'

'Don't know, never tried it before.'

'Alright, alright. I'll do better next week. Are you going to be at the pub tonight?'

'Not sure.'

'Well, maybe see you there. Send my love to Sarah.'

As he set off for the Land Rover, I continued gathering the tools together then stowed them in the old shepherd's hut we used as a lock-up – a funny ancient-looking corrugated tin structure on cast-iron wheels with a stove-pipe sticking through its roof. As I worked, I found I was almost shaking and my insides were tingling like I was a boy on his first date. Like a boy, I knew something momentous was happening – maybe not this time but soon – although I didn't know precisely what.

Sarah arrived at six. She was wearing a long black dress, floaty like the last one but less so, more elegant, and it made her look slim, somehow, not thin.

You could tell from the paleness of her skin she was no sun-worshipper, although she'd caught the sun a little – how could she have avoided it last year? There were freckles around her upturned nose, perhaps brought out by the sun. When she took off her dark glasses the glow on her skin made her eyes seem a deeper green than I remembered. I noticed how bright the whites were, similar to Jill's, making her look so fresh, so young.

I was putting the last bits of kit away in the hut when she arrived. I didn't hear her coming up behind me, just her voice saying, 'Hello.'

She was standing at the foot of the steps looking up at me. She'd taken off her shades and I think it's the image of her face at that moment that has stuck in my mind, her skin dappled by drops of sunlight.

'Have you got Colin hidden away in there?'

'Just me, I'm afraid,' I said, leaning the tushing hook in its corner. 'Right, all done.'

I came down the steps and padlocked the door.

'Col sends his apologies. He was here until a few minutes ago. He's going to watch them cutting the thatcher's field with Andy. I'm not sure he wanted to go, to be quite honest.'

'All the more picnic for you.'

We walked towards the bank.

'Actually I wanted to ask you about Col later,' I said.

'Oh, yes.' She didn't sound surprised.

'He's been behaving a bit weirdly lately.'

'Tell me about it. He drove Griffin up the wall.'

'Not just me then?'

'It's this Winstanley business – gone to his head.'

It was phrases like 'Gone to his head' that made me wonder who exactly Sarah was and what she and Griff were about. There was an upper class Home Counties impatience in her voice at such times, whereas Griff gave the impression he'd been down the mines or in the steelworks most of his life. The apparent disparity intrigued me, though in my experience you could never tell with arty types. They were always putting on an act. Equally, I couldn't square this self-assured Sarah with the self-effacing meek one at the pageant. She was chock full of contradictions.

She'd laid out a picnic rug – I passed some comment like, Dead posh – and on it was a wicker hamper, a half brie, china jars of black olives, stuffed vine leaves, rollmop herrings and anchovies. She'd set out plates on which there was Parma ham and melon covered over with clingfilm and there was a leather case in which were six silver beakers. When we sat down she unzipped her coolbag and uncorked a truly delicious Pouilly Fuissé.

'Did you walk?'

'Only from the end of the track. I brought the car.'

'I was going to say – it must weigh a ton.'

She handed me my wine.

'Is that OK? You wouldn't prefer beer?'

'No. I have been known to try wine.' I slid the ice sleeve up so I could read the label. 'Particularly when it's this good.' We clinked our silver beakers together.

'I wanted to say thank you for all your hard work. You're doing us a favour too, you know. Our land agent's been banging on about sylvicultural management for yonks.'

I wasn't sure which to go for, sylvicultural or land agent. I decided the latter.

'You've got an agent? Like I say, dead posh.'

'Just someone we retain. Of course, there's not much for her to do but, you know, if a tree comes down. And we had a footpath diverted away from the house last year.'

She took another sip of her wine and made a show of tasting it. 'It is good, isn't it?' She turned her attentions to me and began savaging me, playfully, that is. 'I don't quite know what you mean by posh, Mr Dickens. Beneath the street cred and cheery bonhomie, I bet there's a normal middle-class boy. Does your father speak like you?'

Which I have to say caught me off my guard.

'No, he's pure Maldon Chamber of Commerce, as it goes, but I've always spoken like this. It's a generational thing.'

'What does he do?'

'Did – he's retired now. Light engineering – a sort of glorified car mechanic, most of the time, the bread and butter work, but he and the lads could turn their hands to anything. During the war – though this didn't include Dad, he was only a nipper – my grandad, who founded the business, used to service Lancaster bombers.'

She raised her eyebrows. 'Anyway, you know what I mean about, posh.'

'Point taken.'

She removed the clingfilm from one of the plates. 'Help yourself to the other things.'

'Aren't you going to have some?' There were only two plates and she didn't look like she was going to take the clingfilm off the other.

'No, I don't eat much meat. I'll just pick.'

'This is a wonderful feast.'

'So, tell me more about home – where you grew up.'

She was a great listener. She let me chat away, then nudged me into a slightly different area of my childhood and my relationship with my parents by asking a question or passing a perceptive comment. Before I knew what was happening, I was loving talking about myself – well, this aspect of my life, especially. It seemed such a long time since anyone had asked me about it. Mostly people's chat was about Dickens's and business. Talking to Sarah that evening made everything in the world seem right.

She brought over a picnic on two further occasions before I stopped working in the copse. The first was the following week, a Thursday this time. I remember asking her if Friday was out because Griff was coming home. We'd just cheersed a beautiful red Graves (chilled, surprisingly, although she knew what she was doing because the cold enhanced the blackcurrant flavour and the tannins were as keen as mustard).

She looked at me for a moment and her eyes went completely neutral. 'He hardly ever comes down in late summer or autumn. He says London's quiet in August – which is bollocks – and he loves the parks when the leaves start to turn. I'm expected to stay with him at the flat at weekends. But I like it here and last year I started to dig my heels in. This year, apart from an awards ceremony and a couple of dinner parties I can't get out of, I probably won't see him for three months.'

Her voice was cautiously expressive but her eyes didn't change and I detected neither pleasure nor regret as she told me that she and Griff were virtually living apart.

'It's a complicated thing,' she said, as if she realised what I might be thinking or that she'd given too much away. 'He's terribly caught up in his work during this period, so when we do see each other we don't exactly have fun. It's when winter starts and he gets melancholy and can't work that he comes back to the

Folly and we're happy again. It'll be like that this time. And this year's difficult in any case – for a number of reasons. Not the least of which is the fact that my father is ill. He may be dying. But I don't want to talk about that just at the moment.'

'No, of course not. I'm sorry.'

'Not your fault. Now, try some smoked trout.'

I asked her other questions about herself, of course, during those picnics, but soon learnt that many areas were off limits. While she liked listening to me talk about my childhood and adolescence, the conversation went nowhere when I tried to find out what her family life had been like. She mentioned she'd been brought up in the countryside near Bath and that her father was a dentist but that was about it.

The only person from her childhood she talked of in detail was Debbie, the black girl I'd met at the pageant. She told me about a holiday she'd spent with Debbie in Norfolk when they were kids, which gave me the impression of lazy summer days and two romantic, idealistic girls packed full of energy and enthusiasm. It was also a memory we were able to explore together because I then explained about grandad coming from Norfolk. And when she described swimming in the North Sea at night and the water being alive with fluorescent plankton, I knew exactly what she meant.

But such glimpses were rare in those early days and, once we'd negotiated the ground rules, so to speak, we tended to focus on the *recent* past. We spoke about the village, the pub and Folly, and our mutual friends. Colin's name came up a fair bit – and Fiona's. Sarah was fascinated by what Col was like at uni and we both, I'm ashamed to say, felt a certain amount of *schadenfreude* when dissecting his obsessive personality. We dwelt on how driven he was over the pageant and how this revealed the tensions between him and Fi. With hindsight, we were blowing the dust off the fact that there was something seriously the matter with Col, even though we concluded again and again that he'd be fine and otherwise refused to see what was staring us in the face.

When it came to the Folly, Sarah took great pride in describing how she'd furnished the banqueting hall and told me she was still working on the painted ceiling. I was intrigued by how she casually dropped oblique invitations while describing what she was doing, like 'When you see it you'll be astonished at the Victorian craftsmanship'. It was as if she was nerving herself up to ask me to the Folly but couldn't quite get there. I wanted her to invite me directly – I could have called in on the way back – but didn't force the issue. I realised that there was a frisson between us and therefore issuing an invitation was a big step. Bigger than if I'd just been an ordinary friend.

We also entered into this strange conspiracy to tone down our other attachments. I emphasised, when talking about Jill, that we'd split up but completely failed to mention my hopes for a future with her of a few weeks ago.

Sarah's revelation that she and Griff hardly saw each other in the autumn fitted in with our conspiratorial behaviour but was a significantly bolder statement than the kinds of thing she'd said about him before. She'd tended to make a dig at him, or else go vague when I asked about him.

But during that second picnic, when I asked about him, she showed her hand, then hid it again.

After the Griff episode Sarah changed the subject to reading. In one way she was starting on something new but was also, it eventually became clear, keeping Griff's absence in focus.

She asked, 'Do you read much?'

'Not much these days – I've been too busy. But last year, when I split with Jill and sold the business, I had time on my hands and got back into it. I loved reading when I was a boy.'

'What sort of things?'

'It varied. I used to read two or three books by an author then try something different. Not like Col – when we were at university, he used to shut himself away some weekends and plough through a writer's complete works. The worst was Tolkien. I didn't see him for a week.'

'Fast reader all the same.'

'Oh yeah, much faster than me. I imagine that's what happened with Winstanley – Col discovered the guy and immersed himself in his words, only he got sucked under this time. At uni he'd always want to talk about who he'd just read to the exclusion of everything else, but in those days it soon wore off and you'd have a bit of peace before the next craze.'

'We are what we are,' Sarah said and made a clicking sound with her tongue, as if she'd just uttered the last word. 'You still haven't told me who you read.'

'I suppose I began with kids adventure stories – none of which I can remember – then graduated to adult books. The first writer that really made an impression was Ian Fleming. If I'm honest what I was actually after was info about sex (I was thirteen or so) and somehow I felt that because the films were on TV, the books were legitimised. You know, I could read them quite openly and get the sex stuff without upsetting Mum and Dad. They were on display in Mum's library too.'

'Typical boy.'

'Yeah. I read DH Lawrence for the same reason, although I could tell he was a sophisticated writer after a few pages. Then I began to get into the characters and the descriptions of nature. Those two authors, Fleming and Lawrence sort sum up how I read in those days. I bounced between thriller writers like le Carré and Forsyth and serious ones such as Lawrence, Greene – and Dickens, of course.'

'You have read him then? Dickens?'

'Watch it.'

I can still see her smiling at me. I'd provoked a reaction that was part triumph at having rattled my cage, part exultation at the crackling excitement that momentarily fizzed between us.

Then she did something to get us back on an even keel – poured some wine in all probability.

'Do *you* read alot?'

'Like you I used to when I was in my teens but life took off and became very complicated and I never seemed to have the time. It was only when Griff got the London studio and started working up there for months on end that I began reading again – to fill the weekday nights. It's now one of my greatest pleasures because even when everything else is going wrong I can still get absorbed in a book.'

'Yeah, I can understand that. I think I read as a boy to escape from whatever was bugging me, or from insecurities – and there were shedloads of those. If I was down, I'd read and I'd soon feel better or else my mind would get sorted while I was absent in that other world.'

'Have you ever read Hardy?'

'Only a couple.'

'*Return of the Native*?'

'No.'

'You should. I'm reading it now. You can borrow it when I've finished.'

'Thanks.'

'There's an amazing piece at the beginning, where Hardy describes this extraordinary wild heath at dusk and creates an image of a world below in darkness while the sky is still daylight. It's an effect that reminds you of that painting of a streetlamp by René Magritte.'

'I know the one you mean. It's a really weird painting.'

'It's so eerie. Anyway, this trick of the light is something that happens on the heath often and people working there find themselves in limbo, not knowing whether they should pack up and go home or keep working. It's a metaphor for how we're often not quite sure where we are in life or whether or not something has actually begun. Because the boundary between the end of one thing and the beginning of another can be so ambiguous. Not a boundary at all but an area of uncertainty.'

For a moment I'd contemplated making a funny comment but when she stopped what I actually said was, 'Thank you, you've made my day.'

She looked at me, uncertain whether I was being facetious, and I had to move swiftly to reassure her.

'No, no I mean it. I don't know exactly what you're talking about but I get the gist and I'll read the book and think about it. What I'm trying to say is I don't often have conversations like this and really appreciate it.'

She laughed, contentedly.

I read the beginning of *The Return of the Native* – though I didn't wait until Sarah finished her copy but bought one off Amazon later that evening. I did wonder why I felt compelled to do so but to one side of me the answer was becoming obvious. Buying the book was like sharing something with Sarah.

I also believed it was an opportunity to see things from her point of view and understand a little of how her mind worked. I noted down what she said about the dusk and the bright sky and its metaphorical significance.

Even before the novel arrived, I began mulling over the idea of people on the heath not being able to tell what time it was because of the strange trick of the light. The metaphor made sense and I could think of areas of my own life where this sort of ambiguity existed.

My relationship with Jill, for a start. On the one hand we'd split up but on the other we were still good friends and both, I think, harboured a desire to get back together. But then if I wanted her, why wasn't I doing anything about making it happen? Was getting back together an ideal I needed to keep me going while I remained single?

I reckon I knew deep down I would never live with her again. And the reason I wasn't pursuing her was I'd gone through so much since we split. My life had moved on – yet I decided I couldn't be absolutely sure until I embarked on a new relationship. I was in that twilight world Sarah had spoken of.

Another ambiguity was the way me and Sarah played down Jill and Griff. When I thought about this, it was as if the nature of my ambiguous situation altered and I was forced to conclude that the new limbo I was in was one between friendliness towards Sarah and embarking on a relationship.

With hindsight I know I was beginning to fall in love, although at the time the symptoms were difficult to describe. Or more accurately the symptoms were there (once I admitted I was suppressing my feelings about Jill, a list readily supplied itself) and I could describe them perfectly well, but what I couldn't do was accept what I knew. I was split in two.

My rational self was plodding along as normal but then there was this new self. During those picnics and in the weeks that followed, I was overtaken by instincts that were so powerful they scared me. These were emotions I hadn't felt in years. I wasn't even sure they'd been this powerful when I met Jill, though I suppose they were. They were the sort of things I'd experienced in my teens and early twenties – only in those days there wasn't the rational part to reflect on what was happening. I simply did things and couldn't comment on my actions, nor the impulses driving them.

How did these emotions show themselves? Well, first off there was the exhilaration I felt when talking to Sarah. But this was more than little moments of heightened electricity. There was intense eye contact and what she said fascinated me and I found I could respond in more interesting ways than usual. And I didn't have to try. The bravado that was there when I said things like my comment about cannabis vanished.

There was also this persistent tightening in my chest, a feeling that persisted, in fact was almost stronger, when I was away from Sarah and could be at its strongest when I was cycling home.

My instinctive self wanted to make love to her but my rational one could see there were problems. I've never been a great one for sleeping with someone else's partner and even if I detected that things between her and Griff were a bit rocky, equally there was still a definite bond. We all belonged to the same community too. Call me old-fashioned but the thought of the village's disapproval was a live consideration. And this wasn't just down to me having a business to protect but to the way I'd been brought up. You'd have to be pretty smitten to put yourself through a local scandal. There were times when the realisation that I might be on the verge of a relationship with Sarah frightened me.

Another curious problem my rational side came up with was that it didn't find Sarah attractive. She was so slight and frail.

She made Jill, who before her hedge laying malarkey was someone I'd have said was slight and frail, look chunky. The rational me thought there was something odd and undernourished about Sarah. I knew Mum would have taken one look at her and said, 'Sickly little thing.'

But there was a strange enchantment going on because when I was with Sarah I forgot she was thin. The visual got distorted by messages from her eyes, her smile and laugh, and by what I can only describe as the seriousness with which she lived life.

Her face was what you concentrated on. Its miniature beauty and animation drew you in so you forgot – not that she was underweight – but that that mattered. It made you re-evaluate your notions of what constituted beauty, so that you observed her closely and realised that what seemed skeletal was finely-delineated.

I felt moments of irrational jealousy too. When Sarah said she was seeing friends after the first picnic, I imagined a sympathetic artistic type with a shoulder made for crying on who would take advantage of her loneliness.

There was no doubt I was in love. But as the evidence mounted, I'd still find myself staring at it in disbelief and tell myself that one flutter of my heart didn't amount to much. To paraphrase TS Eliot, who Col put me on to at uni, I couldn't yet take much reality.

By the time Sarah brought the last picnic I'd started to look reality in the eye.

It was a couple of days after we talked about Griff and reading and I was setting a fire in the field below the wood. When we began working in the copse back in July, we used to make little fires inside a clearing we opened specially but as it was getting so dry I rethought things. As soon as the cornfield below was cut, I asked the farmer if I could do the burning there. He was fine about it, quipping that he'd prefer that than have the wood go up and his hedges turned to charcoal.

Anyway, I was setting the fire and thinking about Sarah and it suddenly struck me that if I felt like I did and she felt the same, we would end up making love.

It's hard to describe the quality of this realisation because I'd thought about sleeping with her before. This time the thought stunned me like a hammer blow. I could visualise us making love and I knew in a tangible way that this was going to be the outcome. I tried asking myself whether I'd be prepared to actually go that far – as if I was trying to apply the brakes – but the answer came without hesitation. I felt that yes, I would, without a shadow of a doubt. I was terrified.

I was frightened because there was now something pre-meditated about what would happen. This was different to the spontaneous passion between me and Kim which ignited so fast I hadn't time to think. With Sarah, the instinctive side of me was taking over my rational self and forcing it to see things its way.

Yet during the last picnic my situation again seemed ambiguous and I almost reached the conclusion, with a certain amount of relief, that nothing was going to happen after all.

Colin didn't work at the wood that afternoon but when Sarah arrived he was with her. Apparently he'd called round to discuss the management of the field where the pigs were and she made sure he came along.

I pretended to be pleased but inside I was twitching with jealousy. I conjured up a lurid fantasy about there being something between those two. I was struck by how easy they were and how strong their eye contact was. For much of the time I felt like an outsider. I then tried to tell myself that they were bound to be close because they were old friends. It also occurred to me that Sarah wouldn't want to give anything away about us in front of Col.

But soon I began to think that maybe I'd got the wrong impression about how she felt. She was as easy with Col as she was with me, so perhaps that was just her way.

It was only when Col and I finished eating and the wine bottle was almost empty that something happened to tantalise me yet further.

Sarah began packing things away and Col said he should stow

the tools in the shepherd's hut. I offered to do this but he said it was his turn and Sarah teased him by agreeing. She added, 'Colin, if it wasn't for Tom, you'd still be here by Christmas.'

'I know, I know,' he said and looked at me. 'And I really do appreciate all you've done, my old mate. Don't think I don't.'

But despite him saying he must go, he showed no sign of moving. I detected that Sarah was getting a little irritated. She sighed exaggeratedly as she put away the last jars and I remember wondering if she was annoyed with Col.

Whether he picked up on her mood, I don't know, but he soon got to his feet and said, 'Oh dear, can't delay any longer. It's nice here – and it's so civilised having a picnic, Sarah. Thank you.'

After he went, she stood up and closed the lid of her basket.

She moved towards me holding it by its handle and I suddenly realised I still had my silver beaker. We looked at each other and she smiled.

I said, 'Sarah,' and she set down the basket. She looked as if she was about to crouch beside me and I panicked.

I said, 'It's just the beaker. I forgot I had it.' I grinned at her. 'Brilliant picnic. Thanks, as always.'

She smiled back, a tight, abstracted smile. She seemed puzzled if not disappointed. She picked up the basket and said, 'Fine. I think I'll take this to the car and then come back for Col.'

I said, 'Let me carry it,' but she wasn't having that.

'Why don't you help Col. And tell him I need to be home by seven.'

As I gathered together the remaining tools, I thought, 'Why did she put down the basket? Was she really about to crouch beside me? Why did her behaviour make me bluster?'

I think being caught out like that lowered my self-esteem so I was left feeling both that I'd missed a trick and I was imagining things. What was she expecting? That I would kiss her? That was the impression I'd got, as if somehow Col being there made her feel she was being deprived of me in the same way I felt deprived of her.

During the following days I successfully convinced myself I was a fool, that there was nothing in it and this idea that she had wanted me to kiss her when she put down the basket was a big delusion. Yet the fact she put it down seemed so tell-tale and this realisation made me feel foolish for different reasons. I felt inadequate.

But then everything changed for the last time. Ten days later, on the Tuesday of our last week at the copse, she phoned my mobile and asked when we were packing up. I said I was going to finish on Thursday, adding I would be on my own for a change because Col had something important on. She asked if I'd like to look round the Folly afterwards to celebrate the end of the project.

I completed everything at the copse that mattered that Tuesday afternoon and the whole of Wednesday. I wanted to be able to bike over to it on the Thursday around five, tidy up a few last wispy bits on the oaks and have a beer for old times sake.

I had no intention of turning up at Sarah's stinking of smoke nor looking like I'd been pulled through a hedge backwards. I did want to look like I might have done some work, although if she twigged I was cleaner than I should be, I wouldn't mind. The object of the exercise was to give myself the best chance of success.

I dressed myself up in a pair of long shorts with a ton of pockets – a fashion statement suggested by Tara earlier in the summer, after she saw my old ones – and a pale blue, designer sports shirt. In my knapsack were my deck shoes, a pack of condoms and some expensive cologne.

I reached the entrance to the Folly at about 7.20, opened the heavy gate and wheeled my bike to the front of the lodge.

Before heading up the drive, I had a nose round. So far as I could tell – the windows were uncurtained but had vertical bars on the inside – the whole ground floor was a studio. Then, as my eyes adjusted to the light, I realised that the space went right up to the roof, the first and attic floors having been taken out. There was no sign of any actual sculptures, let alone Griff's infamous Armageddon Pots, although there were several giant armatures and three chain pulleys suspended from rails where the attic floor beams should have been.

What with the bars on the windows, it looked like an abandoned S&M brothel, or else a slaughterhouse. Either way, it was creepy.

Walking up the drive, I wondered at Griff and Sarah and asked myself what made them tick? And did they tick at the same rate? One seemed so immediately gregarious but underneath was impenetrable, the other was self-effacing and reserved on the surface but warm, generous, intelligent and kind when she let her guard down. But then there was much she kept hidden too.

Maybe they were well suited.

All of a sudden I was in the throes of another massive loss of confidence. It was as if I was staring down at myself walking between these vast trees, which still looked, despite their unruliness, like the aristocratic specimens they undoubtedly were. Hand picked by a Victorian landscape gardener for a wealthy patron. Jill could tell you the full story just by looking at them.

And here was I, a lad from Maldon who'd dressed himself in his seducing kit, when in all probability Sarah, this modern-day lady of the manor, really did only want to show him her painted ceiling.

What did I know about art and architecture, what with my tacky theme pubs and cartoon pump plates? Culture was Jill's department.

But somehow I kept going. I told myself, just trust your instincts. The culture bit is only superficial. What you're talking about here is a relationship between two human beings. I took deep breaths and began to feel calmer.

About two-thirds the way up the escarpment the drive forked. The main part continued towards where the big house used to be and Sarah told me on one of our picnics that about two hundred yards further on there was a high fence and padlocked gates. Apparently the family who'd lived in the place still owned the site and had hopes they'd one day rebuild it. She thought they even believed they'd be able to buy back the Folly and woods. She felt they couldn't accept they'd lost the high social status that was embodied by the house, and in any case if their son kept losing money on his computer business they'd soon not be able to afford more than a two-up, two-down.

The other, narrower fork of the drive led to a deep terrace in the escarpment, formed by quarrying when the big house was originally built hundreds of years ago. When the house was a nice Tudor manor, not the Victorian dinosaur it became.

The drive to the Folly rose a little then levelled off but even though I was only a few paces from the building I couldn't see any trace of it because the woodland was so impenetrable. There were Irish yews on each side and a huge, thick-trunked cedar of Lebanon to my left, then masses of spindly trees and unkempt shrubs everywhere in between forming dense thickets. I could understand why the land agent kept going on about sylvicultural management.

But then I caught a glimpse of the archway Sarah'd told me about. It was some twenty feet high and built of grey stone, most of which was covered with moss and green, yellow and turquoise lichens which explained why it was so hard to distinguish. I stopped for a moment and tried to make out the architectural details beneath the patina. There were Corinthian columns either side which looked like exotic palms in their green livery. Then there was a hint of some sort of box vaulting on the underside of the arch and above it a rectangular frieze depicting figures that were almost impossible to define. It could have been one of those Indian sexually-explicit bas-reliefs for all I knew or something on a South American temple. This sense of the exotic was added to by the feeling of being in a jungle.

I looked to the right of the arch and began to make out brick outbuildings also covered in moss and lichen, not to mention festoons of ivy. On the left was the Folly itself, again of greened brick but with stone around the windows. Most of the windows were narrow with clover-leaf tops, apart from this massive, and I mean *massive*, traceried one on the second floor. Its overall shape was a flat arch but it was divided into vertical sections by mullions embellished by leaf and branch carvings like they were pollarded trees. Others looked like they had vines growing up them. At the top of the two sturdiest mullions were leafy but empty niches. The upper third of the central bay was occupied by a carved wagon-wheel design like you'd find in a church, complete with stained glass.

Above this window were stone battlements.

I moved on, went through the arch and rang the bell, which you did by pulling a gigantic stirrup-like thing beside the iron-bound door.

It was about a minute before Sarah appeared. She was wearing a long dress, as usual, although this one was very different from its predecessors, which all suggested the classic – to my way of thinking, at least – English summer type. This one was made out of a soft fabric which was almost like T-shirt cotton. It was patterned with dark blue and white diagonal stripes and followed the shape of her body closely. The effect of how the stripes undulated as she moved was immediately mesmeric. It was obvious she wasn't wearing a bra.

The dress made her look elegant and although it enhanced her figure it didn't disguise her thinness. I felt, almost straightaway, that she was saying, this is the way I am – I'm not hiding anymore.

My mouth went dry as soon as I saw her.

She had one of her tiny cigarettes between her fingers, half-smoked. She casually flicked it onto the gravel, smiled and said, 'Welcome to the Folly.'

We looked at each other for a second or two. For half that time I was uncertain what to do but then I stepped forward and kissed her on both cheeks.

'This is an extraordinary place, Sarah,' I said, glancing at the arch.

'It's my pride and joy.'

'I knew it was going to be a humdinger, from what you told me, but I never expected this. It's got a fairytale, magical quality.'

'The outside,' she said pointedly, 'is overgrown. That's my

concession to Griff. But the inside is his concession to me.'

She raised her eyebrows and turned round, saying, 'As you are about to see.'

I followed her inside and shut the door behind me.

I found myself in a large hallway with a bare-stone vaulted ceiling and this amazing black and white tiled floor.

'Is this floor original?'

'Sort of. It's Georgian and came from the dower house that used to stand here before the Folly. When the Victorians built this place they must have salvaged the tiles and reused them. It's quite an odd effect, isn't it?'

'It's because the outside is so medieval-looking. But then there's a clash between the Folly and the arch, isn't there?'

'That's what attracted us. It was about the only time we've agreed! Most things we've done here have involved compromise. Bound to be the case, I suppose – we're both individuals.'

'I thought you said the inside was your domain.'

'What I meant was that it's kept spick and span. OK, I've done most of the designing but I've had to let Griff have his say. Left to his own devices, of course, he'd live in a pigsty and wouldn't have altered a thing from the moment we moved in. But once I began doing it up he wanted to have some input.'

'Sounds complicated.'

We looked at each other and raised our eyebrows.

'Aren't relationships always?' she asked.

'Yeah.'

I wandered over to the long antique table which took up the whole of the far wall. Its top was highly polished and was bare apart from a rectangular granite vase with a single freesia stem in it. I smelt the flower. The scent took me right back to my childhood. Freesias were Mum's second-favourite flowers after chrysanthemums.

'Beautiful – the smell of the flower,' I said turning back towards Sarah. 'I know what you mean about working together being difficult. I once thought of designing pubs with Jill. It was a nice dream but in practice it would've been a disaster!'

Above the table was a vast mirror with a thick stainless steel frame. When I first saw it I thought, how crass. Then, as I smelt the freesia again and took in the tableau with me in the foreground and Sarah some way behind, I noticed the frame was slightly pitted, as if damaged. I looked closer and realised it had some sort of design on it.

'It's a Damien.'

I looked at the frame more closely. Its uprights had these faint, stylised mushroom clouds on them, and along the bottom were scenes suggesting a nuclear holocaust. There were crumbling cities, lines of burnt out cars on fractured highways and in the foreground the tortured remains of churches and warehouses. The images were littered with bodies and body-parts.

'The big buildings are superstores,' said Sarah. She was moving towards me. 'Look carefully and you can see the trade names.'

'It's powerful but there's something strange about the way it's done – it's almost as if the images are being washed away before your eyes.'

'Good way of describing it! He was so proud of that effect. He doesn't usually do mirrors but he played about with some back in 2000.'

She was standing beside me now.

'He did the engravings in full relief first then poured acid on. The ripples were created by blowing it about with drinking straws.'

'Artists, eh? Wild.'

I glanced at her and wondered if this was my moment but she was opening the table's middle drawer.

'And that's not all.'

She produced what looked like a TV remote. She pointed it at the mirror and pressed a button. Immediately there was a blinding flash inside the mirror. This was followed about ten seconds later by great splashes of red light, as if blood was being splattered onto the other side of the glass, which began spreading

286

and merging until the whole thing was red. Within seconds of that the mirror was silver again.

'Wow!'

'I don't much care for Damien's stuff, but I fell in love with this piece and Griff swapped it for an Armageddon pot.'

'Cool. Something else you agreed about.'

She smiled and thought for a moment. 'I suppose we agree more times than I let on. I'm always angry with him at this time of year. Put it down to the heat.'

This wasn't what I wanted to hear although I didn't feel she was being altogether serious. Her smile was turning mischievous and my heart rate increased. But then she was moving away from me and saying, 'Now, the full tour.'

The guest bedrooms, three of them, all en-suite, were on the ground floor. There was also a large laundry room by the back door with a freezer room opposite. There was a service lift from the latter to the kitchen which was on the second floor.

Each bedroom was 'themed', according to Sarah, although I'd have said two were only themed after a fashion.

It was on this floor that Griff's influence was most in evidence, two rooms having been designed by him. One was a sort of wild-west Pandora's box – the kind of theming, I could understand – that had started off as an accurate recreation of a cat-house boudoir in one of his favourite Clint Eastwood movies but was now chock-full of eclectic cowboy memorabilia he'd collected on US promo-trips.

His other room was more of a concept than a theme, which Sarah said took its cue from a London pub several hundred years ago. As soon as she opened the door, I knew exactly what she was on about. The pub was legendary in the licensee trade. One of its bedrooms had been fitted out to confuse drunkards – they were bundled in there after they passed out and when they woke up they found themselves in a living nightmare. As in that room, Griff had had all the furniture – bed, chest-of-drawers, wardrobe, bedside table, even a washbasin in one corner – bolted onto the ceiling, which had a rug in the middle and polished floorboards round the edge. The bed itself was chaos (a 'homage to Tracey') with rumpled, stained sheets littered with beer bottles, sandwich containers, used condoms and porn mags.

The actual floor of the room was black, same as the walls, and had a stiff light flex sticking up in the middle with an upside-down shade on the end.

'How does anybody stay in here?' I asked after I'd got over my initial delighted amazement.

'Simple,' Sarah said and slid open a little invisible cover beside the door. She began pressing buttons and a bed, identical to the one on the ceiling, only neatly made-up, slid out from one of the walls, followed by a wardrobe, chest-of-drawers and bedside table. Then a door sprang open leading to the en-suite.

'Jesus!' I exclaimed.

'Makes my effort next door look rather tame,' she said.

I followed her to the last room. Until she began explaining it I couldn't understand what it was all about. It could have been a room in a council house – well, maybe that's being snobbish but what I mean is it was so banal it felt like just any old bedroom. One that I imagine must be replicated the length and breadth of the UK, amongst poorer households. Or, more accurately, must have been replicated in the fifties and sixties, perhaps even earlier. The furniture was like Utility stuff and while Jill and I had collected some of it, we'd always been choosey. We wouldn't have looked at this lot in a million years. It spoke of student digs and cheap boarding houses. What was the theme?

'I'm not sure I get it, to be quite honest,' I said to Sarah.

She smiled. 'No one does. I always have to explain. It's the bedroom I had when I was a girl – or at least something similar. I suspect it's a little grimmer but that's artistic licence.'

'It is pretty grim, I must say. It's funny, though, I don't suppose it would be that grim if I hadn't assumed you were from a wealthy background.'

'That's the joke – I am. Well, my father's done his best to lose everything, but he started off with a fair bit and Mum came with a small fortune, including a medieval farmhouse.'

'Was that where this room was?'

'Absolutely.'

'Was he cruel, your dad?'

'I never thought so – for a lot of my childhood, at least. It was only when I was in my late teens that the penny began to drop.'

'What about your mum? She must have wanted better for you?'

'I don't think so. She came from a long line of make-doers. I think that for her a bedroom was just somewhere you slept. The remainder of the time she expected you to be outside playing or riding during the summer or inside curled up by the sitting-room fire during the winter. And the rest of the house was jolly nice. She also set great store by hearty meals. I wasn't a deprived child and it was the same for my brother and sister. What mum didn't understand was the idea of you wanting personal space. I liked to read in my own room. She never did get it.'

'My mum was great like that – as I told you, she used to ask me whether I wanted anything doing in my bedroom every eighteen months or so and then she'd get someone in to carry out the work when we were on our summer holidays. I know I was spoilt rotten but I loved it – and loved her for it. Still what she did was tame by the standards of today's kids.'

'I'm sure you're right but you were very lucky all the same.' She looked about her. 'You know, the big thing I asked myself when I was designing this room was why didn't I ever change anything. I could have run up some new curtains or painted the walls a different colour. I don't suppose my parents would've objected. And if they did, at least I'd have tried. What bugs me is I didn't even do that!'

'You put a couple of posters up.'

'Big deal.'

'I like Björk.'

'Do you? That's from *Debut*.'

'I've got it.'

'At least I had music.'

There was a radio-CD player on top of the bookshelves, albeit a fairly primitive one.

'And my books, of course – they were essential.'

'You kept a diary,' I said pointing at the desk.

'For a time, yes. Though that's not the real one.'

She breathed in sharply through her nose. I felt I'd trespassed on something. I remember thinking, girls and their diaries!

'OK,' she said, 'onwards and upwards.'

'This floor is where we sleep,' she said.

We'd just reached the first-floor landing which led off the stone spiral staircase that occupied a corner turret at the back of the building. I expected her to step onto the landing but she stayed put.

'I won't show you our bedroom today – I haven't had a chance to clean. I wouldn't want you to think we were obsessed with Tracey!'

I suppressed my puerile disappointment. 'You're in charge. It's an honour to be looking round.'

'My pleasure. There's also a mini-gym on this floor, and our offices. The bedroom's en-suite, of course, complete with sunken bath. Griff's idea. It's mosaicked and looks Roman. I thought it was far too decadent to begin with but I've got used to it.'

'I considered something similar for the mill, but it wouldn't have looked right. Talking of the mill – you must come and have a butchers sometime.'

'I'd love to.'

So saying, she set off up the stairs.

'And this is it!'

'Shit! Sorry.'

She ignored me.

The first thing you noticed was the gigantic window at the far end, which seemed implausibly vast from the inside. There were two strong beams of sunlight cutting in diagonally like the shafts of giant spears. It was like you were in the nave of a cathedral.

Gradually I began to take in the detail. There were medieval tapestries on the bare stone walls and Gothic furniture that made you think you'd stepped into the great hall of one of Henry VIII's palaces.

I followed behind Sarah, not sure quite where to look next, there was so much to see.

'Well, what do you think?'

'I'm stunned, to be honest.'

'Griff left this room to me. This really is my creation.'

'Astounding.'

'It's taken ages – and it's still not finished.'

She pointed to a kind of alcove beside the stair turret where a tower scaffold was parked.

'I've another four panels to do.'

I looked at the ceiling – there were perhaps forty panels all told, most of which displayed a different coat of arms. The unpainted panels were above the stonking great fireplace half-way down the room.

'You couldn't believe the state of this when we bought the place. Unlike the lower floors, which have stone ceilings, this one's wood and it'd almost completely rotted away. The lead on the battlements had gone – actually there was a Scots pine growing up there.'

'Seriously?'

'Absolutely – it was only a matter of time before the walls started collapsing.'

'So the woodwork's brand new?'

'Yes, but it's a faithful replica of the Victorian ceiling. We had this room done first so the building would have a proper roof. We camped out downstairs until this was completed – all bar the panels – then moved up here lock, stock and barrel while it was done. One of the longest jobs was Griff's upside-down room. You wouldn't believe the health and safety issues! Let alone the technical problems with the computerised electronics! But it's these panels that've taken the longest of all.'

'And you've painted the lot.'

'Yes. I had to be trained first. English Heritage tried to insist we use a specialist firm but I wanted to have a go myself. I told them I had an artistic background but they still made me do training courses. I studied thirteenth century painting and gilding techniques at weekends at the Courtauld. It was eighteen months before I picked up a paintbrush here!'

'It must have been fun, though, learning new skills. Even I can see they're beautifully done.'

'Thank you. By the way, would you like some wine?'

'Yeah, if you're offering.'

She wandered over to the kitchen area which was laid out round another big fireplace on the opposite wall to the window. There was an Aga standing in front of the grate with its flue going up the chimney. The whole front of the fireplace, though, was covered over with fire-resistant glass that the flue passed through. As Sarah told me while she was fixing the wine she and Griff had to seal off the flue to reduce the fire risk – a condition of their insurance – and decided that it was best to use glass so you could see the grate's brick lining and the genuine medieval fireback they'd discovered when they first reopened it.

'You see the Folly was a temple to the Middle Ages,' she said as she handed me my glass of chilled rosé. We clinked our glasses together – perfunctorily because she wanted to get on with her story. She was obviously loving talking about her home.

'Along with a lot of Victorians, the Saxtons who owned this place believed they could get back to a more authentic culture through the study of English Gothic. The family were friends of William Morris, who lived just down the road, of course.'

She opened her tobacco tin and set it down on one of two butcher's blocks and started rolling a cigarette.

'Hence the archaic representation of the shields. Each is the coat of arms of one of the then head of the Saxton family's political cronies or relatives. When the house and Folly were completed he held a huge tournament to which they all came. It took place on the Marsh and there was feasting and jousting and everyone dressed up in medieval costume.'

'Makes Col's pageant seem a bit tame. A bit less mad too, I suppose.'

'I'm not sure about the less mad part.'

She lit her cigarette and inhaled deeply.

'Yeah, you're right. That is going a little far.'

'He's actually been madder since the pageant than before.'

She was walking down the room towards the window. She held her glass and cigarette in one hand, the bottle of wine in the other. I followed.

'He's been all over the place at the copse – when he can be bothered to turn up, that is.'

'What's this about important business?'

'I don't know. Something with Andy, if I'm not mistaken. They're probably weighing up the pros and cons of growing an organic cereal crop – well, that's what I reckon, but you can never tell with them. They're both secretive, although in different ways. You know, it's funny but when I first met Col again, in the Parker, he was with Andy and Andy gave him a computer disc – furtively, like they were a couple of spies. I'd forgotten about that until this afternoon. Don't know what made me think of it.'

'How very odd.'

There was more light streaming into the room than ever from the setting sun. I fancied the light was making her dress see-through as she moved but the effect was so intermittent and teasing I couldn't be sure. But when she bent forward and placed the wine bottle on the stone dais in front of the window I was ninety-nine percent sure she was wearing a thong, something I'd first suspected when we were coming upstairs.

'Yeah, well, anyway.'

'I feel so sorry for Fiona. Has she mentioned anything to you yet?'

'No but she doesn't look any happier.'

'She's not one for complaining. Keeps it all bottled up inside – like my mother. Well, like me, if I'm honest. Like you?'

'I don't tend to talk about my inner feelings, no.'

She was standing in the centre of the window. The big metal-framed casement was open, although you got the impression a room of this size would never be anything other than cool, with or without open windows. On a stifling day like this one, the temperature was perfect. She flicked her cigarette outside, sipped her wine, put her glass on the stone window-sill and turned round.

293

'No you don't,' she said softly. 'You appear to – sometimes I think you're never going to stop but there's much you keep to yourself.'

I stepped towards her, gazing into her eyes. My breathing seemed to slow to nothing but my heart rate got faster. I could not believe what was happening even though I'd dreamt of it. I put my arms round her shoulders, looking up, and we kissed.

Her lips tasted of wine and the spice of tobacco and her. I caressed her body, felt her move beneath the material of her dress. I was surprised how strong she was – she was slight but her skin was lithe and firm.

She slipped her hands under my shirt and ran them over my back.

Then she pushed me away gently.

She crossed her arms and took hold of her dress then pulled it up and over her head. She dropped it on the floor. She was wearing a gleaming white string.

Looking back at suddenly being in that situation with her the moment seems almost like trauma. The single-minded desire surging through me and through her, the sense I'd turned the world upside down, gone from polite conversation to physical intimacy in seconds, the knowledge – and this is maybe hindsight talking – I'd been drawn into something cataclysmic that I could only leave through suffering: all these things blew my mind.

'Come on,' she whispered.

She took my hand and led me to the nearest sofa. It was covered in green velvet and was deliciously soft.

The rest is broken into fragments in my memory. Snatches of seeing amongst the darkness coloured with touch, smell and taste, so that the picture is disjointed, fractured.

The delicacy of eyelashes so lightly closed. The tiny folds of her belly as she leans into me. My shirt sleeve slipping down my arm. Her hands on my chest. My fingers under the elastic of her string moving between her legs. The lipstick smudge of her nipple and my thumb teasing its core. The creaminess of her breasts. My hand in the pocket of my crumpled shorts. The shaved innocence of her. Foil tearing. Pink latex unrolling.

Bright teeth revealed through parted lips. The fineness of her lovely hair. My penis entering her and the seemingly effortless rhythm of our bodies. The gossamer underside of her thigh. Her twisting torso. A glimpse of her rosebud anus. Her tongue pressed against the edges of her teeth. Beads of sweat between her breasts. Tickling, feathery hair bent out over the top of her tiny ear as I sink into oblivion.

It's almost impossible, Mart, to find the words to continue when recalling how happy and confident I imagined myself to be that evening. But I suppose you'd say if I take things step by step, the words will supply themselves. So be it.

We must have lain there asleep in each other's arms for maybe half an hour. We woke at precisely the same time, or so it appeared, and regarded each other with astonishment.

I remember how young and perfect she looked – her face and body were quite flawless in that twilight.

We made love again.

Later she got up and said she'd find us another bottle of wine. I pointed to the one on the dais.

'It'll be too warm.'

'You're the boss.'

'I'll get something to eat too. We can take everything onto the battlements.'

'OK.'

I wandered over to the window and looked at the stained glass. Although it was nearly dark I could clearly make out knights and maidens. Knights slaying dragons with maidens looking on. Knights tilting at one another before a whole crowd of women. I thought of my initial response to the window from the inside – that it made the room seem like the nave of a cathedral – and Sarah saying the Folly was a shrine to the chivalric ideal. I then thought about William Morris and his unusual domestic arrangements with Janie Burden and Rossetti and took some comfort from the fact that the Victorian age was (just like the chivalric age itself) as flawed and morally ambiguous as our own. I don't know why I thought like this. I wasn't conscious of feeling guilty. I felt elated. I felt jubilant. But there must have been some guilt there in retrospect.

We went up to the battlements and Sarah switched on the low level lighting. We hadn't put on any clothes and the freedom of being naked was amazing.

Much of the roof area was covered in decking but there was a broad strip of lawn down one side and numerous natural clay and colourfully glazed tubs of flowers. There was a huge slatted dining table and chairs, recliners, coffee tables, sunloungers on the lawn and several gas heaters for the winter. In the corner opposite the stair turret was a garden shed.

She put down the bottle of wine and a little silk bag which contained her tobacco tin on one of the coffee tables and I set out the dishes of nibbles from my tray. She then poured the wine and switched off the lights using a remote.

'Come and have a look at the view.'

We crossed to the side overlooking the valley. We were above the trees up there and although it was dark you could still make out the fields and the fringe-like hedgerows. There were the pale shapes of the fields of uncut corn, the bright ones where there was just stubble, the grey of the water meadows and the darkness of the plough. Through the middle of the valley ran the river which still caught, here and there, patches of lit sky, even though when you looked up there seemed little evidence of it, apart from a blossom of light where the sun must have only recently passed below the horizon.

'It makes me think of *The Return of the Native*,' I whispered.

'Did I give you it?'

'No, I bought it off Amazon.'

'I meant to put it out but it must have got lost in the chaos of the bedroom.'

'So it really is a Tracey.'

296

'Not far off.'

'Anyway, what do you think – like the heath?'

'A bit but the effect's almost over now. You're right, though, the valley does put you in mind of the heath every so often. The Marsh may have been tamed a long time ago but it's still got a wonderful primitiveness about it. The hedges are so unruly. Remnants of the medieval forest, I daresay. At the time of the Conquest it was described as a wilderness.'

'So Col told me.'

'He is quite good on the history of the area. Better when he talks about that than Winstanley.'

'Can't argue with that.'

She took my hand. 'Come and have something to eat – you must be starving.'

We lay down together on a double recliner and I reached out for food every so often and we sipped our wine and talked about *The Return of the Native*. Sarah rolled a cigarette. After she finished smoking it we began kissing and I said I'd go downstairs and get something.

'No need,' she said. 'There're some in my bag.'

We made love and fell asleep.

Sarah was awake before me.

I was woken by her shouting at me. I'd just been dreaming of the people on Egdon Heath lighting bonfires on fireworks night. Only the bonfire party I was at wasn't Hardy's but one Mum and Dad were organising. My father was in charge of course and me and my friends had to stand behind a rope fence, although Mum was telling Dad he ought to allow me to light one small firework on my own – my very first. 'Oh come on, Dad, let the lad have a go.' Dad wasn't having any of it, although I was sure he'd give in in the end. Mum turned and smiled down at me. 'Health and safety officer, he is,' she said.

But whether he did give in I'll never know because I was suddenly jerked back into the land of the living by Sarah shouting, 'Jesus, Tom, Jesus!'

I remember feeling like I'd been hit over the head with something or maybe that there was a pebble lodged in my brain. Anyway my head was throbbing and the back of my neck ached. 'What's happening? What is it? What the fuck, Sarah?'

'The valley's going up.'

'Going up? Going where? What do you mean?'

'Come and look!'

I stood up and immediately felt giddy. I hate being woken in the middle of the night – always have ever since I was a nipper. I think I started off going in the wrong direction but Sarah screaming 'Fuck!' helped me get my bearings. I staggered over to her and saw what she was on about.

It was a dead clear night with a moon, nearly full, and so many stars you could hardly put a matchstick between them. Though when you looked carefully at the extraordinary panorama of earth and sky you soon realised about a fifth of the heavens were black and there was a stiff breeze getting up from the west which was carrying the smoke from the fire that was gorging itself on the field of maize in the centre of the valley. It could've been the smoke that gave me my headache.

But to begin with I didn't smell the smoke – it was like I needed to see the flames before I could put a name to what I was sensing. And nor, I think, did I realise straightaway how moonlit the night was. The first I knew of it was when I clocked Sarah and saw how silver she was and thought, fleetingly, of how the plankton make you in the North Sea.

'Shit! Shit! Holy shit! What's happening?'

'I don't know. Well, apart from the obvious. It's awful!' Sarah's voice was little more than a whisper.

I looked at her hands. 'Where's your mobile?'

She looked at her hands too. 'I'm sorry, I didn't think. I was paralysed almost. I was fascinated by the flames – and appalled!'

'Sarah! Your mobile!'

Then I remembered her bag. I rushed to it, got the phone and switched it on.

'Here put in the code.'

'No need,' she said and pointed straight ahead.

In the distance were electric blue intermittent flashes coming from the direction of the village where there was a fire station. Then I thought I could see another lot further off and to the south, though I couldn't be sure at that stage.

Seeing those lights was like a release. There was nothing more we could do. I stared into the valley at the flaming field of maize. Like Sarah I was both fascinated and appalled, although I soon noticed that the fire seemed to be dying down. I also saw how there were sudden splooshes of what looked like liquid flame spurting in arcs from the nearest hedgeline. Then pockets of fire raged for half a minute or so before more propellant was chucked on.

'It's deliberate!'

'What? What d'you mean?'

I looked at Sarah. She was standing there hunched forward, arms crossed over her breasts like she was cold. She seemed incredibly slight and vulnerable, as if before she'd made herself bigger by projecting her personality outwards a hundred percent and now had retreated into herself.

I put my arms round her and gave her a hug.

Then I pointed over her shoulder to the near hedge and said, 'Watch.'

Sure enough flames shot out into the field, though this time there were several splashes all coming from the same point and as the fire took hold we could see the silhouettes of four people huddled together. But they were fighting a losing battle because the fire kept dying back no matter how hard they tried to get it going – doubtless because the maize was unripe and was still a green crop. And the next time they threw on more fuel the wind was up and the flames blew back in their faces and there was a scream and shouting.

'Jesus Christ!' said Sarah.

'They're mad,' I said, hugging her to me.

'Who is it? Why are they doing it?'

'Search me. Though the fact they're trying to burn maize is

299

presumably significant. GM, maybe?'

'I suppose – though I haven't heard anything about GM being grown. But then it would be kept secret, wouldn't it?'

'Yeah. By the way do you know what Captain Swing means?'

'Haven't the faintest. Why d'you ask?'

'Fucking sweet Jesus!'

I let go of her.

The arsonists had had another go while we'd been talking – they were obviously a determined bunch – and again the wind carried the flame back on them, only this time the fire leapt over them like an animal, a fiery deer or something, and immediately took hold in the hedge that ran towards the river.

The speed with which the fire spread along that hedgeline was awesome and within seconds the big ash trees in it were going up.

But then we could see the first fire engine careering off the road onto the track leading to the maize field. As they did so this God Almighty bang exploded across the valley.

'They must've taken out the gate!'

'It's madness. But at least it can't go anywhere when it reaches the river.'

'What about the wooden footbridge?'

'Shit, you're right.'

'On the other hand it does seem to be dying down the closer it gets to the river.'

'There's a stubble field on fire to the left.'

'You don't say. But it's not making that much headway in the watermeadows.'

But as soon as I said that one of Col's little pig shelters burst into flames, then another, and out of one sped this poor terrified, squealing animal which soon appeared to be engulfed in flame.

'Col's pigs!' sobbed Sarah. 'I don't believe it.'

'Ssssh,' I whispered holding her tight. 'If it's got any sense it'll jump in the water.'

'Can pigs swim?'

'Given the choice, I reckon it'll have a go.'

Now there were people running everywhere across the

meadow. Three of the black figures were trying to get the other pigs away from the flames and the fourth was chasing after the unfortunate pig that was on fire. Meanwhile the fire crew had started spraying water from their tender onto the maize field from the top of the watermeadow and one of their number was running with a hose down to the river.

You couldn't believe your eyes.

Away to our right came the sound of a powerful motor and we could see blue flashes piercing the trees.

'It's the Faringdon one,' said Sarah.

We watched as the machine lumbered down the hill and turned along the track that serviced the lock keeper's cottage further up the valley.

It was as we were following its progress that we realised simultaneously that far from jumping into the river, the pig was running over the footbridge.

'Oh for fuck's sake!' I shouted into the sky. The wind was extraordinarily strong now and I noticed how black the whole of the sky was – there were swirling clouds, like we were watching a Steven Spielberg film – and the temperature was plummeting.

'It won't take hold,' I reassured Sarah. 'Besides I reckon there's going to be a thunderstorm.'

'I'm going to dial 999. They've got to tell them to send another fire engine – tell them the fire's crossing the river.'

And sure enough, although we'd lost sight of the pig, the rough grass on this side of the bridge was already alight.

But the second crew must have realised what had happened and the big vehicle was grinding through a three-point turn on the track to the lock, before accelerating back towards the road.

'They're on the case, Sarah.'

But she was already talking to someone.

'I'll go and get you a blanket or something,' I said to her. 'You must be freezing.' I set off towards the spiral staircase.

I came back with two white bathrobes from one of the guest bedrooms.

Sarah was sitting on the decking more or less where I'd left her. Her legs were stretched out in front, bent just a little at the knee. Her back was arched, her head was hanging forward, her hands rested in her lap. She was convulsed by sobbing.

I crouched beside her and arranged one of the bathrobes over her shoulders and tried to wrap her body in it as best I could. She was unyielding. And freezing cold – although we were sheltered from the worst of the wind it was blowy down there.

I gave her a big hug and said, 'Come on.' I noticed the mobile on the decking a little way off, almost as if it'd been thrown. 'What did they say?'

She shook her head and sniffed a few times, then sighed, 'It was a joke. They said the firecrews were in full control of the situation and would request assistance if they thought it necessary.' She laughed. 'Fucking, fucking wankers!'

'Did I hear the Faringdon tender go past?'

'Haven't the foggiest. I think I almost collapsed – I was *so* angry! I sort of fainted. What happens if the woods catch fire? This place'll be consumed.'

I patted her back. 'It won't come to that,' I said, although given the success-rate of my predictions that evening, I wasn't convinced I was right.

She smiled, not manically this time, and stared at her bathrobe. 'Where did this come from?'

'The upside-down room. I remembered seeing them in the en-suite.'

'Why didn't you go into our room? It would've been quicker.'

'You said you didn't want me to see it.'

'That's sweet of you.'

'I'm kind of like that.'

'No, I mean it – that was *very* kind of you.'

We looked into each other's eyes then kissed.

A minute or two later I was holding her tightly and gazing up into the sky and it occurred to me that the glow ahead of me meant the copse was alight.

I was about to say something but Sarah had started before me. 'You know what I thought when the operator was talking?'

'No.'

'I thought he was my father. Everything got tangled up. That's why I threw the phone down.'

'Right,' I said, not really understanding what she was getting at.

Just then I felt a big drop of rain fall onto my face followed by another and another. Within seconds it was stair-rods.

I scrambled to my feet and reached out to the heavens.

Sarah got up too, the bathrobe falling from her shoulders. 'Yes!' she cried, leaping up and down. 'Yes! Yes! Yes!'

'Brilliant!' I went and punched the air.

At which point there was a terrifying crack that ricocheted across the sky and a bolt of lightening forked into the valley.

'Jesus!' shouted Sarah.

'We'll get struck by lightning next!'

Fortunately she could see the funny side and burst out laughing.

She leant forward, kissed me and said, 'One of those nights!'

I pulled her to me and kissed her hard.

Then, all of a sudden, there was the sound of people banging frenziedly on the front door.

We both jumped and looked at each other in astonishment.

'What the fuck!' said Sarah.

'Sarah!' someone shouted.

'My God!' she said.

It was Col.

Part Four

Loose Ends

Before I begin on me and Sarah, I reckon I should get the maize and pig stuff out of the way. No, that sounds a bit flippant – more than a bit – and what happened was heart-rendingly sad, for Col, Fiona and the boys especially. Andy was alright even though he ended up on remand and was later sent down. He's resilient – although I have to admit there were times when I worried for his state of mind.

The bare facts of Col and Andy's escapade that night are these: Col, Andy and two mates (or fellow travellers, should I say), Quentin and Bud, dressed themselves up in black boiler-suits and Balaclavas and tried to set fire to the GM maize field using cans of petrol. But because the maize was still green all they succeeded in doing was wreak havoc on the ancient hedges and traditionally-grown crops surrounding it. Only about five percent of the maize was destroyed. Whereas every stook of thatching wheat was turned to ash. Not to mention a mile of hedge, thirty broadleaved hedge trees, five acres of watermeadow and pasture and that labour of love, the copse. Oh, and one New Zealand Kune-Kune pig.

The sort of work only rank amateurs and all-round nice people like Andy, Col, Quentin and Bud could achieve.

It didn't take the police long to track the felons down. Several members of the local fire brigade recognised Andy and Col when Col started racing across the watermeadow after the burning pig and Andy, Quentin and Bud shooed the other, shorter-haired varieties, to safety. I think the firemen would've kept schtum if just the maize was affected. But the sheer irresponsibility of the plan and the threat posed to the Folly, the Trout Inn at Tadpole Bridge, along with a couple of farm cottages, meant they had to come forward.

Raids on the Castle, the smallholding and Quentin and Bud's house ten miles away produced enough digital evidence to convict twenty times over. Col had been particularly obsessive about downloading articles and keeping detailed records of meetings, phonecalls, emails and text messages.

The case came to trial in December. It was disclosed that Andy had chucked in his job with the multinational seed company once he'd learnt it was supporting GM trials, but not before stealing gigabytes of secret data. To his credit, Andy didn't profit from the theft but handed over the discs for free to the agri-terrorist cell he joined subsequently – an outfit based near Godalming.

Andy then got talking with Col one night at the Parker and recruited him. Col in turn signed up Quentin and Bud who he knew through the local branch of the Winstanley Society.

I stood by Andy, even though I thought he'd been a prize pillock and upset Sarah when she thought her house was about to go up in smoke. I liked him, he was a good pub manager and apprentice brewer. I also thought he was the sort that'd turn to drink if he wasn't looked after. I signed an affidavit saying I'd keep his job open for when he was released as part of my character endorsement.

Ironically, I suspect it was this that got him banged up. I reckon the judge thought he was getting off too lightly. Whereas Col, because he was ruined as a land agent and Fiona left him, was worthy of pity. Col got a heavy fine and God knows how many hours Community Service but escaped jail. Quentin and Bud's fines were small and the number of hours insignificant because they were deemed mere accessories.

It was a sorry story that blighted the lives of everyone in the village.

Col and Fiona gave up the smallholding. She and the kids moved to Bath where she got a good job as an accountant. She's nearer her parents, she's living in a city. She's happy. She'd already fallen out of love with Col during the Winstanley business.

Col took a cottage on the edge of the village but hasn't spent much time there. He didn't complete much Community Service neither. Since his breakdown he's been stuck in the Warnford in Oxford, a psychiatric unit. I visit him every couple of weeks. He doesn't say much but I can still force a smile out of him.

As for Quentin and Bud, who knows?

But Andy – Andy's back with me and doing a stonking job. What with my mental health not being so good either, he's a godsend. He'll rival Rajiv one day.

Daddy, I Hardly Knew You

I suppose that title sends Sarah up a bit – which is unfair but tells you something about the ambiguous way I still think and feel about her. I have this almost childish desire to poke fun at her, as if the things she felt and suffered were an act. I know that's not true, yet I can't shake off that desire. It's as if it protects me against human weakness. It's as if acknowledging human weakness would expose me to it, infect me. But then wasn't I infected already? Wasn't I infected way before I ever met her?

It was the day after Dad visited with Gaynor that Sarah first talked about her relationship with her father. We'd been seeing each other for nearly two months and had had some really wonderful times. Griff was still in London. There'd been some spats, of course, and even some darker moments but nothing unusual. That afternoon was the first time she rattled me.

It'd been lovely seeing Dad. He looked years younger and you could tell immediately that he was in love. He was wearing a new tweed jacket and I loved him when he took me to one side and apologised for not bringing the one I bought him. I looked into his twinkling, still-young old man's eyes and we both knew what he was saying. It was Gaynor's choice. I put my hand on his shoulder, squeezed lightly and said, 'Good one, Dad.' Before I could take my hand away he put his on my shoulder and gave me a squeeze. He'd never reciprocated like that before. I said to him, 'I'm pleased for you, Dad. She's one in a million.' He replied, 'So was your mother.' 'Yeah, and not many men meet two like that in a lifetime. You're a lucky man, Dad.' 'And you're a good son, Tom. You've done well here. I wish you lived nearer, but one can't have everything.'

I decided not to tell Sarah too much about Dad when she asked what happened because I knew her father was ill and I thought it would be insensitive to be overly enthusiastic. Yet it didn't take her long to pick up on my joy.

'You're terribly lucky, having such a good relationship with him.'

'Yes, I know. We don't see each other enough, though.'

'Even so.'

'I'm sorry, I didn't intend to say so much about yesterday. I know your dad's not well.'

'You've hardly said a thing. I can see the light in your face, that's all.'

'Suppose you can't disguise that.'

'What do you think I feel about my father?'

'I don't know.'

'I do manage to disguise that.'

'You keep some things private. I realised that from the start.'

'Maybe it's easier to disguise pain, than happiness. Perhaps it's a matter of survival, a greater imperative.'

I didn't quite understand what she was driving at, although I dare say I picked up enough – from her demeanour, if not her words. Selfishly, I didn't want to get too heavy, what with Dad's visit and the fact it was such a beautiful day.

It was a Sunday and I'd driven us to Kelmscott. I'd prepared us a picnic which I packed into a wicker hamper just as Sarah liked. Tara helped me sort out the details, although I chose the wine.

We called at the Plough for a pint, then walked along the lane, past William Morris's manor and onto the watermeadows. Appropriately, we spread out our rug under a huge willow on the river bank.

In the gentle late-autumn sun, Sarah's pale complexion, dark feathery hair and green eyes looked quite, quite beautiful. But there was hurt in her expression. A tension. I'm not the most observant bloke in the world but it'd been there ever since I picked her up. It was like she couldn't let her features respond to the magic of the day. Instead they were frozen by some as yet barely guessed-at ice field spreading across her mind.

After a few minutes, she said, 'I saw Dad last week. I drove to Bristol on Wednesday – he's in hospital.'

As she spoke I detected tenderness and felt that just now I'd been unfair.

'Is he very ill?'

'Yes. Prostate cancer.'

'He's young for that, isn't he?'

'Not really. Its considered medically *normal* if it strikes any time after fifty – according to the websites I've visited anyway.'

'But it's treatable?'

'If caught in time but I think Dad's been silly about it – male pride and all that – and the doctors think it's spread.'

'I'm sorry – you must be devastated. But they don't know for certain?'

'They're doing tests. He's got these terrible chest pains.'

'It's got onto his lungs?'

'No, rib cage. It colonises the bones.'

'Jesus!'

'If they're right, there's not much they can do.'

It was awkward on the picnic rug with all the things laid across it but I pushed myself up and managed to kneel quite close to her. I put my arms round her and gave her a big hug.

'I'm sorry.'

I felt guilty for having tried to avoid talking about her father but there'd been something odd about the way she spoke of him earlier – just as there was about how she was responding to me hugging her. I expected her to lean into me or hug me too but instead she was stiff and unyielding.

I looked up at her then kissed her neck but she pulled away from me.

'Don't be sorry for him,' she said and took a sip of wine.

I stood up and went back to my place.

She was staring at me intently.

'I must seem callous – sorry, but that's the way it is. Only I'm not being callous. He was a real shit to me. He wanted to destroy me.'

I looked into her eyes. I was shocked by her vehemence. But then I'd begun to suspect from a comment she let slip several weeks before that she'd been deeply hurt by her father and this knowledge made me feel tenderly towards her now. And I felt more intense love for her than I had a few minutes before because now it was her who was the victim, not her father – or not just her father, I should say.

And yet I knew better than to try and hug her again.

'Do you want to talk about it?'

'Why not?'

She reached for her tobacco tin, eased off the lid and began rolling a perfect toothpick of a cigarette.

As she did so I poured some more wine then coated my third slice of ciabatta with olive oil spread and topped it with a doubled-over slice of finely-cut honey-roast ham.

Sarah had so far only managed a couple of cherry tomatoes, an olive and the corner of a slice of ham, even though when we unpacked the picnic she said how scrummy everything was and helped herself to loads of different things. I wasn't offended – I was getting used to her eating habits – although I was a little sad. I enjoyed my food and Jill always liked hers, even if she never ate as much as me. With Sarah there was no enjoyment when she ate, if she ate, and you got the impression that she would do anything (smoke, drink, talk non-stop) to avoid taking a mouthful. It was a small thing, maybe, but it made you self-conscious about eating and I found myself willing her to join in. I'd will her to take a decent mouthful so we could feel we were sharing the meal. Instead what I felt was a kind of loneliness. I'd never realised before how natural eating together is, how you take it for granted.

After she lit her cigarette she began telling me about how her grandfather on her mother's side left a largish sum of money in trust for the three grandchildren and that her father was also entitled to borrow some of the capital interest-free on condition it was paid back to the children when they turned twenty-five or else got married.

313

She told me that when she was in her late teens and was working at a pottery near Reading her father took her out to lunch. She was still naïve and vulnerable, she said, and idolised her father, even though he'd always been a bully. She felt in those days that he was somehow straighter than her mother.

Her father chose a fancy restaurant where she ate little and drank too much. She said she often wondered if he knew she had a problem with eating and took advantage of it. Anyway, he got her to agree to him having seventy-five per cent of her capital to invest in some get-rich-quick building scheme. This was well over the odds. He was entitled to fifteen – twenty percent max – by the time she was that age – unless she wrote to the trustees instructing them to give him more. A few weeks later some forms arrived – just a formality, he said – and she duly signed them.

'I didn't give the money much thought, to be quite honest,' she said as she lit another cigarette. 'That probably sounds absurd but twenty-five seemed a very long way off then and I had no reason to doubt Dad would pay it back.'

'What about the trustees? What the hell were they doing?'

'I think they just assumed Dad was honourable. They never asked me what I thought anyway.'

'Wankers. Sorry.'

'No, you're right, although my uncle, Vern, came good in the end.'

'How so? Did you did get the money back eventually? Is that what you used to buy the gallery?'

'Yes, I got it back – and I used some of it to invest in the gallery, although partners put in quite a bit. The rest went on the Folly.'

'So what happened? When you were twenty-five the trustees suddenly woke up?'

'Yes, sort of, only I was twenty-three. I'd been engaged but the whole thing fell through. That's another story. My poltergeist moment.'

'Sounds lively.'

'It was believe you me!'

She flicked the dog end of her cigarette into the river and

314

drank nearly half her glass of wine. She took a deep breath.

'Once the engagement was called off, I went downhill badly. I became skeletal, smoked tons, drank like a whole shoal of fishes. Mum and Dad were mortified about the marriage – the engagement had been in the papers and everyone knew about it, what a good match it was. Jamie, my fiancé, was loaded, a landed gent.'

'You don't go for the minnows when it comes to men.'

'Shut up!'

She threw a cherry tomato at me, which I caught.

'There was a sort of tug-of-war over me. Mum and Dad wanted me to go back home, give up working at the pottery and be decently hidden away. But my boss, Sinéad, decided I should keep working and remain independent. Then, when I was too ill to work, as thin as a bloody rake, she packed me off to her holiday cottage in Wales where I began to put myself back together. She was just amazing!'

'Fairy godmother. Everyone needs someone like that. I used to have, well I wouldn't call him a fairy godfather—' I broke off and couldn't help laughing. 'I had my mentor, Len Banks. Diamond he was, pure diamond.'

'People who have time for those younger than themselves are so precious.'

'Did she pull something off as far as the trust was concerned?'

'Only indirectly. My uncle used to have a boyfriend in the village where the pottery was – there's another extraordinary connection there, but I'll tell you about that another time. Uncle Vern had also started collecting Sinéad's work and one day he visited and asked after me. He'd been told that I was a drug addict living on a Welsh commune, or some such tripe, by Mum and Dad. Sinéad told him the truth and that she didn't like the way Mum and Dad behaved. There was something so proprietorial about it, she thought. That sort of approach was anathema to her.'

'Well I suppose your Dad was worried about when he'd have to pay back the money. I assume the get-rich-quick scheme didn't work out.'

'No, it was hopeless. Dad got an obsession about it – it was to do with developing a building where he had another surgery.'

As she spoke she assumed that cold measured tone I'd heard that second picnic when we talked about Griff spending the autumn in London. She was rolling another cigarette and I had to top up her wine. She was calm on the surface but underneath boiling with anger.

'He even got himself onto the Council so he could obtain planning permission. He failed again and again but wouldn't give up. In doing so he wasted a fortune. Far more than the building was actually worth.'

'Obsession's no good in business. You've got to be light on your feet. Reactive.'

'You wouldn't call Dad that. Where was I? Vern. He rang me up and asked if I needed money. What I hadn't realised was that a proportion of my capital could be advanced to me from the age of twenty-one onwards. When we discussed this, he also began asking about what I actually understood about the trust. It didn't take him long to put two-and-two together.'

'Better late than never, I suppose.'

'Yes, good old Vern. As children we used to think he was a total wet but he really proved his metal. He took Dad on and won.'

'Did he recover a percentage of the money or all of it?'

'Pretty much the lot. Dad had to sell the surgery building and pay me and my brother out. There was enough for him to do that. What he couldn't recoup was his own investment. He was in hock for a fortune which he'd borrowed against Mum's house. They had to sell up as a result. I suspect that's when the prostate problem started.'

'What an awful story. But it had the right outcome for you.'

'Only up to a point. I got the money but the emotional fallout was indescribable.'

When she'd been speaking a few moments before she seemed to be calmer and more matter of fact about what had happened over the trust. But now she fell silent and I could see all the emotion she'd been containing suddenly surge through her from the epicentre of her pain like a tsunami. Her whole body was convulsed with wave upon wave of sobbing. Tears flooded down her cheeks.

I was so stunned by the suddenness of what was happening that for a second or two I just watched unable to take it in. Then I pushed myself up, went towards her – following the same path across the rug as before unthinkingly and in the process overturning a couple of jars which we'd moved – and put my arms round her.

The physical power of those sobs was astonishing but I only held her for a millisecond it seemed before she pushed me back sharply.

She glared at me. 'Don't touch me! *Please*, Tom, I don't deserve your sympathy.'

'Whatever.'

She held out her hand. I took hold of it and gave it a squeeze.

'My father's dying and yet I still hate him. All the time I was with him in hospital I was saying all the right things – yes, giving a perfect performance, putting on a world-class act – but what I really wanted to do was kill him, if I only knew how, and watch him die so he could see in my eyes how much I hated him.'

I was amazed by her harshness. I struggled to find what to say. 'He hurt you badly. I can see that. Although the trust had a good outcome, as you say it's the emotional thing.'

I put my hands on her shoulders and she didn't pull away. She was a little calmer.

I leant towards her and stared into her eyes and continued staring, even though she looked towards the river a lot of the time.

'I remember thinking when you showed me the mock up of your old room at the Folly that your parents must have been cruel to you. You can read your story in that room. It'd been going on all through your childhood, hadn't it?'

She looked at me briefly. 'Yes there is a story in that room. That's why I created it but it's a complex story as I tried to tell you when I first showed you round. When I was putting it together I was still blinded by hatred and from my adult perspective I wanted to show up how appallingly I'd been treated. But you see it wasn't like that at the time, when I was a child. I didn't know any better. OK most friends had far far lovelier rooms but we lived in a really beautiful house with an amazing garden and the farm – which was let to tenants but we could still walk or ride where we liked. And a lot of the time, if I'm honest, I lived in my head when I was in that room, so I could have been anywhere – under Waterloo Bridge even – and it wouldn't have mattered.'

'Yeah but children who're abused often don't know they're being ill-treated and the psychological damage it's doing to them, do they? It takes someone from the outside to come in and see things objectively then get them sorted out.'

'I wasn't abused.'

'You've got this – this eating problem – and that's presumably caused by what happened to you.'

She shook her head and looked me straight in the eye, although she was much more relaxed again now. Docile. She pulled away from me gently. 'I need a cigarette.'

'OK but first—'

I took out my handkerchief and dabbed the remaining dampness from her cheek.

She smiled at me. 'Thanks.'

I sat down again and she started rolling a cigarette. As she did so she gave a little shiver. 'It's getting colder.'

It was overcast now and although the sun was still out much of the sky was leaden. I contemplated where we were for a few moments. Even though it had been unseasonably warm most of the day we were the only people picnicking and there'd been very few people about generally. Just one or two dog-walkers. A young couple, not long before Sarah broke down. The colder air and the change in the sky made the watermeadow seem quite a desolate place. It made me shiver just to look at it, although this was one of those warm, in-love sort of shivers. I remember glancing at Sarah and thinking that for all her sadness she was exquisitely beautiful.

I had to pinch myself to remind me that the day and our new

love were real. That we had days out like this one, being careful not to be seen together but not overly so, and then being closer and making love behind closed doors.

Sarah lit her cigarette and drew deeply on it. 'I don't actually blame anyone for my eating problem, you know. That's my real problem. I used to go and see a psychiatrist and all she did was try and persuade me to blame people for my problem. I started to do that but then I refused. Seems to me that the way I reacted to tensions at home was personal – it belonged to me and would have always come out somewhere along the line. My brother and sister lived through the same things and Alex's way of coping was to take drugs, although he's over that now. Min's way of coping was to be an extrovert, precocious pain in the arse. She's studying to be a psychiatrist by the way. Me, I just threw up.'

I couldn't get my head round what she was saying when she said things like that. I think I heard them but blotted them out. I certainly didn't imagine what she actually did.

'And that is *me*, how I am. No one can change me. Except me, maybe, if I blamed everyone for my misfortunes. But I know that would only be a fiction – a palliative story, not the truth.'

'But the truth can sometimes be a matter of perspective, can't it? You know, like I said, when the social services come in they see things freshly, objectively.'

'Well, whatever. Perhaps I make things worse by turning my anger inwards – I know I do – but the alternative is unthinkable. That's how I am. When I was at the hospital I hated my father, but did I say it? Did I turn off the life support? Did I fuck! I contained my anger behind a façade, a dam, and the dam only bursts when I'm alone, or with you now, or when I'm staring down a lavatory.'

'Oh Jesus, I'm sorry.'

'Sorry for what?'

'I don't know. I just wish I could help.'

'You do – by being here. Listening to me.'

I pushed myself up again and went to her and kissed her.

I was overwhelmed by love. Perhaps too I was protective of her vulnerability. Even so, there was a little voice, ever so faint, that was saying, 'If she was this screwed up and her brother was as high as a kite, some people might've thought her dad had good reason for getting the trust fund out of their clutches, even if his scheme did go wrong.'

Note to Mart

The picnic was probably the best illustration of both Sarah's relationship with her father and the beginnings of her unpredictable behaviour. But what I'm really surprised about is how easy it is to express these things in narrative terms. I thought I'd be scrabbling about trying to pull in details from here, there and everywhere in my desperate efforts to make sense of what happened. And yet if you think hard about which day was pivotal with regard to a particular, important theme, and you start running through the events of that day in your mind you suddenly find yourself noticing more and more. Making more and more sense of life. Suddenly you've got a story to tell – not *War and Peace* exactly but no haiku neither. I remember you saying Mart that human beings are natural story tellers. I hadn't realised before then how fundamental telling stories is as far as unravelling truth is concerned. Yet it's no doddle, this story telling. It's not without its pain. If I were an academic reconstructing the story of the picnic, say, I'd assemble the facts about where we were, what the day was like, what we were eating and so on, and then assess them objectively. There'd be no genuine gut-wrenching pain. There'd be empathy, no doubt, otherwise you couldn't make convincing judgements, but not the actual living experiences. With story telling you revisit, you do relive, you explore, you linger over the past. And that lingering, caused by the relative slowness of writing life down, as opposed to living and breathing it, that lingering makes the pain even worse, second time around. But maybe afterwards the generalised pain and depression those events caused will be less, precisely because you have relived the past vividly through writing. That's what I call the exorcism. Is that how this therapy works, Mart? Am I right? But then sometimes I wonder, what if it isn't exorcism but me opening up this Pandora's box, delving deep inside and pulling out things that should have stayed in the depths. What if it's like that, Mart, this telling stories? I find myself asking these questions quite often, Mart, and they frighten me. And yet I have no choice but to go on. No choice at all. I have to write.

Dad on the Loose

I hadn't realised Gaynor owned a house on Lanzarote and was bowled over when Dad rang a couple of weeks after their visit to say they were going to be staying out there for two months. Of course I was pleased for him, especially when he told me how much better his arthritis was. Mid-winter was always the most painful time. But after a week or two of warm sunshine it went into remission. What's more he's fallen in love with the place. They've spent three months there this year and are about to go again. I must say I'm amazed he likes it – I've checked out photos on the Web and looked at his snaps and I've yet to see a bit that's anything other than grey and hostile. The last lot of pics were digital, sent by email! He's got a new lease of life, has Dad. But I still find it hard to get my head round him being far away. It was reassuring knowing he was there in the old house, doing familiar things, living among the scenes of my childhood. It was like he rooted me by being there in Essex. Now I can't hardly imagine him in his new life. He is – in part at least – a stranger. It's like being a parent when the kids leave home. I sometimes wonder if the Sarah and Griff thing hit me so hard because Dad was away. Ah well, not his fault. Character building. I love you Dad.

A Pagan Act

It must've been about the time Dad and Gaynor flew to Lanzarote, I can't remember for sure, but it was beginning to feel wintry and the leaves when you walked up Sarah's drive were deep and crunchy.

That morning I'd been to see Andy in jail near Bicester. I couldn't believe he was on remand. I'd offered to stand bail but the authorities wouldn't hear of it. He was taking prison well, it had to be said, although I lived in fear he'd get sucked into drugs. He's so chock-full of energy, and sociable with it. I could just see him turning to drugs and getting hooked. When I saw him that time, I told him his job was waiting for him and like every time I saw him I tried to keep him focused on the bright future I just know he's going to have.

After a sandwich at the pub I cycled to the Folly. (The pub incidentally was being run even more tightly than before under Tara's sole-proprietorship. She was doing a cracker of a job but if you were being niggly, you'd say she was perhaps a little too inflexible in Andy's absence.)

I tried to cycle to Sarah's as much as possible. I thought by doing so I was drawing less attention to myself. As if wheeling my bike through the Folly gate was less of a statement than cruising through in my new Beamer.

The front door was on the latch and I went straight up to the first floor. I could hear Sarah and Debbie talking from the hallway. I was allowed into the offices by then, although the master bedroom was still off-limits – and would remain so all the time we were together. When I stayed the night, we'd either use one of the guest rooms or snuggle up in a nest of duvets in front of the fire in the banqueting hall.

Sarah and Debbie were talking by netphone and had their webcams on. Sarah was wearing her tracksuit and had evidently been working out in the gym. I was about to lean in front of her and go, Hi Debs, but realised the conversation was serious. There were tears on Debbie's cheeks.

'I'll text you when we're about to put on *Partie de Campagne*,' said Sarah. 'About an hour and a half? If you go to your church, Tom and I'll head out to the woods. I need some fresh air. Besides it'll remind me of when he came to see me at Aldermaston.'

'—Kay, Babes. Take care.'

'What's the matter?' I asked after Sarah'd signed out.

'I'll tell you in a sec. You OK if we go for a walk?'

'No problem.'

'I've just got to shower and change. I'll see you upstairs in five minutes.'

We were walking along the road towards where the copse used to be.

It was colder now and I'd jammed my hands deep into the pockets of my leather jacket. Sarah had linked her arm through mine – she was wearing mint-green patterned woolly gloves that matched her scarf and hat. This hat, with its ear flaps and pom-pom, was one of those Lapland ones, and made her face appear cheeky. All three items echoed the colours of the swirling design on her heavy blanket coat, an outrageous, expensive-looking creation that came part-way down her thigh. Her leather trousers were black and her work-boots looked so heavy, you wondered how she could pick her feet up.

'So,' I said, 'what's up with Debbie?'

She looked at me. Her face was very gentle. I'd never seen her quite like this before. She'd been relaxed and more open on several occasions just recently, which I loved. But this time her expression was almost maternal, full of deep human sympathy.

'Today is the fourth anniversary of the death of someone very dear to us – to Debs especially.'

'I'm sorry to hear that. She did look pretty cut up. How are you feeling?'

I took my hand out of my pocket and gave her shoulder a squeeze.

'I feel OK – I suppose. I go through so many different emotions on this anniversary. I try to remember that for Debs the pain is much worse but I don't always succeed. There's a nasty little pit of acid guilt that opens up underneath me today and I burn. You being here helps, though.'

She pulled me closer with her linked arm and kissed my forehead.

'Who was it that died?'

'He was someone we were at school with. He was called Karl and Debbie used to go out with him. He overdosed on heroin.'

'I hate drugs – I've been worried sick about Andy. All that energy and no way of letting it out. I can just see him trying something to help him stop climbing the walls and getting hooked.'

'He's not that stupid, Tom.'

'I don't know – I hope you're right. Hope it's just me being paranoid. But it's a scandal he's on remand and you read such horror stories. You know?'

She kissed my forehead again and I looked up at her. She smiled. I felt a kind of connection with her I'd never felt before. She didn't seem cold or vulnerable that day but grown up – that's the only way I can put it – as if she possessed some knowledge about the world that came from having suffered. Having suffered and conquered that suffering. She seemed somehow to have the measure of life that day. She commanded my love and respect.

'Do you want to talk about what happened?'

She hesitated a moment. 'Yes. It'll do me good. I've not talked to anyone about Karl really, apart from Debs. Griff doesn't want to know – which isn't meant to sound as bad as it does. Like you he has no time for drugs, apart from dope now and again. But the big taboo with him is death. I sometimes think he believes he'll live forever. It's as if he was never taught about death properly as a child. If you say to him someone's died, he simply blanks you or says, 'No, no, *cariad*.' Death doesn't seem real to him, and yet if you insist someone's dead he cries, gets angry and throws things.'

'Not a man you can have a heart-to-heart with.'

'No.'

'Did he know Karl?'

'No. I'd not seen Karl for a couple of months when I met Griff and I would never see him again. The last few times were when he came to see me at the pottery after I split up with my fiancé.'

'Your poltergeist moment.'

'Yes.'

'I'm intrigued by that.'

'Well, you'll have to wait. Today's for Karl.'

'I understand.'

She looked into my eyes. 'Thank you.'

I kissed her lightly.

'When Karl died in New York, Debbie hadn't seen him for over a year either. It's because we lost touch with him that we feel guilty. And she was living in the same city, for heaven's sake – two or three miles from where he died! But their break-up had been so acrimonious. In the end, after yet another rehab failed, she went to court to get him banned from seeing her. He was stalking her. She told him through her lawyers she never wanted to see him again. Of course she didn't really mean it and when he died—'

'You say things like that when you're splitting up. Everyone does. You don't mean them literally.'

'No. But it destroyed her. She was working with Woody Allen then. He was amazing. Paid for her to have therapy. Though what saved her was God. That's where she'll be now, in her local church. I couldn't believe it when she told me she'd started going to church. Ever since I'd known her, she'd been so sophisticated and – I don't know – secular. But she explained how her mum used to get her and her brothers to sing in the church choir when they were kids and those memories stuck. When she was desperate she found her way back to them.'

'I've never been religious.'

327

'Me neither. My parents didn't bring us up that way. Mum's stoical old England. Dad's too proud. Even now he's dying, he's still like that. Whatever else you might say about him, he's consistent.'

I laughed and she did too. I thought of how she'd been on the picnic and took this capacity to laugh as a good sign.

'Your way of paying your respects is taking a walk.'

'Yes, though it also reminds me of those last few times I saw him. He was a true friend then. Usually it was me who helped him but when he came to Aldermaston I'd almost lost complete control of my life.'

'I remember you saying. Your boss packed you off to Wales.'

'Where I met Griff.'

'Is that a fact? I did wonder.'

'But before that, after I split up with Jamie, my fiancé, I lost it in Berkshire. I couldn't go back home – wouldn't – so I threw myself into my work. But I also smoked too much, drank madly, didn't eat properly, threw up if I ever let myself have a decent meal— I did some of my best work, though, and didn't let Sinéad down. I did the work of three or four!'

'Work always comes first – I can see that in you. I like that.'

'That *did* come from Mum and Dad. Although they weren't always effective when they did things – we didn't know that at the time, of course – they were always up and doing. And I took that in. Alex and Min didn't, or at least not as much, but with me, not doing anything became unbearable. I had to help in the kitchen or round the house or else I felt terribly, terribly guilty. Eventually keeping busy became an escape *and* a curse – but that's another story.'

I smiled at her. 'You've been through a lot.' I was amazed by how calm she was, even when talking about her childhood and her eating problems. As I say, she was magnificent that day. It made me so optimistic.

She smiled back and shrugged off my compliment. 'Not as much as Karl.'

We were approaching the copse and were both silenced by what we saw. The copse and some of the woodland behind it was just blackened branchless trunks and stumps and things that looked like giant conked-out hedgehogs – all that remained of my two months handiwork. And yet there was hope amongst the drifts of ash. There were already signs of green plants. Also a forester friend of Griff and Sarah's agent had come out a couple of weeks before and was due back in February. He seemed to think there was a chance some hazel would grow back again. Whenever I saw the copse that winter, I found myself clinging to that hope. Not for my sake but for Col and Fi's. All of us who knew them nurtured the fantasy of their differences blowing over and them starting again.

We walked round the edge of the copse. We were no longer arm-in-arm.

'How far are we going?'

'The Leper's Tower. It's the perfect place today. I'll explain. But first—'

She reached into her coat pocket and produced her tobacco tin. Inside was a long fat cigarette with a twisted end. The cigarette was curved so it would fit in. As she straightened it she said, 'I know you think I smoke this stuff all the time, which is bullshit. Do you want to share it with me? I know what you said about drugs but this is a ritual spliff – in honour of the dear departed.'

'I'll take a puff.'

Before linking arms with me again she lit up and drew in a big mouthful of smoke.

We set off up the hill towards Midsommer Plantation. This was the biggest wood Griff and Sarah owned. I'd been there once before with Col, who pointed out the magnificent oaks and sycamores. He was particularly excited by the former, several of which were as broad as an industrial mash tun and were reputed to be the remnants of a vast medieval forest that once extended from here to Swindon. In the centre of the wood, at its highest point, was the Leper's Tower.

'He visited me four or five times – maybe six. I was so out of it, I can't remember. He was in Richmond seeing his mum. Though that was probably a pretext – the real reason was he'd split up with Debbie yet again and was trying to make out he didn't care and was moving back to England.'

'The things people do for love.'

'Here.' She handed me the spliff. 'It's not skunk or anything. Just a token.'

I took a drag. It pains me to say it but it was quite mellow. Gave me a nice tingle.

I handed it back to her.

'I expected him to bang on about Debbie but most of the time he was charming. He was genuinely concerned about me.'

'Was he in between rehabs?'

'No, he went into rehab for the first time a year later. He was really kind and easy in those days, that's all. It was before the hard drugs got to him. He was smoking crack and heroin but seemed to be in control. He didn't do them when he was with me because he knew I wouldn't approve and yet he didn't suffer any withdrawal symptoms that I could see. OK I was out of it myself but not totally – it was a funny kind of out of it.'

She took a long drag on the spliff and thereafter drew on it at the end of every sentence.

'It was as if I was no longer connected to the world around me. Like my head was a burrow and I was peeping out, though not from the mouth – I was deep within the tunnel. Yet I could see everything going on around me, almost more clearly than at any time in my life because my observations were freed from emotion. I was scared because I couldn't relate to people and because they couldn't relate to me. It seemed to me that emotion is itself a drug which makes people oblivious to the loathing and contempt that coexists with kindness. I could detect the slightest hint of cruelty or falseness in people and I avoided them because they threatened my fragile world. It was like I was embedded in this hole that could be stamped into oblivion and yet I was all-seeing, all-knowing. There were only two people I thought genuine – Sinéad and Karl. And Debbie, but she was on the other side of the Atlantic.'

'It must have been very distressing.' I slipped my arm from hers, put it round her shoulder and hugged her. 'Breaking up with someone can ruin you. When Jill left me I almost killed myself drinking.'

'Really?'

'Well it wasn't only that – it was like everything came to a head then. I'd sold my stake in the pub business and all the issues I'd been avoiding for years swarmed in on me.'

'Yep, a lot of things came to a head when I broke with Jamie too.'

She offered me the spliff – there were only a couple of puffs left. All of a sudden I felt protective towards her. I related to what she'd gone through, admired her courage but also hoped her confiding in me meant she wanted my support. I don't know why this should make me accept the spliff but it did.

'Such as?'

We were walking up a fairly steep incline now and we let go of each other so the going was easier. We were following an old cart track with moss-covered stone walls either side that led to the Leper's Tower.

'Well—' she began and immediately broke off. I was handing her back the dog-end of the spliff. 'You finish it,' she said.

'Fair enough.' I took a last pull for appearances' sake before flicking it to the ground.

'Loads of things. Although on reflection coming to a head's the wrong metaphor in my case. Things came to a head way before I got engaged, after which there was attrition. You see, the best way to understand what happened is to think about my engagement as a blessed release for everyone.'

'A blessed release?' I chuckled. I was puzzled.

'Yes, absolutely. Mum, for example, could suddenly see herself being able to talk about me without having to cover things up – no more embarrassment for her. Oh no. An aristocratic suitor – what more could she want? And soon, no doubt, there'd be babies. Bliss. So much better than a dungareed, pot-throwing coat-hanger!'

We laughed. Although it has to be said there was a part of me that sympathised with Sarah's mum. Her hopes for her daughter seemed pretty understandable. I think being that much older than Sarah enabled me to see her mum's point of view.

'Then there was Dad and the trust money. He broached the subject with Jamie at their first meeting – in a roundabout way. Dad asked him if he was expecting anything – you know, like a dowry! As if we were living in the nineteenth century! Of course Jamie said he was OK financially then Dad mumbled something about there being *something* in the pipeline. Yes, having a rich prospective son-in-law took the pressure off the old man beautifully. Never mind that the person he should have been talking to was bloody me!'

'That does sound underhand, to say the least.'

'Then there *was* me. I was either pretending to be grown up or being someone I wasn't, depending on your point of view. I'd even been seen in a twin-set and pearls.'

'I don't think I know what those are.'

'Never mind.'

'I've heard the expression. I can guess the sort of thing you're driving at.'

'Good. So, I was well on the way to becoming Deb of the Year with a healthier appetite. Then suddenly the engagement was off and we had nothing beneath our feet – we were like cartoon people who'd run over the edge of a cliff. Our limbs were whirling away but as sure as eggs we were going to fall. And we did. And how! And our fantasies crashed to the ground with us!'

She was ahead of me. I caught her up and put my arm round her waist. She turned and we hugged each other and kissed. I don't know whether it was the dope but there was an incredible urgency to our kissing, like we wanted to make love there and then.

We pulled our mouths apart and stared at one another hard.

'Come on,' she said, 'let's get to the tower.'

We followed the path to the right and began walking along the brow of the escarpment.

'Anyway, Karl. It's Karl's day. One of the things Karl and I decided,' she said, 'was that my anorexia was like his drug addiction. When I throw up all these endorphins are released in my brain and I feel great. Same as the hit he got from heroin. It was similar to what Alex was doing too. Do you remember I told you Alex's way of coping with Mum and Dad was smoking seriously strong hash?'

'Yeah.'

'Well Alex was like the link between me and Karl. I could understand Karl through Alex. Though Karl knew where I was coming from without any intermediary. He just understood me – like a brother almost. He was able to play the brother's role without all the shared baggage. He was different to Alex – he could understand more because he wasn't damaged by the same things. Though heaven knows he *was* fucked up! It was as if he'd reached a point in his suffering – and was still strong enough mentally – where he could identify with me and be my friend. It was probably the only time he was like that. He'd achieved wisdom of sorts.'

'Were you lovers?'

'No. I loved him and he loved me. Don't think it didn't cross my mind to make love to him. But I didn't, out of loyalty to Debs. I hoped they'd get back together – which they did.'

The track went back down the escarpment for a short way now, then rose again to the tower which was set amongst thick woodland on top of a sort of little hill all of its own.

As we walked up to it, Sarah took my hand and gave it a squeeze.

The tower had recently been restored. Col had mentioned it was a listed building and that Griff and Sarah had been obliged to do it up. It was a simple building – a round tower with battlements and arrow-slit windows following the line of the spiral staircase. The entrance was through a big iron-clad door which was kept locked.

'Did Col let you in?'

'No, he'd intended to get the key off you or Griff but forgot.'

'Well today you're in luck.'

She produced a huge key from her coat pocket.

'He did tell me about the leper, though,' I said as she opened the door. 'How the Lord of the Manor in the Middle Ages had food brought out to him, so long as he stayed at the top of this tower.'

'Which is complete bullshit, by the way.'

'Oh, well shoot me down, why don't you?'

'Sorry. But Col ought to know better.'

We went inside. The stone staircase went round the outside wall – there was no separate stair turret like at the Folly. There was nothing else to see, apart from the wooden walkway around the battlements. It was an empty cylinder.

'The real story is that there used to be a Roman fort here and a *palace*, in inverted commas, of a local English chieftain at the bottom of the valley. According to legend, after the Romans conquered this area, their general went down with leprosy which he'd contracted when he was serving in somewhere like North Africa. As soon as the Roman soldiers realised what he had, they fled. The general's lieutenant is supposed to have told the local chieftain to abandon his palace but he'd become friends with the general and although he sent his family to another part of the valley he himself remained here with some servants and made sure the general had food and water and whatever else he wanted. The only condition was that the general should remain inside the fort. When the general died the chieftain had the fort burnt to the ground.'

'I like that story, Sarah. It's a hell of a lot more interesting than Col's version.'

'I'm glad.' She kissed my forehead.

'So what's this tower?'

'Another folly. Seventeenth century. It's supposed to be based on the ground plan of part of the Roman fort but our architect couldn't find any evidence of it. Not that that matters. It commemorates a story – a story of true friendship. That's just right for today. Come on.'

I followed up the stairs. The view from the top was breathtaking – even better than from the Folly.

'There used to be a tower in the woods near Aldermaston – though it didn't have quite the same outlook, as everything's flat round there. But it was a great place to smoke spliffs in. It's where Karl and I used to go. We were *such* good friends then.'

She took off her gloves and her hat. I ran my fingers through her hair. She put her arms round my neck and we began kissing. I got my hands under her coat and jumper and rubbed her back and her breasts.

'Griff's— not the only— one who hates— death,' she said between kisses. 'I hate death.' Her teeth were clenched when she said that.

Then she pushed me away and whispered, 'Fuck me.'

She unfastened my jeans and pulled out my penis.

She turned away and reached under her coat. She slipped her leather trousers off her bum and I could see she was wearing a mint-green thong.

'I haven't got—' I began, before putting my hand into her coat pocket and finding the pouch she kept her tobacco tin and condoms in.

I felt so turned on that day and despite the fact that she made her fingers bleed, she was clasping the stone so hard as we made love, I thought I'd never been happier in my life.

I couldn't have been more wrong.

Min to the Max

Griff came down from London later in November than usual and didn't move straight back like he normally did but just spent a weekend at the Folly. He claimed London was still boiling and he was loving it so much he wouldn't be returning until there was a cold snap. He was on a creative high.

I found it hard thinking of him and Sarah together at the Folly. Perhaps I should have anticipated how I'd feel – although you don't, do you? I don't suppose I'm the first man having an illicit relationship to lull himself into a false sense of security, to coin a phrase. I'd got used to having her all to myself like we were going out together. Griff might just as well have been an ex-boyfriend given his complete absence.

True Sarah spent a night with him in October when she went to the awards ceremony. But he was so drunk there was no sex. She assured me there wouldn't be this time, but I couldn't help imagining.

I spent a lot of that weekend working at the Castle – apart from Saturday afternoon when I suspected Griff would be down for the rugby. Which he was. I went back to the mill and tried to get some sleep in anticipation of a late night. I didn't sleep a wink – just lay on the bed and contemplated nipping up to the Folly. After I talked myself out of that I phoned Jill. Our weekly chats had got out of synch lately – they were more two or even three weekly ones – and we had a bit of catching up to do.

She said she'd been doing an advanced forestry course and a coppicing course and could come down in the spring to advise us how to regenerate Col's wood. I hadn't let on how bad things were between Col and Fiona, so I brought her up to speed. She was shocked.

Later she mentioned she was doing more with the estate's livestock these days – doing the rounds with the stockman, Adam. I idly remarked that she'd soon be giving up her desk job, whereupon she said she might just do that and started banging on about how marvellous this guy Adam was. He was the National Trust's answer to Doctor Doolittle, it sounded like.

In the past, I have to confess, I wondered if she had a bit of a thing going with Will the estate manager. But her enthusiasm for him was as nothing to the praise heaped on this St Francis of the Home Counties.

I ended the call feeling even more rattled. OK I know I'd moved on but even so, you can't but suffer a twinge when your ex gets the hots for a new man. It was a relief to phone Tara and be given the all clear.

I'd agreed with Sarah that I shouldn't call, text or email until she sent me a message telling me that Griff had left. I assumed he'd leave on Sunday night and spent the whole evening on tenterhooks at the pub. I'd warned Tara I'd probably have to dash out at some point. In the event I ended up drowning my sorrows after closing time and sharing the customary Indian in the Public Bar with Tara, Keith, who occasionally helped out when we were short, and Charlie, one of the regulars. Keith was a prize piss-head but as long as you didn't push him beyond nine, he could sleepwalk anything. That night he'd been propping up the bar as opposed to being behind it. After we'd eaten I tidied the place up, got on my bike and pedalled home to my solitary bed.

To my solitary bed and a silent mobile – silent, apart that is, for one heart-stopping, earth-shifting moment when it did go 'ching-ching'. My trembling hand reached out. I pressed 'read', scrolled and couldn't believe my eyes. I've still got that text. I reckon it did make me smile – it does now certainly. Yes, it must have done. It couldn't fail to: Out with friends. Just been taught how 2 text. Thought I'd send u 1st message. Bit l8 I know-both hour and my age! Tee-hee! Much love from Gaynor and me, Dad. Reading that I wonder how long it took him to get it the right length. Did he use predictive mode? No, probably tapped it out letter by letter. And

337

he'd have had a few beers. It was a labour of love! Good old Dad.

In the end Sarah didn't ring but turned up at the mill at about midday on the Monday.

I opened the door and there she was in her tracksuit as if she'd run from the Folly. She looked tired. We studied each other intently then literally fell into one another's arms and hugged and kissed and pressed our bodies together as if we hadn't seen each other for years.

We staggered back into the house and the front door swung shut of its own accord. We were upstairs in my bedroom within seconds and then I was slipping off her tracksuit bottoms and knickers and she got my jeans and pants down and I was trying to get a condom out of the box in the drawer of my beside table, then we toppled onto the bed and I was inside her and her legs were locked round my waist.

When we woke up she whispered, 'After my run, I drove straight to the pub and when you weren't there, I thought, he's gone somewhere. He got tired of waiting for me. I was so scared.'

'Where would I go?'

'I don't know. I was so afraid, that's all. So irrational.'

I kissed her forehead.

'I didn't even shower. Well, I did. As soon as he left I showered him off me – not that anything happened. He was too drunk – so what's new? Then I just ran and ran him out of my life before driving to the village.'

'I've taken today off,' I said when we were sitting at the kitchen table later. We were eating scrambled eggs with finely-chopped tomatoes and mushrooms and chunks of smoked mackerel mixed in. A special recipe of Jill's. I'd opened a bottle of Beaujolais Villages.

I say we were eating but that's an exaggeration. I was, she was prodding. Soon she gave up and rolled a cigarette.

'Me too. Harriet's looking after the gallery – today and tomorrow. I've got to go down to Wiltshire this evening – talk some things through with Mum and Min. Tomorrow I'm seeing Dad.'

'You're lucky you've got someone like Harriet.' Harriet was Sarah's right-hand. A tall capable girl. I'd only met her the once when I visited the gallery for the first time but I could tell straight away she was on the ball.

'She's one in a million.'

I poured some more wine.

'Sorry I didn't get in touch last night.'

'Well we'd agreed you wouldn't until he left.'

'I know – and I felt sure he'd go back Sunday night. When he stayed I thought I'd text but he was chatty all evening and by the time he went to bed it was gone one.'

'Why did he stay?'

'He wanted to go to Col and Fi's and once we got home he needed to talk through what happened. Fi said the only time Col would be up to a visit was six on Sunday. Apparently Col comes alive then. It's something to do with the depression. Saturday was no good because Griff was pissed after the rugby, so—'

I don't know why but I found Griff wanting to see Col and Fi unsettling. I'd grown so used to thinking of him as not part of the village. His having feelings for Col and Fi and going so far as to reintegrate himself in village life really brought it home what it would be like when he came back for good.

I was haunted by the thought of Griff seeing Col and Fi all next day. I'd always known he'd be back – and that he'd use the Castle – but with him away it never seemed real. In August Sarah and me had two, maybe three months of untroubled courting ahead of us and I don't think I'd moved on mentally. Now I found myself looking up every time someone came into the pub and imagining what it'd be like when Griff was down every day. Things were made worse by Andy being in jail. If he was out I could take more of a back seat like in the summer. I considered recruiting a temp but this went against the grain. I was still paying Andy his wages – it was the least I could do – and while I could afford a temp my business sense didn't like the idea when I could do the work myself.

Having to think along those lines narked me. I hate it when my personal life gets wrinkled up. I like everything smooth. Jill once said in an argument that I was a mummy's boy because I liked things just so. Well, she might more accurately have said I was a daddy's boy – it's from him I get my attention to detail. But then I suppose we were both mummy's boys. And to tell the truth I wouldn't have it any other way. I am who I am – and proud of it.

On the other hand when love comes into the equation you do have to compromise your principles. Which was the situation I found myself in that day at the pub. I was sorely tempted to phone an agency and see who they had on their books. I realised I couldn't abide seeing Griff every day any more than I could give up Sarah.

Still, the pain inherent in the situation remained – though it was as nothing compared with what was about to come.

I wasn't due to see Sarah till the following evening. She was supposed to be working on her next exhibition after she got back from Wiltshire. It was a surprise when she turned up at the Castle.

It was just after five and we'd not long been open. We were in that flat period between the clocks going back and the run-up to Christmas and I'd decided to close at three for a couple of hours on Mondays through to Wednesdays. Jimbo was out front. Me and Tara were in the new kitchen playing about with the cooker and the Star Ship Enterprise extractor hood. We were about to rustle up some trial light meals. If Andy'd been on hand we'd have been launching the full works menu but as it was we'd settled for a selection of gourmet snacks. This was all Tara's initiative. Me, I would have postponed food completely until

Andy was out but she was itching to make a start from the moment the builders left. I'd resisted at first – pure self-interest and laziness, I'm ashamed to say – but there came a point when it would have been cruel not to give her her head. Besides she might have upped and left if I held out too long. That night it was starters.

I'd just popped through to the Lounge to check Jimbo was OK when the door opened and in came Sarah. She looked terrible. She was deathly pale and though she didn't normally wear mascara, not only did she have some on but it had run badly.

I looked at Jimbo and gave him the nod, which he picked up on like a true professional and disappeared into the Tap side of the bar.

I went to Sarah and took her in my arms. As I did so she sort of fell into me like she'd fainted. She burst out crying. 'Tom, Tom,' she gasped, 'they were so cruel. Bitches!'

I whispered, 'There, there, Sarah. There, there,' and stroked her neck and back. She felt so frail. It was as if she'd lost a ton of weight in the last twenty-four hours. Although in truth she was probably no more than a couple of ounces lighter. The way she looked was down to that strange paradox I noticed early in our relationship. On the one hand, particularly when she was with people she trusted, she could be relaxed and outgoing, and her whole demeanour made you forget how skinny she was. At other times, when she was unsure about a situation – like the day of the pageant – she'd make herself disappear. She'd look nice but unremarkable and would simply blend into the background. But when her confidence was dented she crumpled and the illusion was lost.

She was clinging to me tightly. 'Tom, Tom,' she sobbed again.

Then someone else was saying my name behind me. 'Tom I've just thought—'

I looked over my shoulder at Tara and raised my eyebrows. I expected her to fade back into the kitchen but instead she came towards us. She put her hand on Sarah's shoulder and was about to try and turn her with the other.

I must say it had never occurred to me that Tara might know

341

Sarah, except to say hello. Now I suspected she not only knew her socially but had come across her in this state before. I was stunned by these realisations, I don't know why. Maybe because they seemed like yet more things, coming as they did on top of Griff's reappearance, that threatened our private Eden.

Instead of turning towards Tara, though, Sarah continued hugging me, burying her head even deeper in my chest. It was Tara's turn to look puzzled.

I winked at her – it was the wrong expression but I couldn't manage a better one.

She looked at Sarah then back at me and gave a tight little smile. She took her hands away ever so gingerly as if Sarah might fall over. Then she said, 'I'll be in the kitchen.'

I asked Sarah what she wanted to do. I made out, 'Come home with you.'

I got her sitting on the settle by the fire before going through to the kitchen and telling Tara that the tasting was off.

She said that was fine, although she was going to go ahead with the cooking and try the starters on the punters. I could hardly object. Then she said, 'Is she alright?'

I shrugged. 'I've got her sitting down but she's very upset. She's had a row with her mother and sister – I think.'

'Poor Sarah.'

'I'm going to get her back to the mill and talk her down. Sorry for having to—'

'That's OK. Look after her, Tom. Look after yourself too. And Tom—'

'Yeah?'

'Be careful.'

I said I would, although I didn't really know what she meant.

I got my leather jacket, called to Jimbo to unbolt the Tap door and guided Sarah into the yard.

'What happened?'

'What didn't happen?'

She gulped down some more whisky. It was Lagavulin –

342

Cadenhead's As We Get It bottling, 55° proof. It was a beauty – it gleamed like a gem in the firelight and was stuffed with flavours (peat, phenols, iodine, seaweed and salt). Outstanding! Col put me onto it one afternoon up at the copse. He was still a member of a malt club – a leftover from when he lived in Islington and was awash with cash. Poor Col.

'You sure you don't want water?'

'Quite sure, thanks. I love single malts – and this one's a monster!' It was one of the few times she smiled that evening. 'Besides, it'll help numb the pain.' She drank some more then dragged on her cigarette.

We were sitting on the huge leather sofa I'd had delivered a couple of weeks earlier. As soon as we'd got in I lit a fire and shoved the sofa close up. It was a bitter night.

I smiled back but for her the moment was gone. I got my handkerchief out, folded it so there was a little puff of material between my thumb and forefinger, licked this (just like Mum used to when I was a kid), then dabbed at the smudges of mascara on her cheeks, all before she had time to protest.

'Oh God, I'd forgotten. I must have looked like Marilyn Manson. What must Tara have thought?'

'Don't worry about her,' I said a mite too sharply. 'Nor Jimbo. They're professionals.'

She almost smiled again at that. 'That's not really the point.'

'Why were you wearing it?'

'I'm sorry?' She looked hostile all of a sudden.

'You don't usually, that's all.'

'You've noticed.'

'Of course. I love your natural look.'

'Well today I weakened.'

'Weakened?'

'You've picked up on one of the things I *hate* myself for.'

'Hate?' I laid my hands on her shoulders. 'Come on Sarah relax. You're safe now.'

She wriggled away. 'Leave me, Tom. Just give me space, OK?'

'OK, OK, I was only trying to comfort you.'

'Well, you weren't. You made me feel hemmed in.'

She stared at me defiantly. She was angry. I expected her to apologise once I backed off but quickly realised I wasn't going to get anything. She flicked her cigarette butt into the fire.

'Why do you hate yourself?' I asked. I wasn't sure it was the right question. I felt out of my depth. I remember a funny thing came into my head as I watched her – I thought of my grandad's Jack Russells. Although I'm not much of a dog person, I got quite close to successive generations of his lot. They were mostly pretty good but every once in a while you found yourself in a situation where you were gazing at the dog and it would be gazing back at you and you knew, absolutely knew that there was not a spark of understanding between you. It was like that with Sarah. We might as well have been on different planets.

'Oh, it doesn't matter.'

'It *does* Sarah. It does. Do you want a top-up?'

She peered into her glass then nodded.

I reached for the bottle, which was on the floor beside me, and unscrewed the metal cap.

'Cheers,' I suggested.

She raised her glass and I tapped it with mine.

'I hate myself because I put some make-up on to ingratiate myself with Dad. Last night I had such a piss awful time with those bitches that today I felt it necessary to "paint my face", as Mum puts it, so I could get a smidgen of approval from Dad (he just lurves me looking that way). And my God I needed it. I was *needy*, alright. And damn sure I wasn't going to get it from those two wankers. A kick up the arse, more like.'

The intensity of these dysfunctional sentiments disconcerted me. She didn't sound like Sarah. OK she was dysfunctional at the best of times but this was different. The look in her eyes scared me too. It was like she was absent, like she was replaying a video in her mind of what happened with Min and her parents.

'What did they do to you?'

'Fucking bitches – bitches, bitches, *bitches*! They ganged up on me, that's what. I thought going to Mum's when Min was there was a nice way of setting the tone for the future – you know, when Dad's—' And here she paused for a second and her voice went quieter as she pronounced the next word, 'Gone.'

She glanced at me like she wondered if I'd noticed what she did, clocked the expression on my face (I imagine) and drank some whisky as if she was fuelling herself for more of the hard girl stuff. She reached for her tobacco tin.

'That was a laugh! Oh yes, they were as pleasant as can be to begin with – although it was blindingly obvious they'd decided in advance how they were going to play things. Treat her with kid gloves, make her feel safe then put the boot in. Supper was excruciating. Mum made all my favourite things. It was so creepy it wasn't true. I bet it was Min who dreamt it all up – using her psychiatric knowledge to wage psychological war. She ought to be struck off!'

'Surely she wouldn't be that cruel. Anyway, if you saw through it, she wasn't very successful.'

'That's the wickedest thing about her. When she's nice you know she's up to something and yet you're so grateful that she's showing you kindness. You want it to be true. You think, this is what it's like to have a mother and a sister who love you and who you can love back. You know it's a lie but they sucker you into their confidence.'

'I remember Jill and her sister Jemima used to have some right ding-dongs. It used to amaze me, not having brothers or sisters, the things they'd fight about and what they did to each other. You'd think World War Three had broken out and they'd never speak to each other again. But they always did.'

'What I'm talking about, Tom, isn't the same. It's calculated.'

I thought she sounded paranoid but didn't say anything, just shrugged and went, 'OK.'

'What Min can't stand is that Alex and I saw through Dad, got out and made something of our lives.'

'I don't follow.'

'It comes down to money – as everything always does – or rather the lack of it.'

She lit her cigarette.

'Min's trust fund?'

'Yep.'

'Your dad filched money from hers too?'

'Sort of – because she was that much younger than us, he was allowed to invest up to fifty percent of the capital in approved projects. In fact he'd managed to get about ninety percent by lying to the trustees. But as far as Min was concerned, he could have taken the lot and she'd have been perfectly happy. When Uncle Vern forced the sale of the surgery Min objected. She said Dad should be allowed to see the scheme through and we'd all be better off as a result. That was Dad's argument too. He claimed the terms of the trusts were restrictive and he was simply trying to make his children richer than they otherwise would be.'

'You didn't accept that.'

She glared at me furiously. 'No fucking way!' When she said that she sounded like a stroppy teenager – as she did whenever she lost it that night. It was very unlike her. Light years away from the cool maturity (superiority, you might have said) of our first picnics and walk to the tower and far more out of control even than when we'd discussed her father before. I must say I wasn't that impressed by her outbursts – I didn't think they did her any favours when it came to being taken seriously.

'Sorry, it was meant to be a straightforward question. I didn't mean anything by it.'

'Well it didn't come out that way.'

'Sorry.'

'The trustees got a firm of accountants to assess the viability of Dad's scheme – and they said it hadn't a hope. Not that Little Miss Min ever agreed! Daddy could do no wrong. And still can't, even though he's sold her way short!'

'Didn't she get her money back?'

'Nope. She felt so sorry for Dad she allowed him to pay her off in annual instalments. Which he's not always been able to meet – but what the hell, to her way of thinking, that's just fine. She takes the view that his financial embarrassment is all down to him not being allowed to complete the surgery development. Which is our fault, of course.'

'She's close to him, then?'

'She's close to both of them. After the farm was sold and Alex

346

and I got our cash, the three of them huddled together like disaster victims. We were the disaster! They became the new family unit, which was just the way Min liked it. She always did behave like a spoilt only child.'

I knew Sarah would hate me for thinking it, but I could sympathise with Min. She'd been significantly younger than Sarah or Alex and I suspected her bark was worse than her bite. Sarah and Alex were also obviously more independent than her. Her plight reminded me of Jill's – she was the dutiful one, always popping down to see her Mum, whereas Jemima was wayward and a lot of the time seemed like she couldn't care a damn about her family. In my opinion Jemima was caught between needing to reject the family as represented by Jill and their mum, *and* being desperately jealous of their closeness.

'And this blew up again yesterday?'

'Yes. After we'd eaten. I know I shouldn't be paranoid about people taking advantage of my anorexia because ninety-nine times out of a hundred they aren't. It's simply me *being* paranoid. But what with both Min's medical training and her uncontrollable killer instinct, I'm damn sure I'm right.'

'Even if they don't do it consciously they might do it *sub*-consciously.'

'With Min it's conscious. I'm sure of it. She's cruel.'

'OK.'

'Don't patronise me, Tom.'

'I wouldn't dream of it darling.'

'Fuck off.'

I smiled at her hoping I'd diffused the situation. She didn't smile back. Maybe she'd softened a little – it wasn't a sharp, Fuck off – but I wasn't holding my breath.

'What did Min say?'

'It wasn't only her – Mum joined in. They were like a pair of dogs baiting a badger.'

I almost laughed at the image. I thought, Watch out if the badger slips its chains, but kept quiet.

'They've come up with a plan – decided that with Dad dying and the *family* facing yet another financial crisis, it's time we pull together. Things are going to be hard for Mum when Dad dies – and Min needs money for the rest of her studies. So, will I pay my share? Share of what? They expect me to contribute two thirds of the monthly mortgage payments on Mum and Dad's cottage and *repay* two thirds of the outstanding balance of Min's trust fund.'

She took a final drag at her cigarette, sucking it down to almost nothing.

'Why two thirds?'

'Alex is supposed to take care of the other third – he hasn't done as well as me so doesn't have to pay as much! But the number of thirds isn't important. It's the fucking word "repay" that fucking pisses me off! Repay? *Repay*? What the fuck does she think she's talking about?'

'Calm down Sarah. Did you agree to anything?'

'No. It's not my fault that Dad's a cunting crook. Oh, but if I'd let him keep the other surgery, we'd all be millionaires now. Bollocks!'

I got up and chucked another log on the fire. I was getting fed up of listening to her sounding off. There was no way you could reason with her when she was like this. Nevertheless I tried.

'Shall I get us something to eat?' It probably wasn't the most sensible thing to say but I couldn't think outside the box. The *normal* box.

Surprisingly she did calm down for a minute when I said that. 'Have you got any veg?'

'Tons. I get one of these local box things delivered weekly. Usually there's so much I end up throwing most of it away.'

'I'll get myself something later. If I can stay the night?'

'Of course.'

'You fix yourself something.'

'I might just do that.' I was still standing up.

I stared down at her. She was very beautiful but I realised I didn't understand her one bit. I asked myself did I love her. I had deep feelings for her, yes, but had I fallen in love? I was both fascinated and repulsed by her. I was addicted to her. I doubt that amounts to love but at the time it somehow seemed to.

'Did you get so stressed you threw up last night? Is that the problem? I don't understand Sarah and I want to.'

'I toddled off and threw up during it, actually.'

'But they got at you after?'

'Yes.'

'I don't get it.'

'I throw up all the time.'

'OK. So why are you angry? All you had to do was say no.'

'All? Oh don't be so fucking stupid! Anyway it doesn't matter.'

'Of course it does.' I sat down beside her. 'Please explain.'

She was sitting with her legs drawn close against the sofa pointing straight ahead of her. She was hunched up, both hands clasped round her empty whisky glass.

I placed my hand on her wrist and whispered, 'Please tell me. I want to know.'

She was staring into the fire. I half expected her to pull away but for what seemed a long time she just continued staring. Then, all of a sudden, she pulled her arm away sharply and thrust her tumbler towards me.

'More whisky!'

I was so taken aback by the violence of her movements I reckoned she was going to hit me.

I breathed deeply and tried to regain control of the situation. 'I thought I might open a bottle of wine.'

'Do what the hell you like. Whisky!'

I poured her some and she immediately gulped down half.

'OK,' she said, licking her lips. 'I'll *tell* you.'

'Alright. *Alright.*'

Her innocent words stung me. I felt hurt – utterly out of my depth. I almost didn't care whether she told me or not.

'It's not a question of them being nasty and then me throwing up. Throwing up mid-way through the meal is normal.'

She looked hard at me – to see if I was shocked maybe. I hated what she was saying.

'I do it—' she began and took a drink of whisky. 'I do it because— Because most of the time I can't help myself. I don't want to – sometimes I'm determined not to, other times I'm less fussed, I suppose – but I can't avoid it. I'm compelled to. Sometimes I forget to – or maybe that part of me that wants to is as exhausted as the rest of me. Whatever. But those times I usually end up realising I've not been sick and do it anyway. The times I get through a meal and a night without chucking are like a gift from God.'

She again stared at me. I looked away from her. All I could think of was this time when I'd just been starting out in the pub trade. I was managing my first house for Len Banks in Hitchin. It was summer. I was twenty-two, as green as they come but working like a Trojan. The pub was on the edge of the town and I was usually up at the crack of dawn walking through the fields before getting stuck into the cleaning and cellarmanship. That morning was a Sunday and there'd been a rock concert on a nearby farm. It'd been a God-awful racket – Christ knows how they got permission. We objected in the strongest terms – Len's game was about presenting the local as a responsible pillar of the community.

Well, when I went for my walk, the gig was still going on. I chose a route along a stream which would take me close to the farm but not too close before I could veer off towards some woods. It was when I was closest to the farm that I met this woman. She looked middle-aged to me, although thinking back she was probably only in her late twenties. She was out of it. Staggering – pissed out of her skull or on something. She had short, slightly spiky blond hair with tiny multi-coloured bows in it and was wearing a fluorescent pink crop-top and black leggings. She was bare foot. She stopped when she saw me, grinned and made her eyes very wide. Then she shouted, 'Sorry, got to go!' at the top of her voice. She giggled, slipped down her leggings and knickers and squatted in front of me. For a few seconds all I could do was stare, listening to the stream off piss gushing out and running over the ground between her feet. She farted loudly and the sound made me jump. I turned away and set off along the footpath to the woods.

I didn't think I was a prude in those days but the sight of the woman peeing unsettled me. It wasn't just that I saw what should have been private but the fact that she was in such a state. I was saddened that a woman should let herself down like that.

The image of the woman came into my head when Sarah was telling me about throwing up. I had the same set of feelings, both times.

I forced myself to look at her. She seemed defiant as if she expected me to take her on. In truth I couldn't think what to say. If I touched her she'd pull back. Whatever I said would be wrong. I just nodded. Tried to look sympathetic.

'When I forget to chuck up it's like I've set off across a tightrope without thinking about it. You know, how you sometimes do difficult things unconsciously and when you've done them, you think how the hell did I do that and feel scared because you know that if you'd woken part-way through you'd have lost your nerve.'

Again I nodded. I did know what she meant. The number of times I'd experienced that feeling when I ran Dickens's! I smiled at her – she was gentler now.

'Most of the time, of course, I do wake up when I'm still walking the tightrope and I fall.'

She opened her tobacco tin and began rolling yet another cigarette.

'You see, what it is Tom, about throwing up, is that it makes me feel calm, gives me strength, if you like, enables me to carry on.'

'Like Karl and his drugs.'

'Like Karl and his drugs. The trouble is that it's only OK if things in the outside world stay the same. If you're at a dinner party and everyone's being obnoxious, being sick helps you to cope with their bad behaviour. But if you came back from the loo and they were all suddenly nice, you'd freak out. You'd panic, think you'd misjudged them and feel utterly inadequate. Experiences like that tip you over into a new and more desperate cycle of behaviour. You chuck up all the time, lose weight rapidly, drink and smoke too much or take drugs. One time I started cutting myself but I soon stopped. It was too public. If I forgot I'd done it and rolled up my sleeve, people knew instantly what I was about. I want to harm myself discretely. I want to take on suffering, yes, but also to efface myself. I want to fade out. I want to be invisible. Alright, if you starve yourself too much people begin to notice but to an extent you can disguise it with clothes, and anyway you really do start to think you're invisible when you're malnourished. And the weird thing is you create your own reality around you. People notice you're thin but if you keep acting normally they soon forget.'

She finished her whisky and lit her cigarette. Her hands were shaking.

'So when Min and your Mum stopped being nice and ganged up on you – what, you couldn't handle it?'

'I was vulnerable. They made me feel totally useless. I couldn't find the strength to fight back, although I didn't give ground. I was sweet and non-committal, and not telling them how I felt or what they could do with their proposals only made me feel more wretched. It's hard to explain exactly how it was. To understand that, you'd have to know all the things I went through as a child.'

I thought of her room at the Folly. It's sometimes unbelievable what parents do to their kids. But often they don't know they're doing it. As Sarah herself said children react differently to the same thing. You might mention something to one and it screws them up but if said to another it's water off a duck's back.

'All the pain, all the twisted skeins of emotion come back, as if they'd never departed.'

Suddenly she sounded broken. Without thinking I put my hand on her wrist. She didn't pull away.

'I bluffed my way through the rest of the evening like the diplomat I am, making them love me, even though I know that deep down they have nothing for me but hatred. Inside I was burning up. I went to the loo to be sick three times. When I went upstairs I spent all night by the open window smoking like a naughty little girl and feeling utterly, utterly miserable. Like now, I feel broken and I'm terrified of what's to come. I don't have the strength to stop the self-destruction.'

'I don't know what to say. There's too much to take in.'
She laughed. 'I'm sorry for burdening you.'
I waved her apology away. 'That's OK.'

Not long afterwards I left her in the sitting-room for a bit, listening to Björk, smoking roll-ups and guzzling a bottle of Chilean special reserve Chardonnay. I went to the kitchen and cooked myself a light supper – smoked salmon on toast with scrambled egg. I wasn't hungry. I ate it at the kitchen table on my own.

When I'd finished and washed up I asked Sarah what she wanted to do.

She said she just wanted to be quiet.

I'd had enough and told her I was going to walk across the fields to the pub and see how Tara got on – it was a beautiful starlight night. I added that I thought she'd probably feel better being on her own. She didn't disagree. I told her where the veg was.

I had three or four pints at the pub. Tara was a breath of fresh air – and the left over snacks were all of them winners. I began to feel human again.

It was gone midnight when I climbed the last style and approached the house. All the lights were on in the kitchen and I could see Sarah having her supper at the kitchen table.

When I was still in the shadows I stopped and watched her for a little.

After a couple of minutes she stood up and came towards the window, looking tired and pale under the spotlamps. She bent her head over the sink and opened her mouth. A thick stream of sick spilt out. It all happened in slow motion somehow. The extraordinary thing was the sick was white. You couldn't believe the veg had been bleached inside her in such a short time.

When she'd done she stared ahead into the night. I was surprised she couldn't see me, although I've checked since and what she was looking at was her reflection. Then – and I swear this is true, Mart – she licked her lips and there was this big contended grin on her face.

Chaos

Watching Sarah being sick was a surreal experience and the following three weeks, culminating in Griff's death, were no less so.

When I saw her – What? Regurgitate? – it was like the world was turned inside out. What was concealed was suddenly visible. The intensely personal was now public. No not public, that's the wrong word, although me being shown what she did certainly felt public in that I could tell others. The secret was out and I was often nearly overtaken by this desire to proclaim what I'd seen. Other times it was as if people would know what had happened just by looking at me. There were moments when I wondered if I'd been put in a kind of privileged position and could maybe help her. But mostly I felt – well cursed mightn't be overstating it.

Sarah went back to the Folly the next morning. She phoned Harriet first thing to say she wouldn't be in before midday. Then she got up at nine, showered and came down to breakfast. She had a black coffee and, to my astonishment, a slice of toast.

She was quiet, though not I would have said, hungover. She apologised for her behaviour.

I told her there was nothing to apologise for – after all we'd kissed and made up when I got in. In fact we'd made love. Looking back it seems strange to have done that after what I witnessed but somehow it made me tender towards her.

It was in the cold light of day that the mind began to pick over events and I must say I was glad when she left.

During the following week we saw each other twice only. Sarah was busy with her exhibition and I had the pub to look after. I also went up to London for a meeting with Claudette – a blast from the past. She'd detected signs that the pub chain that'd bought Dickens's were prepared to offer me a good price for my shares plus a lump sum as consideration for their early surrender. I was flattered because their interest testified to the quality of the business I'd sold them. Even so I doubted anything more would come of it, although I agreed to meet Claudette again in the new year.

Sarah and I went out for a meal on Friday night and on Sunday had a lovely walk along the Thames. I sensed she was on her best behaviour but I couldn't help but be wary of her. In truth I simply didn't know what to think.

It was a week after I'd seen her being sick that all hell broke loose.

The trial of Col, Andy and the two blokes from the Winstanley Society, Quentin and Bud, took place in Oxford. Griff came down for it the night before and announced he was back for good – well, until next summer, which might just as well have been for good.

After the sentencing Tara attempted to barge her way through the press photographers waiting outside, tripped, fell badly and broke her kneecap. It was a nasty fracture. The bone split into four pieces and it was touch and go whether they'd start floating off and need wiring. As it was she ended up in a fibreglass cast from ankle to thigh. I couldn't believe it when I saw it. She'd had the doctors do it in pink and red. It looked like a stick of rock.

She spent the first night in hospital and the next four weeks at her mum's in Standlake. Which meant I had to move into the pub to satisfy the insurance company.

I'd just about resigned myself to a busier than expected Christmas and New Year and was telling myself it could be worse when Sarah phoned. She was in her car driving across the Marsh. She'd rowed with Griff. She'd packed her bags and left. Could she pick up the keys to the mill? I told her I'd moved to the pub. She said that was no problem – she'd stay with me.

The pub was relatively quiet that evening particularly during the first couple of hours. I was relieved not just because of Tara and Sarah but because Jimbo and Emily had prior commitments. They – plus Keith – had held the fort at lunchtime and I couldn't expect them to alter things, especially as both seemed to have romance on their mind.

I tried phoning Keith but he was well gone. His nine o'clock alcohol-shed had slipped back steadily over the past week. I suspected he was about to go on an almighty bender.

For the first hour after Sarah arrived I phoned round reorganising my diary and checking with Jimbo and Emily which shifts they could do. To be perfectly honest I was glad of the diversion. I needed to keep busy while my brain caught up with events. Jimbo and Emily were very good about me constantly interrupting their amorous pursuits and eventually I put together a half-decent rota. I think they were pleased about the extra money.

We agreed the light snacks had to stop and that we'd close at three for a couple of hours during the week. Obviously if I was doing a lunchtime and there were punters who wanted to carry on and I had nothing better to do... But I couldn't expect the same from the kids.

While I was glued to my mobile Sarah went upstairs, changed Andy and Tara's bed and tidied the flat. I was amazed how calm she was. She was good in a crisis. It was afterwards, when things settled down, that she went to pieces.

Not surprisingly what overshadowed the whole evening was Griff. We kept expecting him to burst through the door any minute. As it turned out there wasn't a dicky-bird but it was still a bloody nightmare!

That night the talk of the pub was Andy and Tara. People were genuinely concerned for me too – which I was touched by. And yet no one batted an eyelid about Sarah being there beyond the obvious. The majority said something like, 'Oh, he's got you working here now, Sarah', although one old boy muttered, 'I'd have thought you'd have got that pyromaniac Colin to help you.

Part of his *community* service!'

What with me phoning and trade picking up from eight onwards we didn't have much chance to discuss what had happened. I got on with serving while Sarah busied herself with other things. She collected glasses, wiped tables and tended the fires. Every so often she sat the other side of the bar for a cigarette and a chat with the customers. You'd never have known she'd just left Griff. With hindsight one might think that was chilling but at the time I found myself feeling good about it. My frame of mind was bizarre that night. She slotted in so neatly I even thought at one point that if this was what it was like to have her there the future was going to be smashing!

At nine she asked if I wanted supper. I was famished but told her I could wait until eleven-thirty. She said she'd put something together but I didn't like the idea of eating behind the bar (Len Banks's professional etiquette kicking in). She explained she'd done a few nights at the Parker to help Jean out when Griff was away last year – which explained how she knew Tara – and would cover for me.

I thought, it gets better and better.

The only thing we talked about after the last punter left was what time we'd get up in the morning. Normally I'd wash the glasses and bottle up before going to bed but I was dog-tired. I said I'd set the alarm for six. She was fine about that because she'd an important meeting at nine. We agreed there wasn't much point going through anything else until the following evening when Jimbo and Emily were on.

I fixed her a treble Bunnahabhain, pulled a pint of Castle Best and we went upstairs.

The way we made love that night was different. It was like we were refugees in a strange land who'd just met and were comforting each other.

It was gone three o'clock when I woke. The first thing I thought was I didn't check the micro.

Since Andy'd been banged up we'd had a retired Master Brewer called Monty Levitt in to do the mashing, copper boil and racking. He was ex-Wychwood and both Rajiv and Andy rated him. All we had to do was keep an eye on the fermenting vessel, skim off excess yeast as necessary and note the diagnostic readings in the fermenting book. Each morning we'd text Mont three sets of figures so he could pick up irregularities.

There wasn't much that could go wrong but it would be just our luck to get caught out. The text idea – Tara's – was designed to limit the damage. If anything did happen we'd be able to get a new batch on the go asap.

Up to now Tara'd done the monitoring, with me as a backup on Saturday and Sunday if she fancied a lie-in. The job made her feel she was close to Andy. But now with her out of action it was down to me. I'd meant to check last thing but what with all the other stuff and, I admit it, the prospect of a beer and a cuddle with Sarah, I'd clean forgotten.

As I stole into my clothes by the light of the alarm, trying hard not to wake her, all I could think of was the disapproving look of Len Banks.

I didn't get back to sleep afterwards. Sarah was dead to the world. Or if she wasn't – she always claimed to be a dreadful sleeper – she was keeping it to herself.

I just lay there, annoyed that I forgot the vessel, and trying to make sense of the previous day. I kept on having these panic attacks when I imagined all the things that might go wrong. For a start this was the pub's busiest time. This was make or break. And here I was soldiering on with a couple of casuals. I told myself to get real and call an agency – which is what Len Banks would have done. He'd have said where the business was concerned you never skimp. But then I was different – and he'd always respected and admired me for it. Whenever a crisis occurred at one of his pubs or later at Dickens's I'd step in and take on the tasks myself, working lunatic hours if need be.

Maybe it was a macho thing – it'd been said, not least by Jill. I don't know.

Then there was Sarah. Above everything else there was Sarah. I thought I've got to get her into the mill as soon as possible. At least that way it'll look right. There was that puritanical part of me which I get from Dad that was concerned about what people would think. And yet there'd been times over the past few months when I'd been reckless, even hoping that somebody would spot us and rumours would start. So what changed? I suppose I'd begun to fall out of love when I saw Sarah being sick. I was loath to admit it, though, because emotions don't disentangle easy. Despite my feelings about propriety there was another part of me that was proud she'd left Griff for me. And while I was to some extent revolted by her eating disorder my heart went out to her too. It couldn't not. Our relationship, though young, had been intense.

At times my feelings were simply sexual. That night lying there beside her I thought, I want her and wish she was awake so we could make love. I also thought of how she helped out in the bar and how possible everything seemed not five hours before.

All next day the different ways I could manage the evening whirled round my head. In the end I decided I wouldn't get anywhere by telling her what to do. In order to persuade her to move into the mill I'd have to use charm.

But charm takes imagination and energy and I was stuffed as far as they were concerned. My instinct – just as it'd been at the mill the week before – was to wine and dine her. I knew this was a no-no but it's sort of hard-wired into your psyche, isn't it Mart? It's the default position. Somehow one of the saddest things about being with Sarah was not being able to share food together. It's what couples do – naturally. I didn't have the reserves to fight my instinct. I settled on the scrambled egg and smoked mackerel because she'd eaten a little when I cooked it before. I got several bottles of Chilean Merlot from the cellar (for me as much as her). I told myself that if she simply wanted to soak herself and puff away to go along with it.

But things went wrong even before she got back.

She phoned at six to let me know she was delayed which left me twiddling my thumbs. She told me she'd had an emergency meeting with her accountant and now needed to catch up on gallery business. She'd be with me at seven-thirty, eight. I said I didn't like the sound of emergency meetings and hoped she was OK. I tried to make light of it but inside was panicking. She said she felt like absolute shit but I shouldn't worry about the meeting because it wasn't what I thought. Her words didn't reassure me.

From her tone of voice, she was firing on all cylinders, despite her claim to be feeling like shit. Suddenly it seemed that any hopes I had of steering our discussion were doomed to failure.

It was quarter past eight when she got in and I was in shreds. I'd been obsessing over the meeting with the accountants. I presumed she meant by saying that it wasn't what I thought that it wasn't about selling the Folly or reaching a settlement with Griff. But if it wasn't about either of those, what was it about?

By the time she arrived I'd convinced myself that her business was in trouble. This would make sense of her erratic behaviour. Had she mortgaged the Folly up to the hilt and was she now trying to cut and run, leaving Griff with a mountain of debt?

True, the more I thought about it I couldn't get my theory to hold much water but I was convinced I was onto something. I needed to pin down what was making her so manic. I was trying to take control of all the other areas of my life and I didn't want this one to elude me.

Looking back I reckon my paranoid thoughts can be likened to me taking on extra work in a crisis. Both strategies are attempts to bring the world to heel. I hate things going wrong which I have no power over.

But the more I thought about Sarah, the more I feared her. There was so much I didn't understand about her and the idea of containing her maverick side seemed laughable.

When she didn't appear at seven forty-five I went downstairs and pestered the kids.

I'd already told them that Sarah was going to be living at the pub for a couple of days. Before doing so I contemplated lying to them but when it came to it I decided that honesty was the best policy. If they found out I'd lied they'd never trust me again. In the event they were OK about it, albeit in different ways. Jimbo gave me the thumbs up and went, Cool! Whereas Emily assumed the manner of a Relate counsellor – her mum and dad had recently split – telling me that although she didn't approve, she understood. I swore them to secrecy.

At ten past eight I went back upstairs and contemplated trying Sarah's mobile. No sooner did I make my decision and retrieve the number than I heard the flat door opening. Seconds later she came into the living-room.

She stopped abruptly and looked at me for a few seconds before giving the room the once over.

She pushed the door to and said, 'Home, sweet home.'

I wasn't sure if she was being sarcastic.

'You look terrible,' she said.

'Thanks.'

'Sorry.'

'That's OK. I've had a lot on my mind. Plus I was worried about you and this meeting.'

'It wasn't much fun – though making a decision was cathartic.'

She reached into the pocket of her blanket coat for her tobacco tin then took the coat off and draped it over the back of the nearest armchair. She was wearing a jade-green mohair jumper, leather trousers – fuchsia-coloured – and brown suede boots.

She looked expensive and unexpectedly fresh. Her eyes were a little puffy, although whether this was from tiredness or crying I couldn't tell.

She came towards me, put her tobacco tin on the coffee table and said, 'I need a drink.'

'I got in a case of wine.'

She laughed. 'Excellent. But first—'

She bent towards me, put her arms round my shoulders and kissed me.

I shifted my legs onto the sofa and she lay on top of me. We pressed against each other hard.

'Forget the drink,' she whispered.

We pushed ourselves off the sofa and went into the bedroom.

Making love felt like the perfect way of releasing the tension that had built up.

Afterwards as we fell asleep, I remember thinking I'd been daft suspecting her business had gone bust.

It must have been near ten-thirty when we woke. I said I'd fetch us some wine but she wanted to get up. She offered to make me supper. I protested that I'd intended to cook her something but she insisted. She told me I needed pampering and apologised for coming back so late.

In the kitchen I pointed out the things I'd bought and explained how I did the scrambled egg and mackerel. She heard me out then surveyed Tara and Andy's herb rack and looked in the dry goods cupboard. 'How about if I make you an invention?' 'Fine,' I said. 'Yeah, that would be great.'

I fixed us some wine and set the table in the living-room. Without thinking I laid a place for her but when she came through with my plate she said she'd eat later.

'Don't worry. I wasn't thinking. This looks amazing! What is it?'

'Mackerel carbonara? Try it. If it needs a bit more marjoram, say.'

I told her it was delicious as it was although to be quite honest I was that knackered if it needed more marjoram I wouldn't have had a clue.

She said she was pleased and sat down.

I nodded towards the coffee table. 'If you want to smoke that's fine.'

'I'll wait till you've finished.'

'No go on. You'll start climbing the walls else.'

'Thanks.'

'Are you ready to talk about the meeting?'

'I think so.'

'It wasn't about Griff or the Folly I take it.'

'No.'

'Nor the gallery.'

'Not directly.'

'How d'you mean?'

'Promise you won't be annoyed.'

'Of course I won't be. You can tell me anything.'

She took a deep drag on her cigarette. 'I arranged to pay Mum's mortgage and raise a lump sum for Min.'

I was dumbfounded. It wasn't any of my business but I'd somehow managed to get my head round her not paying them anything. When she'd spoken about her feelings towards them the previous week I felt uncomfortable but because she was so assertive I fell in line. I thought I don't understand or much care for the emotions here but I've no doubt what she believes.

Because of her forcefulness the issue was kind of loaded and if she'd sat there and said to me she'd told them where to get off, I'd have felt compelled to be right with her. Instead she was calmly explaining that she'd completely changed her mind. This produced an opposite reaction.

'You're joking aren't you? What the hell's going on? Can the business afford it?'

'Tom? I thought you said— Yes, the business can afford it. It's *very* successful.'

'Glad to hear it. But the idea sounds absolutely barking. Sometimes I struggle to make you out, Sarah.'

'Don't, Tom.'

'Have you forgotten what they did to you?'

'Stop, Tom! Please!'

Tears began streaming down her cheeks.

'I'm sorry. I'm sorry. But *Jesus Christ!*' I banged my fist onto the table making my plate jump and she put her hands to her face.

Again I apologised but hard though I tried I couldn't control myself. I felt she'd deliberately involved me in this emotionally-charged stuff and was now twisting and turning my sympathies without any regard for my feelings. I felt used, manipulated. I also felt like all the grunt of the last couple of days had suddenly come to a head.

'What is it Sarah? Is it some need to be liked by everybody? Is it that? I'd like to know. I don't understand. Enlighten me. Please.'

Her hands were pressed against her cheeks puckering her mouth. 'What's wrong with wanting to be liked?' she half-whispered. 'What's wrong with that?'

'By those "bitches"?'

'I can't believe you're talking like this. After what I said. I told you how irrational this bit of me is. I thought you understood.'

She'd stopped crying now. She was calm – icily so.

'I tried to explain. It's my Achilles' heel. I both want to be loved by them and hate myself for being weak.'

Her composure unnerved me. I bowed my head. I said sorry and reached for her face but she beat me away.

'Don't touch me!'

'Oh God—' I thought, Here we go again.

'I'm going to bed.'

I made a grab at her but she dodged.

'Leave me alone!'

She was standing. She looked at me with contempt. She walked across the room, opened the bedroom door then slammed it shut behind her.

I thought, Bitch! I thought, This is a different tactic. We've done hysterics. Now it's a stand-off.

OK Mart, it was not my finest hour. I freely admit it. It'd been a fucking piss-awful two days.

I tried to calm down. I ate a bit more supper but my appetite had gone and I gave up. I poured myself another glass of wine and decided to get drunk but had enough sense to realise that that wouldn't solve anything. I decided to go downstairs and help

Jimbo and Emily bottle up before I checked the micro.

An hour later I came back to the flat and eased the bedroom door open. The bedside light was on and Sarah looked like she was asleep.

I knelt by the bed and laid my hand on her bare shoulder. She opened her eyes. She was wide awake.

'I'm sorry, Sarah. I was out of order. Forgive me.'

She pressed her eyes shut for a moment as if she was in agony then opened them and said, 'Please, Tom, let me get my strength back. We'll talk in the morning.'

I expected her to forgive me there and then but some of the fire had gone out of me and I just nodded, kissed her forehead and got to my feet.

It was next morning that things flared up again. I suppose I thought I'd done my penance and wanted us to apologise to each other and move on. But she sulked. She claimed to have a busy day ahead of her and needed to get her head sorted out.

She wouldn't look me in the eye.

I decided she was playing mind games and trying to make me feel guilty and told her so. She was furious and shouted she didn't play games. We yelled at each other for maybe a minute before she shouted fuck off and stormed out of the flat...

Experience?

I finished the above yesterday Mart before you called.

You asked me how I was and I said OK but that wasn't strictly true. I'd begun to realise things about myself as I wrote which unsettled me.

When I lived through those weeks Mart I was full of self-righteousness. At its most basic, I was convinced I was right and she was wrong. She was the one with the mental illness, I was the sane one with a handle on reality. If I blew my top and hurt her – which I did, a lot over the next fortnight – and she said she needed space so she could heal, I interpreted this as her attempting to wind me up. Her silence compounded her obvious guilt in general. Though in truth she was probably simply trying to sort out her feelings and avoid saying something we'd both regret. I can see that now. She doubtless thought, What the hell have I got myself into! And who could blame her? At the time I could blame her for everything but not now.

Last night Mart, after you'd gone and I was beating myself up for having victimised Sarah I thought about the occasion when I went to see Fiona after Griff died and the police investigation had run its course. We were sitting among the remnants of her and Colin's home. Ben and Nat were at her parents'. We sat on packing cases drinking mugs of tea. She told me some important things that afternoon Mart, some about Griff which I'll come back to later, others about Sarah.

Not surprisingly Sarah refused to see me after Griff's death and I was at Fiona's because I needed to find out if she'd said anything about us. Not that I hoped we'd get back together.

Well, part of me did, part of me thought I'd escaped from the jaws of hell.

It took a while for me to work round to asking about Sarah and when I did Fiona said simply that she had told her we'd had a relationship but hadn't gone into details.

'She's had rather a lot to cope with – just recently.'

'Point taken.'

'Besides, she does tend to keep things to herself. I'm sure she'll talk when she's ready.'

'You'll keep in touch then?'

'Of course. She's my friend.'

She stared at me, her beautiful blue eyes looking hard all of a sudden, as if emphasising her and Sarah's solidarity. I almost abandoned what I was going to say.

'I suppose you know about her eating disorder.'

'Yes.'

'I wondered how secret it was.'

'I don't think she's ever made a secret of it – not since living here, anyway.'

'Other people know about it?'

'Yes. She's very brave.'

'Although sometimes she weakens.'

'It's a *serious* illness.'

'I know, believe me.'

'As a friend, all one can do is be there. Accept her for who she is. She has so many *remarkable* qualities. We all have our weaknesses. And the person her anorexia hurts most is herself.'

'*I* found it quite difficult to cope with, actually.'

'But because you loved her you supported her.'

I couldn't say anything.

Those blue eyes appeared so innocent now. I wanted to ask her why she wasn't supporting Colin but her eyes wouldn't let me.

'Didn't you?' she asked.

'Not enough.'

'Poor Sarah. She told me when you got together that she'd found love.'

She made me ashamed, Mart, although I did try and defend myself by telling her what Griff said. I thought I was like a card player laying down an ace. But I was mistaken. She had the ace. I'll explain in due course.

I left the smallholding feeling humbled but soon – that evening probably – pride got the better of me. Yet over the coming months the more I sought to justify my actions and feelings the more depressed I became. Until I found you Mart.

Wouldn't it have been lovely if I could say I learnt my lessons that afternoon with Fiona but learning them took a long time. Certainly when Sarah was living at the pub I hadn't even started kindergarten.

I've re-read that piece I wrote for you at the very beginning entitled *The Source of my Pain*. I wanted to find out what I said about my feelings towards Sarah in the immediate aftermath of her leaving the pub. I quote:

> In my heart I was glad it was over for the time being. I told myself that as far as the future was concerned, I would take it as it came. But inside I was experiencing relief: the last couple of weeks with her had been a strain. It wasn't the situation with Griff, it was her. Mood swings, playing games, trying to impose some sort of structure on my life I couldn't fathom.

With hindsight my last sentence seems somewhat of an over-reaction. To be truthful the mood swings happened in the weeks before she fled to the pub, that night at the mill especially. They weren't surprising given her old man was about to cop it and there were the inevitable financial and emotional consequences of such an event to be faced. A person can be forgiven mood swings under such circumstances,

Just like the games I accused her of playing, the mood swings could be seen as the direct result of having to cope with a thoroughly insecure chippy bloke. A man who was more worried about twitching lace curtains than getting on and loving his partner.

The trouble was I'd had life too good before Sarah. Businesswise my adult life was a doddle. I simply clicked with the pub trade. Sure, I had to work hard and apply my mind but when you know what you're doing instinctively – you've been fortunate enough to slot into a space that's God-given – and you're on a roll, you just have to play life for all it's worth and it'll pay you back a million-fold. Added to which the market was with me. Consumer demand, tax breaks, technological advances – behind me all the way.

Relationships were easy too. If someone became a pain in the arse, I'd drop them and move on. I wanted life to be a breeze not a flaming nuisance. I didn't have time for complications and I wasn't the only one. Then I met Jill. But we lived our own lives and though I took liberties with the notion of independent people we were both boxed so separately that she worked through her pain and frustration on her own, without troubling me with it. Then one day, bang, she was gone! I know more about her from listening to her rabbit on about her stockman than I ever did living with her in our perfect home.

Before Sarah life was smooth as a mill-pond, as Dad would say. It was a shock to fall in love with someone vulnerable. It took me unawares.

This morning, Mart, I looked at a passage in *The Return of the Native* that I came back to again and again after I broke with Sarah.

"She went indoors in that peculiar state of misery which is not exactly grief, and which especially attends the dawnings of reason in the latter days of an ill-judged, transient love. To be conscious that the end of the dream is approaching, and yet has not absolutely come, is one of the most wearisome as well as the most curious situations along the whole course between the beginning of a passion and its end."

I used that paragraph to explain to myself why I'd been so cruel to Sarah. I decided that as love came to an end my reason began seeing her for the broken thing she was and I'd been fully justified in defending myself against her. But the dream wasn't ending. I was in love, am still in love but I betrayed her.

Sometimes Mart I think we're so astonished to find that the person we love actually needs our help, we're almost insulted that we've allowed ourselves to pick such a dud. It doesn't sit well with our self-image. Nor with what society would have us believe about the way people should be. We lash out at weakness. And yet we're weak ourselves. If Sarah'd known me after Jill left me, God knows what she'd have thought.

Over the past year I've read up on anorexia on the Net. You might say it's become my compulsion. If only I'd done it when I was with her. Instead I preferred not to know. Remaining ignorant was both to live in fear and manage that fear. When things got too much I simply slammed down the shutters. She was mad. I didn't need to know anymore.

Only once during the fortnight did I ask her what it was like. Since discussing it at the mill I'd become squeamish.

We were sitting on the sofa in the living-room having a glass of wine. I was in a good mood because the latest batch of beer was *delicious* and she'd come home and apologised to me for making life hell the previous evening. And I asked what it was like to be anorexic. I said I wanted to understand.

'OK, I'll try and explain it better,' she said.

She looked at her tobacco tin and I assumed she was going to roll a cigarette. Instead she put her glass of wine next to it and said, 'No props.'

I shrugged. 'See how you go.'

'It's a perfectly reasonable question and you've every right to know who you've taken on.'

'Your words not mine – about my right, that is. I wouldn't want to pressurise you.'

'You're not.' She touched my wrist.

She glanced at her wine. 'Perhaps one sip.'

'All I can tell you,' she said as she put the glass down, 'is what happened to me. Anorexia is as individual as people. Everyone has a different story.'

'When did it start?'

'The chucking? When I was eighteen but there'd been periods when I was obsessive about weight and food since way before. *They* began when I was eight, maybe.'

'But why?'

'You said the other day that I wanted to be loved.'

'Yeah. I'm sorry about that. I was probably out of order.'

'Little girls want to be loved by their parents, their brothers and sisters and by boys, most definitely by boys. The special ones, anyway. They also want to be loved by grandparents and teachers – everyone, in fact, whose opinion they value. But it's not just a question of actually being loved by others that's important. In order to feel loved they have to love themselves. Having a sense that they look good is part of the process. Sometimes it's the only meaningful part. A girl can make herself a complete pain but she won't necessarily associate whatever she's said or done with her unpopularity. Instead she thinks people don't like her because of the way she looks. Anther girl might be unhappy because she's growing up in a dysfunctional family but she can't identify the cause – why should she – and starts examining herself for an explanation. She compares her body to those of girls who seem to have everything. She looks at kids on TV and in magazines. She begins studying her shape in mirrors and decides she's ugly or fat or deformed. She doesn't realise that every mirror tells a different story, that if you take a peak at yourself with the mirror on the back of your mum's hairbrush, you're bound to look weird. She starts exercising or starving herself. She sucks in her tummy and adopts postures that make her look like a freak but to her make her look beautiful. She doesn't realise that if you gaze down at your body you see bulges that no one else sees.'

She smiled and shrugged. 'If that makes sense.'

'I think it's different for boys.'

'Is it, though? Lots of boys get anorexia too.'

'So I've read.'

'It's true. There was a feature on Radio 4 the other day and this doctor explained how a fourteen-year-old boy developed an eating disorder. The boy was, in everyone else's opinion, perfectly OK weight-wise. He was a little shy but handsome and had friends, although perhaps because of his shyness, he'd never had a girlfriend. His shyness was to do with not being able to think what to say to people he didn't know, although his intelligence was above average. He wasn't shy because he was self-conscious about his shape. He liked swimming and never appeared bashful – in fact he was confident in the pool and sometimes a bit of a show-off. He learnt to be self-aware by looking at a porn mag a friend bought. It wasn't hardcore, just simulated. Anyway, he tore out a page showing a woman he found attractive and he used to look at her before he went to sleep. Then he started looking at the man and comparing himself. The doctor said that the man's penis couldn't be seen in any of the pictures. Also, the boy told her that for several weeks the man was as good as invisible because he was so fascinated by the woman. There was never any obviously gay interest. It was simply a question of the boy gradually realising that his body was different to the man's. To everyone else the differences would've been insignificant and the only things the doctor noticed were slightly larger than average swellings around the boy's nipples and some fat on his hips. But these were well within what's considered the normal range and the fat on his hips would have gone in any case as he got older. Yet the boy became anorexic. He exercised and starved himself until hospitalised. His real problem was his instinctive shyness but he blamed not having a girlfriend on his weight. The boy hanged himself.'

The story moved me. For a few moments we were both silent. But I still couldn't understand. The boy's case was tragic but he was obviously a thoroughly disturbed person. Sarah wasn't like that – she was vivacious, beautiful and, most importantly, phenomenally successful.

'You're not like that, though, are you?'

'I'm not dissimilar. I used to look at pictures of models in teen magazines. I used to think about what made filmstars so stunning. I even compared my body with that of my dolly! I convinced myself that if I lost weight I'd be happier at home –

and at school. There are no essential differences between me and the boy.'

'But then a lot of people diet without being anorexics. What is it, a question of degree?'

'It's about obsession. You end up thinking about food every minute of the day – because you're starving probably. You obsess about it continually but at the same time you're fucking terrified of it. You read recipes, partly because you think that maybe reading about food will help you satisfy your hunger – in your imagination. Literally food pornography. It's partly because you credit yourself with some intelligence and want to show yourself that there's nothing frightening about a few inanimate ingredients. You study any article on nutrition you can lay your hands on. You find out whatever you can about what you can eat without putting on weight. You become expert in reading food labels and when the legislation changed and companies were forced to give more information about their products I thought, there is a God.'

We both laughed.

'OK I understand what you're trying to do there – control your intake – but what about being sick, where does that come in? I know you say it's like a drug but what are you escaping from? Yourself or the world?'

She stared at her tobacco tin and glass of wine. For a moment she looked blank, defeated. I thought she wasn't going to answer.

She turned towards me and smiled.

'In many ways chucking up saved me. It is like a drug, yes, and like a drug it keeps me going when I'd otherwise buckle under the pain. But drugs weaken you and there's a pay-back time. Being sick every day shares those characteristics. When I spin out of control I get so weak I could easily starve myself to death. So far I haven't and perhaps never will. I believe I'll never lose control to such an extent that I'll let that happen but I can't be sure. Regardless of whether I kill myself I'm certainly doing long-term damage – to my teeth, skin, vision, reproductive organs, heart, kidneys, bone density, my hair, my stomach. You name it, really. But unlike a drug, throwing up seems quite innocuous, somehow. It feels manageable. The effects are slow to show themselves. There's something about me that won't let my illness get totally out of hand. Sometimes I can live with it fairly peaceably. This cycle of ups – well, levels – and downs – downs that are never allowed to sink that far – is what makes me a chronic anorexic. The side-effects of being sick sometimes seem small prices to pay for its benefits. I wish I could be clean, as it were, but accept I probably never will be. I accept in moments of calm, like today, but at other times I would give anything to be well. You said earlier that anorexia was a question of degree. As anorexics go, I guess I'm one of the sorted ones – when my peaks and troughs are averaged.'

'But why do you need to be sick?'

She breathed out sharply, as if she was getting tired.

'When I was a girl the pattern of my behaviour was set. I would get fixated, starve myself, obsess about food then I'd be able to free myself again – not totally, but enough to function quite well. But the downswings eventually got pretty violent. I don't mean I was violent but the feelings inside were strong, debilitating, frightening. It's difficult to describe what it's like. You get into cycles not just of starving then binging and feeling guilty but of walking round supermarkets reading food labels then getting so angry with yourself for frittering your life away doing such vacuous things. But not to do them is unthinkable because they're part of your life. They're almost your good luck charms. Your already poor self-esteem plummets. You hate yourself. You feel suicidal. You can spend a day going shall I shan't I until you've physically hemmed yourself in. Literally, you can't move. Your muscles scream in paralysis. Your mind is whited out. The world has no colour or meaning. You survive any way you can, usually by forcing yourself to do something that will tear your mind away from its obsessions. For me it was studying, which was an escape into the imagination. That and cigarettes – oddly I think their great benefit is that they get me breathing properly.

'But these weren't enough and I knew it. I knew people chucked up but I never wanted to do that. It revolted me. I thought people like that were *really* sick – no pun intended. Then, suddenly, I started. I'd had quite a few good weeks after my A-levels. I went to stay with Debbie. We got drunk a lot. I started going out with someone, I had some fun. I came home and immediately felt trapped. I could tell that the obsessing was about to begin all over again. There was an awful lunch when every invisible wire between me and my family and between them was pulled so tight it cut into me like a garrotte and I thought I was about to break down. But I didn't. I just said, "Excuse me," and walked out of the room. I went to the downstairs loo and threw up. I felt clean and blissfully empty – like an egg that had been blown.'

A couple of tears fell from her eyes. I touched her shoulder – gingerly as if I was touching something very fragile.

'I'm sorry.'

Again, she smiled at me.

'It's not your fault.'

'Isn't there anything anyone can do to help?'

'I tried psychotherapy for a bit. But it isn't geared for adults. I don't know why. The way things are going it'll have to be. I'm not the only adult long-term anorexic. But we're somehow invisible. Doctors can cope with helping children and teenagers but not intelligent, if stroppy, adults. If your illness is acute then it's a different story. You get so weak you can't do anything other than let yourself be helped – unless you're *really* strong and determined. Then you die and you're no longer a burden to anybody. But when you're chronic you're an embarrassment.

'I went along to the psychotherapist and was talked to like a child. I was surprised I wasn't given baby food. I was put in with teenagers and kids who were far gone and who I couldn't identify with. I thought I'm not like them. Even chronic anorexics have their pride. I decided I'd fight my battles on my own.

'I'm sorry, I can't say anymore than that. I'm exhausted. Would you like a drink downstairs?'

I said yes and we sat and chatted by the fire. Talked about anything other than food and eating disorders. At twelve I went out to the micro before joining her in bed. Neither of us had eaten. We didn't make love that night, just held each other and fell asleep. It was the happiest evening that fortnight.

The next morning both of us were irritable, as if she'd said too much and I was struggling to take it all in. We rowed and the vicious cycle started again.

Then Griff came to see me.

He phoned first and asked when would be a good time. It was a Monday and I said three-thirty. It wasn't pleasant hearing his scratchy voice but I couldn't refuse him.

When I opened the door to the Tap I was astonished. He'd lost weight and was wearing a smart suit, white shirt and red tie. His unruly beard was trimmed. It was as if the artist in him meant that everything he did was calculated to subvert expectations. Most people when they hit bad times go from looking kempt to scruffy. He'd gone from being a tramp to looking like Alan Sugar. Maybe it was a Welsh thing.

I sat him down by the fire and offered him a drink. I pulled us both a pint of Stag Beetle and drew up my favourite Windsor chair.

He meanwhile had rolled himself a cigarette. His technique was totally different to Sarah's. For a start the paper and tobacco disappeared inside his huge hands which wiggled about frantically to produce a fat white cigar with a thatch of tobacco sticking out each end. He chewed off the nearest thatch and spat the bits onto the flagstones then set light to the one at the front which went up spectacularly, sending a shower of embers into his lap. He flicked these off without looking at them.

I expected him to be aggressive but during the first pint he made no mention of Sarah or the situation. Instead he asked about the pub and how trade was going. He told me what London had been like and what he was working on. There were fewer 'boyos' and 'bachs' than I remembered and his voice was deeper. The twinkle in his eyes and the warmth of his manner encouraged the kind of male camaraderie I don't always welcome but in his company seemed almost flattering.

It was only when we were half-way through the second pint that he began talking about Sarah. He lowered his eyes and stared at his hands. His voice was little more than a whisper. He told me how much he loved her, that he didn't blame me, he'd always known she'd move on one day, that he wasn't sure he'd take her back, even if she wanted him to.

'She's a bit of a handful, isn't she?' he said and shot a glance at me – part sorrowful, part mischievous.

'You could say that.'

We both chuckled.

'Haven't had to make an insurance claim yet?'

I said, 'No,' then thought, What's he on about?

'I'm not with you.'

'Just that she throws a wobbly every now and then, and—' He tossed his lighter in the air and let it clatter onto the floor. 'Things get broken. And when I say broken, Bach, I mean *broken*!'

'Her poltergeist moment.'

'*Moments*. Yes, that's it, poltergeist moments. Fucking terrifying they are too! Started when she was engaged to that Hooray Henry. Wrecked his place, she did. Why he pulled out. I thought it was a one off when she told me but then I got home one time and the Folly was like a scrap heap. We've done out those theme rooms, must be three times each. Why d'you think it's taken so long to do the place up? Mad, she is sometimes – and you can never tell when it'll happen. Made me a nervous wreck, it has. Why I go to London, see. Recover! But I've never let on. Always been loyal. Never mentioned her activities to a living soul. Suffered in silence, I have.'

I thought, I knew there had to be a reason he hadn't put up a fight. I thought, it all makes sense. From what I'd seen of her, I could imagine her throwing a tantrum and smashing the pub up as clear as if she was doing it in front of us.

But Griff had moved on and was asking about one of the regulars. We chatted about the pub and village for ten minutes or so, had a laugh and parted the best of friends.

Behind the bonhomie, though, I was scared shitless. My

mission was to get Sarah back to the Folly as fast as I could.

The rest, Mart, is, as they say, history. Within days, Griff was dead and Sarah ran into the snow. I sped back to the pub and phoned the police. I haven't spoken to her since.

She was admitted to hospital that night for shock. Fiona told me that one of the doctors knew something about anorexia and was able to put her onto a clinic that catered for chronic adult cases. She'll probably never be cured but she'll learn to manage it – to live with it – better.

There was a police inquiry and an inquest. I imagine, Mart, the plods thought she might have bumped Griff off to begin with. When they came to see me, I certainly got the impression they suspected I might have been in with her.

What the inspector couldn't understand was why I drove back to the pub. I remember him staring at me. We were in the flat. There were two sergeants on the sofa. Me and the inspector were in armchairs, leaning towards each other.

He asked flatly, not a trace of emotion, 'Why didn't you just go back up the drive, go into the house and phone from there? It's what she did.'

I bowed my head. I felt a complete idiot. I was embarrassed. I told him I was in shock. That I couldn't think straight.

He asked if we'd had an argument.

I said yes and explained I suspected she might have lost it and inadvertently helped Griff over the battlements.

I tried to make it sound like everything was chaos that night. I was attempting to avoid both actually accusing her of murdering Griff and giving away how much contempt I showed her. How I wished her dead.

The inspector looked rather bemused when I finished. It was only later that I realised he must have been trying to get me to confess to a conspiracy.

Well, nothing came of their enquiries – neither as far as Sarah was concerned, nor me – and the inquest ruled accidental death.

Griff was buried in South Wales. I didn't attend the funeral.

It was about three weeks later that I went to see Fiona.

When Fiona told me, Mart, that Sarah believed she'd found love when we got together, I seethed. She made me feel about an inch tall.

'Well there are some things about Sarah you don't know, Fiona.'

'Such as?'

'She wrecks things – rooms – she smashes up rooms in a crazy fury.'

'I beg your pardon. Who told you that?'

'Griff.'

She laughed contemptuously.

'You've been had, Tom. Griff was as manipulative as they come. He'd say anything to get what he wanted. Yes, Sarah did lose it once. She did smash up a house. Do you know why?'

I shook my head.

'It was when she was about to get married. It was St Valentine's Day. She'd spent the weekend with her parents. She wasn't due back at her finacé's until the afternoon but she decided to get up early and surprise him. She found him in bed with another— With a man. It wasn't the fact he was bisexual that made her flip but the betrayal of trust. She would never have wanted to share him with anyone. She's not that sort of person. She's very black and white. She was devastated. If only he'd been honest with her, they could have agreed to be friends. She doesn't remember what happened after she found them but, yes, the house was destroyed. His mother decided to say the damage was caused by a poltergeist so the decorators wouldn't suspect anything. She even had the cottage exorcised for show.

'Sarah has never done anything like that since. I'm absolutely sure of it. You've been *had*, Tom Dickens!'

I remember, Mart, Jill used to write, 'Ha-ha! Ha-ha!' in emails sometimes, when she'd just described herself doing something stupid. I always thought she sounded a bit deranged when she wrote that. When Fiona explained to me about the poltergeist moment I thought about Jill's emails and there was this ghastly laughter in my ears: 'Ha, Ha-ha! Ha-ha! HA!'

So, what's it all about, Mart?

It's almost a year since Griff died. Sarah moved away in February – I caught sight of her in the village just before she left but had the good sense not to go up to her. Well it wasn't good sense actually – I couldn't have looked her in the face.

As I say, I haven't spoken to her since that wretched night when Griff died.

At least not to her in person. In my head we've gone on walks and talked through what happened to us. We've made friends, made love, started again. But for much of this year, I could never have done that for real. I didn't have enough self-knowledge nor enough control over my emotions.

Now, though, I think I could make a go of things if we met. But she's gone, I know that.

If we met now I'd know what to think and say – how to accept her and love her right. But when we were together I knew neither of those things.

I've read it's not uncommon for partners of people with eating disorders to pick on that weakness – in their frustration. It's easy to get the problem out of proportion, to lose sight of the remarkable human being you're with. Partners can end up blaming anything and everything that goes wrong in the relationship on the eating disorder and treat the person as if they were mad. If you disagree with what they're saying, you put their 'flawed' opinion down to their instability. Bang! Sorted! Only it's not.

If you give in to your prejudice, you'll no longer be able to separate difficulties that are due to the disorder from those that have other causes. Above all you'll turn your back on your own shortcomings.

A lot of the time I blamed Sarah for problems that arose from my insecurities. It's easier that way. So much better for the ego.

I can see that now, only it's too damned late!

So, what's it all about, Mart?

The tragedy of me and Sarah was that when we met I simply didn't know what I was getting into. I saw this lovely person and yet saw absolutely nothing. Later, all I could see were the flaws. We broke up. I began to realise what I did wrong. A year on and I could be a good partner to her. But the moment's gone.

So here I am, Mart. Older. Wiser? I hope so. But if I meet someone new, will what I've learnt help me to make a go of the new relationship? God, I hope so.

I wonder, now I've reached the end of this therapy, Mart, whether I'll send you what I've written. Maybe not. I'm a proud man, Mart. Self-sufficient. I like to think I can solve my own problems. This therapy of yours, Mart, has helped me do that, for which I'll always be grateful.

I'd like to see you again, Mart, and talk about what I've gone through. Not to show you what I've written. Just meet for a beer and a chat.

Invisible

It's three months since I finished my story.

In the meantime there have been developments. Tara is expecting Andy's baby and Claudette has at last brokered a deal that will set me up for life – if I play my cards right.

When Claudette phoned I went straight out and bought a big Porsche four-by-four. As soon as Andy saw it he nicknamed it the Fat Bastard and said it would make a good bonfire. He's still an anarchist at heart – despite prison. He and Tara are good for me. They keep my feet on the ground. They're like family.

Today I drove to Jill's wedding.

On the way back I decided to turn off the M4 and head for Aldermaston.

I parked up outside the pub pointing towards the pottery.

As I watched, Sarah came out and put up the awning. It looked new.

A man came out and placed his arm on her shoulder.

She looked well. Still thin but healthy and happy. The man was older than her. Older than me.

They kissed.

I thought of Len Banks. Someone who had faith in me, helped me grow.

Maybe that sort of wise, father-figure is what Sarah needs. I hope she's found love.

I know I wasn't right for her.

I turned the ignition, eased the gear stick into first and the Fat Bastard slid away from the kerb.

Note to Mart – (will you ever read it?):

Don't worry, Mart, I've not turned into a stalker. I was just curious, that's all. A lot got stirred up at the wedding.

I couldn't be seen. The Fat Bastard's got this button – press it and the windows get blacked out. Ingenious!

To her, Mart – to them – I was invisible.

THE END

Acknowledgements

I am indebted to Gillie Bolton for her book *The Therapeutic Potential of Creative Writing: Writing Myself* (Jessica Kingsley Publishers, 1999). I would also like to thank: Jess; Frank Cottrell Boyce; the late great and much missed Chris Moss, founder of the Wychwood Brewery; Harriet Stevens; Alan Caiger-Smith; the man on the 18 and 100 buses; Robby Behind Bars; David Flusfeder and Louisa Young for the Arvon course; Keiren Phelan of Arts Council South East; and all at Writers in Oxford.

StreetBooks

StreetBooks is a new Oxfordshire-based publisher.

'My interest is in artisan publishing: which involves high quality, regional fiction, marketed locally in person and globally via the Internet. An analogy I like is that of the micro-brewery: a combination of tradition, passion and the opportunities offered by new technology.' Frank Egerton, editor, StreetBooks

http://www.streetbooks.co.uk

Lightning Source UK Ltd.
Milton Keynes UK
14 August 2010

158417UK00001B/1/P